"HOW DO I KNOW
I CAN TRUST YOU?"

"Good point." He gazed into the fireplace for several moments, then said, "I told myself I wouldn't see you again, that no good could come from it."

"Then why are you here?"

He turned to look at me, his dark eyes intent upon my face. No other man had ever looked at me quite that way, as if every fiber of his being was focused solely on me. My breath seemed trapped in my throat as I waited for his answer.

"Because," he said quietly, "I couldn't stay away."

His voice was so warm and filled with such desire, I was surprised I didn't melt on the spot.

"Raphael . . ."

BOOK YOUR PLACE ON OUR WEBSITE AND MAKE THE READING CONNECTION!

We've created a customized website just for our very special readers, where you can get the inside scoop on everything that's going on with Zebra, Pinnacle and Kensington books.

When you come online, you'll have the exciting opportunity to:

- View covers of upcoming books
- Read sample chapters
- Learn about our future publishing schedule (listed by publication month *and author*)
- Find out when your favorite authors will be visiting a city near you
- Search for and order backlist books from our online catalog
- Check out author bios and background information
- Send e-mail to your favorite authors
- Meet the Kensington staff online
- Join us in weekly chats with authors, readers and other guests
- Get writing guidelines
- AND MUCH MORE!

**Visit our website at
http://www.kensingtonbooks.com**

NIGHT'S MASTER

AMANDA ASHLEY

ZEBRA BOOKS
Kensington Publishing Corp.
www.kensingtonbooks.com

ZEBRA BOOKS are published by

Kensington Publishing Corp.
850 Third Avenue
New York, NY 10022

All Kensington titles, imprints, and distributed lines are available at special quantity discounts for bulk purchases for sales promotion, premiums, fund-raising, educational, or institutional use.

Special book excerpts or customized printings can also be created to fit specific needs. For details, write or phone the office of the Kensington Special Sales Manager: Attn.: Special Sales Department. Kensington Publishing Corp., 850 Third Avenue, New York, NY 10022. Phone: 1-800-221-2647.

Zebra and the Z logo Reg. U.S. Pat. & TM Off.

ISBN-13: 978-0-8217-8063-3
ISBN-10: 0-8217-8063-8

First printing: October 2008
10 9 8 7 6 5 4 3 2 1

Printed in the United States of America

Dedicated to Elizabeth Camp
and her husband, Charlie
And to all the families
in the Armed Forces—
Those who fight to preserve our freedom
and those who stay at home and wait

Chapter One

Most said it was going to be the end of the world as we knew it. Some said that was ridiculous, but those who weren't too busy or too blind to see the signs knew the truth. Mankind had been heading for this showdown ever since the preternatural creatures decided that, although they were small in number when compared to humans, they possessed the strength and the Supernatural power to pretty much run the planet any way they saw fit. And since the nations of the Earth had finally achieved universal peace, most of the world's armies had been drastically reduced or done away with altogether, leaving only local law enforcement agencies to protect the citizens, while national governments debated how to best handle a possible future threat.

In the last six months or so, there had been an escalating number of battles between the two major baddies—the Werewolves and the Vampires.

No one really knew who was winning the war. In the past, when the humans had made war, everyone knew who was winning. The number of casualties, both civilian and enemy, had been reported far and wide. Pictures of those killed in battle had appeared in newspapers, on television, and online. The nightly news had flashed brutal, graphic images of the dead and wounded being carried off the field of battle.

It was different with the Supernatural creatures. Their battles were fought in the dark hours of the night in remote areas around the world. The bodies of the fallen were never found. The Vampire dead disintegrated in the sun's first light. The Werewolves were carried off by others of their kind; some said the dead were eaten so as to leave no trace.

Smart humans quickly learned two things: how to repel the preternatural folks, and how to stay out of their way. Those who weren't so smart usually ended up as someone's dinner. Except for a few reporters who had more curiosity than brains, human casualties had been few so far.

Of course, everyone knew that sooner or later, mankind would have to stand up and defend itself against whichever side won the war between the Werewolves and the Vampires, but until then, the smart thing to do was just stay out of the line of fire.

Being a pretty smart girl myself, I hightailed it out of the big city and took up residence in a small town in the Midwest, figuring there wasn't anything in Oak Hollow to attract either the Vampires or Werewolves. After all, the town wasn't big enough to appear on most maps, and since the Werewolves and the Vampires seemed to like bright lights and big cities, moving to a sleepy little community like Oak Hollow seemed like the perfect solution.

I bought a cute little house made of logs for practically nothing, opened a new and used bookstore on the corner of Third and Main, and figured I'd stay out of danger while the Werewolves and the Vamps killed each other off.

Of course, you know what they say about the best laid plans. . . .

Chapter Two

I spent the next few weeks immersed in fixing up the bookstore. I painted one wall white and the other three a pale apple green. Since I had always loved movies, I put up some framed antique movie posters that I had collected over the years, along with some autographed movie stills. I bought some pretty potted plants and flowers and spread them out as artfully as I could along the tops of some of the bookshelves. I had a collection of stuffed teddy bears I'd had since I was a little girl. Digging them out of one of the boxes at home, I scattered them throughout the store and among the greenery on the shelves, along with an occasional decorative birdcage. I found a fancy automatic coffeemaker and a sturdy table to put it on, stocked up on colorful cups and napkins, and opened the store for business.

After three weeks and three customers, I was thinking maybe I had opened the wrong kind of enterprise for such a small town. Maybe people in rural areas didn't have time to read. Maybe I should have opened a pet store. At least then I would have had some company!

I called the writers' group in the next town to see about setting up a book signing in hopes of drawing customers into the shop.

The woman who answered the phone sounded doubtful that any of the authors in their organization would be willing to drive a hundred miles to sign autographs in such a remote location, but she said she would ask around and see if she could find any writers who lived closer to Oak Hollow. I thanked her for her time and hung up.

One day, out of sheer boredom, I painted a mural on the wall behind the counter. It started off as a flowering peach tree, its branches spreading out along the wall. But as the days went by, I painted a young girl sitting beneath the tree reading a book. Next, I added a gray squirrel on one of the branches, and then a little brown and white dog sleeping beside the girl, and then, in the distance, a fuzzy yellow duck floating on a small blue pond. It wasn't the Sistine Chapel by any means, but it was something to do to pass the time, and it wasn't too bad, for an amateur.

A few days later, while sitting at the malt shop trying to lift my spirits by indulging in a hot fudge sundae with double whipped cream, I overheard a couple of the townspeople talking. Normally, I don't approve of eavesdropping, but in this case it turned out to be highly informative. Apparently, the reason my chosen hideaway wasn't inhabited by Vampires or Werewolves was because it had been designated as neutral territory, a place where the baddies could get together without fear of attack when they needed to parley with one another. Apparently, Oak Hollow was the Switzerland of the Midwest.

I was getting ready to close the store a few nights later when the cheerful jingling of the bell over the door announced that someone had actually come into the shop.

Looking up, I put on my best how-can-I-help-you smile, only to feel it slip away when I got a good look at my first customer in over a week. He was, in a word, magnificent, from the top of his black-thatched head to the polished tips of his expensive black leather boots.

I blinked up at him, all rational thought wiped from my mind as I stared at the Adonis striding toward me. He could have been the poster boy for handsome, with his dusky skin, chiseled features, strong jaw, and full, sensuous lips. Never in all my life had I seen such a drop-dead gorgeous guy.

He glanced around the store, and I could almost see him wondering how I stayed in business, since he was the only customer in the place.

With an effort of will, I managed to stop staring at him long enough to ask if I could be of help.

His gaze moved over me in a way that made me feel as if he had just finished a seven-course gourmet meal and I was dessert.

I had never actually met a Vampire before, but I realized with a sudden jolt that I was looking at one now, although I had no idea how I knew. He was tall, at least three inches over six feet, and solid. As might be expected, he wore nothing but black—black silk shirt, black jeans that hugged a pair of long, muscular legs, and a black leather jacket that covered a pair of broad shoulders. All that black went well with his hair and his eyes. I don't recall ever seeing anyone who had black eyes before, but his were like pools of ebony ink, deep and dark and mesmerizing. I wanted to dive to the bottom and never come up.

Being in the same room with one of the Undead, breathing the same air, made me decidedly uncomfortable. I took several deep breaths, hoping it would calm my nerves. It didn't.

"Are you looking for anything in particular?" I asked, pleased that my voice didn't betray my uneasiness.

"I was hoping you could recommend something." His voice, as deep and mesmerizing as his eyes, danced over my skin.

It had never occurred to me that Vampires liked to read, or do much of anything except wear black, drink blood, and spend the daylight hours resting in their coffins.

"What do you like?" I asked. "Mysteries, suspense, sci-fi . . . ?"

He shrugged. "Have you read any good books lately?"

"Me?" I was unaccountably pleased that he had asked for my opinion. "Well, yes, I thought the latest Jordan Montgomery mystery was his best one to date."

He nodded. "I'll take it."

Aware of his gaze on my back, I hurried to the mystery section and plucked a copy from the shelf.

"That'll be twenty-seven fifty," I said, ringing up the sale.

Reaching into his pocket, he withdrew a crisp fifty-dollar bill. His fingers were cool when they brushed mine, yet I felt a frisson of heat race all the way up my neck to warm my cheeks. I slid the book and the receipt into a sack, also hand painted by me, and handed it to him, along with his change.

"Might I know your name?" he asked.

I hesitated to give it. I'm not really into Supernatural stuff all that much, but I knew that names were powerful mojo.

His gaze locked with mine, and I found myself saying, "Kathy. Kathy McKenna."

"A lovely name for a very lovely lady," he murmured, bowing from the waist. "I hope to see you again."

"Are you going to tell me your name?" I asked. Hey, it only seemed fair that I should know his name now that he knew mine.

"Ah, of course. I am Raphael Cordova."

I stared at him. Raphael Cordova! Good grief. He was the leader or chief or whatever they called it of the North American Vampires.

He smiled, displaying remarkably even, white teeth. "I will see you again, Kathy McKenna."

I wasn't sure if that was a threat or a promise, but before I could ask, or think of a suitable reply, he was gone, as silent as a shadow running from the sun.

The night after Raphael's visit, thirteen people stopped by the store. They didn't just come in because they were curious or to browse, either. They came in to buy. Every one of them bought at least two books; one lady bought four, another bought nine.

I'm not sure when I realized that they had all come into the store after the sun had set, or exactly when I realized they were all Vampires, and that Raphael Cordova had probably sent them. I guess I should have been pleased. Instead, it annoyed me to think that he had rounded up a bunch of his Undead pals and ordered them to throw a little business my way. I didn't need anyone feeling sorry for me, thank you very much. And I certainly didn't want to be beholden to a Vampire for anything.

I had a feeling he would show up later that night, and he did, just as I was about to close up shop. He was clad in unrelieved black again—a short-sleeved T-shirt that emphasized his broad shoulders and muscular arms, another pair of tight jeans, and a pair of scuffed cowboy boots. Just looking at him made me feel good all over.

He inclined his head in my direction. "Good evening, Kathy McKenna." His voice was just as I remembered: soft and low; it caressed my skin like warm, dark velvet.

"Come for another book, did you?" I asked ungraciously.

"As a matter of fact, I did," he replied with a faint smile.

"Don't tell me you finished the other one already." Montgomery novels tended to be long; his newest book was almost nine hundred pages.

Cordova nodded.

"What are you, a speed reader?"

"Not exactly," he replied with a wry grin, "but sometimes the nights can be long."

I was tempted to say, "no kidding," but I restrained myself. "I guess you enjoyed it."

"Yes, very much, which is why I'm here. I'd like to buy everything he's written."

"You might want to narrow that down a little," I said drily. "Jordan Montgomery has written something like fifty books in the last twenty years."

"I'll take whatever you have on hand," Raphael said. "And please order me the rest."

"You don't have to buy all those books just because you feel sorry for me," I said waspishly. "And you didn't have to tell your friends to come in here, either."

"Ah," he murmured, a guilty smile twitching at the corners of his lips. "Don't tell me they all came tonight?"

"I don't know about that, since I don't know how many you asked to show up," I replied, and then, as my exasperation faded, I wondered what was going on that there were so many Vampires in town at one time, which made me wonder if that meant an equal number of Werewolves were also prowling the dark streets. The thought sent a cold chill slithering down my spine.

I glanced out the window, wondering if the moon was full, and if it was safe to walk home now that the town was full of Vampires and Werewolves. Funny that they were enemies. You'd think they would go hunting together, I thought morbidly, since one drank blood and the other devoured flesh.

"Miss McKenna?"

"What? Oh, right, the books." I walked toward the back of the store where the mysteries were shelved, acutely aware that Raphael was following me. I wasn't sure I liked having a Vampire, even a remarkably sexy, handsome one, at my back. Or anywhere else in the vicinity, for that matter.

I had sixteen of Montgomery's backlist in stock, all in hardback. Assuming Cordova read a book a night, I figured I wouldn't be seeing him again for a couple of weeks. The thought left me feeling curiously depressed, but I told myself it was a good thing. After all, who needs a Vampire hanging around?

He helped me carry the books to the front of the store, then handed me his credit card. I stared at it for a moment. Somehow, I had never imagined that Vampires carried credit cards. Apparently, I had a lot to learn about the ways and means of the Undead.

I quickly rang up the books and gave him a copy of the receipt to sign. His signature was a bold scrawl across the bottom of the paper.

I loaded the books into four shopping bags and pushed them across the counter. "Happy reading."

"Thank you." He started to turn away, then hesitated. "Would you care to have dinner with me some evening?"

I stared at him, my mind filling with images of Raphael Cordova bending over me, his fangs poised at my throat. "No, I don't think so."

"I didn't ask you to *be* dinner," he said with a knowing grin. "But if the thought of dining with me makes you uncomfortable, perhaps we could go out for a drink." He held up a hand, silencing the protest he must have read in my eyes. "No blood involved."

As much as I hated to admit it, I was tempted. I hadn't been out on a date in almost six months. I didn't know anyone else in town. And Raphael Cordova intrigued me more than any man I had ever met. But still . . . what was the point in dating a Vampire? I opened my mouth to say, "No, thank you," so you can imagine my surprise when I heard myself say, "Yes, I'd like that."

"Tomorrow night, perhaps?"

"All right." Tomorrow was Thursday. I closed the shop at seven during the week, at nine on Fridays and Saturdays. I was closed on Sundays, like every other business in town except for the gas station/mini-mart located over on Ninth Street, which was open 24-7.

"Shall I pick you up here, or at your home?"

"Here will be fine," I said, uncomfortable at the thought of letting a Vampire know where I lived.

"Until tomorrow night, then." He smiled at me, then left the store.

I stared after him, wondering what I was getting myself into.

Chapter Three

I woke up Thursday morning feeling jittery inside, a condition that grew steadily worse with each passing tick of the clock. I took a long shower, spent half an hour applying my makeup and doing my hair, and another twenty minutes trying to decide what to wear. Since Raphael was picking me up at the store, I wouldn't have time to come home and change for our date later. In the end, I settled on a pair of white slacks and a green turtleneck sweater that made my eyes look a shade darker than they were. I wondered if Raphael liked green eyes. The word *Vampire* whispered through my mind, sending me to my jewelry box where I kept a gold crucifix, not because I was Catholic, but because crosses were supposed to repel Vampires. I had worn it constantly in New York, but it hadn't seemed necessary here in Oak Hollow until I met Raphael.

I fastened the chain around my neck, then took a last look in the mirror, wishing my hair was curly and black instead of long and straight and blond. I slipped into my comfy work shoes, grabbed a pair of white high-heeled sandals to change into for my date with the Undead, scooped up my handbag and my keys, and headed to the bookstore.

To my surprise, I had several ordinary customers that afternoon.

One of them, Susie McGee, was the down-to-earth, outgoing, friendly type. She had a pretty, heart-shaped face, short, dark curly hair, bright blue eyes, and a harried expression. She was about five feet three inches tall, making her two inches shorter than I was. After she paid for her purchases, she lingered at the counter.

"This is a great place," she said, looking around. "We've needed a bookstore for donkey's years, but we're not really big enough to interest a Barnes & Noble or a Borders, you know?"

I nodded, keeping one eye on her three boys, who were playing hide-and-seek in the aisles. They were cute kids. I estimated they were all under the age of seven. They all had their mother's dark curly hair and blue eyes. After twenty minutes of watching them run around my store, I knew why their mother looked stressed out.

"I just love to read," Susie went on. "After a day of looking after my monsters, I need a little time to myself. Of course, the only place I can be by myself is in the bathroom. I call it my reading room," she said with a laugh, and then she sighed. "Honestly, the only time I have to call my own is on the john. Or in the tub. Well, listen to me, running on like that. I'd best be going. Bobby, you stop pulling your brother's hair! Jeremy, put that bear back on the shelf." She looked at me and shook her head. "Honestly, all those kids do is fight! It was nice to meet you, Miss McKenna."

"Kathy, please."

With a smile, Susie gathered up her books and her brood and left the shop.

I glanced at the clock. It was a quarter to seven. Since Raphael was only taking me out for a drink, I had eaten a late lunch. But even if I hadn't, I was much too nervous to think about food.

I turned off the outside lights, locked the cash drawer, then went into the back room to change my shoes. I didn't hear the bell over the door ring, but I knew the moment Raphael arrived. I'm not sure how I knew. Women's intuition, a change in the atmosphere, a sudden internal awareness, I don't know. I just knew he was there, the same way I had known that he was a Vampire.

I ran a hand over my hair, took a deep breath, and made my way toward the front of the store.

Cordova turned to face me, and I felt my breath catch in my throat. Lordy, the man was breathtaking! He wore a white shirt open at the throat, black slacks, and boots. His hair gleamed blue-black in the overhead light.

I felt a blush warm my cheeks as his gaze moved over me, the look in his eyes telling me he liked what he saw.

"Good evening, Miss McKenna."

"You might as well call me Kathy," I suggested somewhat breathlessly.

"Kathy."

The sound of my name on his lips sent a shiver down my spine, made me think of warm bodies intimately entwined on cool satin sheets. Maybe letting him call me by my given name wasn't such a good idea, after all. I touched the crucifix at my throat to give me strength.

Raphael observed the gesture with a wry grin. "The belief that crosses scare off Vampires is an old wives' tale," he remarked. "In any event, it isn't the cross that wards off the Vampire, but the wearer's belief in the power of good over evil."

"I didn't know that."

"And then you have to ask yourself, what if he's Jewish or Hindu?"

I folded my arms under my breasts. "Now you're making fun of me."

He shook his head. "Not really. In any case, if you feel the need to wear one, it should be silver."

"What difference does that make?"

"Silver burns Vampire flesh, gold does not. Not only that, but silver renders us powerless if we're bound with it."

I filed that bit of useful information away for future reference.

"Are you ready to go?" He glanced at the crucifix again. "Or have you changed your mind?"

"I haven't changed my mind," I said. "Just give me a minute to lock up."

He followed me to the door, waited on the sidewalk while I turned off the interior lights and set the alarm.

After I slipped my keys into my handbag, he offered me his arm in a rather courtly gesture and walked me to his car, something sleek and black that looked like it was going a hundred miles an hour even when it was parked at the curb.

He opened the door for me, and I sank into a rich black leather seat that automatically contoured itself to my size and shape. A deep breath carried the rich new-car scent to my nostrils.

My heartbeat kicked up a notch at the thought of being alone in the car with a Vampire. What on earth was I thinking? I had only lived in Oak Hollow a short time, and I didn't really know anyone. If I never came back, would anybody even notice?

Raphael slid behind the wheel in a sinuous movement, started the car with a touch of his hand, and pulled away from the curb. Late-model cars, like most computers, could be operated by verbal command or manually. I wasn't surprised that Raphael opted for hands-on control.

I tried to think of something witty to say to break the silence between us, but my mind had gone blank.

Raphael drove with one arm resting on the edge of the open window, his right hand draped negligently over the steering wheel. I felt a shiver of unease as he turned off Main Street and onto the highway.

"Are you new to our fair metropolis?" he asked.

"You could say that. I moved here a little over a month ago."

"Where did you live before you came here?"

"New York."

"Ah. Oak Hollow must be quite a change from the big city."

"Quite," I agreed with a smile. "So, are you still enjoying Montgomery's work?"

"Very much. I like his voice, the way he turns a phrase. And the fact that I can't always figure out who the murderer is by page three."

"That's why I like him, too," I said with a laugh.

I felt a shiver of unease as Raphael pulled off the highway, turned left at the first street corner, and then made a right onto a narrow dirt road. Stately trees lined both sides of the road, their graceful branches intertwining to form a kind of leafy tunnel. There were no streetlights here, no lights at all until he pulled up in front of a large, rectangular building built of shimmering black stone. The name of the place did nothing to ease my anxiety.

The Stygian Way.

Raphael parked the car in a reserved space in the front, then came around to open my door. Offering me his hand, he helped me out of the car.

A tall, slender man dressed in a black suit and tie stood at the club's entrance. Nodding at Raphael, he opened one of the carved double doors, and I had my first look at The Stygian Way.

I guess surprise sums up my reaction best. I'm not sure what my expectations had been, but the nightclub exceeded them all. Black leather booths lined one wall; small tables covered with pristine white cloths were scattered around the gray and black tiled floor. A crystal vase holding one perfect red rose adorned each table. Dozens of candles filled the room with a soft, warm glow. A long bar made of gold-veined black granite ran the length of the back wall. Glass shelves held an array of sparkling crystal goblets and snifters and stemware.

A young woman wearing a long red dress and a ruffled black apron hurried toward us. "Right this way, my lord," she said with a slight bow.

My lord, I thought. Good grief!

Raphael inclined his head in greeting, and we followed the waitress to a booth in the far corner. I sat down and he slid in beside me, making me feel suddenly like a very small rabbit that had stumbled into the den of a very large, hungry wolf.

Raphael ordered a bottle of red wine that I knew sold for as much as sixty dollars a bottle.

I asked for a glass of 7UP with a cherry.

He lifted one dark brow. "You prefer a soft drink to fine wine?"

I shrugged. "I've never been much of a drinker."

"Afraid I'm going to get you intoxicated and take advantage of you?" he asked candidly.

That was so close to the truth that it made me blush with embarrassment.

Raphael laughed softly. It was a remarkably sexy sound, but then, everything about him seemed sexy.

"So," he said, leaning back, one arm resting along the top of the booth, "how do you like Oak Hollow?"

I shrugged. "It seems like a nice place." I didn't tell him I wasn't sure I was going to stay. Even if the Werewolves and the Vampires didn't live here year-round, it was disconcerting knowing that any number of them could drop in unexpectedly from time to time. "Where do you live?"

"Here."

"As in Oak Hollow here?"

He nodded.

"But I thought . . . I mean, isn't this neutral territory? I didn't think any, uh, Supernatural types lived here year-round."

"Someone has to stay to make sure that everyone follows the rules."

"Oh, of course. How silly of me. I should have known." I was babbling, something I did when I was nervous or afraid. Sitting this close to Raphael Cordova, I was both. I had never been out with a man who was so handsome, or so blatantly male. Or one who was something more than a man.

"You needn't be afraid of me," he said with a quiet smile. "I mean you no harm."

There was no hint of fang when he smiled, but his

teeth looked strong enough to pierce steel. The skin of my throat would offer no resistance. "So, how long have you been a Vampire?"

"My whole life, I guess."

"How is that possible?"

"My father is a Vampire; my mother was mortal when I was born."

I shook my head. Everyone knew that Vampires didn't age once they were brought across. If he had been brought across when he was an infant, he would still be an infant. "I don't understand."

"Neither does anyone else. I was born a Vampire, but it wasn't evident until I turned thirteen."

"I thought Vampires didn't age," I said, confused. "I mean, you look a lot older than thirteen. Not that you look old," I added hastily, since he didn't look a day over thirty, "but you don't look thirteen."

"I can't explain it. I suppose it has something to do with the fact that my mother was mortal. When I reached twenty-five, I stopped aging. Like I said, I can't explain it. No one can."

"So, how old are you?"

"Eighty-five."

It wasn't a vast age. People were living a lot longer these days. But people who were eighty-five didn't look like they were twenty-five. Of course, he didn't look like a Vampire, either. In movies, Vampires were usually portrayed as rail thin and pale, but Raphael was anything but thin and pale. His skin had a nice olive tone, and he looked like a man in his prime, strong and healthy.

He smiled at the waitress when she brought our drinks. I watched him pour a glass of wine, all the while wondering if it was really wine. I had never seen any quite that dark, or that thick. Was it blood, or just my overactive imagination seeing things that weren't there?

He sipped it, then nodded his approval to the waitress.

"Can I get you anything else, my lord?" she asked.

Raphael looked at me. "Are you sure you wouldn't like something to eat? I'm told our filet mignon is excellent."

"*Your* filet mignon? Don't tell me you raised the beef?"

"Not quite," he said, grinning. "Didn't I tell you? I own this place."

I blinked at him. The man was full of surprises.

While I was still assimilating this latest bit of news, he asked the waitress to bring me a filet mignon, medium rare, with all the trimmings.

I waited until the waitress had moved away before asking, "But, if your mother was mortal and your father was a Vampire . . . how . . . I mean . . ." Words failed me. Discussing procreation probably wasn't considered polite dinner conversation, especially on a first date, but everyone knew the Undead couldn't create life.

"My father was brought across by an ancient Vampire," Raphael explained. "He was still new in the life when he met my mother. Apparently, he retained enough of his humanity to sire a child. Two in fact. I have a twin brother, Rane."

"Is he a Vampire, too?"

Raphael nodded. And then, apparently seeing the unasked question in my eyes, he said, "Until we hit puberty, Rane and I were no different than any other teenage boys, but once we turned thirteen . . ." He shrugged.

"Did you know it was going to happen? That you'd become Vampires?"

"No. Neither did my parents."

"It must have come as quite a shock."

He grunted softly. "You have no idea."

I tried to imagine how I would feel if I woke up one day and discovered that I was a Vampire. What would it be like, to be human one day and a blood drinker the next? All the Vampires I had ever heard of had been made, not born, and once made, they were no longer alive, but Undead. But if Raphael had been born a Vampire . . . I frowned. "So, you never died?"

"No. One day I was like any other teenage boy, and the next . . ." He made a vague gesture with his hand. "The day after I turned thirteen, I didn't wake up in the morning. Later, I learned that my mother had tried to rouse me, but to no avail. I woke with the setting of the sun, plagued by a thirst that I didn't understand."

"And your brother?"

"It was the same for him. Our parents weren't sure what to do, but that night my father took me and Rane outside. He told us what he thought was happening, though he couldn't be sure, since no other Vampire had ever sired children. After explaining things to us as best he could, he took us hunting with him. He mesmerized a young woman and took a bit of blood from her. As soon as I smelled it, I knew what I wanted, what I needed. Rane and I both fed from her, and that apparently completed our transformation. We were full-fledged Vampires from that night on."

"What happened to the woman?"

"Nothing. After we fed, my father sent her on her way."

"Just like that?"

"Not quite. He wiped our memory from her mind first." He looked at me for the space of a heartbeat. "You thought we killed her, didn't you?"

I had always heard that Vampires killed their prey, and said so.

"Some do," Raphael said. "The craving for blood, the thrill of the hunt, the power of holding a life in your hands, it's hard to resist, especially for the young ones. Sometimes they get carried away."

I nodded, as if I understood. I didn't, of course. The idea of craving blood was repulsive, the idea of taking a life reprehensible. I reminded myself that he hadn't killed the woman in question. Of course, that didn't mean he hadn't killed others. I would be wise to remember that.

Clearing my throat, I said, "Go on."

"Are you sure you want to hear this?" he asked somewhat dubiously.

"Yes, it's fascinating." And it was, in much the same way any gruesome accident catches and holds our attention.

"Since we could no longer go to school, our parents hired a tutor for us. As long as we lived at home, my mother treated us as though we were no different than we had been before the change." He smiled faintly. "It was a unique experience. We slept by day and met with our tutor in the evening. Because our class held its graduation ceremony after sunset, Rane and I were able to attend. We moved out of our parents' home the next day."

"Just a happy Vampire family," I murmured, intrigued by the story he had told me. I tried to imagine being married to a Vampire, having Vampire children, but it was a concept totally foreign to my way of thinking, to everything I believed in. Try as I might, I couldn't wrap my mind around it. And then I frowned. "What happened to your mother?" I supposed there was a slim chance she could still be alive, but if he was eighty-five, she would have to be well over a hundred.

"She's one of us now," Raphael said. "My father brought her across when Rane and I reached adulthood."

"Did she want to be a Vampire?" I had never heard of anyone asking to join the ranks of the Undead.

"Of course. My old man wouldn't have turned her against her will."

"Was she the same, you know, afterward?"

"Pretty much."

"And she was never sorry?"

"Not that I know of. And you have to remember, her parents, her husband, and her sons were all Vampires. We made the transition easy for her."

"Did you watch it happen?"

"No, although I wanted to."

I couldn't imagine why anyone would want to see such a thing, all that blood. Yuck!

"It's not such a bad life once you get used to it," he said quietly.

"Yeah, right." Drinking blood, living only at night, giving up all my favorite foods, not being able to enjoy a sunny day or take a walk in the rain on a pretty spring morning. I was surprised the whole world wasn't clamoring to join the ranks of the Undead. Not!

"Sure, you have to give up some things," he admitted, "but I'm never sick, never tired, I don't age, all my senses are enhanced. And," he said with a grin, "I don't gain weight."

It would have been a good selling point if Vampires could eat anything they wanted. "Vampires don't eat," I muttered, trying to imagine a life without chocolate or cookies or ice cream. "Of course they don't gain weight."

Rafe laughed. "True enough, but, like I said, it's not a bad life."

Technically, he wasn't alive at all, but I didn't say that. "And now you're the leader of the North American Vampires," I remarked. "How did that happen?"

He shrugged. "My godmother arranged it."

"You have a godmother?" I wouldn't have been any more surprised if he had told me that he was related to Cinderella.

"Yes." He grinned, no doubt amused by the stunned expression that was surely on my face. "Her name is Mara, and she's the oldest living of our kind. When we went to war with the Werewolves, our people decided we needed a leader. She was the obvious choice. She appointed others to positions of authority in various parts of the world. I was given North America, and my parents were given South America. My grandparents are looking after things in Europe. Last I heard, they were in France."

"What happened to your brother? Do you see him very often?"

A dark shadow passed behind Cordova's eyes. "I don't know where he is."

I heard the knife-edge of pain in his voice, a soul-deep sorrow that went beyond tears.

"No one in the family has seen Rane, or heard from him, in the last fifty years."

"What happened? Did you have a fight?"

"No, nothing like that. Not all who are made Vampires react the same way. Some seek it and embrace it. Some are turned against their will. Some accept the change and move on. Some can't adapt to their new lifestyle and quickly end it."

I held my breath. Was Rane one of those?

"For me, it was a natural transformation," Raphael said. "For Rane . . ." The pain in his eyes deepened. "At first, it seemed as though Rane had accepted it as I did. He was gifted with all the powers I had, and more."

"What do you mean 'more'?"

"He has a knack for magic, as well. It's a potent combination."

"I can imagine."

"Oddly enough, my maternal grandmother is also a practicing witch."

"So he inherited it from her?"

"No, our mother was adopted."

"Your family is certainly unique."

Rafe nodded. "Indeed."

"And your brother, he doesn't want to be a witch or a Vampire?"

"So it seems. All his life, he's been torn between light and dark, between good and evil. Becoming a Vampire was more than he could handle. He ran away from us, and from himself. I looked for him. The family looked for him, but he's closed his heart and his mind to us. I don't know how he is, or where he is. All I know is that he's alive." Rafe stared past me, his expression bleak. "I'd know if he were dead."

I had read somewhere that Vampires were incapable of tender human emotions, but whoever had written such a thing would surely have changed his mind if he could have seen the anguish on Rafe's face, the hurt in his eyes, or heard the pain in his voice.

I stared at him, wishing I could help, and thinking that I had learned more about Raphael Cordova and Vampires than I had ever wanted to know.

Chapter Four

Raphael was right about the filet mignon. It was the best I had ever tasted, rare and tender and seasoned to perfection. I have to admit, I felt a little strange enjoying a full-course meal in front of a Vampire. When I offered him a bite of my steak, he made the kind of face I would have made had he offered me a glass of warm blood.

"Don't you ever eat anything?" I asked. I couldn't imagine never drinking a glass of ice-cold lemonade on a hot day, never eating a double scoop of fudge-ripple ice cream, never biting into a cold, tart green apple, or a juicy slice of watermelon. And the thought of never again indulging in a brownie still warm from the oven didn't even bear thinking about. "Don't you miss it? Food, I mean."

He looked at the steak on my plate. It was medium rare, the inside a deep rosy pink, just the way I liked it.

"Sometimes," he admitted, "but not often." Lifting his glass, he took a drink.

I wondered again if it was really wine. I told myself it had to be. I mean, he had obviously planned to share it with me until I ordered something else. Still, when I wasn't looking, he could have signaled the waitress to bring him something more to his taste. I spent a moment debating whether to ask him, and then decided I didn't really want to know.

The waitress arrived to clear our dishes. She asked Raphael if she could bring him anything else.

He looked at me. "Kathy?"

"Nothing more for me, thanks, I'm full."

With a slight nod at me and a smile for Rafe, the waitress gathered my dishes and moved away from the table.

I shifted in my seat. I was all too aware of the silence, of the man beside me, and of the way his thigh was pressed intimately against my own. His scent tickled my nostrils. It wasn't cologne, it wasn't soap. I don't know what it was, just the scent of the man himself, I guess.

"Kathy?"

"What?"

"Would you like to go for a drive?"

I cleared a throat gone suddenly dry. Every instinct I possessed screamed that going for a drive with a man whose scent was more intoxicating than a shot of whiskey straight up was a very bad idea. So naturally I said yes.

Moments later we were flying down the highway at a hundred miles an hour. It was a first for me, and I have to admit that it was exhilarating until I let myself think about what would happen if the car skidded out of control and wrapped itself around a tree. It probably wouldn't hurt Raphael much, at least not permanently. I would most likely end up dead.

Before I could ask him to slow down, he eased off the gas and turned on the radio. Kenny G's "Songbird" filled the air, though I didn't pay much attention. I was too busy watching the speedometer. I didn't relax until we were doing a nice, reasonably safe sixty.

Raphael flashed a grin in my direction. "Sorry, I didn't mean to scare you. Going a hundred miles an hour with my hair on fire has always been my way of letting off steam."

"Really? What are you steamed up about?"

"You."

"Me?" The word emerged from my throat as little more than a squeak.

With a nod, he pulled off the road and put the car in Park. "You." His dark eyes glowed when he looked at me. "I've wanted you since the first night I saw you."

Mindful that a Vampire could mesmerize a human with little more than a glance, I was careful not to meet his gaze.

"Admit it," he said, and there was a rough edge to his voice. "You feel the same about me."

I started to deny it, but the words died, unspoken, as I recalled the image I'd had of the two of us lying entwined in each other's arms. I wasn't about to admit it, though, especially not here and now.

"Kathy, look at me."

"No way."

"Still afraid of me?"

"Darn right! I know all about Vampires. . . ." That was a lie. All I really knew for sure was that they drank blood, slept in coffins, and that the sun turned them to ash in the blink of an eye.

"Do you?" he asked, amusement evident in his tone.

"Well, not all," I amended, "but enough to know better than to look one in the eye." Especially now, when we were parked on a dark, deserted road in the middle of nowhere. I could scream for help until the cows came home, but no one would hear me.

I felt the weight of his gaze on my bowed head, felt the heat of his desire brush my senses like a breath of summer air. It filled the car with an almost palpable energy. I didn't know if it was some kind of Vampire magic or not, but it was all I could do to keep from crawling into his lap and begging him to make love to me. If Vampires had pheromones, his were working overtime.

"I think you'd better take me home."

I shivered as his fingertips slid, slow and sensuous, down my arm. "Is that what you want?"

I nodded. Being this close to him in a confined space was far too dangerous, and far too tempting. I mean, he was the most gorgeous creature, man or Vampire, that I had ever seen, and I'm only human, after all. Add to that the fact that I hadn't been in a man's arms or kissed by anyone other than my mother in a good long time, and well, you get the idea.

"Kathy." He caught my chin between his thumb and forefinger and forced my head up. "Please don't be afraid of me. I won't hurt you. I won't hypnotize you. I swear I'll never do anything you don't want me to do."

There was no safety in that, I thought wildly. I wanted him to sweep me into his arms and make mad, passionate love to me in every way humanly, or inhumanly, possible. I wanted to feel his hands on my body, wanted my hands on him.

I swallowed hard, glad that he couldn't read my mind. "Why me?"

He smiled faintly. "Why not you?"

"But, you've been a Vampire for years. You must have had dozens of women. . . ." I stared at him. For all I knew, he had a wife waiting at home. "You're not married, are you?" I told myself it didn't matter. He was a Vampire, not a potential husband. But I still wanted to know.

He looked offended. "I wouldn't be with you if I was," he said curtly. "I've never been married, although I came close once."

"Really?" Curiosity drove everything else from my mind. "What happened?"

He snorted softly. "What do you think? When she found out what I was, she called me every dirty name in the book, and then she packed up and left town."

"I'm sorry, that must have hurt."

He shrugged, as if it was of no consequence. "It was a long time ago."

But it still hurt. Though he tried to hide it, I could hear the pain in his voice. I resisted a sudden, almost overwhelming urge to comfort him, to stroke the black silk of his hair, to kiss his cheek and whisper that any woman who would walk away from him was a fool. Darn! What was I thinking? Alarmed by the turn of my thoughts, I folded my arms over my chest to keep from reaching for him.

Silence stretched between us, broken only by the chirping of crickets and Brooks & Dunn lamenting a good love gone bad. A capricious wind stirred the leaves on the trees. Clouds drifted over the moon, making the night darker still.

I wished Raphael would take me home. I wished he would take me in his arms and kiss me until I couldn't think straight. I wished I could make up my mind.

"Do you want me to take you back?"

I nodded, even though I didn't really want to go home. But staying here was a really bad idea. I refused to listen to the little voice in my head whispering that I was a coward. Maybe I was, but Raphael Cordova was far too tempting for my peace of mind. I had a feeling that kissing him and then stopping would be like trying to eat just one potato chip. It couldn't be done.

The drive back to the bookstore seemed endless. Raphael didn't seem inclined to talk, and try as I might, I couldn't think of a single thing to say to break the tense silence between us. I stared out the window. Why did I have to find him so darned attractive? Why did he have to be a Vampire?

A short time later, he pulled up in front of the shop. He handed me out of the car, walked me to mine, and waited while I unlocked the door and slid behind the wheel. Rolling down the window, I looked up at him. "Thank you for dinner."

"Can I see you again?" he asked.

As I had on several other occasions, I started to say no, only to find myself saying, "Yes, I'd like that."

I just hoped I wouldn't regret it.

Chapter Five

Raphael Cordova was much on my mind the next day. I thought about him while I fixed breakfast, thinking how sad it was that he couldn't enjoy a good meal anymore. How did Vampires exist without partaking of the finer things in life, like a ham-and-pineapple pizza, or a mug of hot chocolate on a cold rainy night, or chocolate chip cookies warm and fresh from the oven?

After breakfast, I took a shower, dressed in a loose knit gray sweater and a pair of comfy jeans, and left the house.

On the way to work, I made a quick stop at the jewelry store where I bought a pretty silver filigree cross on a sturdy silver chain, as well as a couple of thick silver bracelets for good measure.

Arriving at the bookstore, I read my snail mail, booted up my computer and checked my e-mail, and then spent an hour online reading through various book catalogs and filling out order forms for upcoming releases. The excitement over e-books had faded in the last few years. These days, it was rare for anything other than college and medical texts to be available in electronic format.

Print-on-demand books, once hailed as the future golden goose for publishers, had quickly gained prominence, and just as quickly plummeted to obscurity. As more and more people spent more and more time in front of computers, reading electronic media lost its appeal once the novelty wore off. Readers went back to gathering in bookstores, browsing through the shelves, or relaxing in a comfortable chair with a good book and a cup of coffee. Plus, there was nothing quite as satisfying as the smell or the feel of a new book. Of course, books themselves had changed over the years. New, synthetic paper kept the pages from turning yellow with age, spines were more durable, and the new ink didn't fade. Cover art had become an increasingly sought after art form. There was a big market for original cover art, with some canvases selling for thousands of dollars.

With time on my hands, my thoughts again turned toward Raphael. What was it like to be a Vampire, to sleep all day, to hunt for prey at night? I remembered the hurt in his voice when he talked about the woman he had loved and lost. It was hard to imagine a Vampire having a love life, getting married, sitting around the house watching satellite movies. Or reading Jordan Montgomery murder mysteries, I thought with a grin. I had always thought of Vampires and Werewolves as monsters so consumed with the lust for blood that they had little time for anything else.

Thinking I had a lot to learn, I turned back to my computer and checked the store inventory, looking for anything I could find on Vampires. Nothing came up on the screen, but I knew I had at least one book on the Supernatural. Before moving to Oak Hollow, I had bought up all the stock from a used bookstore that was going out of business. If I remembered correctly, there had been a book on Vampires in one of the boxes.

I finally found what I was looking for. It was at the bottom of a box in the back room, mixed in with a bunch of books I had decided were too outdated or too beat up to put out front.

Book in hand, I poured myself a cup of coffee and settled down in one of the chairs to learn what I could about the care and feeding of the Undead.

In ancient times, Vampires had been blamed for anything and everything that went wrong or couldn't be explained, whether it was a mysterious illness, a loaf of bread that failed to rise, cows that didn't give milk, or chickens that didn't lay eggs.

Fascinating, I thought, and before I knew it, I was caught up in the life and lore of Vampires. The author, Carl Overstreet, had done more than just list the ways to detect and destroy Vampires, he named names. Mara was listed as the oldest living Vampire. It was said that no one living knew how old she was, when she had been made, or who had made her. It was believed that she had been turned in the valley of the Nile during the reign of Cleopatra. It was rumored that she was truly immortal, that she was impervious to blade or stake, and that the sun's light no longer had any power over her.

I read the name again. Mara. Wasn't that the name of Raphael's godmother? Could it be the same woman? I'd have to ask Raphael the next time I saw him.

The book reinforced what I already knew: Vampires needed blood to survive and couldn't abide the sun's light. As Raphael had mentioned, the touch of silver burned their skin and weakened their Supernatural powers.

Reading on, I learned that unless they were very old,

like Mara, or very powerful, they were rendered unconscious during the day.

Vampires possessed a number of preternatural abilities. They could change shape, influence the weather, dissolve into mist, move faster than the human eye could follow, scurry up the side of a building like a spider, and compel others to do their bidding. It was this last ability that bothered me the most. It was disconcerting, knowing that Raphael could mesmerize me with those beautiful, dark eyes. I had been told that when under hypnosis, you couldn't be forced to do anything against your will, but we weren't talking about ordinary hypnosis here, we were talking about preternatural power wielded by Supernatural creatures.

Detecting the Undead was not so easy, which gave me pause to wonder how I had known Raphael was a Vampire when I first met him, or how I had recognized the Vampires he had sent to my shop. Obviously, I had some kind of Vampire radar that had been dormant until recently. Either that, or I'd never come across a Vampire before I met Raphael.

Business picked up a little late in the afternoon. I have to admit, every time the door opened, I felt a flutter in my stomach, even though I knew that, at this time of day, it couldn't be Raphael.

Just before dusk, Susie McGee and her brood trooped in. The boys headed for the children's section, punching each other along the way.

"I promised to buy the boys new books if they behaved at the doctor's office," she said, leaning against the counter.

"They aren't sick, are they?" I asked, thinking I had never seen such active, healthy-looking kids in my life.

"No, the appointment was for me. I thought I had a bad case of indigestion. Turns out I'm pregnant again."

Since I wasn't sure if this was good news or not, I didn't say anything.

"I'm not ready for another baby." She blew out a sigh. "I sure hope this one's a girl."

I smiled, but I couldn't help thinking that a little girl wouldn't stand a chance against three older brothers.

"So," she said, changing the subject, "how's the book business?"

"Picking up a little, but it's still slow." It was easy to see why there wasn't a Borders or a Barnes & Noble in town. The only thing keeping me afloat was the fact that the store was paid for, thanks to a tidy sum my great-aunt had bequeathed me.

"Maybe things will get better in the fall," Susie remarked. "We get a lot of tourists then."

"Really? Why?" From what I had seen of Oak Hollow, there wasn't much to attract visitors.

"Don't you know? Every autumn our town hosts a big Halloween Haunt. People come from miles around to see it."

Funny, that hadn't been in the brochure I'd read.

"It's held the night before Halloween out at the old Carrick place on Cross Creek Road. They have a pumpkin patch, a really scary haunted house, and games for the kids. They give prizes for the most original costume, stuff like that. It's really fun."

Some people believed the Carrick house was inhabited by the ghost of the last man who had lived and died there. It seemed like the perfect place to hold a haunted house. No doubt any Vampires and Werewolves in attendance would feel right at home. I was pretty sure that any Supernatural creatures who showed up would have some really great costumes.

A few minutes later, Susie's kids came running up to the counter, each one waving a book in one hand and punching the nearest sibling with the other.

As loud and obnoxious as her boys were, the store seemed quieter than usual after Susie and her brood left.

Since I kept the store open until nine on Fridays, I went over to the café a little after five for a quick dinner break. I ordered a turkey club sandwich, curly fries, and a chocolate malt. I know, too many carbs, too many calories, but hey, I deserved it.

While waiting for my meal to arrive, I glanced around the café, wondering if coming to Oak Hollow had been such a good idea after all. A Vampire lived here year-round. At the moment, there were a number of other Vampires in residence, which meant there were probably an equal number of Werewolves somewhere in the vicinity. I wondered if they were having a war council or a paranormal conference of some kind.

Maybe I should just close up the store, sell the house, and leave town. The idea wasn't as appealing as it should have been, and I knew Raphael Cordova was the reason.

I read the local newspaper while I ate. Most of the news concerned the new movie theater being built on the south side of town, whether it would have two screens or four, and if it would put the local drive-in out of business. I shook my head. Living in Oak Hollow was like living in the early part of the twentieth century. In a way, I hoped the town and its people never caught up to the present. Since we were pretty much off the beaten path, there wasn't much crime here; life was slower and more laid-back. The people were open and friendly, and when the baddies weren't here in number, the townspeople sat outside in the evening, or strolled down the street, stopping to chat with their friends and neighbors.

Several people nodded or waved to me as I walked back to the store. Flicking on the overhead lights, I went behind the counter, thinking maybe I should buy a portable DVD player so I'd have something to do while I waited for those elusive customers to find their way into my shop. I glanced around, wondering if I would attract more customers if I sold homemade fudge or cookies or something equally fattening and irresistible.

I was in the back room, unpacking a box of new releases, when the bell announced that someone had entered the store. My heart did a little tap dance at the thought that it might be Raphael. Running a hand over my hair, I took a deep breath and hurried toward the front of the store.

I knew a moment of disappointment when I saw that it wasn't my favorite Vampire. This man was fair where Raphael was dark, his eyes were yellow instead of black, but other than that, the two men were of a similar build, although Raphael was a few inches taller, and broader through the shoulders.

My skin tingled oddly as he moved toward me. He was a Were. I knew it immediately, as I had known that Raphael was a Vampire. But the moon wasn't full, so I figured I was safe enough.

I moved behind the counter. "May I help you?"

"I hope so. I'm looking for a book called *Nocturne* by Xavier Valdez. It's out of print, but I was hoping you might have an old copy lying around."

"It doesn't sound familiar," I said, "but I can check for you, if you'd like."

"Thanks."

I powered up my JG5000 and typed in what I was looking for. The JG5000 was the latest in computer technology. It was small, portable, required no hookup or cables, and the battery lasted for five years. You could talk to it or type in your commands; the JG could respond verbally or display the message on the screen. At home, I liked the verbal commands, but here at work, I used the keyboard.

I typed in the title, and when nothing came up, I typed in the author's name. "I'm sorry, nothing comes up. Have you tried the library?"

"No luck there, either. Well, thanks for trying," he said with a shrug. "It was worth a shot."

"Have you looked on WebNet? You might be able to find a used copy there."

"Struck out there, too. You're new in town, aren't you?"

I nodded. His question proved that he wasn't. "I'm sorry I couldn't help you."

"Coming in here wasn't a total loss," he said with a dazzling smile. "At least I got to meet you."

I couldn't believe it. Except for having dinner with Raphael, I hadn't had a date in six months, hadn't met a man who even appealed to me in all that time, and now, in less than a week, I'd met two gorgeous guys, and neither one of them was human. Talk about rotten luck!

"I'm Cagin, by the way."

"Just Cagin?"

"Joseph, but nobody calls me that."

"Kathy McKenna."

"So, Kathy, there's a pretty lake not far from here. How'd you like to go on a picnic Sunday afternoon?"

"I don't know . . ."

"Is it because we've just met?"

"Partly."

"Partly?"

"I'm sorry, I don't date Werewolves."

"No problem, then," he said with a wink, "since I'm not a Werewolf."

Funny, I'd been sure he was. Okay, so, maybe my Supernatural radar wasn't all that reliable.

"Come on," he coaxed, "I promise to be good. I'll even pack a lunch if you'll bring dessert." He glanced around. "I'll even buy something to sweeten the deal."

"All right," I agreed, "but only if I get to pick the book."

"Done!"

Grinning, I walked to the back of the store and picked up an enormous volume titled *Gunmen and Ghost Towns of the Wild West*. I had ordered it by mistake and had been wondering how I'd unload it, since the supplier refused to take it back.

"*Gunmen and Ghost Towns of the Wild West*," Cagin said, grimacing as he read the title. "What am I supposed to do with this?"

"I don't know," I said, stifling a grin. "I guess you could always use it for a doorstop."

"You drive a hard bargain."

"A deal's a deal, and the price is forty-nine fifty, take it or leave it."

With a rueful grin, he lifted his wallet from his back pocket and pulled out a credit card, which he slapped on the counter. "For that dirty trick, you have to pay the sales tax."

It sounded like a bargain to me.

I handed him the book and his receipt, gave him my address, and agreed to meet him Sunday afternoon after church.

The rest of the day dragged on by. Long after the sun had gone down, I kept hoping Raphael would come by, but he never did. Maybe he hadn't enjoyed himself on our date as much as I had, though I had to admit it was one of the strangest dates I'd ever been on.

Later that evening, while taking care of some overdue paperwork, my skin tingled with awareness. I looked up, expecting to see Raphael on the other side of the counter, but there was no one there. Frowning, I glanced around the store, certain that he was there, but if he was, he was invisible. Still, I couldn't shake the feeling that he was nearby, that he was watching me. And then, abruptly, the sensation was gone.

Feeling a little creeped out, I closed the store half an hour early and went home, bolting the front door behind me.

Saturday came and went, and there was still no sign of Raphael. Well, I could take a hint as well as the next girl. I told myself it didn't matter. He was a Vampire, after all, and no matter how attractive he might be, we had no future together. Besides, I couldn't imagine taking Rafe home to meet my folks. *Hi, Mom, Dad, this is Raphael. Oh, by the way, he's a Vampire.* I told myself I was better off without him, but deep down, I didn't believe it. Nor could I believe how much I missed a man I hardly knew.

At least I had Sunday's picnic with Cagin to look forward to.

Chapter Six

Raphael prowled the dark streets of Oak Hollow, his hunger and his frustration growing with every passing minute as he quietly cursed a longing he could not satisfy or ignore. Going out with Kathy McKenna had been as big a mistake as he had known it would be, but he had been helpless to resist. He didn't know what it was about her that drew him. Certainly he had dated other women who were as pretty and as charming, yet none had fired his imagination or his hunger the way she had. Like some exotic siren of myth and legend, she had captured his soul with her smile, his heart with her laughter, and now he couldn't think of anything else. She was in his thoughts by night and his dreams by day. The urge to carry her off to his lair and bed her, to kiss every inch of her sweet flesh, to savor the sweetness of her life's essence, burned through him like a fever with no cure.

Kathy.

Since seeing her on Thursday night, it had taken all the willpower he possessed to stay away from her. In all his existence, he had thought himself in love only twice.

He had killed the first woman; the second one had been the girl he had told Kathy about. He didn't intend to make the same mistake a third time.

But it hadn't kept him from dissolving into mist and entering the bookstore Friday night. Her scent had surrounded him, tantalizing him even in his intangible form as he hovered in the air near her desk. Drifting there, weightless, shapeless, he had recalled the softness of her skin, the warmth of her smile. He had tortured himself with her nearness until he couldn't stand it any longer, and then he had fled the building.

Resuming his own form, he had preyed upon the first man he had seen. Filled with impotent rage, he had taken the man's blood quickly, his hands cruel as he held his prey in place. He had been sorely tempted to drink the man dry. He was a Vampire, after all. Why not loose the beast that lurked within and revel in the power that was his? To what purpose did he cling to his humanity? For the approval of a woman who would never be his? He had released his pent-up frustration in a wild cry that had sent an alley cat scurrying for cover. Overcome with guilt and shame, he had released the helpless mortal, wiped the memory of what had happened from the man's mind, and sent him on his way. Hands tightly clenched, Rafe had watched the man stagger down the street until he was swallowed up in the shadows of the night.

Now, as he stalked the dark streets, Rafe couldn't help wondering what Kathy would think if she could see him at this moment. He didn't need a mirror to know how he looked now, with his fangs extended and his eyes red and glowing with the lust for blood. He had seen his own image mirrored in his brother's face often enough.

Muttering an oath, he vowed it was a side of him that Kathy would never see. To his regret, the only way to guarantee that she never saw him at his worst was to stay away from her.

The thought of never seeing her again was far more painful than he had expected.

Rafe grunted softly. He was eighty-five years old; he had been a Vampire for seventy-two of those years. He should be used to pain in all its forms by now.

Chapter Seven

There was only one church in Oak Hollow, and it was open to everyone who didn't want to drive the hundred or so miles to River's Edge, which was the next closest town and catered to all the major religions and a few I'd never heard of.

Reverend Paul was standing at the door on Sunday morning, welcoming his parishioners with a smile and a handshake, when I arrived. He was a nice-looking, middle-aged man with short-cropped brown hair and guileless brown eyes.

His smile was warm and sincere as he clasped my hand. "Good morning, Kathy. It's good to see you here."

"Thank you, it's good to be here."

I found a seat in a pew near the back, my gaze drawn, as always, to the beautiful stained glass window above the altar. In brilliant shades of blue and red, orange and gold, it depicted the Savior of the world sitting on a rock, a tranquil expression on His face as He stroked the head of a tiny black lamb. The rays of a bright sun gilded His hair and white robe.

I had mixed emotions when it came to religion. I didn't put any stock in the big bang theory. I'd heard it said once that believing in the big bang was akin to believing that you could throw all the parts of a car into the air and it would come down fully assembled. I didn't believe that mankind's ancestors had crawled out of some primordial soup, either. Evolution just didn't ring true. Neither hypothesis made sense to me. I believed in the creation story, though I had no idea where dinosaurs, Vampires, and Werewolves fit into the grand scheme of things. All I knew was that my heart and soul filled with a sweet sense of peace and hope when I looked at the Savior of the world as depicted in that stained glass window.

Reverend Paul took his place at the pulpit. The congregation sang an opening hymn, the reverend offered a prayer, the congregation sang another hymn, and then the reverend turned to his sermon. I guess the reason I liked him so much was because he didn't preach hellfire and endless damnation, but love, accountability, and forgiveness.

Susie sat across the aisle, her three sons sandwiched between her and her husband. It was the first time I had seen her boys sitting still, and the first time I had seen her husband. He had short blond hair and didn't look anything like I'd imagined.

Catching my gaze, Susie smiled at me. I smiled back, then returned my attention to what the reverend was saying. I tried to concentrate on the sermon, but my thoughts kept ping-ponging between Raphael's absence and my upcoming date with Cagin.

After church, Susie introduced me to her husband, Rick. The three of us made polite chitchat for a few minutes before I excused myself. I thanked the reverend for a fine sermon, then hurried home to change out of my church dress and into a pair of jeans and a sweater. I sliced the devil's food cake I had made for dessert and put it into a carrier, along with some paper plates, napkins, and plastic forks.

Cagin arrived right on time. He looked strong and fit in a pair of faded cutoffs and a white T-shirt that had a snarling tiger painted on the back. "Ready?"

"Ready." I grabbed a jacket from the closet, picked up the small basket that held the cake, and followed him out the door.

It was a beautiful day for a drive. The sky was a clear sapphire blue, the weather warm but not hot. The place Cagin had chosen for our picnic was beside a small blue lake. It was a lovely place, flanked by a carpet of thick green grass and tall willow trees. It looked remarkably like the mural I had painted. Ducks and geese floated on the surface of the water. I thought I saw a deer resting in the shade across the way. A hawk soared effortlessly overhead, its wings outstretched.

Cagin spread a blanket in the shade of a tree. Opening a huge picnic basket, he doled out china plates, crystal glasses, silverware, and linen napkins, along with a variety of sandwiches and containers of potato salad, baked beans, coleslaw, dill pickles, and olives.

"This is some picnic!" I exclaimed as he handed me a glass of chilled champagne.

"Nothing but the best."

We passed a pleasant hour over lunch, making small talk and getting to know each other. Cagin owned a number of small businesses in New Jersey, was an only child, had never been married, loved cold beer and fast cars, and collected motorcycles.

"A speed freak," I murmured, smiling. I couldn't help wondering what he was doing in Oak Hollow.

When I asked, he replied, "I'm on vacation, more or less."

"So you're just passing through?"

His gaze raked over me in a way that made me uncomfortable. "I could be talked into staying a while longer."

Since I didn't know what to say to that, I offered him a slice of cake instead.

He took it with a knowing grin, devoured it in three big bites, and stood up.

"That lake looks mighty inviting. What do you say we take a swim?"

"I didn't bring a bathing suit."

He looked at me, a challenge in his eyes. "You don't need one."

"Sorry, but skinny-dipping is out of the question until I know you better. A lot better."

"Whatever floats your boat," he said, and before I knew what he had in mind, he had stripped to the buff and plunged into the water. He swam to the far side of the lake with long, even strokes, then turned and swam back. When he approached the shore, I turned my back to the water. Call me a prude if you will, but he was a little too cavalier about his nudity for me.

Cagin's amused laughter brought the heat rushing to my cheeks.

After he pulled on his shorts and his sandals, we took a walk around the lake, and then, pleading a headache, I asked him to take me home.

I thought he would argue with me; instead, he tossed the dishes and leftovers into the basket, draped the blanket and his shirt over his shoulder, and headed for the car.

I stared after him. If we hadn't been so far from town, I would have walked home. Tempting as that was, common sense won out.

Needless to say, we didn't talk much on the way back to my place. I wouldn't have been surprised if, instead of stopping the car, he had just slowed down and expected me to jump out, but he parked the car and walked me to the door.

Delving inside my handbag for my keys, I muttered, "Thanks for the picnic."

He didn't say anything. Instead, he pulled me into his arms and kissed me, and then, whistling softly, he sauntered back to his car and drove away.

I stared after him, confused by both his abrupt change in attitude and his kiss. It hadn't been a bad kiss, as kisses go, but it hadn't set me on fire, either.

Ah, well, it really didn't matter, since I'd probably never see him again.

The rest of the afternoon stretched before me. Feeling at somewhat of a loss, I grabbed a rag and went from room to room, dusting the furniture. The house wasn't very big—two bedrooms, a bathroom, a living room with a fireplace and hardwood floors, a sunny kitchen, and a small dining room—but it was located on a large lot at the end of a long, narrow street. A white picket fence surrounded the backyard; directly behind the fence was an open field. To the right, a stand of tall timber covered several acres. The only other house on the road was a good distance away.

I had fallen in love with the place at first sight. In my spare time, I had repainted the living room, the bathroom, and one of the bedrooms.

About eleven o'clock that night, I took a long, hot shower, then slipped into a silky tank top and my favorite pajama bottoms, the ones decorated with tiny blue and purple hearts. After fixing a cup of hot chocolate, I lit a fire in the hearth, then settled down in front of the TV to watch a late movie.

I was drifting on the brink of sleep when someone rang the bell. Smothering a yawn, I went to the door. "Who is it?"

"Rafe."

The sound of his voice made my heart skip a beat. "What do you want?"

"To see you, of course. Why else would I be here?"

I glanced at the clock. It was after midnight. It was late for working people like me, but I supposed it was the shank of the evening for a Vampire.

I opened the door a crack. "I never gave you my address. How did you find me?" Since I was new in town and had a private phone number, I knew he hadn't found my name on the Web.

His gaze burned into mine. "Honey, I could find you ten feet down in the dark."

The look in his eyes, the heat in his voice, did funny things in the pit of my stomach.

"Are you going to invite me in," he asked, "or make me stand out here on the porch like some horny teenager?"

Stifling a laugh, I took a step backward. "Come on in."

I felt a peculiar shimmery sensation in the air around

me as he crossed the threshold, only then remembering that a Vampire couldn't enter a home without an invitation from the owner.

Raphael followed me into the living room. "Nice place," he said, glancing around.

I followed his gaze. The room wasn't anything fancy, but it was warm and cozy, from the braided rug in front of the hearth to the oil painting of a herd of wild horses running in the moonlight that hung over the mantel. A pair of red oak end tables flanked a high-backed sofa; a matching chair sat at an angle.

I gestured at the couch. "Please, sit down."

I don't know if he expected me to sit beside him or not, but I took the chair. Sitting next to him while I was wearing a skimpy tank top and pajama bottoms seemed like a really bad idea. Picking up the remote, I switched off the TV.

I was trying to think of something to say when Raphael sniffed the air, and then frowned. "Where have you been?"

The tone of his voice lifted the short hairs along my nape. "I haven't been anywhere, why?"

"Who were you with today?"

"I really don't think that's any of your business, is it?"

"Answer me, dammit! Who were you with?"

"You're not my father. I don't have to answer to you."

He uncoiled from the sofa and stood towering over me, his expression lethal. "Who were you with?"

I looked up at him, my mouth suddenly dry. "Just a guy who came into the bookstore."

"What's his name?"

"Cagin."

Raphael's whole body grew taut. "What were you doing with him?"

"I wasn't *doing* anything. If you must know, he took me on a picnic."

If possible, Raphael's black eyes grew even darker, narrowing to ominous slits. "You're dating a Were?"

"He's not a Werewolf. I asked him if he was, and he said no."

A mild oath escaped Raphael's lips. He raked a hand through his hair, then resumed his place on the sofa. "Werewolves aren't the only Were-creatures. You know that, don't you?"

I shook my head.

"There are a number of Were-creatures," he explained. "There are Were-leopards, Were-coyotes, Were-bears, Were-lions, and Were-tigers, to name only a few. Cagin is a Were-tiger."

I envisioned Cagin with a mouth full of sharp teeth. The better to eat you with, my dear. "I didn't know. I mean, I had no idea." But it explained the funny feeling I'd had when I met him, and it made me wonder anew how I was able to discern Vampires and Were-creatures from other people. I'd never been psychic or anything before. Or maybe I'd just never had the chance to use my gift, if that's what it was, until now.

"There's a big difference between Werewolves and other Were-creatures," Rafe went on. "The Were-tigers and such don't have to change when the moon is full."

"So they're really just shape-shifters?"

"Right. They're born that way, not made. Most of them are harmless, but you never know when one will turn on you. And once a Were-creature gets a taste for human flesh, they're just as dangerous and vicious as the Werewolves."

"So, where do the other Were-creatures stand in the war? Whose side are they on?"

"The Were-tigers are the only other Supernatural creatures involved. The rest have remained neutral so far."

"Why are the Were-tigers involved?"

"They like to fight."

I blew out a sigh, thinking I had been much happier before I knew Vampires and Were-creatures existed. It made me wonder what other monsters were lurking out there in the dark.

"Stay away from Cagin," Raphael said flatly. "You're not safe with him."

"But I'm safe with you?" I tapped my fingertips on the arm of the chair. "Seems to me that it's just a case of choosing who I want to bite me, a Vampire or a Were-tiger."

"You can't trust the Werewolves," he said curtly. "You can't trust Cagin."

"How do I know I can trust you?"

"Good point." He gazed into the fireplace for several moments, then said, "I told myself I wouldn't see you again, that no good could come from it."

"Then why are you here?"

He turned to look at me, his dark eyes intent upon my face. No other man had ever looked at me quite that way, as if every fiber of his being was focused solely on me. My breath seemed trapped in my throat as I waited for his answer.

"Because," he said quietly, "I couldn't stay away."

His voice was so warm and filled with such desire, I was surprised I didn't melt on the spot.

"Raphael . . ."

"I know how you feel. You're afraid to trust me, and

I don't blame you. Hell, I don't trust myself sometimes, but . . ." He blew out a breath that seemed to come from the very depths of his soul. "If you won't be my lover, would you at least be my friend?"

I didn't know what to say. Raphael Cordova was eighty-five years old. He'd been a dyed-in-the-wool Vampire for seventy-two of those years. Yet, at that moment, he sounded far younger than his years. Looking into his eyes, I saw the boy he must have been before his life was turned upside down. He probably hadn't had many friends, what with being tutored at home and all. And later, after he had been turned, it probably hadn't been any easier to find guys to hang out with. After all, not many thirteen-year-old kids were out on the town in the wee hours of the morning.

"What was it like, sleeping during the day and being awake all night? What did you do for fun? Did you get to go out late at night?"

"Not as much as we wanted to." A slow grin spread over his face. "Rane and I snuck out of the house a lot. Worried my Mom no end, the way we were always sneaking out. My dad was more lenient. He understood our need to explore the night, to learn what it meant to be what we had become, especially as we grew older." He grunted softly, and I knew from his expression that he was remembering his past. "Rane and I got into some hellacious situations. There were a couple of times when we'd have been in a world of hurt if our old man hadn't come to our rescue."

"What kind of situations?"

"Nothing too bad until we turned sixteen. It was about that time that we really started stretching our wings, so to speak, testing our powers, seeing how far we could go.

One night we got into a brawl with a motorcycle gang. Those guys really knew how to fight," he recalled with a wry grin, "but they were no match for a couple of teenage Vampires.

"The closest call we had was with a Vampire hunter. He trailed us one night. Being young and stupid and overconfident, we didn't pay any attention to him until he followed us into an alley that dead-ended against a six-story building. We were trying to decide whether to scale the building or turn and fight when he sprayed us with holy water. That stuff burns like hellfire. Some of it splashed in Rane's eyes, momentarily blinding him. While he was trying to shake it off, the hunter came after me. He had a silver dagger in one hand and a thick wooden stake in the other. If the old man hadn't shown up when he did . . ." Raphael shook his head. "I guess I wouldn't be here now."

"I'm glad your father found you in time."

"I guess it's pretty stupid of me to be telling you all this, isn't it?"

"I don't think so. Friends shouldn't have secrets from one another."

He stared at me for a full thirty seconds, and then he smiled. "So I haven't scared you away for good?"

"I don't know. What does being your friend entail, exactly?"

"Whatever you want it to."

"You mean like being there when you're feeling blue, driving you to the airport, and listening when you need someone to talk to?"

"Pretty much," he said with a melancholy smile, "except for driving me to the airport. So, what do you say?"

I couldn't resist the soulful expression in his dark eyes, or the barely suppressed note of hope in his voice. Here was a being with Supernatural powers, a man who could probably destroy me with a glance, and yet he wanted me to be his friend. How could I refuse? Besides, I didn't have any friends in Oak Hollow, either.

I stuck out my hand. "Hello, friend."

His hand, large and strong, engulfed mine. "Friends," he murmured. "Forever."

Forever. Here was a man who could promise me eternity and mean it. "So, friend," I asked, "what do you want to do now?"

His smile was slow and oh-so-sexy.

"Never mind that!" I said. "We're friends, remember? Not lovers."

He was still holding my hand. He squeezed it lightly. "You'll let me know if you change your mind about that?"

I nodded.

"So," he said, releasing my hand, "do you want to watch a movie or something?"

"Sure." Picking up the remote, I turned the screen on, then surfed through the channels until I found a movie neither of us had seen before. After a moment's hesitation, I joined Rafael on the sofa, careful to keep a respectable distance between us.

The screen might as well have been blank, the movie silent, for all that I got out of watching it. I couldn't concentrate on the plot, couldn't think of anything but the man sitting beside me. His presence filled the room; his masculine scent teased my nostrils. He rested one arm along the back of the sofa, his hand tantalizingly close to my nape. Even though we weren't touching, I was aware of every breath he took, every glance he slid in my direction. Every time he moved, I went still inside, waiting, wondering if he would reach for me. *Friends*, I thought. How could I be friends with a man who made me feel this way?

I was almost twenty-four years old. I'd had a number of boyfriends in high school, but nothing really serious until I was a senior. My parents hadn't liked Shane, which only made me more determined to see him. Even when I realized my parents were right about him, I refused to give them the satisfaction of breaking up with him until much later, which pretty much ruined my last year of school.

I didn't get serious about anyone else until Lyle. I was certain he was the man I would marry, the man I would spend the rest of my life with. That, too, had ended badly. Maybe Lyle and I would have lived happily ever after if I'd been willing to compromise my standards, but I'd made it through high school with my virginity intact, thanks to a vow I'd made with my friend, Sherry, who had been my best friend at the time. We had watched the so-called popular girls in school, heard the way the guys talked about the ones who put out, and decided our self-respect was worth more than a one-night stand with the captain of the football team. When I told Lyle I was a virgin and intended to stay that way, he had tried, forcibly, to change my mind. I'd had him arrested. Needless to say, that put an end to our relationship. I'd sworn off men after Lyle.

And now Raphael was here, tempting me with his ebony eyes and his slow, sexy smile. No matter how often I reminded myself that he was a Vampire, it didn't seem to help. He was just the kind of man I had always dreamed of, only he wasn't really a man at all, and I was afraid that allowing myself to care for him wouldn't be a dream come true, but a nightmare. And yet I wanted his touch more than my next breath.

As if he knew what I was thinking, he turned toward me, the heat in his eyes hotter than any fire.

My heart seemed to slow, and then it sped up. I could feel it pounding in my ears. From the way Raphael was looking at me, I knew he could hear it, too, just as I knew that the heat in his eyes wasn't entirely from the urge to make love.

What would it be like, to let him bite me, to know he was drinking my blood?

The thought washed through my veins like ice water, and even though I was loathe to admit it, even to myself, it held a modicum of fascination. In the old *Dracula* movies, the women always swooned when under Dracula's spell. They never resisted; instead, they bared their throats in silent invitation, their expressions bordering on sheer ecstasy as he bent over their necks, his black cloak settling over them like a shroud.

"Does it hurt?" I asked curiously.

Raphael didn't pretend he didn't know what I was asking. "That depends on the Vampire."

That was interesting. "In what way?"

"There are some who feed like wild animals. They take what they want without a care for their . . ." He paused, and I could see him searching for a word that wouldn't frighten or offend me.

"Prey?" I said it for him, since he seemed to be having a hard time.

He nodded. "Others who are more thoughtful make it a pleasant experience."

"So, how come you never hear anyone talking about how wonderful it is to be some Vampire's dinner?"

"Because we wipe memory of us from their minds."

"You can do that?"

He nodded again.

"Have you ever done that to me? Bitten me and then made me forget?"

"No, and I never will."

I hoped he was telling me the truth. "How often do you have to . . . eat? Drink?"

He shrugged. "Once a week is sufficient to sustain life, though not very satisfying."

"What if they're drunk? Do you get tipsy?"

"No," he said, chuckling.

"What if you drink from someone who's got a really bad cold? Or the flu? Do you get sick, too?" Although research scientists had managed to eradicate AIDS and most of the contagious diseases known to man, there was still no cure for the common cold.

"We tend to avoid those who are in ill health, even though their sickness doesn't affect us."

I wondered if that was common knowledge. I mean, if Vampires could drink tainted blood without it affecting them, maybe scientists could use their blood or DNA to find a cure for the new strain of influenza that had recently been discovered.

"Do you like it?" I asked, my curiosity growing by leaps and bounds. "Drinking blood? I mean, isn't it really gross?"

"It should be, but it isn't." His gaze slid to my throat. "It's very sweet, actually."

"Right."

He laughed softly. "Don't knock it until you've tried it."

"No, thank you!"

He laughed again, a husky, sexy sound that wrapped itself around me like warm velvet. The attraction between us flared to life, ignited by the heat in his eyes. I wanted to be in his arms, to feel his body pressed against mine, to taste his kisses . . . and that was all, I assured myself, just a kiss, nothing more, even though my whole body ached with wanting him.

Surely one kiss wouldn't hurt.

"Kathy." His voice was thick with longing.

"Kiss me." The words came out in the barest of whispers, but he heard them.

His arm slid around my shoulders, and I leaned into him, closing my eyes as his mouth claimed mine. His lips were firm and cool, his kiss unhurried. I scooted closer, wanting to feel his body pressed against mine. I slid my hand under his shirt, my fingers moving restlessly over his broad back.

At my touch, he deepened the kiss, his tongue sliding over my lower lip, dipping inside to taste and explore. Heat exploded through me, as if I had swallowed a piece of the sun. That quickly, I was on fire for him.

He cupped the back of my head in one hand while he lifted me onto his lap, so that I was straddling his hips. I moaned softly, scorched by the heat of his arousal. In a distant part of my mind, I remembered my mother warning me to never, ever, sit on a boy's lap. As I had only been ten or eleven at the time, I had been puzzled by her advice. The reason for her warning was blatantly obvious now.

"Kathy . . ." His voice was ragged as he whispered my name.

Lifting my head, I gazed into his eyes, deep black eyes that seemed to glow with a fire all their own.

"If we don't stop now," he said in that same rough tone, "we're going to take our friendship to a whole new level."

I stared at him, every fiber of my being urging me to take him by the hand and lead him to my bed. It was what he wanted. It was what the woman in me wanted. But a little part of me, that one tiny part that was still rational, warned me that it would be a gigantic mistake. Lust wasn't love. One night didn't mean a lifetime commitment. Once I crossed the line and let him make love to me, there would be no going back.

With a sigh of regret, I climbed off his lap, turned my back to him, and took a deep breath. Even if he hadn't been a Vampire, I wasn't about to break my vow and jump in the sack with a man I had known for only a few days. But oh, my, it was tempting.

A tingle of awareness slid down my spine, and I knew he was standing close behind me.

"You're angry."

"No." I turned to face him. "It was as much my idea as yours. But . . ." I blew out a sigh. "Things are moving a little too fast for me, that's all."

"Still friends?" he asked with a roguish grin.

"Still friends."

Lowering his head, he kissed me lightly on the cheek. "Good night, then."

"Good night."

I accompanied him to the door, then stood on the porch, thinking that he looked just as good walking away. I liked the way he moved. I liked the way his jeans clung to his long legs and lean hips. I liked his tight butt. It took all my willpower not to call him back.

He turned when he reached his car. "Like what you see?" he asked, his voice tinged with amusement. Even in the dim light, I could see the smug look on his face. "It's not too late to change your mind."

I felt my cheeks flame with embarrassment. How had he known I was checking him out? Or that I was having second thoughts about sending him away?

I shook my head. It just wasn't fair! Not only was he sexier than any man on two legs had a right to be, but now he was reading my mind!

Chapter Eight

I was unloading a box of new paperback releases on Monday morning when Susie arrived. I was relieved to see that, for once, her boys weren't trailing at her heels. Not that I have anything against kids, it's just that her three seemed more like six. Every time they came into the store, I was afraid they were going to break something, tear something, or just drive me crazy with their constant bickering and punching. I didn't know how she stood it, day after day.

"Hi," I said. "What brings you here so early?"

"Oh, nothing. I was just taking a walk. It's supposed to be good exercise, you know, and . . . did you hear anything out of the ordinary late last night?"

"I don't think so." When Raphael was kissing me, the whole world could have blown up and I'd have been none the wiser. "Why?"

"Oh, it's probably nothing." She smiled, but it looked forced. "Rick says I'm imagining things again."

I came out from behind the counter. "Come on, we can sit down and talk over coffee." I had bought a couple of cute ceramic mugs at the pottery shop. I filled a cup for her and one for myself. "So, what kinds of things are you imagining?" I asked when we were both seated.

"Well, last night I got up a little after midnight to go to the bathroom. Seems like I'm always going these days. Anyway, I heard a wolf howling, and when I looked out the window, I'm sure I saw three wolves attacking a man. Rick said I must have imagined it. He says Oak Hollow is neutral territory, so it couldn't have been Werewolves, and that wild wolves don't attack people."

Susie stared into her coffee cup, her brow furrowed. "I went outside this morning after Rick went to work. There were signs of a struggle and what might have been dried blood on the ground. This has always been such a peaceful place. . . ." She looked up at me, her expression troubled. "Rick doesn't believe there's anything to worry about, but . . ." She placed one hand on her belly. "He says it's just my hormones acting up, blowing everything out of proportion, but I'm afraid something terrible happened last night, and that it will happen again. That it might happen to us."

"I'm sure Rick's right and there's nothing to worry about," I said, hoping to calm Susie's fears, but in the back of my mind, I found myself thinking, what if she was right? What if the Werewolves and the Vampires no longer considered this neutral territory? If they turned this into a war zone, no one would be safe.

Susie stayed another half hour or so and then left to run some errands before she had to pick her kids up from school.

I went back to unloading the box of books—books no one would probably buy—but I couldn't stop thinking about what Susie had said. I knew there were at least fourteen Vampires in town, maybe more. Had fourteen Werewolves showed up to keep things even? Had they had some kind of scuffle last night? Was it time to pack up and leave town? I shook my head. If this remote little burg wasn't safe, no place was. As for the conflict between the Vampires and the Werewolves, I knew someone who could tell me what was going on. Unfortunately, I didn't know how to get in touch with him. And it was just as well. Being able to call him was a temptation I didn't need.

While I was shelving the books, I remembered a conversation I'd had with Raphael. I had been surprised to learn that he lived in Oak Hollow, and he had replied that someone had to stay and make sure that everyone followed the rules. At the time, it hadn't occurred to me to ask if that meant there was a full-time Werewolf in residence as well. But now that I thought about it, it seemed like a logical assumption.

To my surprise, just before noon, several moms trooped into the shop, their children in tow. They all nodded in my direction or murmured hello as they headed toward the far corner of the store where I kept the children's books.

After a few minutes, I went back to see if I could help, and the next thing I knew, I was chatting with the women as if we were all old friends. Two of the mothers asked me to order books for their kids, a third ordered several romantic suspense novels for herself, another asked about a murder mystery for her husband.

Some time later, after the kids had all chosen books, a couple of the moms wandered through the shop, picking up a new book here, a used book there.

It turned out to be quite a profitable day. By the time

the women left the store, it was almost two, and my stomach was growling. I debated closing the shop and running out for a sandwich, but since I'd be closing up at six, I snacked on a candy bar instead and promised myself a healthy dinner later.

A few more customers trickled into the shop throughout the afternoon.

At six sharp, I closed the store. Standing on the sidewalk, my keys in hand, I decided dinner at the café sounded a lot better than going home and cooking a solitary meal.

I slipped my keys into my pocket and strolled down the street toward Carrie's Café, hoping that nothing would happen to change the ambience of this quaint little town. I loved it that the movie theater still played a double feature on Friday and Saturday nights, and that the barber shop still had a red-and-white-striped pole out front, and that the soda shop still served malts in the same shiny stainless steel containers they were made in. I liked it that the stores didn't all look like cement blocks with windows, and that each one was unique. I liked it that the first few pages of the newspaper reported on what was happening in Oak Hollow—Daisy Parker delivered a healthy, seven-pound baby boy on Sunday; Jeffrey Madden pitched a no-hitter at the high school softball game Saturday night; Emma Watson's strawberry preserves won first prize at the River's Edge Country Fair; Ed Stefan and Laura Peterson were engaged.

Crossing the street toward Carrie's Café, I nodded at an elderly couple I recognized from church, although I didn't know their names.

Carrie Watts, who owned the café, smiled at me as I walked in the door. She was a tall, middle-aged woman with curly brown hair, gray eyes, and the biggest dimples I had ever seen. I smiled back at her, then found a small table near the window. A waitress brought me a menu, and after a moment, I decided on a small salad, a cheese-burger, curly fries, and a chocolate malt. So much for my decision to have a healthy dinner.

I had only been there a few minutes when Cagin slid into the chair across from mine.

"Mind if I join you?" he asked.

"A little late to be asking, isn't it?"

He grinned. "I was afraid if I asked first, you'd tell me to get lost."

"You'd have been right."

"Hey, I'm sorry if I came on a little too strong the other day."

"You lied to me."

His brows shot up. "When?"

"I asked you if you were a Werewolf and you said no."

"I'm not."

"Don't split hairs with me. You're a Were-tiger, aren't you?"

"But not a Werewolf," he said with an easy grin. "How'd you find out, anyway?"

I didn't tell him that I had sensed he wasn't human. In the first place, I still wasn't sure how I knew; in the second place, something told me I'd be better off if no one else knew about it.

While I was trying to decide how best to answer, he muttered, "Cordova told you, didn't he?"

"Maybe."

"What are you doing hanging around with a dead man?"

A dead man? Raphael Cordova was the most vibrantly

alive man I had ever met. And since he had never died, "dead man" was hardly an accurate description. I didn't see any need to mention that, either, because if there was one thing I was certain of, it was that I couldn't trust the man sitting across from me.

"Hi, Cagin," the waitress said, returning to my table. "Can I get you anything?"

"Hey, Pam. How about a steak sandwich, rare, and a cup of black coffee?"

"You've got it, you handsome devil."

Cagin licked his lips as he watched Pam walk away. "Cute kid."

"Uh-huh." I had a mental image of Pam as Little Red Riding Hood, and even though Cagin wasn't a Were-wolf, I had a mental image of him lying in wait for her, only this time there would be no heroic woodsman to save her from the big bad wolf, or big bad tiger, as the case may be.

"Kathy?"

Startled from my reverie, I realized he had asked me a question. "What?"

"I asked if you were busy Friday night. I thought maybe we could try again."

"I don't think so."

"Come on, give a guy a break."

"You aren't a 'guy.'"

"You're not holding what I am against me, are you?"

"Not exactly, it's just that I'm still recovering from a bad breakup. I'm really not ready to start seeing anyone again on a regular basis."

"Except for Cordova."

I stared at him, searching for a reply, relieved when the waitress brought my salad and our drinks. The fact that Cagin knew I had gone out with Raphael bothered me, although I wasn't sure why. I mean, I wasn't trying to keep it a secret or anything. Lots of people had seen us together. I guess someone could have mentioned it to Cagin.

I waited until Pam moved away from the table before saying, "What I do, and who I see, are none of your business."

With a shrug, he added two packets of sugar to his coffee and took a drink.

Pam returned with the rest of our order a few minutes later.

Cagin picked up his sandwich and took a bite. Red juice dripped down the corners of his mouth. It looked very much like blood. I knew Raphael drank blood, but he didn't eat his prey.

We said little during the rest of the meal. Cagin ate quickly, then leaned back in his chair, lazily studying me with his amber eyes. As the seconds went by, it made me increasingly uncomfortable. Raphael had gazed at me just as intently from time to time, but it had never made me feel as if I were a piece of meat.

I folded my napkin and laid it beside my plate, placed my fork on top of it, and pushed away from the table. "I'm going home."

"Just like that?"

"Just like that." I reached into my purse and pulled out a twenty-dollar bill. "That should cover my dinner."

He leaned forward, his eyes narrowed. "What the hell do you think you're doing?"

"I think I'm leaving. Good night."

"Sit down," he said curtly. "You're not going anywhere."

I was about to tell him to go to hell when a voice spoke from behind me.

"Are you ready to go home, Kathy?"

Relief poured through me when I looked up and saw Raphael. "Yes, I am."

Cagin's eyes narrowed to ominous yellow slits. "What the hell are you doing here, Cordova?"

"Rescuing my fair lady from the dragon," Raphael replied. He offered me his hand. "Shall we go?"

Cagin sprang to his feet, his eyes blazing with anger.

I clung to Raphael's hand, my heart pounding. Surely they wouldn't fight here, in the restaurant. A quick look around confirmed that everyone in the café was staring avidly in our direction, no doubt waiting to see who would throw the first blow.

"This isn't the time or the place," Raphael said quietly. "Sit down and cool off."

"This isn't over." Cagin spat the words.

"Just tell me where and when," Raphael said. Still holding my hand tightly in his, he walked me out of the restaurant. His car was parked in a red zone at the curb. He opened the door for me, and then closed it with a little more force than necessary.

Still feeling shaky, I watched him walk around the front of the car to the driver's side. Opening the door, he slid behind the wheel.

As Raphael pulled away from the curb, I glanced out the side window to see Cagin standing on the sidewalk.

Raphael drove in silence for several minutes. Tension radiated off of him like heat from a blast furnace. I couldn't tell if his anger was directed toward Cagin or toward me, or if it was even anger I was sensing.

My apprehension kicked up a notch when he pulled

up in front of a large two-story house located at the end of a long dirt road lined with cypress trees. The house was made of faded red brick and had a tile roof. Four steps led to a covered veranda that spanned the front of the house. I only saw one window. It was on the first floor, and barred.

I cleared a throat gone suddenly dry. "Where are we?"

"My place." He cut the engine and got out of the car.

His place. Oh, Lordy. Sitting in the restaurant with Cagin suddenly seemed a lot safer than accompanying a Vampire into his lair.

I was trying to think of a way to convince Raphael to take me home when he opened the car door and reached for my hand. The next thing I knew, he was leading me up the porch stairs. The front door, made of what looked like solid steel, opened seemingly of its own accord. Interior lights came on as I crossed the threshold ahead of Raphael.

The sound of the door closing behind me sent a shiver down my spine.

"Make yourself at home," he invited.

The living room, sparsely furnished, was decorated in earth tones. The main focus of the room was an enormous fireplace that took up most of one wall. I stared at it, thinking it could easily hold an elephant or two. A deep brown leather sofa was situated in front of the biggest television screen I had ever seen. A pair of matching leather chairs faced the sofa. The carpet beneath my feet was a dazzling white. A large painting hung over the fireplace. It depicted a black knight astride an equally black horse. A large green dragon loomed in the distance. A collection of dragons made of onyx, jade, pewter, and carved wood were scattered on the mantel amid several black candles.

"Do you mind if I look around?" I asked.

"Help yourself."

An arched doorway to my left opened onto the kitchen. I peered through the doorway, my gaze sweeping the room, noting that the kitchen was bare except for a small black refrigerator and a microwave oven. The countertop was black granite; the floor was white tile. There were no windows in the room, which I thought was odd, especially for a kitchen, and no back door. I wondered if Rafe had plastered over the windows to block the sun.

A short hallway opened off the kitchen. My feet made no sound on the thick carpet. The first door off the hall was a guest bathroom with a commode, sink, and a small shower. There were no windows in this room, and no mirrors. A small bedroom adjoined the bathroom. The walls were a pale moss green, the carpet white, the furnishings no more than a twin bed made of black wrought iron and an antique chest of drawers made of dark oak. Again, there were no mirrors in evidence, and no windows.

I tried the door at the end of the hallway, but it was locked. It was Rafe's room. I knew it as surely as I knew the sun would rise in the morning.

Backtracking, I returned to the living room, my feet sinking into the carpet's deep pile as I made my way to the sofa. I had never known anyone who had white carpeting before. My first thought was that bloodstains would be really hard to get out, but then I realized that he probably didn't bring his dinner home with him.

Raphael sat beside me. He made a gesture with his hand, and a fire sprang to life in the hearth.

"You should be a magician," I muttered, remembering how he had opened the door and turned on the lights, all with a wave of his hand.

"The Great Cordova," he remarked with a grin. "I like the sound of that." And then his expression turned serious. "What were you doing with Cagin?"

"I wasn't 'doing' anything with him. I was having dinner when he invited himself to join me. How did you know I was there, anyway?"

"As I said before, I could find you in the dark, ten feet down."

I told myself I should be annoyed that he had been following me, or at least looking for me, but I couldn't be angry because it proved that he had been thinking about me, maybe missing me, and that pleased me to no end.

"Why does my being with Cagin make you so angry?"

"I don't like him. I don't trust him. Can I get you something to drink?"

"Like what?" *A glass of blood in a crystal goblet?* I banished the image from my mind.

"A glass of wine, a soft drink, a cup of coffee or tea?"

I blinked at him, surprised that he kept such a variety of beverages on hand.

Apparently reading my mind again, he said, "I bought them the night after we met."

"So, you were that sure of me, were you?"

"Not sure," he replied. "Hopeful."

"Hopeful that you'd get me here and have your wicked way with me?" I asked, only half kidding.

He laughed, the way an indulgent parent might laugh at a precocious child. It reminded me that he was old enough to be my grandfather. Lord, in his eyes, I probably *was* little more than an infant!

"What did Cagin want?"

"What?" The sudden change of topic gave me pause. One minute we were talking about intimate things and the next he was asking about a Were-creature. Was that why he had brought me here, to see if I had any inside information on the Weres? I lifted my chin defiantly. "He asked me out on another date."

Rafe leaned forward, his hands clenched. "You didn't accept?"

I had his full attention now. "A girl has to date someone," I said flippantly.

In a move faster than my eyes could follow, he was towering over me. "We talked about this before."

I stared up at him. The man could be scary as hell when he wanted to.

"I want your promise," he said. "Now, tonight, that you won't see him again."

"I can't help it if he shows up where I am. I mean, what am I supposed to do if he comes into my store? Run away?"

"That's a good start."

"Like I could outrun a Were-tiger," I muttered drily.

Raphael gazed down at me, his expression softening. "Forgive me," he said, resuming his seat. "It's just that I'm worried about you."

"Worried? About me? Why?"

He hesitated, as though debating whether to tell me the hard truth or sugarcoat it with a lie. The truth won out. "You're important to me," he said slowly, "and Cagin knows it. And until I know what side he's on, I'd rather you stayed away from him."

I stared at Raphael, a sudden coldness sweeping through me. He didn't have to spell it out for me. Cagin and Raphael were enemies, that much was obvious. No doubt I would make an excellent hostage for the Were-wolves. Even more frightening was the thought that, even though Raphael seemed fond of me, we hadn't known each other very long. There was no bond be-tween us, no reason to think he would spill any secrets or turn traitor if my life was threatened.

Leaving Oak Hollow was starting to sound better and better.

Raphael shook his head. "It's too late for you to leave."

"Stop that!"

He lifted one brow. "Stop what?"

"Reading my mind. It's very annoying."

He laughed softly. "I'm sure it is."

"How do you do it, anyway? Are you psychic on top of everything else?"

"In a way, although I have to admit, most people aren't as easy to read as you are."

"And what makes me so easy to read?" I asked irritably.

He dragged his hand over his jaw, his expression thoughtful. "I'm not sure, but I've got a theory."

"Would you like to share it with me?"

"You won't like it."

I was sure of that.

"Do you believe in soul mates?" he asked. "One woman made for one man, that sort of thing?"

Feeling skeptical, I asked, "Do *you* believe in that sort of thing?"

He didn't move, but he suddenly seemed closer. "I never used to, until I met you."

A romantic Vampire. Just what I needed. "And what makes me so different from anyone else?"

"Come on, Kathy, I know you feel it, too, that connection between us. It was there the first night I walked into your store."

I wanted to contradict him, but I couldn't. I remembered all too clearly the night I had been in the back room at the bookstore. I had known the minute Raphael had entered the building. I'd had no explanation for it at the time, and while I wasn't sure I believed that we had been made for each other, we did seem to have some kind of extraordinary awareness of one another.

Logic made me shake my head in denial. He was sixty-two years older than I was, and a Vampire to boot. Unless fate was playing a really bad joke, there was no way on Earth that Raphael and I could be soul mates, or any other kind of mates, for that matter. And yet, even now, the attraction between us crackled like a live wire.

"We're supposed to be friends," I said, my voice little more than a husky whisper. "Just friends. Remember?"

He nodded slowly, his gaze locked on mine. Dropping to his knees in front of me, he took one of my hands in his.

"I remember," he said, his voice as rough around the edges as mine had been. "But I don't think it's possible."

The flames in the hearth seemed to burn brighter, hotter. It felt like the room was closing in on me as I tried to draw my gaze away from Raphael's and failed. "Stop that."

"Stop what?"

"Whatever it is that you're doing."

"Honey, I'm not doing anything."

"I don't believe you." It had to be some kind of Vampire magic. I mean, it just had to be. How could I feel this way about a Vampire, even if he was the best looking guy I had ever seen? I shook my head. "This . . . whatever it is I'm feeling, I don't believe it's real. It can't be real."

"How can I convince you?"

"I don't know." I pulled my hand from his and made a shooing motion. "For starters, you can give me some space."

"Whatever you want." Rising, he backed up several paces, putting some distance between us.

It didn't help. My skin felt too tight; my blood felt like it was on fire. It was hard to think, hard to remember to breathe.

"I need to go to the restroom," I said, and then wondered if Vampires had the same needs as humans. After all, they didn't eat. . . .

The look in his eyes told me he knew this for the ploy it was.

Rising, I forced myself to walk sedately out of the room. I stared at the closed door at the end of the hall. Why was it locked? What was he hiding in there? The image of a coffin quickly sprang to mind, something burnished and bronze with white satin lining. Shaking off the morbid mental imagery, I went into the bathroom, closed the door, and turned the lock.

Standing in front of the sink, I soaked a washcloth in cold water and pressed it against my burning cheeks, hoping it would cool me off, although I doubted even a dip in the Arctic Ocean could put out the fire Raphael had ignited. What was I going to do about him?

Sitting on the edge of the oval-shaped tub, I glanced at my surroundings. There were no windows in this room, either, and no mirrors. I noted absently that he had good taste, and I wondered if he had decorated the house himself or had it done by a professional decorator. The sink top was black marble veined with gold; the basin was white, the fixtures antique brass. The deep red towels hanging from the towel bar made a bold statement against the white walls. The stall shower was easily large enough for two. I quickly shook off the all-too-erotic image of the two of us in that shower, our bodies pressed together in a soapy, steamy embrace.

I ran a hand through my hair, then glanced at my watch. I couldn't stay in here forever. Sooner or later, I would have to go out and face him.

I jumped when someone knocked on the door. It could only be Raphael.

"You okay in there?" he asked.

"Fine."

"You planning to come out anytime soon?" There was no mistaking the amusement in his voice.

Muttering under my breath, I unlocked the door and came face-to-face with the man who had troubled my thoughts and haunted my dreams since the moment he walked into my store.

"How long are you going to fight this attraction between us?" he asked.

"Until I get over it," I retorted.

"Take as long as you need," he said, a glint of humor lighting his dark eyes. "I've got time."

Indeed, I thought, he had all the time in the world.

Chapter Nine

Raphael was driving me home later that night when I suddenly remembered what Susie had told me earlier in the day. I glanced over at Raphael. If there had been some kind of Were/Vampire battle fought the night before, he would surely know about it. But would he tell a mere mortal like me? I shrugged inwardly. There was only one way to find out.

"Was there some sort of confrontation between the Vampires and the Werewolves last night?"

He looked at me, his eyes narrowed. "Who told you that?"

I shrugged. "I don't remember. Is it true?"

"An acquaintance of mine was destroyed last night," Raphael said, his voice tight. "He was attacked by three Werewolves."

"I'm sorry."

"How did you know?"

"I told you, someone mentioned it. They heard a noise but thought they might have imagined it." I studied

Raphael's profile. His expression was hard, implacable. "I thought Oak Hollow was neutral territory?"

"It's supposed to be."

"Then why are there so many Vampires and Were-wolves running around? Is something going on?"

"We had a meeting last week."

"What kind of meeting?"

He grunted softly as he pulled up to a stop sign, then made a left turn. "I guess you could call them peace talks. There have been an inordinately large number of deaths among us in the last few months. Some of the older Werewolves and Vampires, my grandparents among them, have been . . ."

"Your grandparents are Vampires, too? All of them?" I'd been taught Vampires couldn't create life. Had I been wrong?

"No, just the ones on my mother's side."

"And they're married?" I couldn't keep the shock out of my voice.

"Of course."

Married Vampires. Who would have guessed? Once again, I realized I had a lot to learn about the Undead. "Go on."

"As I was saying, the older Werewolves and Vampires are trying to persuade the young hotheads that killing each other isn't the answer, and that whichever side prevails will just have to turn around and fight the humans. The Werewolves aren't as vulnerable as the Vampires, but they're still small in number compared to the human population. My grandfather reminded everyone that, once spurred to action by fear or in self-defense, the humans can be a formidable foe. Better to live in the shadows as we have done in the past, he said, than give the mortal population reason to hunt us to extinction."

"Did anyone listen to him?"

"Mara agreed with him. She decreed that the Vampire community would honor a truce, if the Weres would do the same. Clive, who's the head of the Werewolves, also agreed to a truce. Unfortunately, not everyone wants peace. There are hotheads on both sides who want to take over the world, and they don't care how many on either side are killed in the process. The Weres who attacked Cristophe last night did so in an effort to destroy the truce, but Mara and Clive had been expecting something like that to happen sooner or later."

"I'm sorry about your friend."

"He wasn't a friend," Raphael replied. "Just someone I knew." He pulled up at the curb in front of my house and put the car in Park, then turned to face me. "Not a friend like you." His hand slid over my shoulder and down my arm, leaving a frisson of sensual pleasure in its wake. "Losing you, now that would be a real loss."

He certainly knew how to get a girl's attention.

I quivered with anticipation as he got out of the car and came around to open my door. Taking my hand, he helped me out of the car; still holding my hand, he walked me to my front door. It seemed like the most natural thing in the world when he wrapped his arm around my waist and drew me close.

My heart did a happy little joy-joy dance as his mouth captured mine. I moved closer, aligning my body with his, marveling at how well we fit together. The feel of his arousal sent shivers of desire exploding through me. I might have invited him into my house, into my bed, if a bloodcurdling howl of pain hadn't shattered the quiet of the night. The sound, filled with unspeakable agony, sent a chill slithering down my spine.

Raphael released me, his whole body taut as he turned to sniff the wind.

"What is it?" I asked.

"I don't know. Go inside and lock the door."

"I don't want to stay here alone."

"All right," he said, taking my hand, "come on."

I wasn't sure I wanted to go with him, either, but I had no choice now. I followed him around the side of the house and into the dense grove of trees that grew along the north side of my property. It was a good thing he had superior night vision, because I couldn't see a thing. Raphael moved unerringly through the dark, moving deeper and deeper into the woods. As we walked, I could hear rustling in the underbrush. I tried not to think about what might be hiding in the detritus, but thoughts of rats and mice scurrying around quickly came to mind.

A few yards later, Raphael came to an abrupt halt. Shifting a little to his left, I gazed into the darkness. At first I didn't see anything, and then I saw something dark and furry writhing on the ground. Just then, the wind shifted, and I caught the coppery smell of blood.

"Stay here." Raphael's tone warned me not to argue. He didn't have to worry. I had no desire to get any closer to whatever it was that was thrashing on the ground.

Raphael moved ghostlike through the darkness, his feet making no sound even though the ground was littered with dead leaves and broken branches.

I peered into the darkness, but I couldn't see anything other than Raphael's dark figure as he knelt on the ground. A horrible keening wail rose in the air, and I wrapped my arms around my middle, chilled by a cool breeze that carried the scent of blood and death.

I glanced behind me, suddenly overcome with the feeling that we were no longer alone.

Unnerved by the thought of what could be lurking in the darkness, I moved a few steps closer to Raphael.

Another moan rose on the wind. And then a voice, low and edged with pain, whispered, "Do it!"

Raphael leaned forward. I heard a strangled sob, a gasp, and then silence. The stink of urine filled my nostrils.

Before I could make sense of what was happening, Raphael was at my side. Taking my hand in his, he led me back to my house. When we were inside, he locked the door behind us.

"Do you own a gun?" he asked.

"A gun! Of course not."

He swore under his breath. "Whatever you do, whatever you hear, don't leave the house tonight. Do you understand?"

"What happened out there?"

"Not now. Promise me you won't leave the house no matter what, and that you won't open the door for anyone."

It was the look in his eyes more than his words that made me promise. "Where are you going? What happened out there? What was that thing in the woods?"

A muscle throbbed in his jaw. "You're better off not knowing."

"Friends don't have secrets, remember?"

"Dammit!" He raked a hand through his hair, then pulled me roughly into his arms. "A Vampire attacked a Werewolf. He drained him to the point of death, then . . ."

His arms tightened around me. "You don't need to know any more than that except that the Were wasn't going to get better."

"He said 'do it.' What did he mean by that?"

"He wanted me to put him out of his misery."

It was suddenly hard to breathe. "Did you?"

Raphael's gaze slid away from mine. "Yes."

I didn't even want to think about what that meant, how he had done it, or what would become of the body lying in the woods. Was a mercy killing the same as murder?

"I've got to go." Raphael's voice and his expression were distant as he released me and walked toward the door. "Be sure to lock up after I leave."

I followed him to the door. He paused at the threshold, his gaze caressing me, the touch of his hand achingly tender as he stroked my cheek. And then he was gone, disappearing into the night as if he had never been there.

I closed and locked the door, unaware that I was crying until I felt the tears dripping down my cheeks.

Chapter Ten

After leaving Kathy's house, Rafe returned to the woods. The smell of blood and violent death hung heavy in the air.

He stared at the Werewolf's body. Whoever had attacked the Were had caught him in the midst of the change, when he was the most vulnerable. They had attacked him and drained him until there was little blood left in his veins, then ripped out his liver and his intestines, condemning him to die a slow, painful death. Had he been in Werewolf form, he would have survived, but caught in the middle of the change, there had been no hope for him.

Rafe blew out a sigh. He felt no remorse for taking the Were's life. The creature had begged him to do it. It had been the humane thing to do, something he would have done anyway. Still, it was an awesome thing to take a life, even when that life was on the brink of extinction, to drink a man dry, to take his life and his memories and leave only a dry husk behind. There had been little blood remaining in the Were, yet in taking the last of it, Raphael had not only taken the Werewolf's life and his memories, but the power that came from taking that life, as well. No matter that the Were had been nearly dead, his life force nearly gone, his Supernatural power had flowed into Rafe. He could still taste the last of the Were's blood on his tongue.

Draping the body over his shoulder, Rafe carried it deeper into the woods; then, using his bare hands, he quickly dug a grave and buried the luckless creature.

He couldn't prove it, of course, but he was certain that the Werewolf had been killed in retaliation for Cristophe's death. He was equally certain that a young hothead known only as Dawson was the Vampire who was responsible.

Raphael went suddenly still, all his senses on alert, and then, smiling, he turned around. "Hello, Godmother."

Mara smiled. "I never could sneak up on you."

He had always been in awe of the Vampire who was his godmother. She was a beautiful woman, timeless, ageless. Her thick black hair fell to her slim hips in long, rippling waves, her eyes were as green as the waters of the Nile. It was said she had been alive in the days when Antony stood at Cleopatra's side, that the blood of the Pharaohs ran in her veins. He didn't know whether that was true or not, but her powers were unmatched by any Vampire in existence. It wasn't her vast age that fascinated him so much as her ability to walk in the sun's light, an ability that she had passed to his father and, to a lesser degree, to his grandfather. She looked sexy as hell in a pair of white jeans, white high-heeled boots, and a slinky black silk shirt that revealed a good deal of creamy cleavage. She wore a heart-shaped ruby necklace at her throat that Rafe knew was worth a small fortune.

She moved closer to the grave, her nostrils flaring, and then she looked at Raphael, her eyes narrowing in anger. "Explain yourself! Did I not declare a truce? And yet you have defied me by taking this Were's life."

Rafe shook his head. "I killed him at his request, but I'm not the one who attacked him."

She regarded him a moment, her gaze burning into his, and then she turned her attention to the grave once more. "Dawson," she murmured, her eyes narrowing. "He dares much!"

Rafe nodded. Mara had declared a truce. To go against her wishes was a foolhardy thing to do. Dawson's future could now be measured in minutes instead of centuries.

Mara turned her attention to Raphael once again. "The woman in the log house, she means a great deal to you."

It wasn't a question, and Rafe saw no reason to confirm or deny it.

"You are very much like your father," she mused.

"Am I?"

"Indeed. A love for mortal females seems to plague the men in your family."

Rafe couldn't argue with that. His maternal grandfather, Roshan DeLongpre, had traveled back in time to find the woman whose photograph had obsessed him. Brenna Flannagan had not only been mortal at the time, but a practicing witch, as well. Roshan had saved her from a fiery death at the stake, brought her forward in time, and married her. His own father, Vince, had fallen in love with Roshan's adopted daughter, Cara Aideen. His parents seemed perfectly suited to one another, and happier than any couple he knew.

"I've not seen Vince in quite some time," Mara remarked. "How is he? And your mother?"

"Well enough, the last time I heard from them."

"Have you heard from Rane?"

Rafe shook his head. "Not a word," he said, and then, like a bolt from the blue, he realized that Mara knew where Rane was, just as she had always known where they were.

"You know, don't you?" he said, his hands fisted at his sides. "All this time, you've known."

"Of course," she replied coolly. "I'm surprised it's taken you this long to figure that out."

"Where is he?"

"If he wanted you to know, you would have heard from him." She raised her hand, stilling any further questions. "When he has made peace with himself, he'll come home."

Rafe blew out an exasperated breath, knowing he wouldn't get any more out of her.

"Back to the matter at hand," she said, glancing at the grave. "I want this truce to work. I don't know about the Werewolves and Were-tigers, but our people need mortals to survive. I was opposed to going to war with the Werewolves when it began, and I'm still opposed to it. Fighting among ourselves solves nothing. Hopefully, cooler heads will now prevail."

Rafe nodded. A handful of rebellious Werewolves and Vampires had started the conflict. In weeks, it had spread across the world, until the paranormal creatures from nearly every nation were involved. He had been against the war from the beginning, certain that, sooner or later, the humans would realize that their future was at stake, and when that happened, the Supernatural creatures would not only be fighting each other, but the humans, as well.

Turning away from the grave, Mara walked toward the road.

Rafe fell into step beside her. "What now?"

"I'm going to pay a visit to Dawson, and then I'm going to call on Clive. We need to talk. In the last week, several of his people and a number of ours have disappeared without a trace. He's blaming it on the war, but . . ." She glanced at Rafe. "Let me know if you hear of any more unrest in this area."

"You heard about Cristophe?"

"Yes. I was nearby on another matter."

They walked in silence for a time. Rafe couldn't keep his eyes off the woman at his side. She carried herself like a queen, her every movement one of fluid grace. Moments later, they emerged from the woods onto the street.

"How did you get here so quick?" he asked curiously. "The last I heard, you were somewhere in Bolivia."

She looked at him as if he were the dullest knife in the drawer.

Rafe muttered, "Oh, right." With her almost limitless powers, she could think herself anywhere she wished to be.

"Just so," she said, and then she leaned forward and kissed his cheek. "Until next time."

Before he could reply, she was gone.

Rafe stared after her for a moment. What was it like for her, to exist for thousands of years? To be able to walk in the light of the sun? Compared to Mara, he had been a Vampire for a relatively short time, yet he had already forgotten what it was like to feel the sun's warmth on his face, to partake of food and drink in the mortal way. He frowned, wondering if she was able to partake of food and drink again.

With a sigh, he walked back to where he had left his car. He paused on the sidewalk in front of Kathy's house, tempted to knock on her door even though he knew it was a bad idea. As much as he wanted her, hungered for her, they were separated by a gulf that only she could cross.

He stood there for several moments, his arms aching to hold her, and then, muttering a vile oath, he slid behind the wheel and drove home.

Chapter Eleven

I cried for a long while after Raphael left, and then I made myself a cup of hot chocolate topped with lots of marshmallows, hoping it would make me feel better. It didn't. Going to the window, I looked out into the darkness. At first I didn't see anything, and then I saw Raphael standing on the sidewalk. In spite of everything, I hoped he would come back inside, take me in his arms, and hold me close. For a moment, I was tempted to open the door and call his name. I was about to do just that when he looked up at the house. I felt my heart skip a beat when he took a step forward; then, obviously changing his mind, he got into his car and drove away. Perhaps it was just as well.

With a sigh, I turned away from the window, my thoughts and emotions in turmoil. The war between the Werewolves and the Vampires seemed to be escalating. Not only that, but tonight the hostilities had been too close to home for my peace of mind, almost in my backyard. As troubling as all that was, I couldn't stop remembering that Raphael had killed a man. No matter that the man was also a Werewolf and, according to Raphael, on the verge of death. I wasn't sure how I felt about the Werewolves killing Vampires. I mean, except for Raphael, Vampires had already died once. They didn't really die a second time, although their existence came to an end.

Frowning, I went into the bathroom, turned on the taps in the tub, and then added a cap full of lavender-scented bubble bath to the water. How, exactly, did one become a Vampire? All I really knew was that a blood exchange was involved, but how much blood? Did it hurt? What if you changed your mind in the middle? I wasn't exactly sure how one became a Werewolf, either, except that being bitten seemed to be a large part of it.

Turning off the water, I stepped into the tub and sank down into the fragrant bubbles. I had a feeling I'd be spending a lot of time at my computer tomorrow, surfing the Web and looking for whatever information I could find on the Supernatural world and the creatures that inhabited it.

I took a lunch with me to the store the next day, and during my lunch hour, I booted up my computer and surfed the Internet, searching for anything and everything I could find on Werewolves, shape-shifters, and Vampires. I was amazed at the number of Web sites dedicated to Werewolves, and the wealth of information available.

For instance, I learned there was something called lycanthropic disorder, which was in actuality a mental condition wherein a person believed he, or she, was really a Werewolf even though they didn't change shape.

It didn't say if these people went running around the countryside killing things.

And then there was the real deal, where a man or a woman physically transformed into a beast. True Werewolves were immune from aging since their bodies were constantly regenerating. The only way to kill a Werewolf was to destroy the heart or the brain or deprive them of oxygen. I assumed the same was true for any Were-creature. I had always thought that a person had to be bitten to become fanged and furry, but one source said that you could become a Werewolf by birth or by being cursed by a witch. In Europe, between 1520 and 1630, some thirty thousand cases of lycanthropy had been reported.

There were legends of Were-cats, which were also shape-shifters, but instead of turning into wolves, they turned into felines. In days of old in Europe, shape-shifters, including Werewolves, had been considered witches. Were-creature folklore was found on all the continents except for Antarctica, with the Were-creatures turning into whatever wild feline was native to the area, such as domestic cats, lions, leopards, tigers, or lynx.

Researching Vampires proved to be not only interesting and fascinating, but, at times, amusing. For instance, I had always believed that Vampires were made, not born, but according to ancient folklore, those who were born under a new moon or on certain holy days were believed to be predisposed to becoming Vampires, as were those who were born with a red caul, with teeth, or with excess hair. The same was true for those born with a red birthmark, or with two hearts and, of course, being born the seventh son of a seventh son. Others who might be similarly affected were those who were weaned too young, or those who died without baptism. Expectant mothers in Romania were encouraged to eat plenty of salt to ensure that their babies didn't become Vampires.

Others who were good candidates for vampirism were people who committed suicide, prostitutes, and murderers.

Sitting back in my chair, I unwrapped a candy bar and indulged my passion for chocolate. I was about to resume my search when the phone rang. It was my mother, reminding me that my father's birthday was coming up, as if I'd forget.

"So," she said, getting to the real reason for her call. "Are you ready to come back home?"

I blew out a sigh. She was still upset because I'd left New York.

"I saw Jimmy Lee the other day," she said cheerfully. "He's still single."

"That doesn't surprise me," I muttered. Jimmy Lee Brown thought he was the sexiest thing in shoe leather, had no interests other than computers and computer games, and, to put it politely, he smelled bad.

"Honestly, Kathy, don't you think it's time you came home and settled down?"

"Mom, how many times are we going to have this conversation?" It wasn't enough that she called me every week or so, she also sent me e-mails asking the same question.

There was a long silence. I knew she was sitting there, slowly counting to ten, while she asked herself where she'd gone wrong. My brother and sister were both happily married and producing grandchildren, while I, her youngest, remained single with no husband in sight.

"Listen, Mom, I've got to go. Say hi to Dad for me."

After we hung up, I went back to my research. There were a number of references linking wolves with Vampires. In Greece, it was believed that anyone who ate a sheep that had been killed by a wolf was doomed to become a Vampire. In Montenegro, it was believed that all Vampires had to spend a certain amount of time as a wolf. The Gypsies of Kosovo were of the opinion that Vampires were doomed to wander the earth until they met a wolf, which would then tear them to pieces. In Romania, Gypsy villages were supposedly guarded by white wolves that stood watch in cemeteries where they gobbled up any rising Vampires. Totally bizarre, I thought. Who would ever seriously believe such nonsense?

Of course, the dead weren't safe, either. According to folklore, you might become a Vampire if someone passed a candle over your corpse, if your brother was a sleepwalker, or if a cat jumped over your corpse. You were also in danger if you weren't buried with the proper rituals, or you were murdered and your murder went unavenged, or you died by drowning.

There were a number of signs to look for if you wanted to know if someone who had been buried had become one of the Undead. These included disturbed earth around the grave, fallen tombstones, broken or fallen crosses, footsteps leading away from the grave, no birds singing nearby, dogs barking or refusing to enter the cemetery, or horses shying away from the site. Numerous finger-sized holes used by the Vampire to escape his grave in mistlike form were, you should pardon the pun, also a dead giveaway.

Vampires were reputed to have many Supernatural

powers. Raphael had already admitted to being able to hypnotize people, and he seemed pretty adept at reading my mind. According to folklore, Vampires were able to change shape, dissolve into mist, control the elements as well as some animals, and scurry up a wall like a spider. Of course, it was common knowledge that they could create other Vampires, and that they had superior strength.

Reading on, I learned that Vampires couldn't swim or cross running water because water was a purifier which washed away evil and sin. In olden times, a corpse believed to be a Vampire might be placed in a river or a lake. If the body floated, it was a Vampire and the necessary steps were taken.

Destroying a Vampire was a messy business. A hawthorn stake driven into a Vampire's heart was the most common method of destruction. Beheading was also recommended. Sunlight was also fatal, although Vampires in Poland and Russia prowled the streets from noon until midnight.

Most interesting of all was the description of folk Vampires and those in literature, which described the Undead as really disgusting creatures, not only because of their grotesque appearance, which included razorlike, blood-stained fangs, hairy palms, and glowing red eyes, but the stink that clung to them from the dried blood of their victims. Vampires had apparently changed with the times. Modern Vampires were hypnotically and sensually attractive and much more pleasing to look upon, thanks to the influence of Bram Stoker's *Dracula* and suave actors like Bela Lugosi, George Hamilton, and Frank Langella.

And real-life Vampire, Raphael Cordova, I thought with a smile.

Ah, Rafe. I wondered what he was doing. Sleeping, I supposed, and I wondered if he rested in a coffin, and what he wore to sleep in. I couldn't imagine him in anything as mundane as a pair of cotton pajamas. Maybe a black T-shirt and briefs . . . or maybe nothing at all.

Feeling suddenly warm, I went into the back room for a bottle of cold water. What I had read was fascinating. Of course, I had no idea how much of it was based on fact and how much was pure fiction. It occurred to me that I was wasting a lot of time searching the Internet when I had something much better—an actual Vampire. Or did I? After last night, I wasn't sure he was ever coming back. The thought of never seeing him again brought the sting of hot tears to my eyes.

But I didn't have time to wallow in self-pity. The jangle of the bell over the door announced that I had one of those all-too-rare creatures—a customer. Blinking back my tears, I smoothed a hand over my hair, pasted a smile on my face, and went out front.

A pair of elderly women were browsing the romance shelves. One was tall and angular with shoulder-length white hair. The other was short and a trifle plump. Her curly red hair was obviously dyed. In addition to wide silver bracelets, silver crosses, and dangling silver earrings, they both wore designer jeans, brightly colored silk blouses, comfortable sneakers, and fake flowers in their hair. I guessed them to be in their midseventies.

They both looked over at me and smiled, then turned back to the stacks. I watched them for a few minutes as they picked up one book after another, read the back cover copy and the first page, and then either added the book to the growing pile on top of the shelf or put it back. By the time they were ready to go, they had twenty-two paperbacks between them.

"So glad you're here," the redheaded one said. "I don't drive, you know, so whenever new books come out, I either have to impose on my grandson and ask him to drive me over to one of the bookstores in River's Edge, or order them online. But now you're here!"

"Come along, Edna," the other woman said, taking hold of her friend's arm. "I'm sure she doesn't give a fig about your shopping habits."

"Oh, but I do," I said, smiling at the two of them. If they bought this many books every time they came in, I could stop worrying about going out of business.

Edna moved closer to the counter. "I don't suppose you give a senior discount, do you?" she asked in a near whisper.

"Well, I never have," I said, "but I will today. How does 10 percent sound?"

"You see, Pearl," Edna said with a triumphant grin, "I told you it wouldn't hurt to ask!"

"Have you two been friends long?" I asked as I rang up their sales.

"Oh, my, yes," Pearl exclaimed.

"Fifty-five years come January," Edna said. "We met in the maternity ward. I was having my first baby."

"And I was having my second." Pearl looked at Edna, and the two women smiled, obviously remembering the day they had met.

Edna sighed wistfully. "Where does the time go?"

"And you've lived here, in Oak Hollow, the whole time?" I asked.

"Yes, indeed." Edna leaned forward. "Things have

certainly changed, I can tell you that," she said, her voice little more than a whisper. "All these strange people lurking about. Why last night, I heard a wolf howl, right here in the city!"

Pearl nodded. "I don't know which is worse, the Werewolves or the Vampires."

"You've seen them?" I asked, surprised that they talked about it so openly.

"The Vampires tend to be very secretive, you know," Edna remarked. "They never tell you where they take their rest. And they never meet in the same place twice. The Werewolves meet in an abandoned building out at the end of Foster Road."

"How do you know that?" I asked, my curiosity about Edna and Pearl growing by the minute. For that matter, I wondered how they recognized the Werewolves and the Vampires. Unless the Werewolves were in their furry forms, or the Vampires were displaying their fangs, the Supernatural folk looked pretty much like everyone else most of the time. Of course, maybe Edna and Pearl were able to detect them the same way I did. For a moment, I was tempted to ask, but then I thought better of it. My gift, such as it was, might best be kept under wraps, at least until I knew Edna and Pearl better.

The two women exchanged glances, then looked at me with conspiratorial smiles.

"We have our ways, dear," Pearl said. "You be careful now, hear?"

"And remember," Edna added. "Handsome is as handsome does."

I looked from one woman to the other. "Excuse me?"

"Raphael Cordova is a mighty handsome man, dear," Pearl said.

"Nice butt," Edna remarked candidly.

I nodded in agreement, though I was somewhat shocked to learn that a woman of Edna's age would notice such a thing, and more surprised that they knew I was seeing Rafe.

"You do know he's a Vampire, don't you, dear?" Pearl asked.

"Yes."

"His grandmother is a witch," Edna remarked. "Did you know that?"

"No, he never mentioned that."

"Well, just be careful," Edna admonished. "I know he seems like a nice young man . . ."

I bit back a grin. Raphael was anything but young.

"But as my husband always said, a girl can't be too careful," Pearl added.

"Roger was absolutely right," Edna agreed. "But then, he always was."

"You know, dear," Pearl said, "it probably isn't wise for you to go to Raphael's house alone."

I think my mouth fell open. How could they possibly know I had been out to Raphael's house? Or that the Werewolves met in an abandoned building on Foster Road? Or that Raphael's grandmother was a witch? A witch! Good grief! Next they'd be telling me that Susie McGee was a fairy princess and the police chief was a troll!

After I had taken their credit cards, bagged their books, and bid Edna and Pearl good-bye, I poured myself a cup of coffee and replayed the entire conversation in my mind.

A short time later, another woman entered the store. She was young and pretty, with dark blond hair and violet eyes. I thought at first that she was a Werewolf, and it occurred to me once again that there were an awful lot of Werewolves and Vampires in town, although, after what had happened the last two nights, there were at least two less than there had been. But then I realized she wasn't a Werewolf. She was like Cagin, a shape-shifter of some kind.

She looked at me sharply when she handed me her credit card, and I had the distinct impression that she knew that I knew what she was. Taking her receipt and the book, she left the store without ever saying a word.

The rest of the day passed quietly. I ate lunch at my computer and washed the ham and cheese sandwich down with a cup of coffee. I made another sale later in the afternoon, and I closed up early.

Driving home, I felt suddenly melancholy. I hadn't heard a word from Raphael since last night. Of course, he had probably been at rest all day. I wondered if he would come by my house later, or ever again.

Handsome is as handsome does.

Pearl's words echoed in the back of my mind. Raphael Cordova was handsome as sin, and just as dangerous. Last night, he had killed a man in cold blood. Oh, sure, the Were had asked Raphael to end his life, but it was still murder.

Handsome is as handsome does.

Okay, I admit it, it troubled me more than I wanted to admit that Raphael had killed the Werewolf. How many other Were-creatures and humans had he killed since becoming a full-fledged, practicing Vampire?

It was a question that haunted me while I ate dinner. Like an itch I couldn't scratch, it lingered in the back of my mind while I cleaned up the kitchen, and later, while I tried to watch a late movie.

I was about to get ready for bed when the doorbell rang.

I knew before I answered the door that it was my Vampire. Raphael.

Chapter Twelve

Handsome. The word whispered through my mind as I looked at him. Dressed in a dark blue shirt open at the throat and a pair of black jeans, he looked good enough to eat.

"Any chance I could come in?" he asked.

A girl can't be too careful. I blinked at him, and then, ignoring Pearl's earlier warning, I invited him inside.

Nice butt. I grinned as I recalled Edna's assessment of Raphael's behind. Following him into the living room, I had to agree with her.

"Please," I said, "sit down."

I sank into the chair across from the sofa, one leg folded beneath me, suddenly at a loss for words. I had a lot of questions I wanted to ask him, but I wasn't sure I wanted to hear the answers.

"You're still upset about last night," he said, and it wasn't a question.

I nodded. There was no point in lying. "You killed him," I said with a snap of my fingers. "Just like that."

A muscle twitched in his jaw. "Yes."

I took a deep breath, then blurted, "How many people have you killed?"

His gaze burned into mine, and then he rose effortlessly to his feet. "Good-bye, Kathy."

I stared at him, knowing if he left now, I would never see him again.

He was at the door when I called, "Rafe, don't go!"

He glanced over his shoulder, his face impassive. "It's better this way."

"No." I blinked against the sharp sting of tears. "Please stay."

He stared at me for a long moment before resuming his place on the sofa. "Are you sure you want to hear this?"

I nodded, although I wasn't sure at all. Maybe ignorance really was bliss.

"I'm a Vampire," he said, both his voice and his expression devoid of emotion.

I was tempted to say, "duh!" but I restrained myself.

"You have to understand that killing comes easy to us," he went on, "and it gets easier with every passing year. After a while, some of us forget that we were once human. Those who do look on mortals as nothing more than prey, theirs for the taking."

"Is that how you feel?"

"No, but many do. Even so, there have been times when I've taken a life."

I waited, hoping he would say he had killed them all in self-defense.

"When I was a new Vampire, I fell in love with a young woman. After a while, she said she wanted to be what I was, that she wanted us to be together forever." He paused, his gaze looking beyond me into the distant past. "I knew how Vampires were made, and even though I had never brought anyone across or seen it done, I was sure I could do it. I was wrong. She died in my arms."

He looked at me again, his dark eyes haunted. "I've never tried to bring anyone else across."

Feeling suddenly chilled from the inside out, I ran my hands up and down my arms, waiting for him to go on.

"I've killed men and Werewolves in self-defense," he said, his voice cold and flat. "I've killed men when my need for blood was stronger than my self-control, but I've never killed a man in anger." He smiled faintly. "Or a woman."

"Where do you sleep?"

His eyes narrowed suspiciously. "Why?"

I shrugged. "I didn't mean where, exactly, I was just wondering what you sleep in."

"My underwear," he replied, and then frowned. "But that's not what you're asking, either, is it?"

"No."

"These days, only Hollywood Vampires sleep in coffins. The rest of us have discovered king-size beds are more comfortable."

I hoped my relief didn't show on my face.

"Anything else you want to know?"

"Someone told me your grandmother is a witch. Is that true?"

The sound of his deep, rich laughter filled the room. "You've been talking to Edna and Pearl, haven't you?"

"Maybe."

He shook his head. "I don't know where they get their information, but I think those old broads know everything that happens in this town. Hell, maybe they're witches, too."

"You didn't answer my question."

"It's true. My grandmother Brenna is a spell-casting, card-carrying white witch." He canted his head to one side. "Looking for someone who can make me disappear?"

"Of course not. Don't be silly."

"What are you looking for?" he asked, all hint of amusement gone from his voice and his expression.

It was a good question. I wished I had a good answer. "I'm not looking for anything; I was just curious." I blew out a sigh. "Vampires and Were-creatures and now witches. I don't know what to think anymore."

"There are more things in heaven and earth, Horatio, than are dreamt of in your philosophy."

I lifted one brow. "Shakespeare?"

"Hamlet, act one, scene five." He grinned at me. "I had a good tutor."

"Did he know you were a Vampire?"

"No. My folks didn't see any reason to divulge that particular bit of information." He grinned. "Rane and I played some awful tricks on old Mr. Axtell."

"What kinds of tricks?"

"One night, my folks invited him to stay for dinner. While they were all in the living room talking, Rane and I turned his car upside down. Another time, Rane hypnotized Axtell, and when he woke up, he was in a . . ."

"In a what?"

Rafe cleared his throat. "A bordello."

"How'd you manage that?"

"It wasn't easy." Rafe shook his head. "We caught hell for that one."

"I should hope so," I said, but I couldn't help grinning.

"He figured out we were behind it. I don't know how. But a few days later, my old man received a bill for five hundred dollars from the bordello for services rendered. He wasn't happy about that. Neither were Rane and I. Our father decided if we had enough spare time on our hands to play pranks on our teacher, then we could paint the house, inside and out."

Rafe laughed and I laughed with him. And then he looked at me, his expression sober once more. "So, where do we go from here?"

"I don't know. My good sense tells me that I shouldn't have anything to do with you, but . . ."

"But?"

I took a deep breath and let it out in a long, slow sigh. "I can't stand the thought of never seeing you again."

"It could be dangerous for you."

"I know."

"It doesn't scare you?"

"Of course it does."

"You've nothing to fear from me, you know that, don't you?"

"It's not you I'm afraid of. It's what's happening in Oak Hollow. It's knowing, really knowing, that Vampires and Were-creatures and . . . and witches . . . actually exist. I mean, I knew it before I moved here, but I had never met any Supernatural folk. I told myself they didn't really exist. But now . . ."

"Now you can't pretend anymore."

I nodded. "I'm afraid for you, afraid of how all this trouble between the Vampires and Werewolves will end."

"Come here."

Rising from my chair, I went into his arms.

"You don't have to worry about me," he said, his fingertips stroking my arm. "I can take care of myself. And you, too."

I hoped he was right, but only time would tell. Resting my head on his shoulder, I closed my eyes. The future would take care of itself. Right now, I was where I most wanted to be.

"This won't be easy," Raphael murmured, his breath warm against my neck.

"I know."

"For your sake, we'd better take it slow."

I kissed his cheek. "Slow."

He turned his head, his lips seeking mine, his tongue like a flame as it dueled with my own. For a moment, I lost myself in his touch, thinking how amazing it was that he was here, that I was in his arms.

"Rafe . . ."

He drew back a little, his gaze seeking mine. "You want me to stop?"

"No, I . . ." *Might as well just say it,* I thought, then blurted, "I think I love you."

"I think I love you, too."

"This complicates things even more, doesn't it?" I asked. Lust and love were two different animals. Lust was a selfish beast. It had no responsibilities, implied no lasting commitment, no concern for the other's happiness or welfare. But love, ah, love required caring and commitment, it meant putting another's wants and needs before one's own. Lust was fleeting; true love lasted forever.

"In a way," Raphael agreed, kissing the tip of my nose. "On the other hand, it's nice to know where we stand."

Drawing me into his arms once more, he lowered his head and kissed me again and yet again, each kiss deeper and more intimate than the last. His hands moved lightly over my body, as if he wanted to memorize every curve.

Had I been a cat, I would have arched my back and purred with pleasure. As it was, I couldn't restrain the soft moans that rose in my throat as he caressed me, nor could I resist an exploration of my own.

I loved the feel of his skin beneath my hands, the way his muscles bunched and quivered at my touch. I lay back on the sofa and drew him down on top of me, basking in the feel of his body lying atop mine, the heat of his arousal pressing against my thigh.

I was lost in the taste of him, the touch of him, until I felt his fangs at my throat.

It cooled my desire as quickly as cold water doused a fire. "Raphael?"

Muttering an oath, he rolled off me and gained his feet.

I sat up, staring at his back, watching as he raked a hand through his hair, then curled his hands into tight fists at his sides. He was breathing heavily. A leftover remnant of his desire, I wondered, or a sign of his hunger?

"Rafe . . . ?"

He lifted one hand. "Give me a minute."

I grew increasingly nervous as I sat there watching him. Was he subduing his hunger or getting ready to pounce? Only moments ago, he had warned me that our relationship could be dangerous for me.

I glanced around the room, seeking a way out, seeking a weapon. I found neither. Raphael stood between me and the front door, blocking my only exit. My chance of finding a weapon seemed equally slim since I didn't keep a ready supply of holy water or hawthorn stakes on hand. And even if I did, there was no way I could have used either one on Rafe. That fact alone told me I was in far deeper than I'd thought.

A shudder ran through his entire body and then, slowly, he turned to face me, his expression a little sheepish as his gaze met mine. "I'm sorry," he said. "I should have warned you."

"Warned me? About what?"

"With us, the urge to make love and the urge to feed are strongly connected. For us, the taking of blood enhances our emotions and our pleasure."

"Oh." Once again, I had learned more than I really wanted to know.

"The idea repulses you?"

"I don't know about that, but it doesn't thrill me." I wondered how his mother had handled it before she was turned. Had she let Rafe's father drink from her? Dared I ask?

Did I really want to know?

"Kathy . . . I don't want to lose you. . . ."

My heart squeezed painfully in my chest as I waited for him to go on. I had a feeling I wasn't going to like what he was about to say.

"I thought we could make this work, but . . ." He shook his head. "I'd never intentionally hurt you, but . . . dammit, what if I can't help myself? Just now I wanted to taste you, and I was close to taking what I wanted, so close . . ."

"But you didn't."

"What if I can't stop myself next time?"

"I don't know." Maybe he was right. Maybe we shouldn't see each other anymore, yet even as the thought crossed my mind, I knew it wasn't what I wanted. Right or wrong, for better or worse, I was head over heels in love with a Vampire.

Chapter Thirteen

"How did your mother handle it?" I asked. "You know, when your father wanted to, uh, taste her?"

Though we were sitting side by side on the sofa, Rafe was careful not to touch me. I appreciated his caution even as I longed for his touch. I was acutely aware of his nearness. His right shoulder and thigh were only inches from mine. The scent of his cologne tickled my nostrils.

"From what I gather, she wasn't aware of it the first time."

"Really? What did he do," I asked, "drink from her while she was asleep?"

"No, while they were making love."

"Oh. Oh!"

He smiled faintly. "They were making love the second time, too."

"Did she know it that time?" And even as I asked the question, I wondered how he knew the intimate details of his parents' love life.

"Yes, and many times thereafter."

"I don't believe you. How could anyone enjoy being bitten, or having someone drink their blood while they were making love? It's . . . it's . . ." I searched for a word that would describe how I felt without offending him. They were his parents, after all.

He supplied some adjectives for me. "Gross? Disgusting? Barbaric? Repulsive? Nauseating? Horrific?" He lifted one brow. "Should I go on?"

"No, I think you've covered it pretty well."

Ever so slowly and provocatively, he ran the tip of one finger down the side of my neck. It was the lightest of sensations, like a downy feather brushing over my skin. "Why don't you try it and see for yourself?"

I jerked away as if his finger had turned into a venomous snake. "No way! I like my blood right where it is, thank you very much."

"Where's your spirit of adventure?" His fingertips slowly stroked my throat. "Aren't you the least bit curious?"

I was curious, but I wasn't about to admit it, especially to a hungry Vampire! Instead, I said, "Just seeing you is all the adventure I need. As for being curious, you know what happened to the cat."

Raphael looked into my eyes, his gaze smoldering with desire, his voice low and husky as he murmured, "They say satisfaction brought him back."

The man was incorrigible! Those bedroom eyes, that sexy voice . . . how long would I be able to resist? How long until I surrendered to the yearning in his voice, the hunger in his eyes?

"So," I said, "tell me more about your parents."

With a sigh, he settled back against the sofa. "My grandparents are both Vampires. Late one night, they found a young girl giving birth in an alley. The girl abandoned the baby, and my grandparents adopted her. . . ."

"How did two Vampires raise a human baby?"

"They hired a nanny and, later, a live-in housekeeper and a bodyguard."

"A bodyguard? Whatever for?"

"My grandfather is a wealthy man, plus he's made a few enemies in his time. He couldn't protect my mother during the day, so they hired someone who could."

"Where did they find people willing to work for Vampires?"

"No one knew they were Vampires, except for the bodyguard. Even my mother didn't know. They told her and everyone else that they had a rare disease that made it impossible for them to go out during the day. My mother was a grown woman before she found out the truth. Ironically, my mother fell in love with a Vampire, although she didn't know he was a Vampire at the time."

I shook my head, thinking it was the most far-fetched story I had ever heard.

"It's true," he said. "Every word." He stroked my cheek. "Falling in love with mortal women seems to run in my family."

"I'm glad."

"Kathy," he murmured huskily, "I'm dying for want of you." His fingertips drifted up and down my neck again, ever so lightly. "Just one taste, please?"

"And if I say no?"

"I'll expire here at your feet."

I would have laughed if his voice hadn't been edged with pain, his expression filled with such naked yearning that I ached for him. Some said a Vampire's craving

for blood was like a terrible drug addiction for which
there was no cure. Vampires suffered intense agony if
they were forced to go for long periods of time without
feeding. It was a relentless pain, one that grew steadily
worse. The only antidote was blood. In days past, Vampires had been locked up for years at a time. Some went
mad with the pain, but none of them had died from it.
The need just grew more and more excruciating, a hell-
ishly endless torment that only blood or obliteration
could bring to an end.

I didn't want Rafe to suffer even a moment because
of me, and yet . . . how could I let him drink my blood?
He had told me once that it didn't hurt, but I wasn't sure
I believed that. How could someone sinking their fangs
into your neck not hurt? What if he took too much? I remembered the woman he had tried to bring across.
Though he hadn't said as much, I was sure she had died
because he had taken too much, or perhaps he had taken
it all.

"What do they look like?" I asked. "Your fangs?"

"Like this," he said, and bared his teeth.

I guess I had been expecting huge canines, like a
lion's, although I knew that was impossible. Rafe's
fangs were neither as big or as long as I had imagined,
but they were very white and looked needle sharp. Curious, I touched one with the tip of my finger and
quickly drew back as it pierced my flesh. I stared at the
drop of bright red blood. Sharp indeed! I'd hardly
touched the darn thing.

I lifted my hand to my mouth, intending to lick the
blood away.

"Let me," Rafe said, and taking my hand in his, he
put my finger to his lips and sucked lightly.

The heat of his mouth was unexpectedly erotic. A soft "ohhh" of sensual pleasure rose in my throat. If being bitten felt anything like this, I was surprised women weren't lined up for miles on end waiting their turn.

I could see by the look in his eyes that he knew the exact effect his touch was having on my senses. He kissed my palm, his tongue stroking the sensitive skin, and then he let go of my hand.

I looked at my finger, amazed to see that the tiny wound had already disappeared.

"Sweet," he murmured. "Even sweeter than I imagined."

"Blood isn't sweet."

"Not to you, perhaps, but to me it's like the finest wine."

"Well, at least you got your taste," I muttered. "I hope you're satisfied."

"Indeed, but it only whet my appetite for more."

"If I let you drink from me this once, will you promise never to ask me again?"

"Do you think that's fair?"

"I don't care. Is it a deal?"

"Yes, it's a deal," he agreed, "but with one stipulation."

"What kind of stipulation?" I asked suspiciously.

"I will not ask you again, so long as you do not ask me."

"You don't have to worry about that!" I said, completely confident that such a thing would never happen. "So, now what?"

"Now this." He slipped his arm around my shoulders, tilted my head up ever so slightly, and kissed me, a long, lingering kiss that made me forget everything but the taste of his mouth, the heat of his body intimately pressing against mine, and a growing desire that threatened to spiral out of control.

I clung to him, lost in a world of sensual pleasure as he kissed me again, his hands skimming lightly over my back, my thigh, the curve of my breast. His touch was oddly familiar, as if we had made love a hundred times before. My whole being vibrated with need and with the excitement of discovery as my own hands moved over him, measuring the width of his shoulders, the hard wall of his chest, the silky texture of his hair.

His lips were warm as they kissed their way to my throat, his tongue like a living flame as it laved the skin beneath my ear. Moments later, pleasure such as I had never known flowed into me and through me. In a distant part of my mind, I knew that he had bitten me, that he was sipping my life's blood, but I didn't care. He could take as much as he wanted, he could take it all, if it would make this incredible feeling last forever.

I felt bereft when he lifted his head. "Don't stop," I begged softly. "Please don't stop."

"I told you I only wanted a taste." His knuckles stroked my cheek. "Are you all right?"

"I'm better than all right," I said, and then, remembering how I had begged him not to stop, I glared at him. "You knew, didn't you?" I stabbed my finger against his chest. "You knew that once I let you do it, I'd want it again. Didn't you? That's why you made me agree to that stipulation of yours."

He tried to look guilty but failed miserably.

"It certainly explains a lot. I used to wonder why some women were so obsessed with Vampires. I couldn't understand why your mother married your father. Well, now I know."

"Is that right?" Laughing softly, he sat up, drawing me with him. "Kathy, love, you were 'obsessed' with me before I ever tasted you."

"I was not!" I declared hotly. I straightened my clothes, embarrassed by my reaction to what had happened. I'd been so sure it would be disgusting when it was quite the opposite.

"Weren't you?"

"You're mighty full of yourself all of a sudden," I muttered sullenly. "I'm probably no different from the hundreds of other women you've had."

"There's one difference," he said, cupping my cheek in his palm. "I love you. That makes all the difference in the world. When I drink from a woman, I make it as pleasant for her as I can. After all, she's giving me her life's essence, but it's nothing like what you felt. Love makes all the difference."

"And was it different for you, as well?"

"Yes. Drinking from prey eases my thirst, but drinking from you . . . how can I explain it?" He considered a moment, then said, "Drinking from a stranger is like drinking water, but drinking from you is like savoring a rare and exotic wine. Do you see the difference?"

It was impossible to stay angry with such a man. "Stop talking so much," I said, "and kiss me again."

"With pleasure," he murmured, and claimed my lips with his.

He had tasted my blood and found pleasure in it. Even as my body responded to his kisses, I found myself wondering what it would be like to taste a Vampire's blood, Rafe's blood.

The thought had no sooner crossed my mind than Rafe drew back. Wordlessly, he ran the pad of his thumb across the tip of one of his fangs, and then held out his hand. "Go on, satisfy your curiosity."

I don't know which was more disconcerting—having him read my mind, or the thought of actually tasting his blood. "What will it do to me?"

He shook his head. "Nothing. It might heighten your senses for a few days, but nothing more."

"It won't make me a Vampire, will it?"

He laughed softly. "No, love."

I stared at that single drop of dark red blood in morbid fascination. It was thicker, darker, than my own blood. Before I could change my mind, I quickly licked it from his finger. It was like putting my tongue to an electrical wire, and yet strangely pleasurable.

Smiling, he drew me into his embrace again. I wasn't sure what the term was for it these days, but whether you called it necking, petting, or making out, that's how we spent the rest of the evening. I had never in my life been kissed so thoroughly, never been closer to losing my virginity, than I was that night in Rafe Cordova's arms. I experienced each gentle touch, each tender caress, with an intensity I had never known before. Was it love, or was it that tiny taste of forbidden blood that made the difference? I didn't know, and I didn't care. One taste of Rafe's blood had intoxicated me. If I could bottle the sensations erupting inside of me, I could probably make a fortune.

I don't know how far we might have gone if he hadn't stopped when he did.

Caught up in a sensual haze of passion, I stared at him as he gained his feet and straightened his clothing. "What are you doing?"

Taking my hand, he pulled me to my feet and into his arms. "I need to go."

"Why?"

"Because it's very late and you need your rest."

"What's the real reason?"

"I haven't fed yet, and it will be dawn soon."

"Oh." The reality of what he was hit me like a splash of cold water. He was going out to hunt for prey. He was going to drink someone else's blood, and he would be taking more than just a taste.

"I'll see you tomorrow night."

Nodding, I lifted my face for his kiss. No doubt my lips would be swollen and sore tomorrow, I thought drily, but what the heck.

He kissed me lightly and gave me a quick hug. "Good night, love."

"Good night."

I walked him to the door, watched him get into his sleek black car and drive away, and went to bed with a song in my heart and a smile on my face.

I was still smiling when I woke the next morning, partly from my memory of Rafe's kisses, and partly from the dreams I'd had the night before. Never in all my life had I had such erotic dreams. Had Rafe's blood been responsible? Just thinking of my wayward fantasies made my cheeks burn. If Raphael was half the lover he had been in my dreams . . . oh, my!

I made my bed, ate breakfast, dressed, and went to the bookstore. I had no sooner opened for business when a delivery man brought me two dozen long-stemmed red roses. The only time I had ever received flowers before had been from my father. He had sent me an enormous bouquet of yellow daisies on my twenty-first birthday.

I was pretty sure these weren't from my father. Filled with giddy anticipation, I read the card aloud. "For Kathy, lovelier than the fairest flower. Love, Rafe."

Half an hour later, another delivery man arrived. He handed me a heart-shaped box of candy. Smiling, I read the card. "For Kathy, sweeter than chocolate. Eternally, Rafe."

Vampire he might be, but he sure knew the way to a girl's heart.

I was humming softly, counting the hours until sundown, when a man and a woman entered the store. One look and I knew they were both Vampires. The man was tall and lean with powerful shoulders and long limbs. His hair was as black as ink, his eyes a bold midnight blue beneath straight black brows. The woman was beautiful. Her hair, as red as flame, fell unbound to her waist. Her eyes were green flecked with gold. She had a small determined chin, a finely shaped nose, and perfectly arched brows. A necklace of amber and jet circled her slender throat.

Clearing my own throat, I said, "May I help you?"

"You must be Kathy," the man said.

"I'm at a disadvantage, sir," I replied, "since you know my name and I don't know yours."

"I am Roshan DeLongpre," he said, bowing at the waist, "and this is my wife, Brenna."

"Pleased to meet you," I murmured, my thoughts racing. Roshan DeLongpre was Raphael's grandfather. He was a Vampire. His wife was a Vampire. It was a little after eleven in the morning, and they were both awake and in my store. I stared at the two of them, too astonished to think clearly.

"Our Raphael speaks very highly of you," Brenna DeLongpre remarked.

"Does he?"

"Yes, indeed."

At a loss for words, I could only nod. How was it possible for Raphael's grandparents to be awake when the sun was up? Had he been joking when he told me they were Vampires? And what were they doing in Oak Hollow when they were supposed to be out of the country?

"I take it from your expression that Raphael has told you what we are," Roshan said with a wry grin.

"Yes, I believe he did mention it."

Roshan laughed softly. "Please, do not be alarmed by our visit. Brenna wanted to pick up a few books, and since we both wanted to meet you, we thought we would stop by and introduce ourselves."

I made a broad gesture with my hand. "Please, feel free to browse as long as you like."

"Thank you."

He moved toward the science fiction section, the top of his head just visible above the shelf. She wandered among the romances, humming softly.

I wondered what they were doing in Oak Hollow. Rafe had said they were in France.

After fifteen or twenty minutes, they approached the counter, each carrying several books.

"How much do I owe you?" Roshan asked, reaching for his wallet.

"Please, just take them. No charge."

"Nonsense," Roshan said. "You're running a business here, and I can well afford to pay."

I remembered that Rafe had said his grandfather was rich. My fingers were shaking a little as I tallied their purchases. I wondered if Rafe knew his grandparents were in town, and if so, why he hadn't mentioned it the night before. My cheeks grew warm as I recalled how we had spent the night.

Roshan paid for their purchases; I put their books in a bag and handed it to him.

"Thank you," he said. "I'm sure we'll see you again."

"Soon, I hope," Brenna added with a smile. I suddenly remembered Edna telling me that Raphael's grandmother was a witch. *She must be a good witch,* I thought. She was far too lovely to be anything else. I grinned inwardly as I recalled the good witch in *The Wizard of Oz* telling Dorothy that only bad witches were ugly.

Brenna DeLongpre took her husband's arm, and they left the store.

Feeling suddenly weak, I dropped into the chair behind my desk, my mind whirling. What on earth had Raphael told them about me?

"I told them you were beautiful and I was in love with you," Rafe said later that evening. "What did you think I said?"

"You think I'm beautiful?"

"You know I do."

We were still standing on the porch because I had hit him with the question uppermost in my mind the minute I opened the door.

"Okay if I come in now?" he asked drily.

"Of course." I stepped back so he could cross the threshold.

He closed the door, then followed me into the living room and sat beside me on the sofa.

"I was just surprised to see them," I said. "I mean, really surprised, especially since it was still daylight. Shouldn't they have been home in their beds or whatever?"

"You'd think so, wouldn't you?" Rafe said with a grin.

"So, why didn't they burn to a crisp?"

"You remember I told you about Mara?"

"The oldest Vampire around?"

"Right. Well, she made my father and because Mara's blood is so powerful, he can be awake during the day. Mara also shared blood with my grandfather, who then shared his blood with my grandmother. Consequently, they can all be active during the day."

It was beyond amazing. His Vampire father had sired twins. His father and his grandparents weren't rendered unconscious when the sun rose. "What about your mother?"

"Naturally my father shared his blood with her."

"So she can walk around during the day, too?"

Raphael nodded.

"What about you?"

"The Dark Sleep has no power over me."

"Then why haven't I ever seen you during the day?"

He shrugged. "It's when I choose to take my rest. Even though I can be awake and active, it's more natural for me to rest when the sun is up. My parents and grand-parents also prefer to rest in the afternoon."

"So, why doesn't Mara share her blood with all the Vampires?"

"It would weaken her. There are hundreds of Vampires, you know."

I nodded. It made sense. Even if she doled it out over time, it would take years to share her blood with all the Vampires.

"But that's not the only reason," Rafe said. "Being able to walk in the daylight gives her an edge over most of the rest of our kind. You understand?"

Oh, I understood, all right. It gave her a decided advantage to be able to be awake when all the other Vampires were asleep and helpless.

"What are your grandparents doing here?" I asked. "I thought they were in France."

"Mara summoned them."

"Another council of war?"

"Another council of peace," Rafe said. He slipped his arm around my waist and drew me closer. "Do you want to talk all night?" he asked, nibbling on my ear.

"I don't know," I murmured. "What did you have in mind?"

"Oh, a little of this," he said, trailing slow, hot kisses along my neck. "A little of that." His hands skimmed over my body, leaving a quivering mass of desire in their wake.

"I'll give you an hour to stop that," I said, and surrendered to the magic that was Raphael.

Chapter Fourteen

I woke smiling the next morning. It was getting to be a habit, I thought, one I didn't want to break.

Humming softly, I turned on the radio in the kitchen while I poured myself a cup of coffee.

". . . in other news, longtime resident Susie McGee is still missing."

Susie, missing? I turned up the volume.

"According to her husband, Mrs. McGee went to a parent-teacher conference three nights ago and never returned home. Her car was found on the edge of Brawley Woods late last night. Mr. McGee was questioned at length by the Oak Hollow Police Department and later released. In what may be a related story, Mark Littlejohn has also been reported missing. According to his wife, Mary Littlejohn, Mark went bowling with a couple of friends three nights ago and never came home. The police are currently questioning Mark Littlejohn's associates at work. If you have information relating to either of these missing persons, please call the Oak Hollow Police Department. In the meantime, local police are advising residents to be sure to lock their doors and windows and to remain inside after dark. In stock market news . . ."

I switched off the radio. Two people had gone missing on the same night. That didn't sound good. I didn't want to believe that anything bad had happened to Susie, so I searched my mind for some other explanation. Maybe she and Mark had run off together. I shook my head. Even if such a far-fetched scenario was true, Susie would never have left her kids behind. She might leave her husband, but never her sons. What if Mark was the father of Susie's new baby and Rick had found out and . . . and what? Killed them both and buried the bodies? I shook my head. There had to be another explanation, something a little less gruesome.

I couldn't imagine Susie sneaking out to meet another man. As for Mark Littlejohn, I had never met the man and knew nothing about him except that he owned a roller-skating rink on the outskirts of town.

Susie was still much on my mind when I opened the store later that morning. Who would want to hurt a pregnant woman? Poor Susie . . . I thrust the thought from my mind. Until I knew otherwise, I refused to believe the worst.

Edna and Pearl stopped by later that afternoon. Instead of their usual colorful attire, they both wore black from head to foot, relieved only by tinkling silver bracelets, dangling earrings in the shape of crosses, and silver necklaces.

"Isn't it awful, dear?" Pearl murmured. "Poor Susie! And Mark. Such a nice boy."

Edna clucked softly. "I knew something like this would happen, what with all those Vampires and Werewolves stalking the streets after dark."

Pearl laid her hand on my arm. "Susie was a friend of yours, wasn't she?"

"Yes. Have you heard anything?"

"No, only what they said on the news this morning. But when people go missing in Oak Hollow . . ." Pearl's voice trailed off.

Edna nodded. "It's so sad. I don't know how Rick will raise those boys without her."

"Stop it! She's not dead. I can't believe it. I won't!"

"I know how you must feel, dear," Pearl said kindly. "But it's better to face the truth, however ugly it might be, and then put it behind you."

"We're on our way over to see Rick and offer our condolences," Edna said. "We just wanted to stop by and see how you were doing."

"Be sure to go right home tonight," Pearl said.

"And lock your doors," Edna added.

"I will. If you hear anything . . ."

"We'll let you know, dear," Pearl said.

I stared after them. They had to be wrong. Susie couldn't be dead. She just couldn't be.

I was thinking about closing the shop early when Rafe arrived.

It was the first time I had seen him when it was still light outside. "You're here early."

"I heard about Susie."

Tears stung my eyes. "Do you know what happened to her?"

"No, but I have a pretty good idea."

"She's not . . ."

"I don't know. I was going to go look for her, but I wanted to make sure you were all right first."

"I'm fine," I said. "And I'm coming with you."

"I'm not sure that's a good idea."

"We're wasting time."

He didn't argue further. I grabbed my purse, locked up the store, and followed him to his car. By the time we reached the cutoff to Brawley Woods, the sun had set, plunging the world into darkness. There were only a few houses out this way, and they were set a good distance from the road. There were no streetlights, no illumination of any kind save for the car's headlights and a few scattered stars.

I tapped my fingertips on the armrest, trying not to think about what we might find.

Thirty minutes later, Rafe pulled off the road. There was no sign of Susie's car. I supposed her husband or the police had taken it back to town. How many other people had disappeared that no one knew about? I fingered the cross at my throat, wondering if it would really protect me.

Rafe came around to open the door for me, and I got out of the car. "Now what?"

He signaled for me to be quiet; then, closing his eyes, he lifted his head and sniffed the wind.

He stood so still and blended into the shadows so perfectly, it was almost as if he was a part of the night. He looked so otherworldly standing there that it sent a shiver down my spine. The word *Vampire* whispered in the back of my mind, reminding me once again that there was an immense gulf between us that I could never cross.

Abruptly, Rafe took my hand in his. "This way," he said, and plunged into the woods. The trees grew thick here, their branches intertwining to form a thick canopy overhead. The ground was covered with pinecones, bits of bark, and broken branches.

As I stumbled along behind Rafe, I wished my night vision was as good as his obviously was. I couldn't help thinking that looking for someone in Brawley Woods was like looking for a needle in the proverbial haystack. The woods covered thirteen square miles of ground that were crisscrossed with deep crevices and gullies and pockmarked by dozens of caves. What chance did we have of finding Susie, if she was even out here?

We had been walking about twenty minutes when Rafe stopped. He sniffed the air again; then, veering to the right, he continued on.

The trees weren't so thick here. I shivered as the wind shifted. Glancing up, I saw that dark gray clouds were gathering overhead.

Another ten minutes ticked into eternity, and then I heard it, a funny whimpering sound, almost like an animal in pain. It made the short hairs prickle along my nape. "What was that?"

Before he could answer, I saw a dark shape huddled on the ground beside a tree. My foot hit a branch, and the creature's head jerked up, its eyes wild.

"Susie!" I stared at her in disbelief. She was naked, and as the moon emerged from behind the clouds, I saw that she had been crying.

"Go away!" She scooted backward, her hands awkwardly covering her nakedness.

"Susie, it's me."

"Go away!" A sob was wrenched from deep inside her as she continued to scramble backward. "Please, just go away."

"Susie, listen to me." Rafe's voice, low and mesmerizing, brought her to a halt. "We're here to help you."

"No one can help me," she cried, her voice filled with soul-deep anguish. "No one!"

"Trust me." Rafe moved toward her as he spoke. "I'm not going to hurt you."

She looked up at him, her arms crossed over her breasts, tears running unchecked down her cheeks. Leaves and debris were tangled in her hair, there were scratches on her arms and legs, scratches that were healing, fading, even as I watched. Most troubling of all was the dried blood on her inner thighs. Had she been raped? I glanced around, wondering where her clothes were.

Rafe knelt before Susie. Gently, he wiped the tears from her cheeks. Removing his shirt, he draped it over her shoulders. "There now," he said. "You'll be all right."

She shook her head. "No, I'll never be all right again. My baby, oh, my poor baby."

"Susie, what happened?" I asked, coming up behind Rafe.

"Not now," he said, and lifting Susie into his arms, he turned and headed back the way we'd come.

I hurried after him, a thousand questions screaming in my head.

When we reached the car, Rafe opened the rear door and settled Susie in the backseat. I crawled in beside her. She was shivering convulsively now. I put my arms around her, hoping to help warm her.

Raphael started the car and turned the heater on full blast.

"You'll be home soon," he said, speaking to Susie over his shoulder.

"No! No, I don't want to go home. I can't go home! Please!"

Seeing that she was on the verge of hysteria, I said,

"We won't take you home, I promise. You can stay at my place, all right?"

Still shivering, she huddled against me, silent tears tracking her cheeks. Feeling helpless, I patted her shoulder, murmuring that everything would be all right.

When we reached my house, Raphael carried Susie inside. I marveled at how gentle he was with her, how the very sound of his voice seemed to soothe her.

I followed him inside, taking a quick moment to admire his bare back before I closed and locked the door behind us.

"Rafe," I said, "bring her into the bathroom." Leading the way, I turned on the taps and added some scented bubble bath, hoping it would relax her.

Rafe held Susie until the tub was full, then slipped his shirt off her shoulders and lowered her into the water.

"Anything else I can do?" he asked, looking at me.

I shook my head.

"I'll be in the other room," he said. "Call me if you need me."

With a nod, I closed the door. Susie lay in the bathtub with bubbles up to her chin. She stared blankly at the ceiling.

"Can I get you anything?" I asked.

She shook her head, then whispered, "I wish he'd killed me."

"Who?" I asked. "Who did this to you?"

"I don't know. I was coming home from a meeting with Mrs. Blythe. It seems Jody has been causing some trouble in class." She smiled wistfully. "He's a good boy, you know."

I nodded. Jody was her youngest son. "Go on."

"I stopped at the light on the corner of First and Elm,

and a man got into the car. He made me drive out to the woods and then . . ." She shuddered. "He dragged me out of the car. I thought he was going to rape me. I told myself I could live with that, if he'd just leave me alive. But he didn't rape me. He . . . he turned into a wolf. A wolf." She shuddered again. "He bit me. . . ."

She pushed her hair aside, and I saw an ugly red wound smeared with dried blood. I thought it odd that her other scrapes and scratches had disappeared, but the bite mark remained.

"I don't remember anything after that except . . . I had a horrible nightmare. I dreamed I was a wolf." A single tear ran down Susie's cheek. "When I woke in the morning, I couldn't find my clothes and I . . . I panicked and started running, but I got lost in the woods."

She laughed, a dull, humorless sound. "I remembered reading somewhere that if you got lost, you should sit down and wait for someone to find you, so that's what I did. I told myself that Rick would find me, that everything would be okay, that nothing worse could happen to me."

She looked at me, her expression bleak. "Just proves how wrong you can be. Hours passed and no one came." She folded her arms over her breasts. "I was about to start walking again when the same man suddenly appeared. I told him to go away and leave me alone, but he just laughed. He said he'd come to help me."

"Help you? Help you how?"

"I didn't know at the time. I thought he was some kind of lunatic, because he wouldn't let me go, but he gave me food and water. I slept the rest of the day. When I woke, he told me the moon was full and that I was going to change. Before I could ask what he meant . . ." She closed her eyes. "It happened."

"What happened?" I had to ask, even though I was afraid I already knew the answer.

"I turned into a wolf. It was horrible, painful, frightening." She placed her hand over her abdomen. "I miscarried in the middle of it."

"Oh, Susie, I'm so sorry." And even as I spoke the words, I was overcome with relief. Thank goodness the moon wasn't full tonight. And then I frowned. "You need to see a doctor."

"No!"

"But . . ."

"I'm all right. Don't you know? Werewolves heal quickly."

I stood there, feeling totally helpless as I tried to think of something to say.

"It's probably for the best," she said in that same lifeless tone. "No baby should have a Werewolf for a mother." She opened her eyes and looked at me. "How can I ever trust myself to be alone with my children? What will Rick say? What will my parents say? The ladies at church?"

Moaning softly, she clutched her stomach. "My baby, I want my baby."

Never in all my life had I seen such anguish reflected in anyone's eyes. I yearned to comfort her, to tell her everything would be all right, but the lie tasted like ashes in my mouth.

"Why?" she asked in a hoarse whisper. "Why didn't he just kill me?"

* * *

Later, after I bathed Susie and helped her into one of my nightgowns, I put her to bed in the guest room and tucked her in. I stood there a moment, my heart aching for her. I couldn't begin to imagine the horrors she had experienced as she felt her body transform, nor could I truly understand her pain at losing a child. I had been tempted to tell her she could have other children, but I had quickly realized she wouldn't find any comfort in that. Having another child, or ten, would never make up for the one she had lost.

Blinking back my tears, I tiptoed into the hallway and closed the door behind me.

Rafe was waiting for me in the living room. "Is she all right?"

"She's asleep." I sat beside him on the sofa. "Why would anyone do such a thing to Susie?"

Rafe didn't answer, but then, I hadn't expected him to. There was no answer, at least none that made sense. None that would heal Susie's wounded heart. Only time could do that. Still, I wanted an explanation.

"It isn't fair," I said bitterly. "She's not involved in your war."

"That's where you're wrong," he said. "Everyone's involved whether they want to be or not."

"I don't understand how either side can win. I mean, do the Werewolves intend to destroy every Vampire in the world? And what about the Vampires? Do they expect to destroy all the Werewolves? Even if it was possible, it would take years."

"The hotheads who started the fight don't care about that. They're like the old-time terrorists. They don't care who they hurt or how many innocent lives they take, all they want to do is kill."

"And innocent people like Susie are going to be caught in the middle?" I shook my head. "It isn't right!"

"Hopefully, Mara and Clive will resolve it soon."

"How will they do that?" I wanted an answer, and I wanted it now.

"I don't know, exactly. I just know they're working on it." I must have looked doubtful, because he added, "They're trying to talk some sense into the more militant ones on both sides."

"And if that doesn't work?"

"The ones who refuse to listen, who refuse to end the fighting, will be stopped."

"Oh." I didn't have to ask how that would be accomplished. Justice among the Supernatural creatures was notoriously swift and final.

Worrying about the future, mine or Susie's or Rafe's, wouldn't help. It never did. Feeling suddenly tired and depressed, I rested my head on Rafe's shoulder and closed my eyes.

I must have dozed off, because the next thing I knew, Rafe was shaking me gently.

"Oh, sorry," I murmured. "I didn't mean to fall asleep."

"It's all right." He kissed the tip of my nose. "You should go to bed. I'll see you tomorrow."

I walked him to the door where he took me in his arms and spent a few moments kissing me good night. One last hug and a warning to keep my doors and windows locked, and he vanished into the darkness. I stared after him for a moment, wondering if I would ever get used to the way he seemed to just disappear into nothingness.

With a shake of my head, I locked the door, then went through the house, checking the back door and the windows before I went into the guest room to look in on

Susie. She was sleeping on her side, her head pillowed on her hand. Her cheeks were damp with tears. It made me hurt inside to look at her, to know what she had been through, to know that she would have to live with what had been done to her for the rest of her life.

Heavy-hearted, I went into my room to get ready for bed.

I wasn't sure what woke me. Sitting up, I turned on the light beside my bed and glanced around. Everything was as it should be. And then I heard it, the faint creak of the loose floorboard in the hallway.

Thinking that Susie might need something, I got up and slipped into my robe. I was headed for the guest room when I noticed the light was on in the kitchen.

I sighed, thinking a nightmare had probably awakened her.

I came to a dead stop in the doorway, my stomach churning at the scene before me. "Susie! What have you done?"

She looked up at me, her eyes wide and scared. Blood dripped like crimson raindrops from the ugly gash in her left arm.

I stared at her a moment longer, then grabbed a dish towel and wrapped it tightly around her wrist. Grabbing my keys and my handbag, I urged Susie outside and into my car. Settling her in the front seat, I slid behind the wheel and drove to the hospital as fast as I dared, grateful all the while that Oak Hollow was a small town and that the hospital was less than five minutes away.

I hit the brakes hard, tires screeching as the car jolted to a halt in front of the emergency entrance. Getting out of the car, I practically dragged Susie inside.

One look at her pale face and the bloody towel wrapped around her wrist stilled any questions the night nurse might have had. Calling for a doctor, stat, she led Susie into the nearest examination area and drew the curtain.

A short time later, a doctor hurried down the hall and into the ER.

I paced the ugly green hallway from one end to the other and back again. I had known Susie was upset, but I had never expected her to do anything like this.

"Rafe, where are you when I need you?"

I had no sooner murmured the words than he was there beside me.

I was too happy to see him to question his abrupt appearance. He opened his arms, and I went into them gladly, grateful for his nearness and his strength.

"What happened?" he asked quietly.

"Susie slit her wrist."

Rafe muttered an oath. "Is she going to be all right?"

"I don't know. The doctor's with her now. Oh, Rafe, if I hadn't woke up when I did . . ." I buried my face against his chest. Another few minutes, and I would have been too late.

After a time, he guided me to a chair. I sat down, and he took the chair beside mine, my hand clasped in his. I don't know how long we sat there. It might have been two minutes, it might have been two hours, but finally the doctor came out of the cubicle.

I stood as he approached; Rafe stood beside me. "How is she?"

"She's lost quite a bit of blood, but I'm confident she'll recover. I'll have to report this to the police." He pulled a pen from his pocket. "I'll need your name for the report."

"Katherine McKenna."

"Are you a relative?"

"No, just a friend."

"Have you notified Mr. McGee?"

"No." I wondered how he knew who Susie's husband was, and then it came to me. She'd had three kids and this was the only hospital in town.

The doctor made a note on his pad.

"Can I see her?" I asked.

The doctor scrubbed a hand over his jaw. "I don't see why not, but only for a few minutes. We've given her a sedative to help her sleep, so she might be a little groggy. She's been moved to . . ." He checked the chart in his hand. "To Room 14," he said. "Last door on the right."

"You go on," Rafe said. "I'll wait here."

With a nod, I hurried down the hallway. I hated hospitals. I hated the sounds and the smells. It seemed to me that Death was always lurking in the shadows, waiting for the weak and the unwary.

I paused outside Susie's room; then, taking a deep breath, I pushed the door open. Susie lay on a narrow bed, a thick white bandage wrapped around her wrist. There were hollows in her cheeks, dark circles beneath her eyes. She was hooked up to an IV.

"Susie?" Standing beside the bed, I smoothed a lock of hair from her brow. "Susie, can you hear me?"

Her eyelids fluttered open. "Kathy? Forgive me . . . I'm so ashamed."

"You're gonna be fine, just fine."

"Rick won't be able to say it was just my imagination this time," she said weakly, and burst into tears.

Words failed me. Sitting on the edge of Susie's bed, I

took her hand in mine and prayed that would be comfort
enough.

I stayed with Susie until she fell asleep, and then,
feeling as though I'd been run through an emotional
wringer, I tiptoed out of her room.

Rafe was waiting for me in the hallway. "How is
she?"

"Sleeping."

He took my hand as we left the hospital. When we
reached my car, he didn't ask if I wanted him to drive
me home, he just opened the door for me and then got
behind the wheel. Neither of us spoke until we were
heading back to my place.

I thought about all the things that I had read about
Werewolves. Most of it had been based on speculation,
rumor, and myth. But what had happened to Susie was
all too real.

"What will become of her now?" I asked. "How can
she raise her family, be a wife and a mother, when she's
a . . . a Werewolf?"

"That's up to her," Rafe said.

"Up to her? What does that mean? She didn't ask for
this. And what about the monster who did it to her?"

"She can learn to control what she is, or she can let
what she's become control her. She can accept it, or she
can wallow in self-pity. Being a Werewolf isn't the worst
thing in the world. She'll be the same as she's always
been except for those nights when the moon is full."

"And then what? She'll turn furry and run around the
countryside killing people?"

"I'll get in touch with Clive. He can send one of his

pack to help her learn to adjust to her new life, teach her how to control her beast."

"Her beast." I repeated the words. If this seemed like a nightmare to me, how much worse was it for Susie? I couldn't help wondering how her husband and children would react when they heard the news. I had only met Rick McGee once, briefly, after church. Susie had never said much about him, making me wonder what kind of man he was, what kind of marriage they had. I just hoped he would be as supportive as possible under the circumstances.

"We all have problems to deal with," Rafe remarked. "Some people are born with physical deformities, some have mentally handicapped children, some people are married to alcoholics." He shrugged. "I've never known anyone who had a perfectly carefree life."

"So, do you think of being a Vampire as a problem?"

He shrugged. "In a way. I could have let it ruin my life. I could have turned my back on my humanity and let the lust for blood consume me. Instead, I chose to look at it as a kind of sickness that imposes limits on what I can and can't do. On the other hand, it's given me some remarkable powers."

"So, you're saying that Susie should just look on this as some kind of monthly inconvenience, like retaining water and cramps?"

Rafe chuckled. "I guess you could put it like that," he said, and then his expression turned serious once again. "I don't want to make light of this. It's going to take some serious readjusting on Susie's part, and on her family's, as well. Whether she can handle it or not depends on how strong she is, both mentally and physically. And spiritually, I suppose."

Rafe's words troubled me. How strong could Susie be, mentally anyway, if she had already tried to take her own life?

I looked over at Rafe, admiring his profile, the spread of his shoulders, the way his hair framed his face. "Do you like being a Vampire?"

He glanced in my direction. "Most of the time. Why? Are you thinking of becoming one?"

"Of course not! Do you think you'd like being a Werewolf?"

"I don't know." He slowed to make the turn onto my street. "I never gave it a lot of thought."

"Would you be mortal again, if you could?"

"I'm not sure I was ever mortal, at least not in the true sense of the word."

"Would you like to be?"

"I don't think so. It's a moot point, anyway, since there's no cure for what I am."

"I don't guess there's a cure for being a Werewolf, either."

"Not that I know of." Pulling up in front of my house, he killed the engine.

"Do you want to come in?" I asked, smothering a yawn.

"I'd like to, but I think you'd better get some sleep."

"Maybe you're right."

Leaning toward me, he cupped the back of my head in his hand and kissed me, slow, sweet, and deep. "Honey, I'm always right."

Chapter Fifteen

After leaving Kathy's house, Rafe made a brief stop at his place, and then returned to Brawley Woods. Following Mara's standing orders, he went searching for the body of Mark Littlejohn. He found what was left of the man at the bottom of a deep crevasse, the grisly remains covered by rocks and debris.

Rafe had seen death in many forms, but never had he seen a body as badly mutilated as this one. Had Littlejohn been unmarried, Rafe would have left the body where it was, but Littlejohn had a wife and a little girl, not to mention parents, who would miss him. Learning of his death wouldn't be easy on his family, but never knowing what had happened to him would be even more cruel. This way, they would have closure if nothing more.

He wrapped the man's remains in the blanket he had brought from home, then carried the body back to his car and placed it in the trunk.

When he reached town, he pulled up in back of the Oak Hollow emergency room and left Littlejohn's remains where they were sure to be found. He felt bad about leaving the body outside, but he wasn't a fool. Any Vampire who waltzed into a hospital carrying a dead body was just asking for trouble. And whether Littlejohn's body was found tonight or tomorrow morning wouldn't matter. The man was beyond help, both mortal and Supernatural.

It was near 2:00 A.M. when Rafe met up with Mara, Clive, Cagin, and his grandparents in one of the vacant rooms in the Hollow Tree Hotel. They didn't bother to tell the clerk at the desk they were there. The fewer people who knew, the better.

Rafe was the last to arrive. He hugged his grandmother and Mara, shook hands with his grandfather, and acknowledged the presence of the two Were-creatures with a nod of his head. He didn't like Clive, and he didn't trust Cagin, but it was time to put his personal feelings aside, at least for the moment.

"You've all heard of the recent attacks," Mara said without preamble. "Clive and I agree that a Werewolf is responsible. However, neither Clive nor Cagin recognized his scent."

Roshan looked at Clive. "Are we dealing with the possibility of a rogue Werewolf?"

"I'm afraid so," Clive replied. "I followed his scent for several miles, and then it disappeared."

"How is that possible?" Brenna asked.

Clive shook his head. "I don't know. I have several of my people out scouting the area."

"Even if he transformed, wouldn't he still smell the same?" Rafe asked.

"Yes," Clive said. "That's what troubles me."

"What are you thinking?" Mara asked.

"I don't know how he did it, but I'm thinking he's either found a way to mask his scent or change it altogether."

"Are we sure Littlejohn was killed by a Were-creature?" Roshan asked.

Mara turned to look at him, her green eyes glittering like polished jade. "Who else could it be?"

"One of us, perhaps?" Roshan said quietly.

"I've never known a Vampire to rip his victim to shreds," Mara remarked. She looked at Rafe. "Was the body drained of blood?"

Rafe shook his head. "I don't think so, but it was hard to tell from what was left."

"Are we sure the woman and Littlejohn were both attacked by the same person?" Brenna asked. "Maybe there's no connection. After all, it could just be coincidence that both of the humans were taken on the same night."

"And in the same place?" Clive said. "I don't think so."

"Did you pick up any Vampire scent at either scene?" Mara asked.

"No." Rafe glanced at Clive. "It smelled like dyed-in-the-wool Werewolf to me."

"Maybe it was a blood sucker," Cagin said, his yellow eyes narrowing as he looked at Rafe. "Maybe it was a Vamp smart enough to mask his own scent. Maybe he mutilated Littlejohn to make it look like one of us did it."

"Maybe it wasn't a Vampire or a Werewolf," Roshan suggested.

Clive snorted. "Who else would have done it?"

"A mortal," Roshan replied. "Maybe a group of mortals who don't want the war to end."

"I'm the one who found Littlejohn," Rafe said flatly. "He smelled of Werewolf. As for the girl, I know for a fact that she was bitten by a Werewolf, since she transformed when the moon was full."

"All right," Mara said. "Until we learn otherwise, we're going on the assumption that there's a Werewolf in town who has deliberately disobeyed Clive's command to cease any and all killing within the city. Our first order of business is to find him before he kills again, or before he bites anyone else. Clive, I want you to determine the whereabouts of all your people on the night the McGee girl and Littlejohn were taken. Once you're convinced that none of your people is responsible, I want you to send them all away.

"Roshan, when the girl gets out of the hospital, I want you and Brenna to keep an eye on her. I want you to watch her house day and night, and follow her if she leaves."

"Any particular reason why?" Roshan asked.

"I don't want any more human casualties in Oak Hollow. There have been too many already. Rafe, I want you to get in touch with our people and tell them all to go home."

"Hold on a minute," Clive said. "Including you, that leaves four Vamps in town and only two of us."

Mara lifted one brow. "And your point is?"

"I want an equal number of my people in town."

"We're not going to war," Mara said impatiently, "we're trying to stop this one from escalating."

Clive shrugged. "If you don't like it, then send two of your people away."

"That's how this whole war between us started," Mara reminded him. "The thirst for power has brought us to the brink of war with the humans. At one time, I thought it was a battle we might win, but I see now that the old way was better for all of us."

"You mean when we tucked our tails between our legs and hid out in the woods?" Clive asked disdainfully.

"The humans outnumber the Supernatural community ten thousand to one," Mara said impatiently. "Even we can't beat those odds."

"Sure we can," Clive retorted. "All we have to do to lower the odds is kill them, one at a time."

"And how will you survive when the prey is gone?" Roshan asked.

"This is getting us nowhere," Mara said, rising to her feet. "It's time to end the feud between us now, once and for all, before the humans do it for us."

"They'll never defeat us," Clive said with a sneer. "They're too weak."

"But they're not stupid," Mara said. "They have found cures for almost every disease known to mankind. They have conquered space and harvested the oceans. They have found a way to overcome any and all obstacles that they have encountered. Do you doubt that they can find a way to destroy your kind, as well?"

Apparently, Clive had no argument for that. Rising, he motioned to Cagin, and the two Weres left the room.

"He's a fool," Mara said. "Even now, I've heard rumors that human scientists are working on a drug that will cure lycanthropy. If they can come up with a viable concoction that won't harm the humans, all they'll have to do is add the drug to the water supply. The Werewolves will be cured whether they want to be or not. Perhaps the shape-shifters, as well."

Rafe grunted softly. "And how will that affect us?"

Mara shook her head. "Since we are not truly alive, I have no idea."

On that troubling note, Rafe bid Mara and his grandparents farewell, dissolved into mist, and floated out the window of the hotel.

Materializing inside his car, he pulled away from the curb. What Mara had said about ending the war before the humans ended it for them made good sense; he just hoped Clive and his Weres were smart enough to see that. The Vampires and the Werewolves had been waging open war among themselves for less than a year with heavy casualties on both sides. Rafe had no idea which side was winning. As far as he knew, no one had ever taken a census among the Werewolves. It was rumored that a Vampire hunter had a record of many of the known Vampires, but as far as Rafe knew, it was only a myth. Still, it was unusual for Supernatural creatures to disappear without their kind being aware of it.

As for some miracle drug that would cure the Werewolf community . . . Rafe shook his head, wondering again what kind of effect such a concoction would have on the Vampires and the shape-shifters, if any. That thought was followed by another, far more troubling one. Before the humans could drug the water supply, they would have to test it, not only on humans to make sure it was safe, but on Werewolves to make sure it worked. Would they think to test it on Vampires, as well? Maybe they were testing it already. Maybe that accounted for the missing Werewolves and Vampires.

He swore softly. There was nothing he could do about that. Putting the thought out of his mind, he let himself think about Kathy instead. He had never been one to believe in karma or fate, but in the deepest part of his being, he knew she had been born for him.

When he was with her, he could almost forget he was no longer human. Almost. He was amazed that she had so quickly accepted him for what he was. Her curiosity about his lifestyle and his paranormal powers amused him, her nearness aroused him, her blood was the sweetest he had ever tasted. A few sips had satisfied his craving in ways nothing else ever had.

And she loved him. That was the most amazing thing of all. But did she love him enough, was she brave enough, to spend the rest of her life with him?

Only time would tell, he mused ruefully.

And that was one thing he had plenty of.

Chapter Sixteen

Friday morning dawned cold and wet. Dark clouds hung low in an angry gray sky. My first thought was for Susie. Picking up the receiver, I called the hospital and gave the operator her room number.

A man answered the phone.

"Hi," I said. "This is Kathy McKenna. Is Susie there?"

"This is her husband. She's not taking phone calls just now."

"Oh." I didn't like the tone of his voice at all. "Is she feeling any better?" I heard Susie's voice in the background. It sounded like she was crying. "Mr. McGee, please, if I could just speak to her for a minute."

"Perhaps another time," he said curtly.

"Excuse me, Mr. McGee, but I'm the one who found her. I think I have a right to speak to her."

There was a pause, the sound of muffled voices that told me Rick had his hand over the receiver, and then Susie's voice came over the line.

"Kathy, I'm sorry, but I really can't talk right now."

"Are you all right?"

"Not really."

I had the feeling her husband was standing over her, listening to every word. Before today, I'd never said more than three or four words to the man, but I was starting to hate him. "I understand. Why don't you call me when you get home, or when you can talk?"

"I will."

"Promise?"

"Yes, thank you for calling," Susie said politely, and hung up the phone.

I stared at the receiver, wondering if I dared call back. She had sounded so . . . I don't know, so completely forlorn, so lost. I had hoped her husband would comfort her, but I didn't think the man had it in him. He had sounded angry, as if what had happened to Susie was her own fault.

But there was nothing I could do about it now, not while he was there. If he didn't want me to talk to her on the phone, I was pretty sure he wouldn't want me coming to visit.

After a quick breakfast, I showered, got dressed, and went to the bookstore.

In spite of the rain, or maybe because of it, a number of people came into the shop to browse. Even more surprising, they seemed in no hurry to leave, and most of them actually bought books.

"I'm going home to curl up in front of the fire," one woman remarked. "A good book and a cup of hot chocolate—I can't think of anything that sounds better on a day like this."

An image of Rafe flashed through my mind. I could think of several things I'd rather do on a day like this, I mused, imagining the two of us curled up on my bed.

I didn't say it out loud, of course, merely nodded in agreement.

Shortly after two o'clock, things went back to normal, as in, no customers. I closed up for thirty minutes and went to lunch, then returned to the store. Shortly after three, the Were-girl I had seen once before entered the shop.

She picked out a couple of paperbacks. Ringing up her purchases, I wondered what would be the best way to start a conversation with her and decided on a simple, "Hi, Jennifer, it's nice to see you again."

She looked at me, her violet eyes wide and suspicious. "How'd you know my name?"

I held up her credit card.

"Oh," she said, blushing, "of course."

I smiled as I returned her card, then bagged her books. I wanted desperately to question her about what it was like to be a shape-shifter, but the words stuck in my throat. She didn't look like she was anxious to talk about it, and I wasn't sure it was a good idea to let her know that I knew what she was. Besides, she probably couldn't answer my questions anyway, since being a shape-shifter wasn't the same as being a Werewolf.

"Come again," I said.

She smiled uncertainly as she picked up her bag and left the store.

With a sigh, I stared after her, then picked up the phone and dialed the hospital. I asked for Susie's room, only to learn that her husband had already taken her home.

The hours seemed to drag by. And it was Friday, which meant staying open until nine. Of course, I was the boss. I could always close up early. Heck, I could close up now.

Moving to the door, I stared out into the gloom. Jagged bolts of lightning speared the clouds; thunder rolled across the lowering skies. The sidewalks were empty; there was little traffic on the street.

I'd stay another half an hour or so, I thought, and then I was going to go home and, like the woman who had been in earlier, I was going to curl up in front of the fire with a cup of hot chocolate and a good book.

The prospect was so appealing, I decided not to wait any longer. With that thought in mind, I turned away from the window and felt my heart skip a beat when I saw Rafe standing by the counter. He wore a long black leather coat over a pair of black jeans and a dark green shirt.

"Oh!" I pressed a hand to my heart. "You startled me!"

"Sorry."

I studied him for a moment. He was as handsome as ever, his appearance impeccable, his long black hair framing a face worthy of a Botticelli, but something wasn't right. And then it hit me. "How come you're not wet?"

He shrugged. "Vampire magic?"

I grunted softly. It seemed to be his standard answer for anything related to his Supernatural status. "Susie went home today."

"She's better then?"

"I don't know. I didn't really get to talk to her. I'm worried about her, Rafe. Her husband seems so unsympathetic and, well, I'm just worried about her."

"You don't think he'd hurt her, do you?"

"I don't know, but I can't believe they let her go home already. I mean, she lost a baby and . . . and, you know."

"We can stop by there later, after you close up," Rafe said.

"I'm closing now," I said. "Let's go."

Rafe parked his car a block away from Susie's house. I looked askance at him. Did he expect us to walk in the rain? Maybe he wouldn't get wet, but I would.

"I'm going in alone," he said.

"What?"

"The best way to find out what's going on is for me to go in there, unseen."

"How are you going to . . . oh. Can you really do that? Make yourself invisible?"

He winked at me. "Yes, ma'am."

"I don't believe it."

"No?"

Before I could say anything else, Rafe's body shimmered and dissolved into a faint silver mist, kind of like shimmery specks of dust. I stared at him in astonishment, all the while wondering what other Supernatural powers he possessed, and then the mist was gone.

"Be careful," I murmured, but there was no one there to hear me.

Staring out the window, I listened to the rain beating down on the roof of the car. Lightning flashed in the distance. I was wondering what was going on in Susie's house when the strangest thing happened. One minute I was watching jagged bolts of lightning flash across the skies, and the next it was like I was inside Susie's house. It took me a minute to realize I was seeing things through Rafe's eyes, hearing what he heard.

Susie was sitting up in bed, her hair pulled back into a ponytail. It made her look like she was about fifteen years old. Her husband, Rick, sat in a rocking chair beside the bed. I suppose he was a good-looking man, though it was hard to tell, his expression was so grim. His eyes were gray and as hard as iron; his hair was blond and he wore it cropped close to his head. I couldn't say how tall he was, since he was sitting down, but from his physique, it was obvious that he worked out.

". . . don't know what we're going to do about this," he was saying. "If you think I'm going to leave you here alone with my sons while I'm at work, you really are out of your mind."

"I'd never hurt them," Susie said, though her voice lacked conviction. "This isn't easy for me, either, you know."

Rick dragged a hand over his jaw. "I can't handle this now," he said, "not on top of everything else. I'm going to call my folks tomorrow and see if they'll take the boys for a while."

"I'd never hurt my babies," Susie repeated, her eyes bright with unshed tears.

"You already killed one of them."

Susie pressed her hands over her womb, her face white with shock. "It wasn't my fault," she whispered. "How can you blame me for that?"

"I shouldn't have said it," Rick muttered. "You know I didn't mean it. I know how much you wanted another baby." He shook his head. "I just don't know what to do."

"Maybe you're right," Susie said, her expression bleak. "Maybe it would be best if the boys went and stayed with your mother." She hesitated a moment, then said, "I think you should go, too."

There was a long pause. I had the feeling Susie was hoping that Rick would refuse to leave her, that he would take her in his arms and tell her that no matter how bad things seemed at the moment, they would work it out together.

He said nothing of the kind. "What are you going to do while we're gone?"

"I'll ask my mom to come down and stay here with me."

"Does she know about . . . about what you've become?"

Susie nodded.

"It's settled, then. I'll call my folks first thing in the morning." Rising, he gave her a quick kiss on the forehead. "Why don't you try and get some sleep? Everything will look better tomorrow."

Leaving the bedroom, he closed the door behind him.

Susie stared at the door. "No, it won't," she murmured, and dissolved into tears.

My own eyes were wet when Rafe materialized in the car beside me. "How did you do that?" I asked. "How could I see what you were seeing, hear what you were hearing?"

"I've tasted you. You've tasted me. We're connected now in a way that I can't explain."

"Poor Susie," I said, swiping at my tears. "I wish there was something I could do."

Rafe blew out a sigh. "It's worse than you think."

"Worse!" I exclaimed. "How could it possibly get any worse?"

"There's an underground movement among the mortals. As Mara and Clive feared, the humans are starting to worry. That worry has prompted some of them to band together. They're forming groups, hunters, if you will."

I stared at Rafe. "Hunters?" I thought about Susie

and her husband. But surely Rick wouldn't tell anyone, especially a hunter, that Susie was a Werewolf. And yet I couldn't forget the expression on his face when he looked at her. I was very much afraid that his revulsion for what she had become was stronger than whatever love he'd once had for her.

Rafe nodded. "As far as I know, there haven't been any active Vampire hunters in the last twenty-five years, but from what I hear, mortals from all over the world have gone off to some school down in Texas that was supposedly started years ago by a couple of the best hunters in the business. The school hadn't been attracting any interest until recently. Other hunters have gone underground in hopes of finding our lairs. No one knows where these men meet, or how many there are. Right now, all we have are rumors, but when rumors abound, there's usually some truth behind them."

"But . . . why? I mean, the Vampires and the Were-wolves are only killing each other, aren't they?" But even as I spoke the words, I thought about Mark Littlejohn. How many other people had disappeared that no one knew about? How many innocent people, like Susie, had been transformed into monsters?

"It seems there have been scattered incidents of Vampires and Werewolves attacking humans," Rafe said. "Until recently, most of the mortals killed have been drifters, you know, people who wouldn't be missed. But late last night there were two attacks that changed all that. In New York, a Werewolf killed the son of a well-known actor, and another Werewolf attacked the daughter of the governor of New Jersey. She's not expected to live."

A coldness swept through me at his words. It was one

thing for the Supernatural creatures to kill each other; quite another when they started openly attacking humans.

"How do you know all this?" I was pretty sure it hadn't been reported on the six o'clock news, or on the front page of the *Oak Hollow Clarion*.

"Bad news travels fast. Mara and Clive met early this morning. The Werewolves involved in the attacks have been dealt with, but that won't end it."

Dealt with. A polite way of saying they had been executed.

I looked at Rafe, realizing for the first time that he was also in danger from hunters, and his family with him. I told myself not to worry. His grandfather had existed for hundreds of years. His grandmother and his parents were all strong, able to walk in the sun's light. Surely they could all protect themselves. Couldn't they?

By the time we reached my house a few minutes later, the rain had stopped. I was glad to be home. I quickly turned on the lights, as if that could chase away the evil that lurked outside in the shadows.

When I shivered, Rafe obligingly started a fire in the hearth, then drew me down onto the sofa beside him.

I snuggled against him, grateful for his nearness. "You're in danger now, too, aren't you?"

Rafe draped his arm around my shoulders. "Don't worry about it."

"How can I help it?"

"Kathy, love, I appreciate your concern, but . . ."

"But you're a big, bad Vampire and you can take care of yourself," I said, elbowing him in the ribs.

"Exactly." His fingertips caressed my cheek. "Now that that's settled . . ." His lips brushed mine. "I've been needing to do that since last night."

"And I've been waiting since last night." But even as I closed my eyes and surrendered to Rafe's caresses, concern for Susie continued to niggle at the back of my mind, until I felt Rafe's tongue sweep the side of my throat. Excitement rose up within me as his fangs lightly scraped my skin.

He hesitated, his breath warm against my neck as he waited for my consent.

"Do it," I murmured, and surrendered to the dark ecstasy of my Vampire's kiss.

The faint sting of his fangs was quickly swallowed up in the almost painful pleasure that followed. For a time, I was lost in a world unlike any other, a hazy red wonderland where nothing existed save one exquisite sensation after another—the heat of his mouth against my skin, the touch of his hand in my hair, the pressure of his thigh against mine.

Gradually, vague figures rose in my mind, like pale images emerging from the mists of time.

I saw Rafe playing football with a dark-haired boy that I dimly realized must be his twin brother, Rane. A woman with blond hair hovered in the background, her expression one of maternal amusement as the two boys tussled on the ground like rambunctious puppies. That scene blurred as a new one took its place, and I saw Rafe and his brother prowling the shifting shadows of the night. A tall, handsome man accompanied them, and I realized I was watching Rafe's father teaching Rafe and his brother how to hunt. The image became sharper, clearer. I felt the coolness of the evening air, the pounding of Rafe's heart as he summoned a young woman to his side. I felt his excitement and her fear as he wrapped her in his embrace and then, like magic, her fear vanished and she stood quiescent in his arms. I shivered as his fangs extended and his eyes took on a faint red glow. I gasped when he bent his head over her neck. The scent of blood and lust filled my senses and then, as if someone had turned off a light, the images disappeared.

It took me a moment to realize that Rafe was no longer nuzzling my neck, but holding me in his lap.

I stared at him, feeling oddly disoriented. "What happened?"

"What do you mean?" He was watching me, his face carefully blank.

"I'm not sure. If I'd been asleep, I would have thought I was dreaming, but . . ." I met Rafe's gaze, and he looked away. "I wasn't dreaming, was I?" Even before Rafe answered, I knew I had been seeing bits and pieces of his past.

"What did you see?" he asked, his expression guarded.

"You and your brother," I said, smiling at the memory. "You were scuffling."

"We used to do a lot of that when we were younger," Rafe said, a melancholy note in his voice.

"You must miss him. I mean, I've always heard twins are really close, that sometimes they feel what the other is feeling, even when they're far apart."

Rafe nodded. "It used to be that way, until he shut me out. Sometimes I feel I'm only half alive."

"I'm sorry."

"You'd think I'd be used to it by now. So," he said briskly, "did you see anything else?"

"I saw the two of you, hunting with your father."

A muscle twitched in Rafe's jaw. He didn't say anything, didn't draw away from me, but I suddenly felt like there was a wall between us.

"He's very handsome, your father," I said, hoping to change the subject. "You look a lot like him."

"You know what they say," he said flatly. "Like father, like son."

"What's wrong? It's not as if I didn't know you were a Vampire."

"I never wanted you to see me like that."

I stared at him. Was he embarrassed because I had seen him feeding?

"Not a pretty sight, is it?" he asked, his voice brittle.

I had a sudden image of Rafe and Susie running through the night together, their heads lifting as they paused to scent the wind for prey. Would they fight over the first luckless mortal who crossed their path, or would Rafe take the blood and leave what was left for Susie? The thought made me sick to my stomach.

Rafe swore softly, and I knew he had been reading my mind. Gently, he moved me from his lap onto the sofa, then gained his feet in a fluid movement no human could ever duplicate.

"Rafe . . ."

"You should get some rest."

"Are you going to run away from me every time I learn something new about you, about how you live?"

He looked down at me, his eyes narrowed. "Is that what I do?"

"You know it is."

"I don't want to hurt you. I keep telling myself to stay away, that no matter how I feel about you, about us, no good will ever come of it, but . . ."

"Stop thinking so much." I rose from the sofa and wrapped my arms around his waist. "I'm a big girl. I know what I'm doing."

"I only wish that was true," he said, but he didn't back away.

Hours later, after Rafe had gone off in search of prey, I curled up on the sofa and thought over the events of the last few days.

I had met Rafe's grandparents.

The war was no longer between the Werewolves and the Vampires, but between the Supernatural creatures and the rest of the world.

The only friend I had in town was now a Werewolf.

I was falling deeper in love with Raphael Cordova with every passing day.

I was able to see what he saw and hear what he heard. Even more amazing, I was now seeing images from his past.

Oak Hollow was no longer a safe haven; perhaps it never had been.

On that happy note, I put on my favorite comfy nightgown and went to bed.

It was raining again when I woke on Saturday morning. The gloomy weather perfectly suited my mood, which only grew worse when I sat down to breakfast and read the paper. A man's body had been found out near Brawley Woods; a teenage boy was missing.

I'd barely opened the shop when Edna and Pearl arrived. Today, they were wearing brightly colored turtleneck sweaters, jeans, fur-lined boots, and floppy hats. The dead man and the missing boy were all the two women could talk about.

Edna informed me that the dead man was Ezra Solomon, a thirty-year-old computer programmer who had stopped in Oak Hollow on his way to South Carolina. The teenager had been the oldest son of Jack and Alpha

Cameron, who owned Oak Hollow's only bed and breakfast. They had two other kids—a boy about twelve, and a girl a few years younger.

"How do you two know all this?" I asked, looking from Edna to Pearl and back again. As far as I knew, the names of the deceased hadn't been released to the public yet.

Pearl and Edna exchanged that conspiratorial look that I was quickly becoming familiar with, and then they changed the subject.

I knew they weren't Werewolves or Vampires, but what if they were witches, like Rafe's grandmother? Like Werewolves and Vampires, witches were Supernatural creatures. For all I knew, Edna and Pearl met in the woods late at night and read deer entrails or something.

"I'd close up early tonight if I were you," Edna said, dropping a load of books, mainly romantic suspense and sci-fi, on the counter.

"Oh? Why?"

"Let's just say the streets won't be safe after dark," Pearl said. "When you see Raphael, you might suggest that he leave town for a while."

I couldn't help noticing she said "when" and not "if".

"There's a hunter in town," Edna explained, lowering her voice. "His name is Travis Jackson. He's from Amarillo, Texas, and he's staying at the hotel."

And with that bit of ominous information, Edna and Pearl gathered up their purchases and left the store.

Standing behind the counter, I looked out the window at the rain and wondered what other surprises the night would bring.

Chapter Seventeen

The night brought Travis Jackson and a flurry of raindrops into the store just as I was getting ready to close up. Of course, I didn't know who he was at first, just a tall, good-looking man with short brown hair and dark, piercing eyes. In spite of the inclement weather, he wore a cream-colored shirt with the sleeves rolled up to his elbows, a pair of faded jeans, and scuffed brown boots. I guessed he was in his midthirties or thereabouts. He nodded at me as he passed the front counter and moved toward the murder mystery section.

I would have told him I was closing and asked him to leave, but hey, I couldn't afford to turn away a customer.

He returned a few minutes later with a couple of paperbacks and swiped his credit card through the machine. Cash money rarely exchanged hands these days. In fact, it was getting to be a rare commodity, as were checks. Nearly every transaction was paid for by credit card. Businesses no longer wrote checks to their employees; instead, whatever amount was due was deposited in a personal bank account.

I rang up the sale, then asked to see his driver's license.

I murmured, "Thank you, Mr. Jackson," and then it hit me. He was the hunter from Texas. I stared at the silver cross that hung from a thick silver chain at his throat, and then glanced at the door, hoping Rafe wouldn't show up.

Jackson followed my gaze then looked back at me. "Are you expecting someone?"

"What? Oh, no." I dropped the books into a bag and placed the sack on the counter. "Please, come again."

He smiled, revealing a dimple in one cheek. "I'm new in town," he said. "I don't suppose you'd consider going out to dinner with me? You know, sort of a gesture of goodwill from one of the town's prettiest citizens."

I should have moved to Oak Hollow sooner, I thought. I had only been here a short time and three men had already shown an interest in me. Of course, a Vampire and a Were-tiger weren't men in the usual sense of the word. And this man, though handsome, repelled me, though I couldn't say why.

"I can't," I said. "I'm sorry."

He glanced at my left hand. "You're not married or engaged, so I guess it must be me."

"No, it's not you," I said quickly, but it was. There was something in his eyes I didn't like. I wasn't sure what it was, but I had the feeling he was hiding something dark and ugly.

"If it's not me, then what is it?"

Persistent cuss, I thought. "I'm in a relationship."

He leaned one hip against the counter. "Hmm, a one-on-one kind of thing, where you don't date anyone else?"

"I'm afraid so."

He made a tsking sound. "Just my luck."

I had to smile at that.

"If your relationship goes south, I hope you'll let me know."

"Does that mean you're here to stay?"

"Pretty much."

I filed that bit of news away for Rafe. "What is it that you do?" I asked, wondering if he would tell me the truth.

"Are you sure you want to know?"

"Of course. Why wouldn't I?"

"I might never get you to go out with me, once you know my line of work."

"I already know," I said, and then bit down on my lower lip, thinking maybe I should have kept that bit of information to myself.

"I don't believe you. How could you possibly know?"

"It's hard to keep a secret in a small town. Didn't you know that?"

His eyes narrowed. "So, what is it you think I do?"

I'd never been much of a liar, so I blurted the truth. "I think you're a Vampire hunter."

He swore a pithy oath. "How the hell did you find out?"

I was somewhat surprised that he admitted it. "Is it supposed to be hush-hush?"

"Not exactly. On the other hand, the fewer people who know, the better."

Leaning forward, I whispered, "Don't worry, your guilty secret is safe with me." *Well, pretty safe,* I amended silently. "Do you just hunt Vampires?"

"And Werewolves," he admitted, "and anything else that goes bump in the night. So, am I dead in the water?"

"No more than you were before," I said. "How many Vampires and Werewolves have you killed?"

"All together, or just this year?"

I would have thought he was kidding except for the

sudden tightening of his jaw muscles. This was interesting news, indeed. Rafe had told me there hadn't been any Vampire hunters in the last twenty-five years. Apparently, he'd missed one. I wondered what else he might be mistaken about. "So, how many?"

"Thirty-six Vamps, eighteen Werewolves, and one Were-leopard."

"You must be good at it," I muttered. He had to be, or he would have been dead long before now.

"It's a gift."

"A bloody one, I should think."

He rested his elbow on the counter. "At times," he admitted, "but a necessary one. Have you noticed any increase in paranormal activity in town lately?"

"No, why?"

"I'm getting a strong sense of Supernatural presence in the area."

"Really?"

He nodded.

"How do you find these . . . creatures?"

He dragged a hand over his jaw, and then he smiled a cat-that-just-ate-the-canary kind of smile. "Like I said, it's a gift."

"What do you have, some kind of voodoo that tells you when they're nearby?"

"Something like that."

"So, how does it work?"

"I don't know how to explain it," he said, "but when there's a Were or a Vamp in the vicinity, I just know it."

It occurred to me that Travis Jackson had the same sort of "gift" that I had, which made me wonder if all Vampire hunters possessed it, which then made me wonder what I was doing with it. I certainly wasn't a hunter, nor did I have any desire to be one.

"Do all Vampire hunters have that peculiar ability?"

"No. Just the best ones." His tone of voice suggested that he was among the best of the best.

"And the others?"

"They just want to kill things."

"So, how many hunters are there?" I asked, thinking this was something Rafe might need to know, if he didn't already. "I mean, I've heard there are hunters in training, I guess you'd call them, but I didn't think there were any already working."

"How'd you know about that?" he asked, his voice sharp.

I shrugged. "I must have overheard someone mention it. Why? Is it a secret?"

"Well, it's not news that we want the Supernatural community to be aware of. I'm sure you can understand that."

"Of course. So, where does one train to be a Vampire hunter?"

"In school, naturally," he said with an easy grin.

I would have thought he was kidding if Rafe hadn't told me about that school down in Texas. "You must have some interesting classes."

"You could say that."

"Like what? Bloodletting 101? The ten best ways to kill a Werewolf? How to stake a Vampire without getting blood on your clothes?"

His laughter didn't reach his eyes, making me think I'd hit close to home.

"There's a place in Amarillo," he said. "For all intents and purposes, it's been closed for the last twenty-five years. Used to be the number one school in North America, but a lot's changed since then."

That had to be the understatement of the century!

"We've been underground for a while," Jackson went on, "keeping a low profile, so to speak, but the Weres and the Vamps are getting more aggressive every day. It's no secret that they're not just killing each other anymore."

Rafe had mentioned that, too. I thought about Susie. I needed to warn her that there was a hunter in town. I wondered if Jackson would spare Susie's life if I told him that she was my friend and that she had three young children, but something told me to keep that information to myself. "So," I asked, "are you the only hunter in Oak Hollow?"

"No."

"I don't suppose you'd tell me who the other one is?"

"Not a chance. If he wants you to know, he'll tell you."

"Fair enough. Well, it's been nice talking to you," I said, "but I need to close up."

"Good idea," he said. "The streets aren't safe after dark."

I nodded. He was the second one to tell me that today. Like my mother always said, if two people tell you you're sick, lie down. When two people tell me the streets aren't safe after dark, you can be sure I'll be inside behind locked doors before the sun sinks below the horizon.

"I hope to see you around . . . I never got your name."

"Kathy."

"Pleased to meet you." He glanced out the front window, then back at me. "It's getting dark," he said, scooping up the bag from the counter. "Why don't you lock up and let me walk you out?"

"Thanks, but I'll be all right. That's my car, parked out front."

With a nod, he headed for the door.

I stared after him, thinking that the Supernatural community was in a world of hurt if Travis Jackson was a typical Vampire hunter.

I said as much to Rafe later that night. We were at my place, sitting on the sofa in front of the hearth. It was raining again. I snuggled closer to Rafe, thinking how cozy it was to sit next to him in front of the fire and listen to the rain.

"So, do you know him?" I asked.

"I've heard of him. They say he's got a high body count."

"Thirty-six Vamps and eighteen Werewolves. Oh, and one Were-leopard."

Rafe whistled softly. "I guess he is good."

"You think?"

"Well, he's not going to have anyone to hunt in Oak Hollow after tonight. Mara and Clive are telling all their people to get out of town."

In spite of the heat of the fire, I felt suddenly cold all over. "You're leaving?" I told myself it didn't matter. He was a Vampire, and even though I loved him more than I had ever loved anyone else, there was just no future for the two of us.

His gaze moved over me. "If I was, would you miss me?"

"Don't tease me, Rafe. Are you leaving?"

"No." He slipped his arm around me and drew me closer. "Not even if Mara told me to."

Relief washed through me, and I sagged against him. If I'd had any doubts about how much I cared for him, the ache I'd felt at the thought of his leaving town had chased them all away. Though I had only known Rafe for a short time, I could no longer imagine my life without him in it.

The words *Mrs. Raphael Cordova* whispered through the back of my mind. Even if I'd wanted to marry him, it was impossible. Two years ago, legislation had been passed forbidding Vampires to marry mortals. Anyone getting married after sunset was required to submit to several blood tests to prove that both parties were human. No such law existed for the Were-creatures, perhaps because they were still technically human and alive.

Rafe looked at me, one brow raised. "Marriage?"

I blew out an exasperated sigh. "Do you read all my thoughts?"

"No, but some of them come through loud and clear." His gaze searched mine. "Do you want to get married?"

"Of course. What girl doesn't?"

He nodded, his gaze narrowing. "Do you want to marry me?"

I stared at him for the space of a heartbeat. "Are you proposing?"

"If you want me to."

I didn't know what to say. Yes, I loved Rafe, madly, truly, deeply, but I couldn't help wondering how much of what I felt for him was from the depths of my own heart, and how much came from the Supernatural glamour that all Vampires possessed? And even if my feelings were 100 percent my own, did I want to be married to a Vampire? Did I love him enough to accept him as he was, to give up all thought of living a normal life, of having children and grandchildren? Once the excitement and the first thrill of falling in love wore off, as was bound to happen sooner or later, would I regret my decision? Did I want to live with a man who needed blood to survive, a man who would never age, never look any different than he did now? I was mortal, subject to sickness, old age, and death. What if he grew disenchanted with me when the passage of time began to leave its mark on my face and figure?

Rafe stroked my cheek. Had he been reading my thoughts again? Was that disappointment I saw in his eyes?

"It's all right, Kathy," he said quietly.

"I do love you," I said, fighting the urge to cry. "You know I do."

"I know."

"It's just . . . I just don't know . . . I don't want to be a Vampire."

"It's all right."

"But everyone in your family is like you. I'd never fit in, never really be a part of your family. I'd always be different, an outsider."

"It's all right," he said again in that same quiet tone. "I'm not asking you to change."

I thought about his mother. She had lived with a Vampire husband until her sons graduated from high school, and then she had asked to be brought across. Had she ever been sorry she had given up her humanity? Did she miss doing mundane things like grocery shopping and going to lunch with a girlfriend? And what about his grandmother, Brenna? Had she asked to become a Vampire? The mere idea of anyone wanting to be one of the Undead was inconceivable. And yet . . . what would it be like never to grow old, to never be sick, to have a wealth of Supernatural powers? The fact that I was even thinking about it unnerved me. Thoughts gave birth to deeds.

I could tell, just by looking at Rafe, that he was reading my thoughts again.

"Do you want me to leave?" he asked.

"No! Can't we just go on the way we have been?"

"If that's what you want."

"It is," I said. "It really is." But I couldn't help wondering whom I was trying to convince, Rafe or myself.

I thought about our conversation long after Rafe went home that night. Everything was changing. Oak Hollow was no longer the safe, peaceful place I had imagined. Susie had been attacked by a Werewolf. The Camerons' oldest son was still missing, presumed dead. The governor's daughter remained in the hospital in critical condition. The latest news bulletin stated she wasn't expected to recover. I wondered if Mara and the leader of the Werewolves would be able to put an end to the war between the Vampires and the Werewolves, if Susie's husband would be able to accept the radical changes her new lifestyle was bound to cause in their marriage, if Susie would be able to adjust to her new life, and how she would explain it to her children. I thought about Rafe's mother asking for the Dark Gift. Had it really been her own idea, or had his father coerced her? And what about his grandmother, the witch? Had she been a willing victim, or had the change been forced upon her?

Later, lying in bed, I stared up at the ceiling, wondering how things had gotten so complicated. I had come here looking for a quiet place to live and ended up in a hotbed of Supernatural activity.

I considered moving to another town, but where would I go? And how could I leave Rafe? Even as I asked myself that question, I knew that leaving now, before our relationship went any further, would be the smart thing to do. Just as I knew that I wouldn't go. No matter how things played out between us, I had to stay until the end.

I didn't feel like having cold cereal for breakfast Saturday morning, and I didn't feel like cooking, so I headed over to Carrie's Café. I wasn't the greatest cook in the world, and Carrie's buttermilk hotcakes were the best I had ever tasted. Besides, it was no fun cooking for one . . . something I would be doing for the rest of my life if I married Rafe.

Rafe. How had he managed to get under my skin so deep and so fast? Sooner or later, he would grow tired of me. I pushed the thought aside. He had said he loved me. I loved him. For now, that would have to be enough. But even as I tried to convince myself that the present was all that mattered, I couldn't help wondering what the future held for us. When we were together, I was certain that we could make it work. I loved the way he made me feel. I had never been happier, never felt more beautiful, more desirable, or more cherished. And when he kissed me . . . Lord have mercy, when he kissed me it took every ounce of restraint I possessed to keep from dragging him into my bed and having my wicked way with him, although, never having slept with a man, I didn't know exactly what my wicked way would be. But one thing I knew for sure. Making love to Rafe would be wonderful.

But now, with the sun shining high in the sky, I couldn't ignore the doubts that beset me. We were so different, how could we ever hope to make a life together?

I shook my head. Today had its own problems. Tomorrow would take care of itself.

I was wondering if I had enough time to run over and visit Susie and still open the store on time when Pearl and Edna breezed into the café. They spotted me immediately and came over to say hello.

This morning, they wore long-sleeved, frilly white blouses, broomstick skirts, white sneakers, and ribbons in their hair. I wondered if they called each other to confer about their wardrobe choices.

"Good morning, ladies," I said. "What brings you out so early?"

Pearl held up a sheaf of papers. "We're posting flyers for the Halloween Haunt, dear," she said. "Is it okay if we drop one off at your store later?"

"Sure. Or you can give it to me now and I'll put it in the window."

Pearl beamed at me. "Thank you, dear. You're going to come, aren't you?"

"I don't know. I guess so."

"You must come," Edna said. "And you must wear a costume."

"It's the day before Halloween, dear," Pearl said. "You don't want to miss it. It's *the* highlight of the year."

"I'll do my best to be there." Halloween had never been my favorite holiday. One Halloween, when I was about five, the son of our next-door neighbor had come over wearing a hideous mask and a fright wig and scared the living daylights out of me. I could still remember how terrified I'd been. Even after John took off the mask, I had refused to go near him. I'd had nightmares about him and that horrid mask for weeks after that. Even now, when I knew, rationally, that it had just been a rubber mask, the memory of that night still gave me chills.

"Well, enjoy your breakfast, dear," Pearl said as the waitress arrived with my order.

"We have a lot of stops to make."

I watched Pearl and Edna as they moved toward the door. They stopped to chat with several of the diners before leaving the café. They were a strange pair. On the outside, they looked pretty much like any other women their age, although their clothing was sometimes a bit on the flamboyant side. But there was something just the slightest bit off about them, something I could never quite put my finger on.

I was drinking the last of my juice when Travis Jackson slid into the chair across from mine.

"Morning," he said, smiling affably. "Mind if I join you?"

"Not at all. I was just leaving."

"Aw, come on, sit with me while I have something to eat."

I didn't want to sit with him, but then, what the heck, maybe I'd learn something that could be useful to Rafe. "Maybe just for a minute. I have to open the store."

"You're the boss, aren't you?"

"Yes. So?"

"So, who's to complain if you open at ten-thirty instead of ten?"

As much as I hated to admit it, he had a point. Still, it gave me a good excuse to leave if I was of a mind to. Besides, I was hoping to squeeze in a visit with Susie.

Travis ordered a stack of hotcakes, bacon, and coffee. I asked the waitress to bring me a cup of tea.

"So," I said, "why aren't you out doing whatever it is Vampire hunters do?"

"Plenty of time for that," he said, sitting back in his chair. "It's hours until dark."

"How do you find them?"

"Hey, I can't divulge the tricks of the trade."

"Took a blood oath, did you?" I was kidding, but the sudden wary look in his eyes told me I had touched a nerve. "You didn't really? Tell me you didn't."

"I can't tell you anything, so don't ask." For someone who'd been so eager to talk the other day, he'd become suddenly taciturn.

My imagination immediately kicked into overdrive as I pictured Travis Jackson and his cronies huddling around a fire, swearing an oath of allegiance that they would never reveal their secrets or their meeting place, and sealing it with blood.

I was glad when the waitress arrived with Jackson's order. I drank my tea as quickly as I could, burning my tongue in the process, said a quick good-bye to Travis, and grabbed my check. After paying the bill and giving Carrie a couple of dollars to give to the waitress, I hurried out of the café.

Outside, I took a deep breath of the cool, crisp air, and then frowned. Something was different. Not wrong, exactly, just different. I glanced up and down the street and then, not knowing why, I walked toward the end of the block. The whole atmosphere of the town had changed. At the corner, I turned around and headed back toward my car. Why did everything feel so different? And then it hit me. On Mara's orders, most of the Vampires had left Oak Hollow. I was certain that most of the Werewolves had also moved on. The latent weight of preternatural power no longer hung over the town.

The very air felt lighter, less oppressive. I wondered if Travis Jackson had also noticed the difference.

I got into my car and drove down Main Street. Funny, I hadn't noticed how oppressive all that Supernatural power had been until it was gone.

I glanced at my watch. It was almost ten. I tapped my fingertips on the steering wheel, debating whether to open the store or look in on Susie, and then I decided that Travis was right. I was the boss. If I decided to open the store late, or not at all, it was nobody's business but mine. Of course, with that cavalier attitude, I would soon lose the few customers I had. But today Susie had to come first.

A few minutes later, I pulled up in front of her house. It was a nice place, with a wide front porch. A couple of pink hydrangeas grew on either side of the porch steps, a hummingbird feeder hung from a tree in the side yard. Bicycles and baseball bats littered the front yard. A late-model silver Caddy was parked in the driveway.

When I rang the bell, a taller, older version of Susie opened the door. "Yes?" she asked in a cultured voice. "May I help you?"

"I'm here to see Susie."

The woman smoothed a hand over her ice-blue, tailored silk skirt. It had probably cost more than my whole outfit, including my shoes. "I'm afraid she's not having visitors just now."

"I think she'll want to see me. If you could just tell her that Kathy is here."

"Kathy!" The woman's cool demeanor evaporated like morning dew. "Please, do come in. I'm so glad to meet you! I'm Myrna Lancaster, Susie's mother."

She ushered me into the living room, then took my

hand in hers. "I can't thank you enough for what you've done." Tears filled her eyes. "Susie's my only child . . . I . . . her father and I . . . how can we ever repay you?"

"That's not necessary. Susie's a friend of mine. Is she all right?"

The woman's face sort of crumpled. Her shoulders slumped, and she sank down on the sofa. The tears she had been holding back trickled down her cheeks.

"All right? How can she ever be all right again? Her life's ruined. And Rick . . . I told her not to marry him." Myrna Lancaster shook her head and squared her shoulders. "I'm sorry, forgive me. Of course she'll be all right."

"Of course," I said.

"Her father is, at this minute, discussing her case with our family doctor. We'll do whatever has to be done, no matter what it costs."

I didn't like the sound of that. If Susie's parents thought they could buy a cure for their daughter, they were sadly mistaken. As far as I knew, there was no cure for being a Werewolf. I hoped I was wrong. "Can I see her now?"

Myrna Lancaster led me down a narrow hallway lined with pictures of Susie and her family. We passed a couple of small bedrooms. A peek inside one of them showed neatly made twin beds and a Spiderman toy box overflowing with cars, trucks, and dinosaurs.

Susie's room was at the end of the hall.

Myrna knocked on the door. "Susie, are you awake? You have company."

"I don't want to see anyone."

"It's your friend, Kathy. She's anxious to see you."

"Oh, come in."

Myrna Lancaster opened the door, and I followed her

into the room. She smiled at Susie, who was sitting up in bed. "Can I get you anything, sweetie?"

"No, thanks, Mom."

Myrna Lancaster nodded and then looked over at me. "Well, I'll just leave you two alone to visit," she said, and closed the door behind her.

Susie didn't look much better than she had the last time I had seen her. There were hollows in her cheeks, dark shadows under her eyes. She was still unusually pale and seemed thinner than I remembered. But it was the expression in her eyes that tore at my soul. She looked forlorn, haunted, but worse than that, she looked like she had lost the will to live.

I sat in the rocking chair beside the bed and conjured a smile. "So," I asked with forced cheerfulness, "how are you feeling this morning?"

"How do you think I feel? Rick's taken my boys to his mother's house. My mother is afraid of me, and next month, when the moon is full, I'll turn into some kind of furry monster." She waved her hand in the air, then let it fall back into her lap. "Other than that, everything's just fine."

"Do you want me to leave?"

"No, please." She reached for my hand and gave it a squeeze. "I'm sorry. This is just so hard for me. I don't even know who I am anymore."

"I wish I knew what to say, some magic words that would make it all better, but . . . but maybe it won't be so bad. I've met a couple of Werewolves, and they don't seem any different from anyone else, at least most of the time. I don't know what they're like when the moon is full, but maybe you could just think of this as another kind of monthly curse," I said, remembering my conversation with Rafe. "You know, like your period and cramps, and maybe you could, I don't know, just make the best of it."

Susie stared at me, blinked twice, and then, to my astonishment, she burst out laughing. "I sure hope I don't get both curses at the same time of the month! Can you imagine a Werewolf with PMS?"

I looked at Susie, and then I laughed with her, because I knew she was going to be all right.

It was a little before eleven when I made it to the store that morning. Surprisingly, I was busy all day. And I was glad of it. I didn't want time to think about Susie's future as a Werewolf, or what my future with Rafe might be.

Even though most of the Vampires and Werewolves had left town, at least for the moment, I decided it would still be a good idea to close at dusk from now on so I could be safely home by dark.

With that thought in mind, I turned off the lights, set the alarm, and headed for my car just before sunset. I was punching in the code to unlock the door when a hand closed over my forearm.

I shrieked and jerked away.

"Hey, sorry, I didn't mean to scare you."

"Travis!" I pressed a hand over my pounding heart. "Are you out of your mind? What are you doing, sneaking up on me like that?"

I wanted to smack him when he laughed.

"Sorry," he said again. "I was hoping we could go out for a drink."

"Didn't we already cover this?"

"Come on," he coaxed. "One drink. What can it hurt?"

"Oh, all right. I'll meet you at Sugar Babe's."

"Great."

With a shake of my head, I got into my car. I sat there for a minute, waiting for my heart to stop pounding, and then I drove the six blocks to Sugar Babe's Tavern. It was the only place within the city limits where you could legally buy mixed drinks. Even though it was still early, the place was crowded. I paused just inside the door to wait for Travis. A three-piece band occupied the small stage at the far end of the room. Saturday night was open mic night at Sugar Babe's, and anyone who had a mind to could step up on stage and entertain the customers. I winced as the lanky singer making love to the microphone hit three sour notes in a row. Several boos and catcalls filled the air, but the man kept on singing, his gaze focused on a skinny redhead who was looking at him as if he might be the next Elvis.

When Travis arrived, we threaded our way through the crowd looking for an empty table. Luck was with us. A couple vacated a table for two near the back wall as we approached. I sat down, and Travis dropped into the chair across from mine.

"What'll you have?" he asked.

"Just a Coke with a couple of cherries."

"That's it?"

"I don't drink."

"All right. Looks like there's only one waitress working. Might be faster if I go over to the bar and get our drinks. Don't let anyone else have my seat," he said with a wink.

I made a face at him, then blew out a sigh. It felt good to sit down. A couple of women in their early twenties were on stage now. They wore white off-the-shoulder blouses, full skirts, and cowboy boots. I listened as they broke into their rendition of the latest country hit, but my mind wasn't on the music. Instead, I was thinking about Rafe, wondering where he was, what he was doing, and if he would come by my place later.

As if my thoughts had conjured him, he suddenly appeared in Travis's chair.

I pressed a hand to my heart, wondering if I was going to survive the night. One more unexpected surprise just might do me in.

"Rafe, what are you doing here?"

"You're here," he said in that seductively masculine voice that sent tendrils of longing shooting through me. "Where else should I be?"

"Not here!" I glanced toward the bar where Travis seemed to be in deep conversation with another man. "Not now."

He reached for my hand and covered it with his own. "Why not now?"

"Because I'm . . ." I started to say "on a date," but I didn't like the sound of that. Besides, this wasn't a date, it was just a drink with a casual acquaintance. "Because there's a hunter here."

His eyes narrowed as he turned to survey the crowd.

Did Rafe have an ability similar to Travis Jackson's? Could hunter and prey recognize each other the way lions recognized zebras and coyotes recognized rabbits?

"Come on," I said, "let's go."

Rafe's gaze met mine. "You haven't had your drink yet."

I cringed at the accusation I read in the depths of his eyes. He knew why I was here, and whom I was with. I wondered if he had done that little turn-to-mist trick of his and followed me.

"Rafe, it doesn't mean anything. He invited me for a drink, that's all, and I . . . I didn't see any harm in it."

He didn't say anything, just continued to look at me.

"I'm sorry," I said, though I wasn't sure what I was sorry for.

"You've got nothing to apologize for," he replied. "Enjoy your evening."

Before I could say anything else, he was gone.

Moments later, Travis returned to the table. "Where'd he go?"

"Where did who go?"

"The Vampire that was here." Travis put our drinks on the table, his narrow-eyed gaze scanning the crowd.

I widened my eyes in what I hoped was a look of innocence. "There was a Vampire here? Really? Where?"

"Here," Travis said, his voice tight. "You were talking to him."

"Oh, him," I said lightly. "He was just a guy who asked me to dance, that's all. Was he really a Vampire?" I glanced around the room, as if I was afraid. "Is he still here?"

Travis looked at me suspiciously for stretched seconds before he sat down. "No, he's long gone by now."

"Good." I reached for my drink, wishing I had ordered something stronger than a Coke.

I was thoroughly depressed by the time I got home, by turns angry with Rafe for being so possessive and for checking up on me, and then angry with myself for apologizing for what was a perfectly innocent evening, and then feeling blue because it seemed like the fabric of our relationship was slowly unraveling.

I was too upset to eat dinner; instead, I curled up on the sofa, a pillow clutched to my chest, and thought about Rafe.

I wasn't sure what had drawn us together other than great chemistry and the inability to keep our hands off each other. I told myself yet again that there was no future in dating a Vampire, even one as mouthwatering as Rafe Cordova. At best, we might have had a few years together. At worst, I might have become one of the Undead.

With a sigh, I hugged the pillow closer, thinking that a few years with Rafe would have been better than a lifetime with anyone else, even though I knew that staying with him wasn't a good idea. Sooner or later, we would have made love. Given his effect on my senses and the way I felt about him, it was inevitable, only I wasn't sure I wanted to give my virginity to a Vampire, even a gorgeous, sexy Vampire.

More depressed than ever, I brushed my teeth and went to bed.

There, alone in the dark, I buried my face in my pillow and let the tears flow.

Chapter Eighteen

Feeling out of sorts after his meeting with Kathy, Rafe went to Susie McGee's house to see his grandparents, who were standing watch. He found them sitting on the grass in the side yard, playing gin rummy by the light of the moon.

"Raphael, what brings you here?" his grandmother asked. "Is something wrong?"

He dropped down beside her. "No, I was just . . . bored."

His grandfather grunted softly. "Sometimes the nights can be long."

"But beautiful," Brenna remarked. "Just look at that sky."

Rafe looked up. Mortal eyesight was limited, but he could see millions of stars scattered across the heavens. For all the years that he had been a Vampire, he had rarely taken notice of the skies.

"How is that lovely girl?" Brenna asked. "What was her name? Kathy?"

"She's fine," Rafe replied flatly.

"Oh, dear," Brenna said. "You've had a fight, haven't you?"

"Not exactly." He blew out a sigh.

"What, exactly?"

"She doesn't want me."

"Is it you she doesn't want?" Roshan asked. "Or what you are?"

"She doesn't want to be a Vampire."

Brenna made a soft, thoughtful sound. "Did you ask her to become one?"

"No, I asked her if she wanted to marry me. She said she loved me, but . . ." He shrugged as if it didn't matter one way or the other. "Not enough, I guess."

"It's not an easy decision to make," Roshan said. "Maybe she just needs more time. After all, you've only known her a few weeks."

"Your grandfather's right, as always," Brenna said. "Did you tell her she doesn't have to become one of us?"

"Yes."

"Are you going to see her again?" Roshan asked.

"I don't know. She wants us to go on like before, but . . ." Rafe dragged a hand over his jaw. "I don't know. It might be best for both of us to end it now, before things get any more complicated."

"You love her, don't you?" Brenna asked, though it was more a statement than a question.

"Yeah, dammit."

Roshan laughed softly. "Love makes fools of us all."

"Listen!" Brenna said. "What's that?"

Rafe stood, his senses probing the night. And then he heard it: footsteps, followed by the sound of the McGees' garage door opening. Moving toward the corner of the house, he saw Rick McGee get into his car and back out of the driveway.

"I thought he moved out," Rafe remarked.

"He came by a few hours ago. Brought the kids for a visit," Roshan said, coming up behind Rafe.

"Where do you suppose he's going this time of night?"

"I don't know," Roshan said. "He doesn't have the kids with him. What do you say we go find out? Brenna, you stay here and keep an eye on the girl and her mother."

Brenna rose, her hands fisted on her hips. "I always have to stay behind."

Roshan kissed her on the forehead. "It's a good thing, too. You never know when I might need rescuing again."

Rafe grinned. Years ago, his grandmother and his father had rescued Roshan from a witch who had been determined to resurrect Anthony Loken, her deceased lover. To do so, she had needed the blood of an enemy, and his grandfather had fit the bill nicely, having been instrumental in taking Loken's life.

Brenna laughed softly, as if she, too, was remembering that time, and then she kissed her husband and patted Rafe's cheek. "Be careful, you two."

Rick McGee's car was easy to follow. Because Roshan felt like running, Rafe ran alongside him. The exercise eased some of his tension, and Rafe wondered if that had been his grandfather's intent.

They stayed back far enough that McGee couldn't see them, then fell back even farther when the man made a sharp left on Oak Tree Road and pulled up in front of an abandoned meat-packing plant. McGee got out of the car and, after glancing around, he knocked on the door, knocked again, and then a third time, before a tall man in dark clothing opened it.

"You're late," the tall man said.

Rafe frowned, thinking the man looked familiar, and then he realized it was the man Kathy had been with at Sugar Babe's.

"Yeah, well," McGee was saying, "one of my kids got sick. He wanted me to sit with him until he fell asleep."

With a look of disdain, the tall man stepped back. McGee went inside, and the tall man closed the door. And not just an ordinary door, Rafe noted. It was reinforced with heavy steel.

"Guess we'd better go see what's going on," Roshan said cheerfully, and dissolving into mist, he drifted toward the building.

Grinning, Rafe did the same. Slipping under the door, he rose in the air and hovered near the ceiling. From the outside, the place looked like it hadn't been used in years, but the inside had been spruced up some. The room was empty save for a dozen or so metal folding chairs pushed up against the walls, a long wooden table, and a beat-up old wooden chest with some mystical symbols painted on the top and sides.

There was what looked like an old meat locker in one corner of the room. Curious, Rafe drifted into the other area. There were no windows. The heavy iron door had been reinforced on the outside; the inside panel had been plated with a thin coat of silver, as had the floor, walls, and ceiling. He didn't need three guesses to figure out why. All that silver must have cost them a fortune, he mused. The faint coppery scent of blood hung in the air. He wondered how many of the missing Vampires had been imprisoned in that room before they were destroyed.

Muttering an oath, he turned his attention back to the

two men. They were sitting at the end of the table, across from each other.

"So," the tall man was saying, "can you do it or not?"

McGee shook his head. "I don't think so. Dammit, Jackson, she's the mother of my kids."

"You can't trust her with your kids, not anymore," Jackson said, and though his words were cruel, his voice was kind. "If you want me to take care of it, I will."

Rick McGee buried his face in his hands. "I don't know. Dammit, I just don't know."

"You don't have to decide tonight, but don't wait too long."

"Are you sure it's the only way?"

"What do you think? She's no longer the woman you married. I know it's hard, but you'll all be better off once it's done. Besides, it's what she wants, isn't it?" Jackson reached over and squeezed McGee's shoulder. "She already tried to kill herself once."

McGee nodded, though he looked none too happy.

Jackson slammed both hands on the table. "All right, on to new business. We're meeting at Barney's early next Saturday morning. One of the hunters over in River's Edge has discovered a Vampire's lair, and he wants some backup. I'll pick you up around six."

"Six, right."

"Another thing. There's a Vampire here in town."

"Yeah, Cordova. He's supposed to keep the peace."

"Cordova," Jackson said. "I've heard of him."

"Are you planning to take him out, too?"

"All in good time," Jackson said, smiling. "All in good time." Rising, he slapped McGee on the back. "I'll see you next Saturday. And remember what I said about the missus. Don't wait too long. The closer it gets to the full moon, the harder it will be on her, and on you."

Looking miserable, McGee rose from the table and left the building.

Still hovering near the ceiling, Rafe was tempted to materialize and put one Vampire hunter permanently out of commission, and then he smiled inwardly. *All in good time,* he thought, mimicking Travis Jackson's words. *All in good time.*

But first, he had to warn the River's Edge Vampire community that their lair had been discovered.

Chapter Nineteen

I went to church Sunday morning, but I was so lost in my own misery, I didn't hear a word of Reverend Paul's sermon. Staring up at the stained glass window over the altar, all I could think about was Rafe. Would I see him later? If he came over, would things be the same between us, or had I ruined everything?

At home, the hours dragged by. Determined to put Rafe out of my mind, I called my mom and dad, and then I called a cousin I hadn't talked to in months, and then I called Susie's house, but no one answered the phone. I didn't know whether to be worried about that or not. Her mother could have taken her out to lunch, or maybe Rick had taken the boys back to his mother's house and Susie had gone to visit them.

I wandered through the house and then, feeling thoroughly depressed, I curled up on my bed and took a nap.

It was late afternoon when I woke. Sitting on the edge of the mattress, I blew out a sigh and then, on the spur of the moment, I decided to get out of the house. I'd been spending too much time alone. I'd go for a short walk, and then drive over to Carrie's Café for an early dinner.

I hadn't realized how cool and cloudy it was until I stepped outside. I considered going back inside for a jacket, then decided a brisk walk in the chill air was just what I needed to clear my head.

Shoulders hunched against the cold, I set out with no particular destination in mind. I guess I shouldn't have been surprised when I ended up in front of Susie's house. She was my friend, and it still bothered me that she hadn't answered the phone.

I paused on the sidewalk. The house looked closed up tight. I was trying to decide what to do when I felt a sudden chill that had nothing to do with the cold slither down my spine.

"What are you doing here?"

I practically jumped out of my skin as Cagin's voice whispered in my ear. Before I could reply, he grabbed me by the arm and dragged me behind the tall hedge that separated Susie's house from her neighbor's.

I pressed a hand over my heart. "What are *you* doing here? I thought all the Vampires and Weres had been ordered to leave town."

He shrugged nonchalantly. "I didn't feel like leaving."

"Won't you get in trouble for staying?"

"I've been in trouble before."

Shivering, I folded my arms across my chest. "Why are you watching Susie's house?"

"Because two Vampires have also been watching her."

I didn't like the sound of that. "Why would Vampires be watching a Werewolf?"

"Beats the hell out of me," he replied, his gaze sliding away from mine. "That's why I'm here."

While I was trying to make sense of Cagin's answer, Susie's garage door opened. In the overhead light, I saw that Rick was behind the wheel. Susie sat beside him. There was no sign of the boys. I wondered if they were at her mother-in-law's, or if her mother was watching them.

Cagin swore under his breath as the car backed out of the driveway and onto the street.

A moment later, a tall, dark shadow emerged from the side of the house and then, in the twinkling of an eye, it was gone.

Cagin's hand tightened on my arm. "DeLongpre! Dammit!"

I frowned. Were Rafe's grandparents the Vampires Cagin had referred to? Why would they be watching Susie? Was Rafe's grandmother here, too? Time to worry about that later, I thought. Right now I feared Cagin was going to rip my arm from its socket.

"Let me go; you're hurting me," I said, and then, seeing the feral light in his eyes, I wished I had kept my mouth shut. Staring into those yellow eyes, I felt like one of the three little pigs confronting the big bad wolf.

His eyes changed, until they were no longer human. His lips peeled back in a silent snarl, baring his teeth.

I stared at him, suddenly fearing for my life. Surely he wouldn't transform and devour me here, in a public place! Even as that thought crossed my mind, I realized that the thick shrub would prevent anyone from seeing us.

I opened my mouth to scream for help, but all that emerged from my throat was a pathetic sob.

And then, in the blink of an eye, Rafe was there.

"Let her go." His voice was mild, but there was nothing the least bit passive in his expression or the taut line of his body. His eyes glowed red, and when Cagin didn't release me immediately, Rafe's lips peeled back, displaying his fangs.

Feeling like a rabbit trapped between two predators, I glanced from Rafe to Cagin and back again. Would Cagin let me go, or would I be caught in the middle of a fight between two Supernatural creatures, either one of which could destroy me in a heartbeat?

"I said let her go," Rafe repeated, and though his voice was still soft, I heard the steel underneath.

Apparently, Cagin did, too. With a growl, he shoved me aside.

I fell hard, scraping my knee against a decorative rock, but I was hardly aware of the pain as I stared at the battle being silently waged in front of me.

I told myself to hightail it out of Dodge while the getting was good, but I couldn't move. I could only huddle there in morbid fascination as Cagin transformed into a beast. It was an awesome thing to see. He shook off his clothing and kicked off his sandals as he changed. Fear tore at my heart. Surely Rafe didn't stand a chance against a Were-tiger! But even as the thought crossed my mind, Rafe's body was also changing shape. Somewhere in the back of my mind I registered the fact that his clothing simply disappeared. An instant later, a large panther stood in Rafe's place, its coat sleek and black.

The two creatures came together in a rush, teeth and claws rending fur and flesh as they rolled on the ground.

I scrambled out of the way, my heart pounding with dread.

It was a fearsome sight, mesmerizing in its intensity;

frightening, yet beautiful, like a savage ballet. I backed up another step and realized I wasn't alone. Glancing over my shoulder, I saw Rafe's grandmother standing behind me, her eyes glowing red as she watched the battle.

"Do something!" I cried. "Can't you do something?"

"I could," she replied, "but Rafe would never forgive me for interfering."

I wondered how she could be so calm when her grandson's life was in danger.

The creatures parted for a moment. Panting heavily, they stared at each other. Blood smeared their mouths and dripped from the numerous bites and scratches that appeared on both of them. Cagin seemed to be favoring his right foreleg.

I held my breath, hoping the fight was over. Both were injured. Both were bleeding.

Rafe took a step toward Cagin, his lips peeled back in a silent snarl.

He froze, as did Cagin, at the sound of voices coming toward us.

Between one heartbeat and the next, Cagin and Rafe resumed their own forms. Cagin turned and disappeared into the darkness between the two houses. Rafe vanished in a swirl of silver mist, as did his grandmother. If Cagin's clothing hadn't been scattered on the ground, I might have thought I imagined the whole thing.

Tossing Cagin's clothing under a bush, I quickly made my way up to Susie's front porch and knocked on the door as if nothing untoward had happened and I was merely stopping by for a visit.

On the sidewalk, a man and a woman strolled by,

completely unaware of the life-and-death struggle their presence had interrupted. I wished I could thank them.

As soon as they were out of sight, I ran down the street and didn't stop running until I was at home behind a locked door.

With a sigh, I closed my eyes and rested my forehead against the wood.

"Kathy."

Rafe's voice, so soft I thought I had imagined it. And then I heard it again, louder. Opening my eyes, I turned around, and he was there, his clothing stained with blood, his face, neck, arms, and no doubt the rest of him, covered with nasty-looking bites and deep scratches. Even as I watched, the smaller wounds were healing, fading, until only a deep laceration across his left fore-arm remained.

I stared at him, at the faint red glow that lingered in his eyes, and knew what he wanted. I waited for him to ask, and as the seconds ticked by, I realized he wasn't going to. I was going to have to offer.

My legs were shaky as I walked to the sofa and sat down. I was acutely aware of his gaze on my face. Lean-ing my head back against the sofa, I closed my eyes.

"Just don't take too much," I said, and my voice was every bit as shaky as my legs had been. He had bitten me before, but his desire then had been fueled by pas-sion, not physical need. I wondered if there would be a difference. Would his bite still bring me pleasure? Did he see me now not as a lover, but as prey?

My hands clenched as he sat beside me. His knuck-les stroked my cheek, the length of my neck. Kisses fol-lowed in the wake of his touch, and then I felt the prick of his fangs at my throat. Pleasure flowed through me.

I felt lighter than air, felt as though I could soar through the heavens. I wondered what he was feeling, and no sooner had I done so, then it was as if I was walking in his mind. There was pleasure there, too, mingled with an easing of physical pain. I felt his strength returning, and with it, his desire.

I opened my eyes to find him staring down at me. His eyes were no longer red; the wounds that I had seen had healed, leaving no trace of a scar. *Amazing,* I thought. He looked strong and fit while I felt light-headed and a little disoriented.

Muttering "stay here," he went into the kitchen.

I closed my eyes, wanting nothing more than to go to sleep, though I was certain to have nightmares after what I had seen.

I must have dozed off, because the next thing I knew, Rafe was shaking my shoulder, pressing a glass of orange juice to my lips, insisting I drink. When I emptied the glass, he filled it again and coaxed me to drink that, too.

"I'm all right," I said. "Don't look so worried."

He stroked my cheek. "What am I to do with you?"

"Anything you want," I murmured.

I closed my eyes. Had I imagined it, or had I heard Rafe whisper, "No bad dreams tonight" before I slid into welcome oblivion?

That night, I dreamed a wonderful dream. In it, Rafe and I were holding hands as we walked along a sandy beach. A full moon cast silver highlights on the surface of the water. The sand was warm beneath my bare feet, the air tangy with the scent of salt and surf, but it wasn't the ocean or the night that held me in its spell, it was the man beside me. He wore nothing but a pair of black trunks, and I couldn't stop looking at him, couldn't stop admiring his well-muscled physique. I was jealous of the moonlight that danced in his midnight black hair and caressed his tawny skin.

A wave washed up on the shore, and I gasped as the icy water splashed over my legs. In an instant, Rafe had me in his arms, cradled against his chest.

"Better?" he asked.

Locking my arms around his neck, I murmured, "Oh, yes," thinking that nothing could be better than being held in his embrace.

He proved me wrong by showering me with kisses, one deeply erotic kiss after another, until I was on fire for him. "Rafe."

Just his name, but he knew what I wanted. He carried me across the sand to a sheltered cove. Miraculously, a blanket sprinkled with bloodred rose petals awaited us there. The light from a dozen candles cast flickering shadows on the rocks and sand.

He lowered me onto the blanket; then, stretching out beside me, he drew me into his arms and kissed me again. Whether it was one kiss or many, I didn't know. His hands played lightly over my oh-so-willing flesh, making my body sing a new song. He was the master and I his eager student, anxious to discover the secrets behind his fathomless black eyes, willing to follow wherever he led. His body was taut beneath my questing fingertips, his skin smooth, cool to my eager touch, exhilarating to my senses. He let me explore to my heart's content, let me touch and taste whatsoever I desired.

Ah, desire . . . it hummed through my veins, sizzled

over my skin. The prick of his fangs only heightened each sensation, carrying me to dizzying heights, yet I climbed them unafraid because I knew Rafe was waiting for me there, just as I knew that he would never let me fall. . . .

I woke to the sound of my alarm, amazed that I had slept so late. I set the alarm clock every night as a precaution, but I always woke before it went off.

Sitting up, I realized I was wearing a pair of pink bikini briefs and a T-shirt and nothing else. Funny, I didn't remember undressing or getting into bed.

Rafe, I thought, *he must have undressed me and put me to bed.* I glanced at the other side of the mattress, frowned when I saw a faint indentation in the other pillow, as though someone had been there only moments ago. I ran my fingertips over the pillowcase, smiling as I realized that Rafe had spent the night beside me.

The dream I'd had flashed through my mind. Had it been a dream? It had seemed so real, the smell of the ocean, the feel of the sand and the sea beneath my feet, the taste of salt water on my tongue . . . the taste of Rafe on my lips, the heat of his body intimately pressed to mine.

I shook my head. Of course it had been a dream. What else could it have been? We were nowhere near the ocean.

Brushing away my confusion, I went into the bathroom and turned on the shower, only then remembering my visit to Susie's house and the fight that had ensued between Rafe and Cagin. Thinking of it now made me shiver. I had never seen such a bloody battle before, nor realized the extent of Rafe's ability to heal. And my blood had helped. It pleased me that he had come to me instead of going to a stranger. Everything about him pleased me, I thought, smiling.

Ten minutes later, wrapped in a towel, I went to the phone and dialed Susie's number, felt a surge of relief when she answered on the second ring.

"Susie! How are you?"

"Hi, Kathy, I'm fine, why?"

"Nothing. I mean, I called you last night and you didn't answer and . . . and I was worried." I decided not to mention that I had gone by her house, or that a Were-tiger and a pair of Vampires had been lurking in the dark.

"Oh, I'm sorry, I heard the phone, but Rick and I were on our way out. I'm surprised the machine didn't pick up."

"That's all right. I was just, you know, worried. Where's your mother?"

"Oh, she had to go home. My dad was in a car accident. He's got a broken leg and a few bruised ribs. The doctor said he'll be okay in six or eight weeks, but right now, he can't get around on his own."

"Are you staying by yourself?"

"For now."

"Do you want me to come and stay with you?"

"No, I don't think that's necessary. I'm fine, really."

"Well, I'm glad you're all right. You sound a lot better."

She laughed softly. "You know what they say, anything that doesn't kill you only makes you stronger. I'm not crazy about what's happened to me, but I think I can live with it, although I guess I won't know for sure until the next full moon. The head Werewolf said he'd send someone to talk to me before then, sort of help me adjust, you know?"

"That's great. How's Rick these days?"

"I think he's getting used to the idea. He took me to see the kids last night. We haven't told them yet . . . Rick wants to wait a little longer. He's probably right. There's plenty of time, Anyway, I'm not sure they're old enough to understand what's happened."

"I'm sure it will all work out. Speaking of work, I've got to go; I just wanted to make sure you were okay."

"Thanks, Kathy. You're a good friend. Let's get together for lunch soon."

"Sounds good to me. I'll talk to you later."

After hanging up the receiver, I ran a brush through my hair, applied my makeup, and pulled on a pair of black jeans and a green sweater. I ate a quick bowl of cereal for breakfast, brushed my teeth, then grabbed my handbag and my keys and drove to the store.

It was ten after ten when I arrived. Almost on time.

I was surprised to see Cagin come into the shop later that day. He wore a pair of tight jeans and a black T-shirt that emphasized his muscular torso. Amazingly, he looked none the worse from last night's brawl. It really was remarkable, the way the Supernatural creatures healed. I imagined there must be doctors in hidden labs all over the world trying to discover the secret ingredient to the recuperative powers of the Werewolves and the Vampires. Anyone who could bottle it would soon be rich beyond their wildest dreams.

"What are you doing in here?" I glanced out the front window, praying that someone else would come into the shop. After last night, Cagin was the last person in the world I wanted to be alone with.

"I came for a book, what else?"

"I don't know." I shrugged, grateful for the counter between us, even though I was pretty sure he could leap across it with no trouble at all. "I guess I just didn't expect to see you."

"Hey, I'm sorry about last night. Things got a little out of hand, that's all."

"A little out of hand? Right."

"We're all on edge these days, what with that new hunter in town, although I don't imagine he'll last long. Or the other one, either. Mara or Clive will see to that."

"Two hunters," I repeated. "Right." Travis Jackson had mentioned there was another hunter in town, but he'd refused to divulge the man's name. Cagin had no such qualms.

"Jackson and McGee—damn their eyes."

"Rick McGee?" I shook my head. "You must be mistaken."

"We can't afford to be mistaken about things like that."

It couldn't be true. If Rick was a hunter . . . the possibility of what that might mean to Susie's future was frightening. But surely Rick wouldn't kill his own wife! Even as I tried to reassure myself, I knew Rick wouldn't have to. Travis Jackson would destroy her without a moment's hesitation.

I had to call Susie, I thought desperately. I had to warn her before it was too late, but what could I say? How could I convince her that her life might be in danger from her own husband?

I didn't think Cagin was ever going to leave but, finally, he picked out a couple of sci-fi books and left the store. As soon as he was gone, I grabbed the phone and punched in Susie's number. After four rings, her answering machine picked up.

"Hi, this is the McGees' home. We can't get to the phone right now, but you know what to do. Ta-ta for now."

I broke the connection. Just because she didn't answer the phone didn't mean she was in danger. She could have gone to visit her kids again or run to the market. Maybe she'd gone for a walk . . . and maybe she was lying dead in a ditch somewhere.

As the day went on, I tried her number half a dozen times, until I wanted to scream in frustration.

I was thinking of closing up at five when I was suddenly inundated with customers all clamoring for the latest installment of the young adult series titled *Ghost Wind*. Written by a nineteen-year-old boy, bookstores all over the country were touting it as the next Harry Potter.

For the first time since I'd opened the store, I was praying for customers to leave. Instead, they seemed determined to hang around, exchanging stories of how *Ghost Wind* had turned their nonreaders into fanatics. I listened, I rang up sales, I bagged books, and all the time I was silently screaming at them all to go home so I could lock up.

It was almost six when I ushered the last customer out the door and turned out the lights. I was locking up when Rafe appeared. I'd never been so glad to see anybody in my life.

"What's wrong?" he asked.

"Susie doesn't answer her phone."

He lifted one brow. "That's what has you so upset?"

"Is that why you're here? You knew I was upset?"

He nodded, sniffed the air, and then frowned. "Cagin was here."

"He came in to buy a book. He told me there are two hunters in town, and that Susie's husband is one of them! I've been calling her house all day, and she doesn't answer. You don't think he'd . . ." I couldn't say the words aloud.

Rafe rubbed a hand over his jaw. "It's possible."

"You know something. What? Tell me?"

"My grandfather and I followed McGee the other night. He met up with Jackson."

I stared at him, my heart pounding with dread. "And?"

"Jackson asked McGee if he could take her out, or if he wanted Jackson to do it."

"I don't believe it! How can they expect Rick to kill her! How can Rick even associate with someone crazy enough to expect him to kill his own wife! It's . . . it's insane!"

"All the hunters I've known are dedicated to destroying the Supernatural. They take a blood oath to do their duty or die trying."

"I can't believe you didn't tell me this before!"

"I don't want you involved in this."

"I'm already involved. Susie's my friend." I grabbed Rafe's arm. "We've got to stop them before it's too late."

"I'll see if I can find her. You stay here."

"No! I'm going with you."

He shook his head. "Not a chance. These guys are killers. If you get in their way, they won't hesitate to kill you, too. You got that?" He slipped his arm around my shoulders and gave me a squeeze. "For all you know, she could be at the movies." He kissed my cheek. "Stay here," he said again. "I'll be back as soon as I can."

I grabbed his arm. "I need to go. If you won't take me with you, then I'll . . . I'll . . ."

"You'll what?"

"I'll find someone who will. Someone like . . . Cagin."

Rafe glared at me. I knew he was trying to intimidate me, but I refused to back down.

"Dammit, Kathy . . ."

"We're wasting time."

With a shake of his head, he stalked out of the building.

I turned off the lights, locked the door, and followed him outside, half expecting that he would be gone. But he was leaning against the front fender of his car, waiting for me.

I told myself not to worry, that if anyone could find Susie, it was Rafe. After all, he'd done it before.

But I couldn't shake the feeling that something terrible was about to happen.

Chapter Twenty

I gazed out the window as Rafe drove up and down the streets of Oak Hollow. I was counting on him to find Susie, but as it turned out, I was the one who found her, in a roundabout sort of way.

We had been searching for over an hour and were about to give up and go back to my place when I sensed the presence of a Were.

"Slow down." I glanced up and down the street. "Over there."

Rafe pulled up in front of the house I indicated. A large FOR SALE sign hung from a post in a corner of the yard. A smaller sign read VACANT. I thought I recognized Susie's car in the driveway.

I glanced at Rafe. If it was Susie's car, what would she be doing here, in the dark, in an empty house? I was surprised at the number of ghastly possibilities that quickly flitted through my mind, each one worse than the last.

"I'm going inside to have a look around," Rafe said. "Any point in my telling you to wait here?"

"Probably not."

"Stay behind me."

I didn't have any problem with that. I followed him up the walkway to the front porch, waited while he listened a moment, then tried the doorknob.

It opened at his touch.

Apparently, he didn't need an invitation to enter a vacant house. He crossed the threshold on silent feet, and I tiptoed in behind him, my heart pounding as I glanced around. I couldn't see much, but even in the darkness, I could see that the room was empty.

Rafe stood just inside the doorway for a moment, then moved unerringly through the living room and down a narrow hallway, with me close on his heels.

There was the sound of a scuffle followed by a sharp cry that was quickly cut off, but not before it lifted the short hairs along my nape. The scent of blood brought the taste of bile to the back of my throat.

Rafe stepped through a doorway to the left, then glanced at me over his shoulder. "Stay there."

His tone left no room for argument, so I waited until he moved farther into the room before I peeked around the door frame.

And wished I hadn't.

There were no curtains on the windows. In the faint light cast by a streetlamp, I saw Susie sitting on the floor, her back against the wall, her expression stricken. A thin ribbon of red marred her throat. It took me a minute to realize it was blood.

Her husband lay sprawled on his back at her feet, a gaping hole where his throat had been. A large knife with a wicked-looking silver blade lay on the floor beside him.

Cagin, wearing only a pair of jeans, stood beside the body. His yellow eyes were glowing. Blood was splattered across his chest and stained the corners of his mouth.

"What happened here?" Rafe asked.

It was Cagin who answered. "He brought her here to kill her. I couldn't let that happen."

Cagin had saved Susie's life. . . . I frowned, remembering the night outside Susie's house. Maybe the look on his face hadn't been anger, as I had supposed, but worry. Or affection.

I stepped into the doorway. "You were protecting her the other night, too, weren't you?"

"Maybe."

"And you were going to shift and go after her, weren't you? Only Rafe's grandfather beat you to it, and then Rafe showed up. . . . You didn't want to fight him, did you? You were just angry because we interfered."

Rafe glared at me. "What the hell are you talking about?"

"He's in love with Susie."

Rafe's brow furrowed thoughtfully, and then he looked at Cagin. "Is that right?"

"What if it is?"

"Wolves and tigers don't mix," Rafe said.

"Mind your own business," Cagin said, his voice a snarl.

I looked at Susie. She hadn't moved, hadn't said a word. "Susie?"

Slowly, she lifted her head and looked at me. "Joe's been helping me adjust," she said, her voice so low it was barely audible.

Joe, I thought. *Who's Joe?* And then I realized she meant Cagin.

"He promised to stay with me when the moon is full." She looked at Cagin, the horror in her eyes changing, softening. "He understands me."

Good grief, she sounded like she was in love with him! But how could that be? She couldn't have known him for more than a few days.

"We need to get out of here," Cagin remarked.

Rafe nodded. "We need to get rid of the body."

"You two can take care of that," I said. "I'm taking Susie home."

She was silent in the car. Now and then, a long shuddering sigh escaped her lips, but other than that, and a few tears, she just stared out the window, her hands folded so tightly in her lap, her knuckles were white.

When we reached Susie's house, I pulled into the driveway. I cut the ignition, then helped her out of the car and up the walk. Inside, I urged her to sit down; then I went into the kitchen and fixed her a cup of tea heavily laced with some brandy I found in one of the cupboards.

Refusing to meet my gaze, she drank it without question, then put the cup aside.

"He was going to kill me," she said, her voice devoid of emotion. "He said he was sorry, but it was his duty. He told me not to worry, that he'd look after the boys, and then he pulled a knife. . . ." She looked up at me for the first time. "He had the knife at my throat, and then Cagin was there, and . . ." She began to tremble. "I'm cold," she murmured. "So cold."

I went into her bedroom and pulled a blanket off the bed. I tried to imagine what it had been like for her, feeling the knife against her skin as she waited for her husband to slit her throat, then watching while Cagin attacked and killed her husband.

Returning to the living room, I draped the blanket around her shoulders, then sat beside her.

Susie lifted a hand to her throat. "If it wasn't for Cagin, I'd be dead now."

"You seem very . . ." I searched for the right word. "Very fond of him."

A blush stained her cheeks. "He's been very kind to me. He listens when I talk. He makes me feel like what I have to say is worthwhile." She smiled faintly. "He makes me feel beautiful."

It just proved that you could never tell, from the outside, what was going on in someone else's life, or someone else's marriage. Had anyone asked, I would have said that Susie was happy with her husband and her marriage, but in just a few short sentences, she had proved me wrong.

She looked at me through haunted eyes. "What am I going to tell my children? What if Rick was right? Maybe they would be better off without me."

I didn't know what to say to that. For all I knew, Werewolves made wonderful mothers. Then again, maybe they didn't.

Susie rested her head against the back of the sofa and closed her eyes. A moment later, she was asleep.

With a sigh, I carried her empty cup into the kitchen, rinsed it out, and then stood at the sink, my hands braced against the edge of the counter as I stared into the darkness beyond the window. Where was Rafe? What had they done with Rick's body? How was Susie going to explain his absence to her children, her parents, his family, the townspeople? And what of Travis Jackson? No matter what story Susie concocted to cover her husband's disappearance, Travis would suspect the truth.

Feeling a headache coming on, I fixed myself a cup of tea, then went into the living room and sat in the chair next to the sofa. Susie had been crying in her sleep. Her cheeks were damp with tears.

My heart ached for her. I wished there was something I could do to help, some words of wisdom that would ease her fears. It just wasn't fair for such a sweet lady to suffer so much. But she wouldn't have to suffer alone. It was obvious that Cagin was in love with her. Given the chance, he would take care of her.

And then I frowned. Cagin had said two Vampires were watching Susie's house. Having seen Rafe's grandmother there, I had assumed the other Vampire was Roshan, which begged the question, where had Rafe's grandparents been tonight? Why hadn't they followed Rick and Susie?

It was a little over an hour later when Cagin and Rafe showed up.

Cagin didn't say a word. Lifting Susie from the sofa as if she weighed no more than a small child, he brushed a kiss across her brow, and then carried her out the door.

"Is she okay?" Rafe asked.

"As okay as she can be, I guess, all things considered. Where's he taking her?"

"To his place, for tonight. Tomorrow, he's taking her away from here."

"Away where? And what about her kids? What's going to happen to them?"

"I don't know. I guess they'll stay with their grandparents for however long it takes for Susie to get a handle on her new lifestyle." He grunted softly. "No doubt her kids will have a new father soon."

"You think she's going to marry Cagin?"

"I'd bet my next fifty years on it."

"But . . . what kind of life will that be for her boys, having a Werewolf for a mother and a shape-shifter for a stepfather? And how can they marry? I mean, he's a Were-tiger and she's a Werewolf."

"They'll work it out. It won't be the first time such a thing has happened."

I shook my head, amazed at his nonchalant attitude, but then, I guess after being a Vampire as long as he had, there wasn't a whole heck of a lot that surprised him.

"Where were your grandparents tonight?" I wondered aloud. "I thought they were watching Susie's house."

"Mara needed their help with another matter. That's why Cagin was there."

"He would have been there anyway," I muttered. "You know, I don't understand you two. One minute you're trying to kill each other and the next you're both looking out for Susie."

"I don't care for him much, but he's all right. He's just got a bad temper."

"Are Mara and Clive having any luck ending the war?"

He nodded, his expression suddenly grim. "Most of our people and the Werewolves have decided to sort of fade into the woodwork, so to speak, until things die down. Mara had a hard time convincing Clive it was the smart thing to do. Sometimes I think he's got more pride than brains, but he finally agreed. The hunters are more organized and more numerous than we first thought.

From what I understand, more than fifty Werewolves have disappeared without a trace in the last three months or so, and about half that many Vampires, and that's just here, in the States."

"Maybe they were killed in the war."

"A few perhaps, but not that many with no one knowing what happened to them or where they are. Come on," he said, "we should get out of here."

He was right. I didn't want to be in Susie's house if the police came by. I wondered again what Rafe and Cagin had done with Rick's body, and then decided I really didn't want to know.

When we reached my house, Rafe walked me to the front door, then took me into his arms. "You should get some sleep."

I started to say I wasn't sleepy, but I yawned instead. It wasn't that late, but it had been a trying night. "Will you stay with me until morning?"

"If that's what you want."

"I do." After all that had happened, I didn't feel like being alone.

I unlocked the door, and Rafe followed me inside. He locked the door and then followed me down the hall to my bedroom. He sat on the foot of the bed while I went into the bathroom to change into my nightgown and brush my teeth. Even with the door closed, I could sense his presence in the next room, feel the tension stretching like a fine wire between us, taut and quivering. Right or wrong, I couldn't help wanting him.

Feeling a little nervous, I smoothed my gown over my hips, took a deep breath, and opened the door.

Rafe was still sitting on the bed. He hadn't been idle, though. He had removed his shirt, T-shirt, boots, and socks. His chest and shoulders were a study in masculine perfection, like a handsomely sculpted work of art. I yearned to run my hands over every inch of him, but I wasn't sure I was prepared for what would surely follow.

He rose as I walked toward the bed, his eyes glowing with need, but a need for what?

Trembling, I pulled back the bedspread. My gaze met his for a long moment, and then I slid under the covers, my heart pounding wildly as Rafe settled down beside me.

"Relax," he said quietly. "We're just going to sleep."

Relieved and yet a little disappointed, I closed my eyes. I had always heard that Vampires were cold-blooded creatures, but there was nothing cold about the man lying beside me. Warmth radiated from him like heat from a blast furnace, or maybe it was just my own overheated imagination.

"You must think me an awful prude." I wished I could be as blasé about sex as most of the girls in my home-town had been. Some of them had embraced the New Morality with open arms. They had changed lovers as often as they changed their hairstyles and nail polish. Marriage was old-fashioned, they'd said. People were living longer now. How could anyone be expected to stay with the same person for seventy or eighty years? I pictured Rafe in my mind, thinking that seventy or eighty years would never be long enough.

My friend, Nancy Gale, had been of the opinion that a woman needed at least three husbands. Number One should be dependable and of good stock, the kind of man you'd want to father your children. Husband Number Two should be carefree and full of fun, able to show a girl a good time, while Number Three should be easygoing and good at conversation, someone to spend your declining years with.

"An awful prude," I repeated with a sigh.

"No, I think you're a woman who knows what she wants and won't settle for less."

I wished he was right. I wasn't sure what I wanted. One day I wanted Rafe more than anything in the world, the next I was swamped by doubts. Could a big-city girl find lasting happiness in a small town? Could a mortal woman be truly happy with a Vampire? Tune in tomorrow, same time, same channel.

Rafe's fingertips lightly stroked back and forth across my brow. "Go to sleep, Kathy. You don't have to decide anything tonight."

"I hate it when you do that," I murmured.

"Sorry, love."

"Love . . . I do love you, you know. . . ."

His lips brushed my cheek, light as butterfly wings. "I know."

His words, and the sweep of his lips on mine, lulled me to sleep.

Chapter Twenty-One

Rafe held Kathy close to his side. As always, her nearness was both pleasure and pain. Her skin was like smooth satin beneath his fingertips, her breasts were warm and softly rounded, tempting him almost beyond his ability to resist. The lingering fragrance of her perfume teased his nostrils, the scent of her blood aroused all his senses.

So easy to take her, to make her his, to make her what he was. So easy . . . if he didn't mind incurring her hatred, perhaps for however long he lived. Ah, but what a beautiful Vampire she would make, forever young, forever his. . . .

He shook the thought from his mind. She was smart not to get too involved with him. The world was turning, changing. The war between his kind and the Werewolves had jolted humanity out of its lethargy. He was amazed at how swiftly they had recognized the danger, how quickly they were responding, recruiting hunters, destroying Vampires and Werewolves alike. He wondered if the hotheads who had started the war were still alive, if they realized the full extent of what their folly might cost, or if Mara and Clive had hunted them down and destroyed them before they could cause any more trouble.

He recalled what Mara had said about humans finding a cure for the Werewolves. How like humankind, to assume the Werewolves wanted to be cured. And what of his kind? If he had a choice, would he want to be mortal again?

He caressed Kathy's cheek. She loved him, but would she ever be able to accept him as he was? If it meant being with her, he would willingly embrace being mortal again if such a thing were possible, and yet, how much better if she would accept the Dark Gift. Instead of sixty or seventy years together, they could have centuries.

But it was a moot point at best, at least for now.

He thought of Joe Cagin and Susie McGee. Though Cagin was a shape-shifter and Susie a Werewolf, they had a far better chance of making a life together than did a mortal and a Vampire.

He grunted thoughtfully. Perhaps he should ask Mara to share her blood with him. For all intents and purposes, his parents and grandparents seemed to be nearly human again. They still needed blood to survive, though not as much as ordinary Vampires and not as often. The sun no longer had any power over them; they could rest by day or by night.

But before he could contemplate any kind of life with Kathy, he had to make sure that the war between the Vampires and the Werewolves was over once and for all. He wondered if the Supernatural creatures understood that their only hope of survival was to disappear for a while, to lull the human world into believing that life had returned to normal, that the Supernatural creatures were no longer a threat to their way of life, or to their existence. Once there was peace between the Supernatural community, once mortals assumed that they were again in control of their world, that would be the time to pursue his feelings for the woman sleeping at his side.

Rafe stayed with Kathy until the first pink glow of dawn lit the sky. After dropping a kiss on her cheek, he left her house, quietly cursing himself for staying so long. Though he could be active during the day, he was not yet immune to the effects of the sun's light. He ran to his car, felt the sun's rays burn through the back of his shirt as he opened the door and flung himself behind the wheel. Grabbing his sunglasses, he put them on and raced the rising sun toward his lair.

Reaching home, he drove into the garage and closed the door behind him. Removing his sunglasses, he got out of the car and went into the house.

He stood inside for a moment, waiting for the blistering pain to pass, and then, blowing out a deep breath, he made his way to the room where he spent the daylight hours. There were no lights in this room, only blessed darkness, a king-size bed, a small satellite screen, and a floor-to-ceiling bookshelf crammed with books— mostly murder mysteries.

But he was in no mood to watch the news or lose himself in another Montgomery mystery. At the moment, he had far more pressing matters to think about. Although the war between the Supernatural creatures was virtually over, another battle loomed on the horizon, this one bigger and perhaps more ferocious than the one between the Werewolves and the Vampires had been. The Supernatural creatures hadn't been fighting to exterminate one another, only to see who would reign supreme. Thanks to Mara and Clive, they would be fighting on the same side now, fighting for their survival. The Werewolves would carry the battle during the day, the Vampires after dark.

The first task would be to locate the hunters and neutralize them, which would be no easy task, since no one knew exactly how many there were. The Werewolves and the Vampires could work on that together, he thought, perhaps in pairs. The Werewolves could locate the hunters during the day, the Vampires could catch them unawares at night and erase the desire to destroy Supernatural creatures from their minds. Clive was of the opinion that the hunters should be killed, but Mara had been against that, arguing that murdering them would only stir up more trouble. The second task would be to find out if talk of a cure was true, and if so, what effect it would have on the Werewolves and the Vampires. The shapeshifters would no doubt be immune. Since they were born, not made, there was nothing to cure.

Rafe stripped down to his briefs and slid beneath the quilt his grandmother the witch had made for him when he was still in his teens. She had sewn it with needle and thread and love, and imbued it with a touch of magic to keep his bad dreams at bay.

It embarrassed him now to remember that he had once been plagued by nightmares. Or daymares, he thought ruefully, since he slept when the sun was up. The dream had begun shortly after his thirteenth birthday. Every day, the same dream. He was walking down a dark street, searching for prey, and then he would see her, a woman with long blond hair. He approached her from the back, lifted her hair from her neck to drink. And then, to his horror, he was unable to stop. He took it all, her blood, her thoughts, her memories, and then he opened the vein in his wrist and poured it all back into her. When the deed was done, she looked at him through eyes as red as hellfire, and then she buried her fangs in his throat and drained him dry, until only a withered, empty husk remained. Helpless, he lay there, writhing in agony as he waited for the sun's light to find him.

He had never told anyone about his dream until, without meaning to, he had mentioned it to his grandmother. The quilt had been on his bed the next day. He had never had that dream again.

Kathy's image rose in his mind and with it, as sharp as a dagger, the realization that her hair was the same golden color as that of the woman in his nightmare.

Chapter Twenty-Two

The rumble of thunder woke me. I shivered, thinking it sounded ominous somehow, then chided myself for letting my imagination get the best of me. It was just thunder.

Rising, I showered, dressed, ate breakfast, and went to work.

It was still raining when I opened the shop. Thinking that I probably wouldn't have much business if the downpour continued, I booted up my computer and read my e-mail. Nothing particularly exciting—a lot of jokes I had received a dozen times before, the usual amount of spam. I shook my head in disgust. With all the advances in technology, you'd think they could do something about unwanted e-mail from companies offering everything from male enhancement to get-rich-quick schemes. I loved the ones from supposed foreigners who were willing to split millions of dollars with me if I would just give them access to my bank account. Like that was ever going to happen!

I looked up as the bell over the door rang, surprised to

see Travis Jackson enter the store. Rain dripped from his hat and the hem of his coat. Belatedly, I realized I should have put down some rugs or towels so I wouldn't have to mop the floor every time somebody came into the shop, although, up until now, it hadn't been a problem.

Travis smiled as he sauntered toward me. There was something decidedly smug in his expression. I wondered if he had spent the previous night destroying the Undead.

"Afternoon, Kathy," he said cheerfully.

"Hi." I had to force myself to be civil to the man. I didn't want him wondering why my attitude toward him had changed, didn't want him asking questions I didn't want to answer. "What brings you out on a day like this?"

"I figured you wouldn't have much business, and I thought maybe you'd like to go out for a cup of coffee."

"I don't think so." I had no desire to spend time with a man who had cheerfully offered to kill Susie if her husband wasn't up to the job.

"Come on," Travis coaxed. "It's just a cup of coffee."

Since I couldn't tell him why I didn't want to have coffee with him, I needed a good excuse. I just wished I had one. "I'm sorry, I can't," I said. "I'm . . . I'm expecting an important phone call from . . . from one of the major book distributors back east."

He didn't believe me; I could see it in the sudden narrowing of his eyes.

"There was a mix-up in one of my orders," I said, making things up as I went along. "I need to get it resolved right away, you know, and with the time difference between here and New York . . ." I shrugged. "You know how it is."

He grunted softly. "Yeah, sure, maybe I'll see you later."

The tone of his voice sent an icy chill down my spine.

I breathed a sigh of relief when he left, bemused by the realization that if it came to a choice between spending time with Travis Jackson or with the Supernatural community, I felt safer on the dark side with the Vampires and the Werewolves.

I finished reading my mail, then moved through the stacks, straightening a book here, turning a couple of the newer ones face out. With nothing else to do, I swept the floor, dusted the shelves, watered the plants.

I was thinking about going out for a late lunch, or maybe just closing up for the day, when Jackson showed up again.

"I figured since you wouldn't go out for coffee with me, I'd bring it to you."

I didn't want to take anything from the man, but it smelled divine. "Thank you."

He handed me one of the cups. "Careful, it's hot." He rested an elbow on the counter. "So, how do you like Oak Hollow, now that you're settled in?"

I shrugged. "It's a nice place."

He grunted softly, then sipped his coffee.

Removing the lid from my cup, I took a drink and then frowned. "What kind of coffee is this? It tastes kind of . . . of . . ." I blinked, then rubbed a hand over my eyes as everything seemed to go kind of gray and hazy.

Travis smiled an odd little smile as he took the cup from my hand, and then everything went black.

* * *

Cold, so cold.

Hard floor beneath me.

Bad taste in my mouth.

I opened one eye, closed it, and opened both eyes. The scene didn't change. Bare walls, a naked bulb overhead. I was dreaming, I thought, having a nightmare. I closed my eyes, waiting for it to end.

I got colder, the floor beneath me seemed to get harder, and I had to go to the bathroom.

I wasn't dreaming.

I opened my eyes again and sat up. What the hell? In the faint light cast by the low-watt bulb dangling by a cord, I could see that I was in a room of some kind, but a very strange room. The walls were silver, the floor was silver, the ceiling was silver. I ran my fingers over the floor, thinking it was just paint, but when I tapped my fingernails on it, it sounded like metal, not concrete.

I tried standing, but my legs refused to support me, so I crawled toward the door, which was also coated with silver.

I frowned, trying to think why silver was important, but my mind was fuzzy, and I couldn't concentrate. Reaching up, I tried to open the door. It was locked, of course.

I wrapped my arms around my waist and closed my eyes. This had to be a nightmare. It just had to be, but when I pinched myself, it hurt. It wasn't supposed to hurt in a dream, so where was I and how had I gotten here?

The last thing I remembered was talking to Travis Jackson. He had brought me a cup of coffee. It hit me, then. Travis had drugged me, but why?

Rising to my knees, I pounded my fist on the door. "Travis? Travis, are you out there?" I pounded on the door until my fist ached. "Travis! Dammit, let me out of here!"

Sinking down on the floor, I blinked back the tears that stung my eyes. Crying wouldn't help me now.

Closing my eyes again, I tried to focus. Travis had drugged me and brought me here, but why, and where was here?

I guess I dozed off, because the sound of the door opening woke me. Blinking, I stared at the figure hovering over me.

Now I knew I was dreaming.

"Hello, dear," Pearl said. "We thought you might like something to eat." She placed a tray on the floor in front of me. "I hope you like chicken salad sandwiches."

"What are you doing here?" I asked. "What am I doing here?"

Pearl make a little tsking sound. "I'm afraid you're the bait, dear."

"The bait?"

She nodded.

"What are you hoping to catch?"

"Why, a Vampire, of course," Edna said from the doorway. "We're sorry it had to be you, but . . ." She blew out a sigh of regret. "Rafe chose you."

"You want to catch Rafe?" I shook my head, hoping to clear it. "But why? And why do you need me? You know where he lives. . . ."

"It's not wise to go to a Vampire's lair," Pearl said. "We told you that, but you didn't listen."

"Why do you want Rafe?"

"We need another Vampire guinea pig, one with power. Now that all the other Vamps have left town, he'll have to do." Edna glanced at Pearl. "We'd hoped to get Rafe's grandfather, or maybe Mara herself, although I'm not sure we could have held her."

"We'll get her, dear," Pearl said reassuringly. "Sooner or later, we'll get them all."

I glanced from Edna to Pearl. "You're hunters?" I looked at their colorful skirts, their outrageous hats and comfortable shoes, and found it inconceivable that these two women, both grandmothers well into their seventies, went around staking Vampires and lopping the heads off Werewolves.

"Of course, dear."

"We used to run a school down in Texas," Edna said wistfully. "Those were the days!"

Texas, I thought. Travis Jackson was from Texas.

Pearl smiled. "We were important then! People looked up to us, respected us." She sighed wistfully. "Now, when the new hunters look at us, all they see are a couple of has-beens, but we'll show them!"

"Yes, indeed," Edna said, a hint of madness shining in her eyes. "We'll destroy more Vampires and Were-creatures with our formula than all those hunters with their stakes and silver bullets combined."

Hunters. A school in Texas. I frowned. "You said you'd always lived in Oak Hollow."

"We've always maintained a residence here, dear, even when we lived in Texas. My grandson took over the family business when Edna and I retired."

"Retiring," Edna said. "It was a big mistake."

Pearl nodded. "Yes, indeed, but they'll remember us now."

I shook my head again. It didn't make sense. Edna and Pearl had told me about Travis, told me where the

Werewolves met . . . warned me not to be alone with Rafe. Why?

"Travis," I said with sudden clarity. "He's your grandson, isn't he?"

Pearl beamed at me. "Yes, indeed. Such a good boy."

"And the best hunter to come along in years, except for my Jeffrey," Edna added with a grin.

"Let's not have this argument again," Pearl said with some asperity. "Travis is the best, and he has the kills to prove it."

I stared at the two of them, unable to believe they were standing there arguing about who was the best hunter while I sat on the floor suffering the aftereffects of being drugged and kidnapped.

"Eat your lunch, dear," Pearl said, moving toward the door. "It'll be dark in an hour or so, and we have a lot of work to do before the sun goes down."

Sundown, I thought, and Rafe would be looking for me. He was the only hope I had, but I didn't want him to find me, didn't want his life to be in danger because of me. Closing my eyes, I tried to send him a mental warning to stay away, but I couldn't focus, couldn't think past the growing fear in my heart and the nagging pain in my head.

I stared at the food on the tray. How did they expect me to eat when my life, and Rafe's, were in danger? Still, I forced myself to pick up the sandwich, to take one bite and then another. Even though I wasn't hungry, I had to eat, had to regain my strength for whatever the night might hold.

When I was finished, I pushed the tray away, then curled up on the floor and closed my eyes. All I could do now was rest, wait, and pray.

I lost track of time as I lay there. I dozed and woke and dozed again, and then, as clearly as if I could see him, I knew Rafe was nearby.

Scrambling to my feet, I pressed my ear to the door, hoping to hear what was going on in the next room, but to no avail.

Though my legs still felt like rubber, I paced the floor, all the time wondering what was going on in the other room. Where was Rafe? Were Edna and Pearl still in the building somewhere? What about Travis? And Susie? Was she still with Cagin?

The ache in my head grew worse. Pressing my hands against my temples, I leaned against the wall, quietly cursing Travis Jackson and his crazy grandmother.

I jerked upright when the door opened and Travis sauntered inside, looking smug. Before I could ask what was going on, he cuffed my hands behind my back, grabbed me by the arm, and hustled me outside and into the back of a large, nondescript gray van.

"Where are we going?" I had to ask, even though I knew he wouldn't answer.

My heart skipped a beat when he dropped a black hood over my head. Visions of being shoved against a wall and executed crowded my mind, making it hard to breathe.

I heard the door slam, and then the van lurched forward. I sat on the floor a moment, then lowered my head and shook off the hood. It didn't help much. The inside of the van was dark, the windows painted over so that I couldn't see outside. A sliver of light penetrated the crack in the double doors.

With a sigh, I stretched my legs out in front of me, gasped when my foot hit something. Peering into the darkness, I saw a large cage pushed up against one wall of the van. Looking closer, I realized there was a man locked inside, his hands bound behind his back. His feet were also bound. A thick black hood similar to the one I had shaken off covered his head, and even though I couldn't see his face, I knew it was Rafe.

I took a closer look at the shackles around his ankles. I couldn't be sure, but I thought the restraints were silver. A sense of hopelessness fell over me like a shroud as I recalled Rafe telling me that silver burned a Vampire's flesh and rendered them powerless.

It was creepy, riding in the back of the van, unable to see where I was going. I kept hoping I was having another nightmare, but the ache in my head and the growing ache in my shoulders was all too real. I wondered what time it was.

It seemed we had been driving for hours before Rafe stirred. He lifted his head, as though sniffing the air. "Kathy?"

My spirits rose a little at the sound of his voice. "I'm here."

"Are you all right?"

"I guess so. For now, at least."

"Where are we going?"

"I don't know. What happened? How did they get you?"

"Half a dozen hunters, including our old friend, Jackson, were waiting for me at your place. They're good," he said with grudging admiration. "They blinded me with holy water and had me trussed up in less than a minute. I should have sensed them," he muttered, "but . . ."

"You were too busy thinking about me."

"Yeah, but that's no excuse. Don't worry, I'll get you out of this."

I clung to his words as the vehicle made a wide right turn and came to an abrupt halt.

Travis Jackson's expression was grim when he took hold of my arm and hauled me out of the back of the van. Night had fallen, though the moon had not yet risen. Gazing into the darkness, I couldn't see much of anything except for a huge two-story building surrounded by a high block wall topped with barbed wire.

Once I was out of the van, four men built like pro linebackers climbed into the vehicle. I tried to hang back so I could see what they were doing to Rafe, but Travis dragged me down a narrow walkway that ran along the side of the building. Up close, I could see that the structure was built of stone and weathered wood. When Travis unlocked the door, two rows of recessed, overhead lights came on. He gave me a little push, and I stumbled inside. Before I could turn around, he was gone.

I glanced at my surroundings. I was in a large, sterile-looking room that was outfitted with two metal examining tables, complete with tie-down straps. The walls were puke green, the floor was gray and black tile. Several glass-fronted cupboards lined the walls; the shelves were filled with test tubes and beakers in varying sizes, along with several nasty-looking instruments that reminded me of the Spanish Inquisition. Two windows, set high in one wall, were covered by iron bars

Turning my back to the door, I turned the knob, but it was locked, of course. No surprises there. I was looking for another way out when the door opened and Travis stepped into the lab.

"Where's Rafe?" I demanded.

"In his cage, like a good little guinea pig."

A cage! "What are you going to do with him?"

"Whatever the hell I want."

Taking me by the arm, Travis led me out of the lab, then guided me, none too gently, down a narrow corridor. He turned right into another corridor and opened the last door at the end of the hall. When he switched on the light, I saw a small, square room. The white walls and the tile floor were bare. The only furnishings were a narrow cot topped with a dark gray blanket, and a three-legged table. A pedestal sink and a toilet occupied one corner.

"Make yourself at home," Travis said, and pushed me into the room.

It was getting to be a habit with him. One I didn't like. I spun around to face him. "I want to see Rafe."

Travis snorted. "I don't give a rat's ass what you want."

"Why are you doing this?"

"It's us or them, missy. Haven't you figured that out yet?" He snorted softly. "Too bad you're on the wrong side." Moving behind me, he removed the handcuffs.

I rubbed my wrists. "How long are you going to keep me here?"

"Until the tests are over." He winked at me. "You're a guinea pig, too."

My insides turned cold. "What do you mean?"

"My grandmother and Edna think they've found a way to cure the Weres and the Vamps and restore their humanity, but before we add their formula to the world's water supply, we need to test it and make sure it's harmless to the general population."

"Vampires don't drink water."

"But they drink human blood. They'll ingest the formula that way."

"You can't do this! What if it doesn't work? What if . . . what if it kills the Werewolves and destroys the Vampires?" Surely Pearl and Edna realized their so-called cure wouldn't work on the Undead. Vampires didn't have a disease. Did Pearl and Edna really think they could restore life to the Undead? And what about the shape-shifters? They weren't made or brought across, they were born that way.

"If they die, they die," Jackson said with a shrug. "Either way, there will be a sudden decrease in the Supernatural population. Either way, we win."

"I'm not a Supernatural creature."

"True, but that's why you're here. We need to test the effects on a few regular people, too." He ran his hand across my cheek. "I'm sorry you had to be one of them."

I jerked away, repelled by his touch and the merciless look in his eyes. "What happens when the tests are over?"

A muscle worked in his jaw.

It was all the answer I needed. Whether the cure worked or not, they couldn't leave any witnesses behind. Feeling suddenly numb, I sat down on the edge of the cot. What they were doing was not only against the law, it was inhuman, immoral.

"Try and get some sleep." Travis looked at me a moment, the way a man might look at a pet dog that was about to be destroyed. "I'm sorry you got involved in this," he murmured, and left the room.

The rasp of the key turning in the lock sounded ominous.

And final.

Chapter Twenty-Three

Rafe took several slow, deep breaths in an effort to breathe through the pain. The silver binding his wrists and ankles burned his skin like the very fires of hell, stripping him of his strength, making it hard to think of anything else. All he wanted to do was sleep and escape the pain sizzling through him, but rest eluded him.

Lying there in the dark, he quietly cursed himself for being caught like a rat in a trap. If he had been paying attention to his surroundings, Jackson and his cronies would never have taken him unawares, but he had been thinking about Kathy and how good she had felt in his arms the night before, and how much he missed her when they were apart. In spite of the obstacles between them, he couldn't imagine his future without her. He had been trying to decide whether or not he should propose to her again when Travis Jackson had stepped out of the shadows and thrown holy water in his face.

Rafe had yelped in pain. Before his vision cleared, Jackson and five of his buddies had wrestled him to the ground and cuffed his hands behind his back. He had tried to dissolve into mist, but the silver manacles had quickly drained his strength, leaving him weak and powerless.

Bound like a hog for the slaughter, they had shoved him into a cage and dumped him in the back of a van. Hours later, he had been carried out of the van, cage and all, to wherever the hell he was now. He tried to shake off the hood that covered his head, but it was tied in place, leaving him in darkness. He reached out with his feet, measuring his prison. The cage was barely large enough to hold him. He swore under his breath. Trapped in the dark and bound with silver, he was virtually helpless.

Where was Kathy?

He closed his eyes, focusing on her image. She was near, he was sure of it, but he couldn't find her, couldn't concentrate.

Dammit, where was Mara when he needed her? And then he remembered; she had gone to Rome to confer with the Italian Vampires. She had taken Roshan and Brenna with her; his parents were still in South America. And Rane, who the hell knew where he was?

Rafe swore softly. For the first time in his life, he was truly alone. He swore again, wondering if Kathy, like the woman in his dreams, would be the means of his destruction.

Chapter Twenty-Four

The hours dragged by. Eventually, exhaustion took over, and I collapsed onto the cot. Pulling the blanket over me, I closed my eyes and slept. My dreams were fragmented, filled with images of Cagin caught between the transition from man to beast, his face and body hideously distorted. I turned away from him, running for my life. Seeking shelter, I clawed my way up an icy mountain to Susie's house, realizing too late that there would be no help for me there. She was one of them now, no longer human, no longer my friend. Travis Jackson rose up out of a dark mist, the blade of a knife shining like molten silver in his hand. Edna and Pearl loomed behind him, their faces wreathed in insincere smiles. There was only one person I dared trust, one man I could turn to, and I ran on and on through the endless night, chased by the fear of what I might become if I couldn't find him. . . .

I woke to my own screams echoing off the walls and ringing in my ears.

The sliver of light streaming under my door told me

the night was over. I worried about Rafe, wondering if they had provided a dark place for him to spend the day.

Rising, I relieved myself, then paced the floor, my thoughts chasing themselves like a cat chasing its tail. Where was this place? Where was Rafe? Tests, Travis had said. Tests to see if the formula concocted by his grandmother and Edna could cure the Werewolves and the Vampires. Tests to see how the shape-shifters, and ordinary people like me, would react to their so-called cure. I broke out in a cold sweat. What if it had no effect on the Supernatural community? What if it turned me into some kind of ravenous monster? Suddenly, being a run-of-the-mill Vampire didn't seem so bad.

The hours passed with agonizing slowness. A man wearing a mask and a white lab coat brought me a breakfast tray. The smell of scrambled eggs and sausage made me sick to my stomach. I drank the coffee, ate a slice of toast, and left the rest.

Agitated, worried for my future and Rafe's, I paced the floor again.

Lunch arrived a little after noon. Even though I wasn't hungry, I forced myself to eat a little of the turkey sandwich, felt a rush of unwanted gratitude for whoever had included a chocolate malt.

Sitting on the edge of the cot, I stared at the opposite wall. Time hadn't passed this slowly since I was a little girl waiting for Christmas morning.

Rising, I paced until my legs ached, then stretched out on the cot and closed my eyes. What were Edna and Pearl doing now? Where was Rafe? Had anyone noticed that I hadn't opened the store today? If I never returned to Oak Hollow, would anyone even miss me? I wished that I had told my mother that I loved her the last time we talked, just in case it really was the last time.

As the hours passed, I grew increasingly more fearful. "Rafe." I whispered his name, wondering if I would ever see him again, wishing that we had made love when we had the chance. "Rafe, where are you?"

Kathy?

His voice whispered in my mind, calming my fears. "Rafe!"

I'm here.

"Are you all right? I'm so afraid."

I know. Strange, I tried to contact you before and couldn't.

"That is odd," I agreed. He was the one with the Supernatural powers. I had always seen things, heard things, through him. I was about to ask him if he knew where we were when the door to my room opened and two men wearing white lab coats stepped inside.

Without saying a word, they took hold of my arms and escorted me back to the lab I had seen the night before.

Something new had been added, a double row of large animal cages, six on each side of the room, facing each other. Seven of those who were locked inside were strangers to me, but I knew the people in three of the cages—Cagin, Susie, and Rafe. The fourth was a pretty girl with dark blond hair and violet eyes. I frowned, thinking she looked familiar. Of course, Jennifer Something-or-other. She had come to the bookstore once or twice.

The last cage was empty, the door open. I knew it was for me.

I fought a losing battle as the two men dragged me

toward the cage. They locked me inside and then left the room.

I stared at Rafe. He sat hunched over in the middle of his cage. He stared back at me, but said nothing. His face and neck were badly burned where the holy water had touched him. I felt his pain as if it was my own, wondered what drug they had used to subdue him.

This couldn't be happening. Any minute now I'd wake up in my own house in my own bed. Yet even as I told myself it was nothing but a nightmare, I registered the fact that the cages held two human men, three Werewolves, three Vampires, and three shape-shifters. The Vampires and Werewolves were bound with silver, which drained their Supernatural strength. Each group consisted of two males and one female, all between twenty and thirty years old.

Edna and Pearl were totally insane, I thought. Effectively testing something as radical as this would take years. You couldn't test a new drug on twelve people and call the results conclusive. And what about its effects on dogs and cats, on birds and fish and livestock? On the water supply and agriculture, the atmosphere itself?

I noticed that Cagin was holding Susie's hand through the bars, though she seemed unaware of it. I was surprised to see them there, since Rafe had told me that Cagin was taking Susie away from Oak Hollow.

The other prisoners sat in silence, their faces reflecting nothing of what they felt, if indeed they felt anything. Drugged, I thought, all the Supernatural creatures had been drugged to render them incapable of fighting back.

I tensed as the door to the lab opened and Edna and

Pearl walked briskly into the room. In addition to their usual colorful skirts and sneakers, they wore lab coats, rubber gloves and hospital masks. The two men who had brought me into the lab earlier followed them inside. I fought down a rising tide of panic as Edna and Pearl moved around the room. Why had I never noticed that insane gleam in their eyes before? Hard to believe it had always been there and I had never seen it. I had been amused by their outrageous appearance and eccentric behavior and dismissed them as two slightly unconventional grandmothers. How could I have been so blind?

I couldn't help wondering where Travis was. I thought it odd that he wasn't there to watch the tests.

"We'll start with the shape-shifters," Pearl decided. She picked up a small glass bottle, removed the cap, filled a nasty-looking syringe with dark green liquid, and moved toward the first cage.

One of the lab assistants unlocked the door. He grabbed hold of the shape-shifter inside and held him down while the second assistant extended the shifter's arm. Quickly and efficiently, Pearl injected the serum into his vein. The assistant locked the cage door, and then Pearl and her assistants moved to Jennifer's cage. She offered no resistance.

Cagin was next. He snarled when they opened the door. In spite of being drugged, he tried to put up a fight, but in his weakened state, he was no match for the two burly assistants who held him down while Edna administered the dose.

"The Werewolves next, I think," Edna said, filling another syringe, "and then the Vampires."

Pearl looked at me. It was hard to read her expression

behind the mask, but it seemed her eyes were sad. "And then the humans," she murmured.

I could only watch in horror as Pearl and Edna moved from cage to cage, injecting the Werewolves. My stomach clenched when they opened the door to Susie's cage. She seemed unaware of what they were doing to her.

Rafe's gaze locked with mine when they opened his cage. Bound with silver chains, he was helpless to resist, but his eyes never left mine.

The other two Vampires were quickly inoculated.

I glanced at the shape-shifters. They sat as before, unmoving, and I wondered how long it would take to see what the serum's effects would be, if any.

Minutes passed and then the first Werewolf that had been injected howled with pain as he changed into a wolf and then quickly resumed his human form. He howled again and then, foaming at the mouth, he collapsed and lay still.

In moments, the second Werewolf let out a long wail that sent chills down my spine, and then he, too, collapsed.

I stared across the aisle at Susie. She lay on the floor of her cage, her teeth bared. She moaned piteously as her body convulsed.

In the cage beside hers, Cagin growled softly.

I glanced at the other two Vampires and then at Rafe. They didn't move, only sat there, unblinking. And then, one by one, they toppled sideways and lay still.

"Rafe." His name whispered past my lips. He didn't seem to be breathing.

I watched with mounting horror as Pearl injected the two human males, and then one of her assistants unlocked the door of my cage. I stared at the needle in Pearl's hand, more frightened than I had ever been in my life.

I screamed, "No! Let me go!" when the two men grabbed me. Though there was little room in the cage to maneuver, I kicked and bucked for all I was worth in an effort to free myself, but I was no match for their greater strength.

Terrified and helpless, I stared up at Pearl. The needle in her hand looked huge and deadly. "Please," I begged, "please don't do this."

"I'm sorry, dear," she said, and jabbed the needle into my vein.

I watched the sickly green liquid disappear into my arm. A burning sensation shot through me, and I went limp as the two men released me. My blood felt like it was on fire, my body felt heavy, numb. Helpless, I could only lie there, wondering if I was going to die like a lab rat in a cage.

As from far away, I heard Edna's voice. "It's obvious the formula doesn't work on the Werewolves."

Pearl picked up a long stick and poked Susie with it. She didn't move. "Perhaps it was too strong, or we used too much."

"Yes, perhaps," Edna murmured thoughtfully. "We'll have to change the dosage and round up more subjects."

"Yes, dear, I think you're right," Pearl agreed. Removing her mask and gloves, she tossed them on a table.

"I didn't expect the results on the others to take so long," Edna said. She peered into the cages that held the two human males. Like me, they lay unmoving and unresponsive when she poked at them.

"Why don't we go have dinner while we're waiting?" Pearl suggested.

"We might miss something."

"Nonsense! The cameras are recording," Pearl said, glancing up at one of the monitors mounted on the wall. "We can watch from the kitchen."

"You're right, as always," Edna said with a smile. She peeled off her gloves and removed her mask.

"Let's go, dear," Pearl said. "Travis should be back by now."

Unable to move, I lay there for what seemed like forever, only gradually becoming aware that some of the others were moving.

And then I heard Rafe's voice. "Kathy? Kathy! Are you all right? Dammit, answer me!"

With a great deal of effort, I managed to roll over so I could face him. "You're alive."

He grunted softly.

"Are you still a Vampire?" Even as I asked the question, I wondered if I wanted him to be cured. I had fallen in love with a Vampire. Would I feel the same about him; would he be the same man, if he were human?

"I don't know." Head cocked to one side, he touched his elbow to one of the silver bars that imprisoned him and quickly jerked away. "I'd say so."

I was relieved and disappointed, but mainly glad that he was still alive, still my Rafe.

"Can you move?" he asked.

"I think so." I sat up cautiously. The world spun around me for a few seconds before righting itself. So I could sit up. Big deal. I was still locked inside a steel cage.

Moving carefully, Rafe sat up. "Dammit." He closed his eyes for several minutes. I could almost see him conquering the pain the silver caused him, feel the effort it cost him to gather his power and focus his energy. He stared at the lock on the door of my cage.

I held my breath, afraid to move or speak for fear of distracting him, even though I wasn't sure exactly what he was doing.

Several long moments passed into eternity and then, miraculously, the padlock fell open.

"Find the keys," Rafe said. "Hurry!"

I found a set on the counter, near several bottles of serum. Grabbing the keys, I opened Rafe's cage. Moving cautiously, careful to avoid touching the bars, he crab-walked out of the cage. It took me several tries to find the key to the shackles that bound his hands and feet. My stomach churned when I saw the angry red burns at his wrists and ankles.

But there was no time to do anything about them now. I quickly unlocked the other cages. The two male Werewolves were dead. Susie lay unmoving. Her face was pale and sheened with perspiration, but she was still breathing.

As soon as I unlocked the door to Cagin's cage, he scrambled out and drew Susie into his arms. I freed the other two Vampires, then removed their restraints. I had the feeling they were both very young in the life.

"What now?" I asked when the last cage had been opened.

"We need to gather up everything we can find," Rafe said. He pointed at the two human men. "You two, gather up all these bottles and anything else you can find."

Without a word of argument, the two men quickly found a couple of empty wooden crates and began filling them with bottles of serum, along with the contents of the drawers and cupboards.

It took only a few minutes.

"Cagin," Rafe said, "take everybody to my house. Kathy, go with him."

"No way."

Cagin looked at me. "You staying or going?" he asked impatiently.

"Staying."

For once, Rafe didn't waste time arguing with me.

"Be careful, you two," Cagin said. Opening the door, he glanced up and down the hall before leaving the lab. The shifters moved out behind him, followed by the Vampires and the two men.

"What are we going to do?" I asked.

"Look for the formula to that damn serum."

"Do you think it's here?"

"I don't know." He checked the drawers to make sure nothing had been left behind. "Come on, let's check the rest of the building."

I followed Rafe down the hallway. He stopped at each room along the way to peer inside. Most of them were empty; two contained cots, no doubt for the guards. A third was the room where I had been held. The last room was an office.

Rafe went inside, and I closed the door behind us. Several large metal filing cabinets lined one wall. They were locked, but that was no problem for Rafe. I stood lookout while he went through the drawers, pulling out the files that looked promising.

He had scanned a dozen or so when he said, "Got it!"

"Someone's coming."

Folding the file in half, he shoved it under his shirt, closed the drawer of the cabinet, then grabbed me by the hand. "Shh, not a word."

Pearl's voice. The sound of footsteps coming closer.

My heart was pounding a mile a minute when Pearl opened the door and stepped inside. To my amazement, she walked right by us as though we weren't there.

She rummaged around in the file cabinet a moment, muttered an oath that sounded even worse coming from a grandmother, and hurried out of the room.

"Come on," Rafe said, "let's get out of here."

"Why didn't she see us? Never mind, don't tell me. A little Vampire magic?"

"Right, let's go."

I stayed close behind Rafe as he searched for the nearest exit. Twice, he stopped as men in white lab coats appeared in the hallway. Both times, the men walked past us as if we weren't there. A handy trick, I thought, surprised they couldn't hear my heart pounding.

We finally found a door that led outside.

"Where are we?" I asked.

Rafe shook his head. "Beats the hell out of me. Come on."

We walked away from the lab until we came to a block wall that must have been twelve feet high.

"Now what?" I asked.

Before Rafe could answer, the wail of a siren split the air.

"Looks like they've discovered our absence," Rafe said. He held out his hand. "Here, get on my back."

"What?"

"Do it."

Muttering, "This is a heck of a time for games," I took his hand and he swung me around until I was riding piggyback. I choked back a shriek as he vaulted effortlessly over the wall.

He landed softly on the other side. I slid off his back, then fell into his arms when he turned around.

"You okay?" he asked.

"I guess so. I wish they'd turn that siren off. I feel like we're breaking out of prison."

His teeth flashed in a smile. "Don't think we aren't."

"Do you have any idea where we are?"

He glanced around, then lifted his head and sniffed the air. "We're in Clear Glen," he said, "about fifty miles from home."

I groaned. Fifty miles! Did he expect us to walk? I gasped in surprise when he lifted me off my feet and settled me on one hip, the way a mother might carry a child.

"What are you doing?"

"Going home the fastest way I know how."

The next thing I knew, he was running, or maybe flying, through the night, so fast that, to my mortal eyes, the world was nothing but a blur.

In less time than it takes to tell, we were at Rafe's house.

My admiration for Vampire powers was growing by leaps and bounds.

"No one's here," I said, and then realized that, unless Cagin and the others could fly, they couldn't possibly have arrived before we did. "What are we going to do now?"

"Destroy those vials," Rafe said, "and hope that no one else knows how to make the damn stuff."

"Do you think that's what Pearl was looking for in the office? The formula?"

"I don't know." He removed the file from inside his

shirt and tossed it on the coffee table. "I'm hoping they were too paranoid to give anyone else a copy."

"Why didn't it kill Susie? It killed the other two."

"I don't know. Maybe it doesn't have the same effect on males and females. Maybe it affected her differently because she hasn't been a Werewolf very long." He ran his hands up and down my arms. "How do you feel?"

"I don't know. All right, I guess." I stared at the raw, angry-looking skin on his face and neck. It must have hurt like the very devil. "What about you?"

"Same as always." His gaze met mine. "Were you hoping it would make me mortal again?"

"I thought about it," I admitted, "but I love you just the way you are." I touched his cheek with my fingertips. "Does it hurt terribly?"

"More than you can imagine, but it'll heal."

"How long will it take?"

"A few days, a week, maybe longer." He took my hand in his and kissed my palm. "Stop worrying about me."

"Somebody has to. How long do you think it will take for Cagin and the others to get here?"

"An hour or so. What do you say we wash away the stink of that place and change clothes?"

"I'd like that."

Moments later, we were in Rafe's shower. For a few blessed minutes, as he washed me and I washed him, I forgot all about Pearl and Edna, until I washed Rafe's face. He flinched at my touch.

"Sorry. Would it help if you . . . you know?"

He nodded, his gaze intent upon my face.

"Do it, then," I said, and tilted my head back, offering him my throat.

Murmuring my name, he bent his head over my neck.

It was a remarkably erotic sensation, standing in his arms with the water sluicing over us while he drank from me.

He took only a little, then released me.

"That can't be enough," I said.

"It will do, for now. I don't want to weaken you too much after what you've been through."

"What about you? The silver restraints, the drug . . . how were you able to draw on your powers so quickly?"

"The silver has no after-effects. As for whatever drug they used, it wasn't long-lasting."

"Neither was the serum," I muttered, "unless it killed you." Except for its lethal affect on the two Werewolves, the serum was a failure. Would Pearl and Edna try again? Would the Supernatural creatures give them a chance?

Rafe caressed my cheek with the back of his hand, and then he lifted his head, his nostrils flaring. "We'd best get dressed. They're almost here."

Since I didn't have a change of clothes, I put on one of Rafe's T-shirts over my bra and panties, then slipped into his robe, belting it tightly at my waist.

He put on a T-shirt and a pair of sweats.

Five minutes later, there was a knock at the door.

"That'll be Cagin and the others," Rafe said, and went to let them in.

The two humans came in first. They set the boxes on the coffee table, then stood there, silent and unmoving. It took me a minute to realize they were under some sort of spell.

Rafe frowned when the two Vampires entered his house. I wondered if he was annoyed because they hadn't asked permission, and then wondered why they hadn't.

Perhaps the Undead only needed an invitation into the homes of the living.

Jennifer and the other male shape-shifter followed them. She looked at me, her eyes widening with recognition. "I know you," she said. "The bookstore . . ."

I nodded.

Cagin came in last, carrying Susie in his arms. He sat on the sofa, cradling her against his chest. No one else sat down.

"Now what?" the male Vampire asked. He was a nice-looking kid, no more than twenty-two or twenty-three, with fine blond hair and sleepy blue eyes.

"How do you feel?" Rafe asked.

"Weak," the male said, looking confused. "And hungry."

Rafe's eyes narrowed. "Hungry? For what?"

"A chili dog and a Coke," he said, and then frowned.

"What about you?" Rafe asked the female. She was a pretty little thing, with curly black hair and heavily-lashed brown eyes. She couldn't have been more than twenty or twenty-one at the most.

"I feel empty inside," she said. "Just . . . empty." She took hold of the male's hand. "Jimmy, I want to go home."

Rafe regarded the two of them a moment. "How long have you two been Vampires?"

"Only a few weeks," Jimmy said. "Gina was turned on our honeymoon. I asked her to bring me across the next night."

Rafe grunted softly. "I don't think you're Vampires any longer."

"Really?" Jimmy asked, his eyes wide. "You mean it worked?"

The girl smiled as if they had just won the lottery. "Human again!" She threw her arms around her husband.

He picked her up and swung her around in a circle, then drew her close to his side. They stood there, beaming at each other, no longer aware of the rest of us. So young, I thought, and so much in love.

Rafe turned toward the shape-shifters. "What are your names?"

"I'm Jennifer," the girl said. "Jennifer Westover."

"Gary Linden," the man replied.

"How did the formula affect the two of you?" Rafe asked.

"It hurt and it made me a little dizzy," Jennifer said, and Linden nodded in agreement.

"What about you?" Rafe asked, speaking to Cagin.

"The same," Cagin said, "but it didn't last long."

"Can you still shift?" Rafe asked, looking at each shape-shifter in turn.

"I don't know," Linden said, frowning. "I think I can." Jennifer nodded. "Me, too."

"I know I can," Cagin said. "I can feel it inside me."

Rafe looked at me. "How did it affect you?"

"It burned like acid and left me feeling numb all over."

Rafe gazed at the two men standing across the room. "How did the serum affect you?"

"It was like she said," the taller of the two replied.

"Yeah," the second one agreed. "And then, for a little while, I couldn't move."

Rafe swore softly. "So, it works, at least in part. Most effective against Vampires, by the look of it." He glanced at Susie, who seemed to be sleeping now. "We don't know for sure what its effect is on the Werewolves. Maybe it only kills the males, or maybe it only kills those who've been Weres for a long time," he mused. "But that doesn't make sense. You'd think the oldest would be harder to destroy."

He shook his head, then looked at the two human males. His eyes took on a faint red glow. "After you leave here, you will not remember this night, this place, these people, or anything that happened here."

The two men nodded.

"Go home now," Rafe said, "and forget everything you've seen and heard."

Gina regarded Rafe curiously. "Why didn't it affect you?" she asked after the two men left the house.

Rafe shrugged. He stood unmoving for a moment, and then he moved closer to the two former Vampires, his gaze locking with first one and then the other. "You will not remember this night, this place, or anyone in this room, do you understand?"

Jimmy and the girl nodded.

"You will not remember that you were once Vampires. You will not remember whatever lives you may have taken, or feel any guilt. You will not remember this place or anything that happened after you were turned. Is that understood?"

Again, they nodded.

"Don't go home. You won't be safe there. Leave town now, tonight. Do you understand?"

They both nodded.

"Go now."

Looking a little lost and confused, Jimmy took Gina by the hand and they left the house.

"What about us?" Jennifer asked. "Are you going to take our memories, as well?"

"No. But I wouldn't advise either of you to go home."

Rafe's gaze hardened. "Few people who know where I live survive to tell the tale. I hope you'll remember that."

"Don't worry," Jennifer said. "I'm getting out of Oak Hollow tonight."

"I owe you my life," Gary Linden said. "I won't betray you."

Cagin waited until the two shape-shifters left the house, then looked up at Rafe. "What do we do now?"

"Destroy the serum we have," Rafe said, "then get in touch with Mara. I've got the formula, but there may be other copies. I'll give mine to Mara when she returns. She can get in touch with Clive. Maybe they can come up with an antidote, just in case the hunters make another batch."

Cagin stroked Susie's brow. "Can you do anything for her?"

Rafe shook his head. "I'm not a doctor."

"She's dying," Cagin said quietly.

"No!" I looked at Rafe. "Please, don't let her die."

"What do you want me to do?"

Cagin stroked her hair. "Make her a Vampire."

Rafe stared at Cagin as if he had asked him to turn a chunk of lead into gold.

"It's worth a try," I said. At this point, making Susie a Vampire seemed better than the alternative. Vampire or not, Susie had three children who needed her.

"It could kill her," Rafe said flatly. "I could kill her. I've never brought anyone across."

"You can't hurt her," Cagin said. "She's already dying."

Rafe shook his head. "She's barely accepted being a Werewolf. What makes you think she'd want to be a Vampire instead?"

"I want her to live!" Cagin said, a low growl in his voice. "Dammit, just do it! What have we got to lose?"

Rafe looked at me. "I haven't fed."

I knew what he was saying. He was hurting from the effects of the holy water and the silver manacles, but, more than that, he needed to be in control so that he didn't savage Susie, so that he didn't take her past the point where she would be able to recover. The small amount of blood he had taken from me hadn't been enough to restore his strength or satisfy his hunger.

"Take what you need," I said. "Hurry."

Rafe swore under his breath. Then, his face set in hard lines, he took me by the hand and led me into his bedroom.

My heart was racing like a runaway train when he closed the door.

Chapter Twenty-Five

"Couldn't we have a light?" It was so dark in his room, I couldn't see a thing.

"Sorry, there aren't any."

"Why not?"

A soft sound of amusement rose in his throat. "I have no need for them."

He placed his hands on my shoulders and urged me to take a few steps backward. When I felt the edge of the mattress against the backs of my knees, I sat down, relieved to discover that he did, indeed, sleep in a bed.

I felt the mattress sag when he sat down beside me.

"Relax," he murmured.

"Right."

"Why are you so tense?" he asked. "We've done this before."

"I don't know." It was the truth. Maybe it was because we were in his bedroom for the first time; maybe I was just too keyed up after all that had happened.

"You don't have to do this," he said quietly.

What other choice did I have? If I refused, Susie would

die. "No," I said, "it's all right, really. Just . . . just do whatever you need to."

Even as I spoke the words, I couldn't help wondering if I was doing the right thing. Would Susie hate me for what was about to happen to her, or thank me for helping to save her life? And how would it affect her relationship with Cagin, whatever that was? Before tonight, they had both been two-natured creatures—both human and Were; now, she would be a Vampire, a blood-drinking child of the night. It would make their relationship more difficult, more like mine and Rafe's, I thought, and then frowned as I realized I wasn't sure exactly what our relationship was.

It was a strange sensation, being near Rafe but unable to see him. He caressed my cheek, rained kisses along the side of my neck. I shivered at his touch, stilled as his tongue laved my skin. In a distant part of my mind, I wondered why it didn't hurt when he bit me, and then all thoughts and fears were forgotten, swallowed up in the waves of sensual pleasure that washed over me. A delicious heat engulfed me, driving everything from my mind but the need to give him whatever he desired, my heart, my soul, the very breath from my body.

I moaned a low protest when his tongue skimmed my neck, sealing the wounds. The bed shifted as he rose, and I reached blindly for his hand. "Don't leave me."

"I'll be back in a few minutes."

"No. I want to be there."

"I don't think this is something you want to see."

"How do you know? You said you'd never seen it done."

"But I know how it's done. You don't, and you don't need to."

"Yes, I do." Feeling light-headed, I rose on legs that were none too steady, and would have fallen if Rafe hadn't slipped his arm around my waist.

"You're the most stubborn woman I've ever known," he muttered irritably.

I smiled into the darkness, pleased by his words though I wasn't sure why. When he opened the bedroom door, I squinted against the light, which seemed brighter than it had before.

Cagin was sitting on the sofa where we had left him, Susie still cradled against his chest. His hand, large and calloused, lightly stroked her hair. She didn't move, didn't seem to be breathing. Were we too late?

Rafe settled me in one of the leather chairs. "You sure you're all right?"

"I'm fine, stop worrying about me."

"Yeah," he muttered, "like that'll ever happen."

He regarded me a moment more, as if he expected me to collapse any minute, then moved toward the sofa. Wordlessly, he lifted Susie from Cagin's lap. Shape-shifter and Vampire exchanged glances—Cagin's yellow eyes filled with suspicion, Rafe's dark ones narrowed and impatient—then Cagin rose and went to stand in front of the fireplace.

Rafe took Cagin's place on the sofa. He looked at me over Susie's head and then, ever so gently, he smoothed her hair away from her neck. For a moment, his finger-tips stroked the skin beneath her ear. His lips were moving, but I couldn't hear what he was saying.

The air seemed suddenly charged with Supernatural energy. The hair along my nape prickled, and I knew Rafe was gathering his power.

My breath caught in my throat as he lowered his head

over her neck. His hair swung forward so that I couldn't see what he was doing, but I knew. I could smell the scent of Susie's blood, feel the rush of preternatural energy that filled the room.

Cagin took a step forward, a feral gleam in his amber eyes, his hands tightly clenched at his sides.

I was surprised by the sharp stab of jealousy that swept through me as Rafe continued to drink.

Susie stirred in Rafe's arms, a small moan rising in her throat. Her hands clutched his arms, her fingers digging deep into his skin, and then she went suddenly limp.

Cagin took another step forward, his face terrible to see.

When Rafe lifted his head, I saw a single drop of bright red blood at the corner of his mouth. His eyes were red and glowing. He looked at me, only for a moment, but it seemed to stretch into eternity. I could hear his voice in my head.

This is who I am, he said. *This is what I am.*

And then, his gaze still locked on mine, he bit his wrist and held the open wound to Susie's lips.

"Drink." He spoke softly, yet his voice rang with authority.

Susie obediently licked at the blood oozing from his wrist, once, twice, and then her hands grabbed his arm and she sucked greedily.

Once again, preternatural power flowed through the room. Susie's cheeks bloomed with color, her hair and skin took on a luster they'd never had before.

Cagin swore softly, his gaze focused on Susie.

It seemed she would drain Rafe dry before he said, "Enough!" and broke her hold on his arm. A flick of his tongue sealed the wound in his wrist.

Depositing Susie on the sofa, Rafe gained his feet.
He wiped his mouth with the back of his hand, then
looked down at Susie. "Do you know who I am?"

She nodded, though her eyes were filled with confusion. "What happened?" She glanced around the
room. "Where am I?" When she saw Cagin, she smiled
tentatively.

"What do you remember?" Rafe asked.

"I remember . . ." She frowned. "I remember some
men came to the house. I don't know who they were.
They took me outside and put me in a van. . . ." She
worried her lower lip with her teeth. Teeth that seemed
much whiter than they had been before. "I don't recall
anything after that." She looked at Cagin again. "I remember you," she said softly. "You saved my life."

Cagin blew out a breath that seemed to come from
the soles of his feet. "Go on."

Susie put a hand to her head. "Why do I feel so
funny?" She wrapped her arms around her middle. "I
hurt inside. Why? What's happened?" She looked at me
for the first time. "Kathy, what's going on?"

I wondered again if she would hate me for my part in
her transformation.

Cagin moved to Susie's side and sat down. "I'll explain it all to you later," he said, stroking her cheek.
"When we're alone."

"You two should spend the night here," Rafe said.
"I've got a spare room. You won't be safe at her place,
or yours."

"What happens now?" Cagin asked.

Rafe glanced at Susie, then at me. "Kathy, why don't
you show Susie where the bathroom is. Run a bath for
her."

"All right. Come on, Susie."

She followed me into the bathroom. I was relieved when she didn't ask any questions I didn't want to answer.

Once the tub was full, I turned my back so she could get undressed and then, after assuring her that everything was all right, I went back into the living room.

Cagin was sitting in one of the chairs, staring into the cold fireplace.

Rafe was standing at the window looking out. When I entered the room, he took me by the hand, led me into his bedroom, and quietly closed the door.

I sat on the edge of the bed. "Can't we please have a candle or something?" I asked. After what I'd seen earlier, I needed the reassurance of light.

Rafe left the room. He returned a few minutes later with half a dozen candles, which he placed on the dresser and the tables on either side of the bed. A wave of his hand brought them flickering to life. The tiny flames cast dancing shadows on the walls, which were painted a lovely blue-gray. The ceiling was white, to match the carpet. A quick look around showed a very large room with a fireplace in one corner. An enormous television screen was mounted on the wall across from the bed. There were no windows, of course.

"Why did you want Susie out of the room?" I asked.

Rafe closed the door, then came to sit beside me. "She'll die tonight."

"What? But I thought . . . didn't it work?"

"It worked, but there's more to it than just an exchange of blood. Her mortal body will die in an hour or so, and when she rises tomorrow night, she'll be

Nosferatu. Cagin needed to be prepared for what will happen, for himself, and for her."

I ran my hand along the edge of the bed. "So, she's going to die, like, die?"

"In a manner of speaking, but only for a few moments."

"Why didn't the serum work on you when it worked on the other two?"

He shrugged. "Probably because I wasn't made a Vampire in the usual way."

I supposed that made sense. Technically, he had been born a Vampire. No one had brought him across, there had been no exchange of blood. It was the same with the shape-shifters. They had been born, not made, so there was no disease to cure, nothing to heal.

"Would you have been sorry if it had worked?" I asked.

"Before I met you, I would have said yes, but now . . ." His knuckles brushed my cheek. "I'm starting to hate what I am."

"Why?"

"Because," he said, his voice endearingly soft and sensual, "it's keeping me from what I want."

I licked my lips. "What do you want?"

"To spend the rest of my life with you."

"Rafe . . ."

"You should get some rest," he said. "You've had quite a night."

"What was it like, bringing Susie across?"

"I'm not sure I can describe it." He looked past me, his thoughts obviously turned inward. "You can't imagine what it was like, the wonder of holding her life in my hands, the rush of power that flowed through me as I took her to the point of death, and then gave her life back to her." He paused. His eyes, as dark and deep as eternity, burned with bright intensity as they gazed into mine. "I wish it had been you."

Looking into his eyes, hearing the heartfelt longing in his voice, for that one brief moment in time, I, too, wished it had been me.

At my request, Rafe left the candles burning after we went to bed. I wasn't sure I would ever be able to sleep in the dark again. Every time I closed my eyes, I saw Rafe bending over Susie's neck. I smelled the coppery scent of her blood, saw the hellish red glow in Rafe's eyes as he took her to the brink of eternity, and then brought her back. I saw the gleam of insanity in Pearl's eyes, the madness in Edna's, the hatred in Travis Jackson's. I remembered being locked in a cage, the sting of the needle and the helpless terror that had followed, the fear that I would die in that cage, that my parents would never know what had happened to me.

Rafe woke me twice during the night, his touch and his voice soothing my fears, chasing the nightmares away.

He'd been right, I thought, I never should have watched him bring Susie across.

Toward dawn, when he thought I was asleep, he went into the living room. Curious, I slipped out of bed, padded silently down the hall, and peeked around the door frame.

Rafe stood in front of the sofa, his back toward me. "How's she doing?" he asked.

"She was scared," Cagin said, "but she calmed down some when I explained what was happening. She even made a joke, saying she'd never been a morning person, and now she wouldn't have to worry about it anymore."

"How do you feel about it, about what she's become?"

"It doesn't matter. I'm thirty-five years old and I've never been in love until now." He shook his head. "I loved her from the minute I saw her. If anyone had ever told me that was possible, I wouldn't have believed it."

"It happens," Rafe said quietly. "She'll sleep until the sun sets. When she wakes up, she'll be ravenous."

Cagin nodded.

"She'll probably attack the first person she sees, which will most likely be you. If she does, don't let her take too much."

"What would happen if she . . . can shape-shifters be turned?"

"I don't know why not. Might be interesting to find out."

"Interesting," Cagin repeated. "Yeah, right."

"I've got some bottled blood I keep for emergencies," Rafe said. "If you can get her to drink it, it will take the edge off her hunger and help her to control it. It will make it easier on you, too, if she wants to feed off you."

Cagin grunted softly.

"I've never known a Vampire to feed off a shape-shifter," Rafe went on. "I don't know what the effects, if any, will be on either of you."

"I guess we'll find out."

"Maybe so. Just don't let her get away from you. Every fledgling reacts differently to being turned."

"This just keeps getting better and better," Cagin muttered.

"If it goes sour," Rafe said, "just remember it was your idea."

"Right."

The two men regarded each other for a moment, then Rafe started to turn away from the sofa.

I hurried back to the bedroom as fast as my legs would carry me. Diving into the bed, I pulled the covers over my head and pretended to be asleep.

I heard the soft click as Rafe closed and locked the door. I could feel him standing there, staring down at me.

He pulled the covers back on his side of the bed. "I know you're awake."

Blowing out a breath of exasperation, I sat up. "Is Susie going to be all right?"

"I don't know. I hope so."

"Your face . . ."

"Pretty bad, I guess."

"No. It's . . . I . . ." In the light of the candles, I could see that the ugly burns were almost gone. Only a rough redness remained in the worst places. The rest of his face was healed, as if he'd never been hurt.

He rubbed his hand over his cheek. "I told you it would heal."

"You said days, maybe weeks."

He shrugged.

"It was the blood, wasn't it?"

"Yeah."

"Was it mine? Or Susie's?"

He slid into bed and pulled me down beside him. "Yours, of course."

I snuggled against him, my head resting on his shoulder. "This is getting to be a habit, our sleeping together."

"I'd like to do more than sleep," he muttered.

"I know." I couldn't help but admire his restraint, couldn't help but wonder how much longer it would last.

For that matter, I was beginning to wonder who I was saving myself for. I wanted Rafe, no one but Rafe. Loved him as I had never loved anyone else. Did it really matter that he was a Vampire? As for getting married, for couples like us, it was against the law. What if we made our own vows? What if I promised to love him, and only him, for as long as I lived?

As long as I lived . . . I looked up to find Rafe watching me intently.

"Will you?" he asked, and I knew that he had been reading my mind again. This time I didn't care.

My heart seemed to skip a beat. "Yes."

He turned onto his side, so that we were facing each other, and then he clasped my right hand in his. "I promise to love you and protect you for as long as you live. I will give myself to you and none other. I will cherish you in this life and the next."

Blinking back my tears, I said, "I promise I will love you and only you for as long as I live. I will give myself to you, only you, and stand by your side, for now and forever."

"Then I take you as my wife, to love and to cherish, from this night forward."

"And I take you as my husband, to love and to cherish, from this night forward."

Murmuring my name, he drew me into his arms and kissed me. Sighing with sweet surrender, I closed my eyes and gave myself into his keeping.

His lips moved over mine, gently, almost reverently. I basked in his touch, surprised when bare skin met bare skin.

"Better?" he asked.

"Much better." I didn't ask how he had managed to

free us from our clothing. It was a night made for magic, and it was all around us. Flames crackled in the hearth. The scent of roses filled the air, music played ever so softly in the background, or maybe it was all in my mind. I didn't know and I didn't care. All I knew was that I was in Rafe's arms, his body pressed close to mine. His hands caressed me, his lips adored me, his touch lit a fire deep inside of me that only he could quench.

Curious and eager, I explored the taut lines of Rafe's body, marveling at the hardness of his biceps, his six-pack abs, the width of his shoulders, the feel of his skin beneath my fingertips and my tongue, the sheer masculine beauty of his face and form.

When I was desperate for him to take me, when I thought I would surely go up in flames if he didn't possess me, he rose over me, his dark eyes burning with desire as his sweat-slick body merged with mine, and I knew I had been waiting for this moment since the night we met.

Heat exploded deep within me. I clung to his shoulders, my hips rising to welcome him. I felt his tongue lave the skin alongside my neck, waited impatiently for the prick of his fangs. I cried his name as wave after delicious wave of pleasure washed over me.

And then I was floating, drifting lazily on a tranquil sea of afterglow. Whispering Rafe's name, I opened my eyes, startled to realize that we really were floating, about a foot off the mattress.

His lips nuzzled my ear. "It's all right, don't be afraid."

My hands tightened on his shoulders. I wasn't afraid of falling. After all, there was a mattress right below me.

I wasn't afraid of Rafe, either, not really, but sometimes the reality of his Supernatural powers was a little over-whelming.

"You know, you really are the most amazing man," I murmured, smiling.

"Honey, you don't know the half of it," he said, and then he kissed me again, and nothing else mattered. I loved him, adored him, wanted only him, in bed, over the bed, under the bed, it didn't matter, as long as we were together.

Slowly, we drifted back down to the mattress. We lay there, locked in each other's arms, while our breathing returned to normal and the sweat cooled on our skin.

Rafe ran his fingertips over my brow and down my cheek. "Regrets?"

"Of course not. Why would you even ask?"

"I was afraid I might disappoint you."

"You, afraid? I don't believe it! You're the most confident man I've ever known. I've never seen you the least bit unsettled."

He grunted softly. "I was plenty unsettled in that cage."

"We all were. What's going to happen now? Do you think Edna and Pearl will come looking for us again? I can't believe they're hunters."

"It's a stretch, isn't it? As for whether they'll come after us again, I'll take care of that."

"You're not going to kill them?" Even after what they had tried to do, I couldn't stand the thought of Rafe hurting them.

"If I have to."

"Rafe, no . . ."

"I'm going to try something else first, but if it doesn't work . . ." He let the sentence hang, unfinished.

I knew what he was saying, and what he wasn't saying. Edna and Pearl posed too big a threat to the Supernatural community. They had to be stopped, one way or another.

Rafe's lips brushed my cheek. "This isn't the kind of conversation I expected to be having on my wedding night."

"No?" Excitement fluttered in the pit of my stomach when his hand cupped my breast.

"Have I told you how beautiful you are?"

"Am I?"

"More beautiful than any woman I've ever known."

I didn't believe that, but it was nice to hear.

His hand moved in my hair, sending shivers of delight down my spine. "Kathy, do you know how much I love you?" His voice, low and husky, moved over me like rough velvet.

"As much as I love you?"

"More." His clever hands moved over my willing flesh, teasing my desire back to life.

"That's impossible," I said, grinning as I felt the evidence of his own desire stirring against my belly.

"Shall I show you?" His voice was lower now, almost a growl. Hunger glowed faintly in his eyes.

Even as I murmured, "Yes, please," I couldn't help wondering how much blood I could afford to lose in one night.

"You needn't be afraid," he said, "I took only a small taste."

"You're reading my mind again," I said with mock severity.

A slow smile lit his eyes. "How do you think I knew how to please you so well?"

"In that case, I give you leave to read my mind for the rest of the night," I said.

And he did.

I woke feeling deliciously warm and achy in places where no man but Rafe had ever touched me. Smiling, I thought of the night past. We had made love all through the night, each time more thrilling, more satisfying, than the last.

Opening my eyes, I glanced at my watch, surprised to see that it was almost three o'clock in the afternoon. And then I blushed, thinking that maybe it wasn't so surprising at all. After all, we had made love until the early hours of the morning. Unlike human males, Rafe never tired, never needed to rest.

Taking a deep breath, I turned on my side to look at the man sleeping beside me. I wasn't sure what to expect. I had always heard that Vampires slept like the dead, but he didn't look dead. Far from it. Was he trapped in the daylight sleep? He had told me he could move around during the day, but maybe once he fell asleep, he couldn't wake until the sun went down. If I touched him, would he feel it? If I spoke his name, would he hear me?

My heart skipped a beat. The old adage said to let sleeping dogs lie. I wondered if the same was true for sleeping Vampires.

"I'm not asleep."

I punched him in the arm. "Stop that." His fingertips

skated down my bare arm, sending a familiar shiver down my spine.

He regarded me through heavy-lidded eyes. "You said it was all right last night."

"That was last night. This is today."

"And what are your plans for today, Mrs. Cordova?"

Mrs. Cordova. The words filled me with warmth and a sense of belonging I'd never known before. How could I have forgotten that we had exchanged vows last night? Vows that were, in my mind, just as binding as if they had been spoken in front of a minister in church? As far as I was concerned, I was now Mrs. Raphael Cordova. And then I frowned. What would Rafe's parents think? I'd never even met them. Would we stay in Oak Hollow? Would Rafe expect me to sell the bookstore?

"The shop!" I exclaimed, sitting up. "I should have opened hours ago." I wondered again if anyone had missed me, or even noticed that my store had been closed for a few days.

Rafe tugged me back down beside him, his arm slipping comfortably around my shoulders. "There's no need for you to work any longer."

"No?"

"No. I make more than enough to support you."

"Well, that's nice to know, but if I don't work, what will I do during the day?"

"Whatever you wish." His hand slid up and down my spine, and then he brushed a kiss across my cheek. "I need to rest a while."

"Okay. I think I'll go home and change my clothes and then go over to the store for a few hours."

"No. It's not safe for you to leave here."

He was right, of course. Why hadn't I thought of that?

No doubt Travis, Edna, Pearl, and their henchmen were frantically searching Oak Hollow from one end to the other looking for their escaped guinea pigs. It wouldn't do for word of their nefarious activities to become public knowledge. I was pretty sure the townspeople would be up in arms if they discovered Edna and Pearl's plan to dump their formula into the water supply. It would be even more dangerous for Jackson and the women if the Supernatural community got wind of their scheme.

As soon as that thought crossed my mind, I knew that Edna and Pearl's days were numbered, one way or the other.

"I'll take you home tonight so you can get whatever you need and bring it here," Rafe said. His voice sounded different, heavy somehow.

Last night, we hadn't talked about where we would live. I doubted Rafe would be happy at my place. It was too open to the sun, too easily breached. On the other hand, I didn't think I could be happy here, in his place, either. It was too dark, and while I understood the reason for it, I knew that, in time, it would leave me feeling depressed and claustrophobic.

I ran my fingertips over his chest. "How long will you sleep?"

"Until sundown."

"What's it like, when you're sleeping? Is it really like death?"

"I wouldn't know," he said with a wry grin. "Since I've never died. All I know is that it's different from mortal sleep."

"Different how?"

"Sleeping Vampires, except for the old ones, are helpless during the day, and they don't dream."

"So, what's it like for you?" I slid my hand over his biceps, admiring the latent strength beneath my palm. "If I touch you while you're sleeping, will you feel it?"

"Yes."

"And if I call your name, will you hear me?"

"I will always hear you."

I smiled at that. "Do you dream?"

His heavy-lidded gaze held mine. "Sometimes."

"What do Vampires dream about?" I ran my hand down his arm and over his abs.

"If you don't stop that," he said, his voice husky. "I'll show you what I dream about."

Warmth spread through me. If he hadn't been on the brink of oblivion, I would have made those dreams come true. As it was, I kissed him lightly. "Will it disturb you if I take a shower?"

"No." He smiled faintly. "Next time, perhaps I'll share it with you."

"I'd like that." The image of the two of us, soapy from head to foot, stirred something deep within me. I kissed him again, then went into the bathroom and closed the door.

For a moment, I stood there, my fingertips pressed to my lips as I remembered all that had happened between us the night before.

Smiling, I took a quick shower. Later, while drying off, I wished I had some clean clothes and a change of underwear. I wasn't happy with the thought of putting on my dirty clothes. I never wanted to wear them again. I pulled on a pair of Rafe's sweatpants and one of his T-shirts. Both were too big, of course, but they were clean, and they smelled of the man I loved.

I tiptoed out of the bedroom and went into the living

room where I found Cagin sitting on the sofa, his hands dangling between his knees.

He lifted one brow when he saw me.

"What?" I said.

"You slept with him." There was no censure in his voice; it was simply a statement of fact. "I wondered how long it would take."

He could have meant I slept beside Rafe during the night, but that wasn't what he meant and we both knew it. I felt my cheeks grow hot. I started to deny it when he lifted his hand.

"I can smell it on you," Cagin said.

I lifted my chin and squared my shoulders. "It's none of your business."

He shrugged.

"I don't suppose there's any food in the house," I remarked.

"There's coffee, orange juice, and donuts in the kitchen."

"Oh?"

"I went out early this morning."

"Do you think that was wise?"

Cagin made a dismissive gesture with his hand. "We've got to eat. The coffee's cold, but you can nuke it in the microwave."

"Thanks." Coffee and donuts weren't the most nutritious meal, but this morning they suited me just fine.

Going into the kitchen, I glanced around while I heated the coffee, thinking that the room was going to waste with nothing in it but a small refrigerator to keep an occasional bag of blood fresh and a microwave to warm it in. The thought made my stomach churn. I'd have to get used to his ways, I thought, and he'd have to get used to mine, which included buying a stove and a larger refrigerator, as well as a table and chairs.

I took the cup from the microwave, wishing that Cagin had thought to pick up a few packets of sugar. Plucking a buttermilk donut from the box on the counter, I returned to the living room.

"How's Susie?" Plopping down in one of the chairs, I set my cup on the coffee table, then took a bite of the donut.

A sigh rose from deep inside Cagin's chest. "Sleeping peacefully now."

"Was it . . . terrible? Watching her change?"

"Terrible?" The word seemed torn from his throat. "Terrible? Yeah, it was terrible. Damn near broke my heart to watch her."

"But she's all right?" I took a sip of the coffee. It was black and strong and bitter. I drank it anyway.

He nodded. "I owe Cordova a debt I can never repay."

"And she's all right with being a Vampire now?"

"She said she was glad to be alive, but she's worried about her kids."

That was understandable. She would have to find someone to look after them during the day now, someone to take them to school and pick them up, drive them to the dentist and Little League. How would she explain her sudden aversion to light, the fact that she didn't eat, or sleep at night?

"Tell me about you." I put the empty cup aside. "What's it like to be a shape-shifter? Do you like it?"

"What's it like to be human?" he asked. "Do you like it?"

"Touché."

"It's what I am, what I've always been. A leopard can't change his spots," he said, grinning, "or, in my case, his stripes."

"It's different than being a Werewolf, though, isn't it? I mean, you don't run around killing people, do you?"

He shrugged. "It's been known to happen, on occasion."

I had a sudden mental image of Rick McGee lying on the floor in a deserted house.

"So, how serious is it with you and the Vampire?"

"I don't know what you think of me," I said sharply, "but I don't sleep around."

"You're in love with him?"

"Yes, I'm afraid so."

"He drank from you last night. It wasn't the first time, was it?"

When I didn't answer, he shook his head in disgust. "How can you let him do that? It's disgusting."

I lifted a hand to my neck. "That's what I thought, too, until it happened to me." And then I frowned. "Susie's a Vampire now, remember? What if she wants to taste you? Are you going to refuse?"

"Damn right," he said, but I heard the hesitation in his voice and knew he was thinking about it, even if he wouldn't admit it.

"It's quite wonderful."

He looked at me as if I had lost my mind. "He's brainwashed you, hasn't he?"

"No, although I guess he could if he wanted to."

Cagin grunted softly. "Life sure as hell gets complicated sometimes, doesn't it?" he muttered, and I knew he wasn't just talking about himself and Susie.

Complicated, I thought. That had to be the understatement of the century.

"I'm still hungry," he said. "What do you say we order a pizza? With lots of garlic?"

I grinned, happy to see that his good mood had been restored.

We spent the next hour watching TV and eating pizza, and then we played cards with a deck I found while snooping in the kitchen drawers.

"So," I asked during a lull in the conversation, "what are you and Susie going to do now?"

"I asked her to marry me."

"Oh?"

"Yeah. She said she'd think about it." He rubbed his palm against his thigh. "I probably spoke too soon. Hell, I killed her husband. She's never going to forget that, no matter how long she thinks about it."

"You saved her life," I reminded him. "Twice." Once when he'd saved her from Rick, and again last night, when he had insisted that Rafe bring her across.

"I guess it's all in how you look at it," he muttered.

"She cares for you. Anyone can see that."

"She's the first woman I've ever loved." His voice was so low, I could scarcely hear it. "And she'll be the last."

The look in his eyes and the fervent tone of his voice touched a chord deep inside me.

We played another hand of cards, and then Cagin pushed away from the table and stood. "I'm going to go look in on her."

"All right." I went to the room's single window and drew back the heavy drapes. Through the thick iron bars, I could see that the sun had gone down. Rafe had said he would rise at sundown. Was he awake? Maybe waiting for me to join him in bed?

While I was deciding what to do, Cagin returned to the living room. "She's gone."

"Gone?" I shook my head. "How can that be? We'd have seen her leave."

"Would we?"

I hurried down the hallway to Rafe's bedroom. Opening the door, I peered inside. The sheets were rumpled, but the bed was empty.

I glanced over my shoulder at Cagin, who was standing in the doorway behind me. "Where can they be?"

Chapter Twenty-Six

Susie stared at the young man who stood, unmoving, in front of her, then glanced at Rafe. "I don't think I can do this."

"Sure you can."

She looked back at the man that Rafe had mesmerized, her expression doubtful.

"Susie, stop thinking like a mortal. You're a Vampire now, and you need to feed. I know you can feel the hunger inside you. Surrender to it, to what you are."

"You want me to drink his blood?"

"It's what you're craving," Rafe said patiently. "It's the only thing that will relieve the pain. And it's natural for you now. Sweet, like nothing else."

She made a face. "Yuck!"

"Trust me on this. Here, this will make it easier." Grasping the man's shoulders, Rafe scraped his fangs along the side of the man's neck. A thin ribbon of bright red oozed from the shallow incision. The coppery scent of blood rose in the air.

Drawn by the scent, Susie took a step forward, her

nostrils flaring. Slowly, her eyes took on a faint red glow. Her lips parted, and Rafe saw her fangs, sharp and white and ready.

"That's it," he said. "Take him in your arms, gently now. You don't want to hurt him."

A harsh laugh rose in her throat. "Why are you worrying about my hurting him? I'm going to kill him."

"No, you don't have to kill."

"I don't? But I thought . . . isn't that what Vampires do?"

"Not all of us. Whether you kill him or not is up to you."

"What if I can't stop myself?"

"That's why I'm here."

With a soft cry of resignation, Susie wrapped her arms around the man and buried her fangs in his neck. His head lolled back against her arm, his body quivering, but he made no sound, offered no protest, no cry of pain.

Rafe stood nearby, his own hunger rising as he watched Susie feed. When he judged she had taken enough, he put his hand on her arm and drew her away.

She turned on him with a feral hiss, her eyes blazing.

"No more," Rafe said. "If you're still hungry, we'll find someone else."

She stared at him, her gaze fixed on his throat.

"Vampires don't feed on Vampires," Rafe said, his voice sharp. "They take a drink now and then, but never more than that."

Rafe spoke a few words to the man, erasing the memory of what had happened from his mind, and then sent him on his way.

Susie stared after him. Gradually, the heat faded from

her eyes as her fangs retracted. "I have a lot to learn, don't I?"

"It'll come to you, bit by bit. Or," he said, grinning, "bite by bite. How do you feel?"

"Wonderful! Like I could fly."

Rafe grinned. "You will, in time."

"What about my kids? Will they be safe around me? And what about my parents, my friends? How will I explain my sudden aversion to food and the fact that I can't go out during the day and . . ." Her shoulders slumped in defeat. "Maybe you should have just let me die."

"Stop it. You've got a lot to live for. And, unless I miss my guess, Cagin will be right there to help you."

Her expression softened at the mention of Cagin's name. "He asked me to marry him."

"I'm not surprised."

"How can I? How can I trust myself to marry anyone, or trust anyone I marry?"

"Do you love him?"

"I don't know. I think so, but . . ." She shook her head. "He killed Rick, and even though he did it to save my life . . . how can I live with the man who killed the father of my children?"

"How can you live without him?"

"I don't know."

Rafe put his arm around Susie's shoulders and gave her a squeeze. "It'll all work out, one way or the other. Now, do you want to go back to my place, or are you still hungry?"

She licked her lips, her eyes glowing. "I want some more."

Chapter Twenty-Seven

I was watching the news, or pretending to, when Rafe and Susie entered the room. I hadn't heard them come in and couldn't hide my surprise at seeing them, nor could I stop staring at Susie. She had been a pretty young woman before, but now she was radiant. Her skin seemed to glow, her eyes looked brighter, her hair appeared thicker and more lustrous. Apparently, becoming a Vampire was better than a face-lift or a day at the spa. Of course, there were a few trade-offs, like giving up food and sunshine for blood and moonlight.

Cagin sprang to his feet when he saw her. "Where the hell have you been?"

She looked at Rafe, as though for reassurance.

"We've been hunting," Rafe said calmly. He glanced around the room, making me wish I had cleared the empty pizza box and plastic coffee cups from the coffee table.

Eyes narrowed, Cagin looked at Susie as if he had never seen her before, and then he sighed. "I shouldn't have yelled at you like that, but, dammit, didn't you think I'd be worried when I went in to check on you and you were gone? For all I knew, those crazy hunters had you again."

"I'm sorry," she murmured, moving closer to Rafe. "I didn't think about that."

"All right, everybody just calm down," Rafe said. "If anyone's to blame, it's me. I thought it would be best for all concerned if Susie went hunting with me the first time."

"So," Cagin said, obviously ill at ease with the idea of his lady love hunting for prey, "how was it?"

Susie smiled up at Rafe. "Not as bad as I thought it would be. Rafe was very kind and patient with me."

Cagin glared at Rafe. "Is that right?"

"Back off, Cagin," Rafe said, bristling. "She needed someone to teach her what to do. If I didn't do it, who would? You?"

Cagin clenched his hands at his sides.

For a minute, I thought the two of them were going to fight again.

"Joe, please don't be angry," Susie said, moving to his side. "Please don't make this any more difficult than it already is."

Cagin muttered an oath, but the anger washed out of his eyes. "I'm sorry." He glanced at Rafe and then at me. "If you two will excuse us, I think Susie and I need to talk."

Rafe inclined his head, and Cagin and Susie left the room.

"Where did you go?" I asked. "What happened?"

"Just what I said. I took her hunting, just as my father once took me."

"You're not her father."

"That's where you're wrong. She's my fledgling, and I'm her sire. She belongs to me now, in a way she'll never belong to Cagin."

"I don't think I like the sound of that. In fact, I'm sure of it."

Rafe smiled indulgently as he sat beside me on the sofa. "We're not bound the way you and I are bound," he assured me. "No one else will ever share what we have." His knuckles slid over my cheek. "Don't you know that?"

When he looked at me like that, how could I doubt him?

"So, she's going to be all right, then?"

"I think so."

"She looks different. Does becoming a Vampire affect everyone that way?"

He nodded.

"Too bad you can't bottle it," I muttered. "You could make a fortune."

"You're angry."

I tossed a lock of hair over my shoulder. "Why should I be angry?"

"Jealous, then."

I would have denied it, but what was the point? He could read the truth in my mind. I blew out a sigh, annoyed with myself for being jealous of a Vampire, no matter how pretty she was. So what if she would never grow old, never get sick? She would never enjoy a good meal again, never take her children to the park on a sunny day, never share her whole life with her sons, or with the man she loved. Shape-shifters lived longer than humans, but not as long as Werewolves or Vampires. Susie, it seemed, was destined to live a long life as one creature or the other. Barring accidents, she might outlive Cagin.

"Kathy?"

I didn't want to talk about Susie anymore, didn't want to delve too deeply into the reason for my jealousy, so I changed the subject. "What do you suppose Edna and Pearl are up to?"

"I don't know," Rafe said, his voice brittle, "but I intend to find out."

"How are you going to do that?"

"I'm going after them, back to the lab, if necessary."

"Are you crazy?"

"Don't worry. They won't take me unaware this time."

"But . . ."

"Someone has to stop them," he said. "If I don't do it, who will?"

"What about Mara?"

"Mara's not here."

"What about Clive? Or . . ."

He silenced me by pulling me into his arms and kissing me.

Mumbling, "You don't fight fair," I closed my eyes and lost myself in his touch.

I forgot everything else until I heard Cagin clear his throat.

"What do you want?" Rafe asked gruffly.

"We need to decide what to do. Susie and I can't stay here forever."

Rafe kissed the tip of my nose, then drew me against his side. "I'm going after Edna and the others."

"When?"

"Later tonight."

"I'll go with you," Cagin said.

"Me, too," Susie said.

Rafe nodded. "We'll wait until after midnight."

"Where do you think they'll be?" Cagin asked. He sat in one of the chairs, and Susie sat in the one across from him.

"No telling. We'll start at Edna's place. If she's not there, we'll assume they're out at the lab."

"And if they aren't there?" Susie asked.

"Then they're probably out looking for us," Rafe said.

"Maybe we should bait a trap and let them come to us," Cagin suggested. "Take them on our turf, on our terms."

Rafe frowned. "What do you have in mind?"

"We could let the girls go to Kathy's house. Sooner or later, one of the hunters will come looking for them there, and when they do, we'll be waiting."

Rafe shook his head. "Forget it. I'm not using Kathy for bait."

"I think it's a good idea," Susie said. "Don't you think so, Kathy?"

"I guess so."

Rafe glared at me. "I said forget it."

"Susie will be with me," I argued. "She's a Vampire now. Doesn't she have the same powers that you do?"

"More or less," Rafe admitted grudgingly.

"No matter what we decide to do, I need a change of clothing," Susie declared. "I can't stand my own smell." She looked at Cagin and wrinkled her nose. "You could do with a change of clothes, too."

"Dammit," Rafe said, "we've got more important things to worry about than that."

"Easy for you to say," I remarked, "since you're wearing clean clothes! Besides, you said you'd take me home tonight."

A muscle worked in his jaw.

"Just let Susie and me go home and get some clean clothes and whatever else we need. Then we can stay at my house for a while and see if anyone shows up. If nothing happens by say, 2:00 A.M., we'll come back here and regroup."

"Sounds like a plan to me," Cagin said.

Rafe shook his head. "I don't like it."

I laid my hand on his arm. "I know you don't. But I'm in this, too, and whatever plan you come up with, I intend to be a part of it."

"Stubborn woman," he muttered, not for the first time. "Come on, let's go."

We went to Susie's house first. She packed a bag, and then Rafe drove us to my place.

"We'll be nearby," he said. "I've taken your blood, Kathy, and Susie's, too. If anything happens in there, I'll know it as soon as you do."

"I'm not worried," I said.

"No?"

"All right, maybe a little." I slid my arms around his waist. "I love you."

"I know."

"Reading my mind again?"

He shook his head. "I can see it in your eyes." Drawing me closer, he kissed me, and then whispered, "I can't wait to get you alone."

His words and the husky tone of his voice sent a shiver of anticipation down my spine.

He kissed me again and then headed for the door. Cagin kissed Susie on the cheek, then followed Rafe out of the house.

The sound of the door closing behind them echoed in my mind. *Rats in a trap,* I thought as I locked the door, that's what we were, and then I told myself I had nothing to worry about. I had a Vampire in the house with me, another one outside, along with a Were-tiger. If the three of them couldn't protect me, no one could.

I looked at Susie. "So," I asked, "do you want to wash up first, or should I?"

"Go ahead," she said, "it's your house, after all."

"All right. Make yourself at home."

I went into the bathroom, turned on the water in the tub, set the controls for hot water, and added lavender bubble bath. While waiting for the tub to fill, I went into the bedroom and packed a bag—nothing fancy, just jeans, T-shirts, and sweaters. I thought fleetingly of the bookstore. I hadn't been there in days, but that didn't seem important now.

Returning to the bathroom, I undressed and stepped into the tub, reveling in the blessedly warm water. I soaked for a good fifteen minutes, then, mindful that Susie was waiting, I scrubbed from head to foot and got out of the tub. Wrapped in a towel, I dried my hair and then, feeling 110 percent better, I pulled on a pair of navy blue-and-white-striped pajama bottoms and a navy blue T-shirt and went into the living room.

"Nothing like a hot bath," I said, taking a seat on the sofa.

Susie looked up from the magazine she had been thumbing through. "Finished so soon?"

"I figured you were as anxious to wash off the smell of the lab as I was. I'll fix us some coffee while you . . . oh, sorry."

Susie smiled uncertainly; then, picking up her bag, she left the room.

I stared after her. If I had to choose between being a Vampire or a Werewolf, I'd pick Werewolf, hands down. They might not have all the Supernatural powers Vampires had, they might not live as long, but at least they could eat regular food and enjoy a cup of hot coffee.

I wandered through the house while I waited for the coffee to heat. I'd probably have to close the bookstore and leave town. The thought saddened me. I liked it here, but I didn't see how we could stay after all that had happened.

I had started a fire in the fireplace and was sipping a second cup of coffee when Susie padded into the room. She wore a long pink robe over a pink and white night-gown, and a pair of fuzzy pink slippers. Her dark curly hair framed her face. She looked more like a pixie than a Vampire.

Her gaze slid away from mine as she curled up in one of the chairs. She seemed uneasy in my presence. Was it because she was uncomfortable with her new state of being, or because I was now prey?

Unnerved by her silence, I turned on the TV and began surfing through the channels. I wasn't really paying attention until I saw Susie's picture pop up on Oak Hollow's community station.

"That's me!" she exclaimed. "What's going on?"

"I don't know," I said, startled to see my own photograph and Cagin's appear beside Susie's, along with photos of the other men and women Edna and Pearl had kidnapped. We were all there, except for Rafe and the other Vampires, of course, since they didn't photograph.

I leaned forward as the reporter, who looked extremely serious, stared into the camera and said, in a somber tone, "If you have any information regarding the whereabouts of any of these people, please contact the Oak Hollow Police Department immediately. The men and women in question are believed to have been inadvertently exposed to a rare and deadly virus that is extremely contagious. Symptoms include paranoia and delusions. Do not attempt to intercept these people yourself as they are considered armed and dangerous. Again, call the police if you have any information. In other local news . . ."

"I don't believe it!" Susie exclaimed. "Edna and Pearl have all the nerve in the world."

"We're going to have to leave town," I said, thinking the decision had been taken out of our hands. "After tonight, we won't be safe anywhere in Oak Hollow, and probably not in River's Edge."

"We'll have to tell the guys when they get here," Susie said. "They'll know what to do."

"I hope so." I quickly flipped through the other news channels. "Let's hope it's only been reported on the local station."

We stared at each other a moment.

I sipped my coffee. If Edna and Pearl managed to get our photographs broadcast on the major news channels, we wouldn't be safe anywhere.

After a moment, Susie ran her fingers through her hair, then folded her hands in her lap. "Kathy . . ."

"What?"

"Are we . . . are we still friends?"

"Of course," I said, frowning. "Why wouldn't we be?"

"Because of what I was, what I am. . . ."

"Susie, I'm in love with a Vampire. Why would I object to having one for a friend?"

She laughed, but there was no humor in it. "I can't believe my bad luck. Just when I tell myself things can't get any worse, they do! How am I going to raise my children?" A sob rose in her throat; a single red tear slid down her cheek.

That, more than anything else, seemed to emphasize the change in her.

"You're still alive," I said. "I'd call that lucky."

"Yeah, right."

"Cagin loves you."

"He's just another complication." Susie pulled a tissue from the pocket of her bathrobe and blew her nose. "He asked me to marry him. Did he tell you that? How can I? He killed my husband. Oh, I know, Rick was about to kill me, but . . ." She wiped the tear from her cheek with a corner of the tissue. "I just don't know what to do anymore. How could I have lived with Rick for so many years and never known what kind of man he was? Never suspected he was a hunter? If he hid that from me, I can't help but wonder what else he was hiding. My mother always said I was too trusting. I guess she was right." Another tear slid down her cheek, and she wiped it away. "I miss my sons. They must think I've abandoned them."

"You can call them tomorrow night," I said. "I'm sure they're anxious to hear from you."

She sighed heavily. "What can I say? Even if they were old enough to understand, I couldn't tell them the truth about what happened to their father, or about anything else, for that matter."

"You can tell them you love them."

"Yes," Susie said, very quietly. "I can tell them that." She toyed with the sash on her bathrobe. "Maybe I should give them up and let my mother raise them."

"Susie . . ."

"Maybe they'd be better off without me."

"Stop that! Rafe's grandparents were both Vampires, but they raised his mother. I'm not saying it was easy. They had to hire nannies to look after her during the day, but they managed, and she turned out just fine. If they could do it, so can you."

"You're a good friend, Kathy. You always say just what I need to hear."

"Can I ask you something? You don't have to tell me if you don't want to."

"You want to know what it's like, being a Vampire."

"How did you know that?" Geez, I hoped she couldn't read my mind, too. It was bad enough knowing that Rafe could do it.

"It's what I'd want to know, if I were in your place."

"So, what's it like?"

She ran a hand through her hair again, then looked at her fingernails, as if seeing them for the first time. "I haven't been one very long, you know, but, well, so far, it's quite amazing. I think I'm going to like it."

It wasn't the answer I had expected. Oh, I knew Rafe

was happy being a Vampire, but he wasn't like other Vampires. He hadn't sought it out; no one had brought him across. He had been born to it, grown up with a Vampire father and Vampire grandparents, but Susie . . . I shook my head. "Are you serious?"

"You can't imagine what it's like." She leaned forward, her words coming quickly now. "Everything looks the same, yet different. Your T-shirt, for instance, I can see every individual thread. Colors are brighter, sounds are clearer. I don't need my contacts any more," she said, smiling. "I can see better and farther than I ever could. I can hear things I never did before. The flutter of a moth's wings, the whisper of the wind in the trees, the ticking of a clock from somewhere upstairs . . . the beating of your heart."

Her words made that heart beat a little faster. She still looked like Susie, but she was a Vampire now. I needed to remember that.

"You don't have to be afraid of me," Susie said, and I heard the hurt in her voice, the disappointment.

"I'm sorry."

"It's all right. I guess I can't blame you."

"What was it like, hunting with Rafe?" Even as I asked the question, I couldn't stifle a twinge of jealousy because Susie had shared a part of Rafe's life that I never would.

"So much different than I thought it would be. I didn't think I could do it, drink blood, but he made it easy."

"Wasn't it disgusting?"

Her gaze slid away from mine. "It should have been, but it wasn't. It was . . . pleasant."

Pleasant? Pleasant! I didn't know what to say to that.

A day at the beach was pleasant. Spending time with your loved ones was pleasant. Getting a full-body massage was pleasant. But drinking blood? No way!

Silence fell between us. It wouldn't have bothered me before, but it bothered me now. I wondered what Susie was thinking, couldn't help being somewhat amazed that she had adjusted so quickly to being a Vampire when she'd had so much trouble being a Werewolf. The absurdity of it all made me want to laugh and cry at the same time. Susie's life would never be the same again; but then, neither would mine now that I had pledged my life and my love to Rafe.

"At least the four of us can still be friends," I said, thinking aloud. After all, I didn't really have any other friends in town, certainly none Rafe and I could share an evening with.

"That's true, isn't it?" Susie remarked with a winsome smile. "I won't have to pretend with you, or make excuses about why we can't go to lunch."

I grinned at her. "Right." I suddenly felt a lot better. Maybe everything would work out after all.

But later that night, curled up on the sofa, hovering on the brink of sleep, I wondered if I had made the right choice in deciding to stay with Rafe. I loved him, loved everything about him, but now tiny doubts insinuated themselves into my thoughts. In choosing to stay with Rafe, I had distanced myself from my family. I would never have children or grandchildren, never cook a big Christmas dinner for my husband and kids, and while I didn't want kids right now, I had hoped to have one or two in the future. After all, I was only twenty-three years old. I still had a few good years left in me. . . .

I shook off my doubts. I had made my choice, and I would make the same one again.

Yawning, I checked the time. It was almost two. "The guys will be here any minute," I said, switching off the TV.

"I can't decide if I'm relieved or disappointed that nothing happened," Susie said. "I sort of expected Edna and company to show up any minute."

"I know what you mean. Maybe we should just leave town, now, tonight."

"Don't you think they'd come after us?"

"I don't know. Actually, I'm surprised *they* didn't leave town. We should have gone to the police and pressed charges." Funny, none of us had thought of it earlier.

"Do you think they would have believed us?"

I shrugged. The police weren't known for being sympathetic to the Supernatural community, or to those who associated with them. "It doesn't matter now."

"Edna and Pearl must have some powerful friends somewhere," Susie said thoughtfully. "I mean, how else did they get our pictures on the news? For that matter, how did they get our pictures, period?"

"Beats me. They must have taken them while we were drugged." Now that I thought about it, we'd all looked sort of spaced-out in the photos. Hopefully, the national news media wouldn't pick up the story. "I've been wondering about something else, too."

"What's that?"

"How did two elderly women who aren't doctors convince the Oak Hollow police chief that we were infected with some mysterious virus?"

"Maybe the police are in on it, too."

Now there was a scary thought. "You might be right," I said, warming to idea. "Being a police officer would be the perfect cover for a hunter. The cops can come and go pretty much as they please, poke into other people's business, snoop around at any hour of the day or night without arousing suspicion, lock up anyone they want for twenty-four hours without a warrant."

Susie nodded in agreement and then, for no reason that I could see, she sat up straighter, her body tensing as she stared at the front door.

"What is it?" I asked. "Are the guys here?"

"No." She stood up, and I saw her eyes begin to change.

I felt a whisper of power flow through the room as Susie's eyes took on a reddish glow.

"It's Travis Jackson," she said, "and he's not alone."

Chapter Twenty-Eight

A sudden rush of adrenaline had me jumping to my feet. This was the visit we had been waiting for, but now that it was here, I suddenly found myself wishing I was anywhere else. I had no Supernatural powers at my command, no weapons with which to protect myself. Why hadn't I bought a gun? But then, I had never thought I would need to defend myself against my own kind. I remembered telling Rafe earlier that I had Susie to protect me, but looking at her now, even with her eyes red and glowing, she didn't seem like she would be much help. She was shorter than I was and slender as a willow. And she had been a Vampire only a couple of days. Maybe that didn't make any difference; maybe Vampires came equipped with all their powers immediately on being turned. And maybe they didn't. Why hadn't I asked Rafe about that sooner?

I froze as someone knocked on the door. There was no point in pretending we weren't home. The lights were on, smoke would be visible rising from the chimney.

"I'll get it." Susie was moving toward the door as she spoke.

My gaze darted around the room as I searched for a weapon. When this was over, if I survived, I was buying a gun! Since I didn't have one now, I grabbed the fireplace poker and held it behind my back just as Susie opened the door.

"Susie." Jackson's voice was filled with wry amusement. "I didn't expect to find you here, but it saves us a trip, doesn't it?"

"What do you want, Travis?" Susie asked.

"I think you know." He looked at her a moment, his eyes narrowing. "Vampire?" he murmured, looking momentarily confused.

"We're not going back," she said. "Your serum doesn't work."

"That's why we need to try again." His hand delved into his jacket pocket and reappeared with a small glass vial. "I don't want to hurt you."

"Really? Is that why you kidnapped me, locked me in a cage, and stuck a needle in my arm?"

From where I stood, I could see his jaw tighten. "Let's do this the easy way, shall we?" he asked, and threw the contents of the bottle into her face.

Susie reeled backward, an inhuman shriek of agony hissing from her throat. I watched in horror as the skin on her face and neck began to blister. *Holy water,* I thought.

The two men behind Travis lunged forward. Grabbing Susie by the arms, they wrestled her to the ground, flipped her onto her stomach, and cuffed her hands behind her back.

Shouting, "Leave her alone!" I lifted the poker and

slammed it across the back of the nearest man as hard as I could.

He let out a roar of pain as he rolled away from Susie.

I was lifting the poker to hit the other man when Travis came up behind me. He jerked the poker from my grasp, then backhanded me across the face. I reeled backward, my cheek burning from the force of his blow, my eyes watering.

I heard someone let out a shriek filled with pain and terror. I blinked to clear my vision, and when I looked again, I saw one of the men who had been holding Susie sprawled on his back on the floor, a bloody hole where his throat had been. The man I had hit was frantically trying to crawl toward the front door, but the angry Were-tiger biting his leg wouldn't let go.

Travis Jackson stood with his back against the far wall, his eyes wide with fear as he stared at Rafe.

I stared at him, too. This was Rafe, my Rafe, I told myself, but it was hard to believe. Clad in black from head to foot, his eyes blazing like the fires of hell, he looked like the angel of death come to call.

Travis shook his head as Rafe's hand closed around his throat. "No," he gasped. "Please, no."

"Only brave when you're on the winning side?" Rafe's voice was as cold and unforgiving as the grave. "You'll never hurt me or mine again."

All the color drained from Travis Jackson's face. "Please." His voice was little more than a hoarse whimper. A dark stain spread over the front of his trousers, filling the air with the strong scent of urine as he begged for his life. "Please."

I must have made a noise of some kind, because Rafe turned his head to look at me, his eyes glittering. He was every inch a Vampire now, more powerful and frightening than I had ever seen him.

I looked at him, my heart pounding. *Don't do this.* The words rose in my mind. *Please don't do this.* I couldn't bear the thought of watching Rafe kill Travis Jackson. I knew Rafe wanted the man dead, and maybe Jackson deserved to die for what he'd done, but not like this.

Rafe's hand tightened around Travis Jackson's throat. I could feel Rafe's struggle as he fought down the urge to kill Jackson. Because of the blood bond between us, I knew what Rafe was thinking, feeling. The desire for vengeance, the lust for blood, and the urge to surrender to what he was burned strong within him.

And yet, for my sake, he fought it back. I saw it in the fading red glow in his eyes and in the gradual relaxing of his grip on Jackson's throat, though he didn't release him completely.

"Jackson, look at me."

Travis lifted his fearful gaze to meet Rafe's.

"You don't deserve it, but I'm going to let you live." Rafe's gaze locked with Jackson's. "You're going to go back to Texas. You're going to forget everything you ever knew about hunting, about Supernatural creatures, and about the formula your grandmother concocted. No matter what anyone says to you, you will never remember any of this. To try to do so will cause you unbearable pain. You will forget everyone in this room, everyone that was in the lab. When you leave here, you will forget this place. You will go home and destroy any and all records and photographs that have anything to do with the Supernatural community, and then you will destroy any and all records, correspondence, and photos held by

Edna or your grandmother or the school in Texas. Do you understand?"

Travis nodded woodenly. "Yes, master."

"If anyone mentions the word Vampire or Werewolf to you, it will make you violently ill and you will refuse to discuss it. If you ever attempt to hunt me or my kind again, I will find you, and I will kill you. Do you understand?"

Travis nodded again. "Yes, master."

Rafe's eyes narrowed to mere slits. His power flowed through the room, making it hard to breathe. It whispered over my skin and caused the short hairs to prickle on my nape.

Travis's body tensed, then began to tremble. All the color drained from his face as he pressed the heels of his hands to his temples. "Stop," he gasped. "Please."

"Remember the pain," Rafe said, his voice harsh, "And do not betray me or mine again. Now get the hell out of here."

Moving like some kind of movie zombie, Travis left the room, one hand still pressed to the side of his head.

Only then did I look at Susie. Cagin had freed her hands and was wiping her face with a washcloth. She moaned softly every time he touched her, and I recalled Rafe telling me that holy water burned Vampire flesh like hellfire. The left side of her face was raw and red, the right side didn't look quite so bad. Rafe's face had healed in a remarkably short time, but he had been a Vampire longer than Susie. I wondered if she would heal as fast as he did.

I glanced around the room. The bodies of the two men Cagin had savaged were nowhere to be seen. They couldn't have just disappeared, which made me think

Cagin must have dragged them outside while my attention was focused on Rafe and Travis. Were they both dead? What had he done with the bodies?

"Kathy."

I looked at Rafe, relieved to see that he was my Rafe again.

"We need to get out of here," he said.

"You got that right," Cagin agreed. "Let's go."

I didn't argue.

I pulled a long sweater coat on over my pajamas, grabbed my keys and my handbag. Rafe picked up my suitcase, and we followed Susie and Cagin out the door. Rafe waited while I locked up, and then we got into Rafe's car, which was parked out front.

I glanced out the window as we pulled away from my house, wondering if I would ever see it again.

"Drop us off at my place," Cagin said when Rafe pulled away from the curb.

"Do you think that's wise?"

"We're not staying," Cagin said. "I just need to pick up a few things."

I glanced over my shoulder. "Where are you going?"

"I'm not sure," Cagin replied. "Just somewhere the hell away from here until Susie has a handle on things. Then we'll come back and get her kids and find a new place to live."

I looked at Susie. She sat very still, as if the slightest movement caused her pain. Fine white lines bracketed her mouth. The burns on her cheeks and down the left side of her neck looked raw and red, as if someone had tried to scrape away her skin with a dull knife. I hoped she would heal as quickly as Rafe.

"I'll miss you," I said.

"I'll miss you, too." She delved into her handbag and came up with a pen and a small notebook. She tore out a page. "This is my cell number, and my e-mail address." She quickly wrote them down and handed me the paper. "Let's keep in touch."

I tore off the bottom of the page she gave me and wrote down my cell number and e-mail and passed it back to her.

A few minutes later, Rafe pulled up in front of Cagin's house.

"Thanks for the ride and everything," Cagin said.

"Yes," Susie said, "thank you so much."

"Watch your backs," Rafe said. "Don't trust anybody."

With a nod, Cagin opened the door and got out of the car, Susie's bags tucked under his arm.

"Be careful, both of you," Susie called before following Cagin into the house.

I looked at Rafe. "Do you think they'll be all right?"

"I'd lay odds on it." Reaching over, he gave my hand a reassuring squeeze.

"Do you think we'll be all right?"

He slid a glance in my direction before putting the car in gear. "Don't you doubt it for a minute."

With a sigh, I rested my head against the back of the seat and closed my eyes. Hard to believe I had moved to Oak Hollow for some peace and quiet. I sure hadn't had much of it.

After a time, I sat up. We should have been back at Rafe's by now. A look out the window showed we were on a narrow two-lane road.

"Where are we?" I asked. "Where are we going?"

"A place I know where we can spend the rest of the night."

"There isn't much night left."

"We'll be there before dawn."

"Good thing," I muttered. If there was one thing I didn't want, it was to watch Rafe go up in flames. "Do Vampires really go up in smoke if the sun touches them?"

"Yeah."

"Have you ever . . . never mind."

"Seen one?" A muscle clenched in his jaw. "Just once."

"Was it someone you knew?"

He nodded.

"A friend of yours?"

He shrugged. "More of an acquaintance."

"What happened? Was it an accident?"

"No, Thor wanted to die. He was an old Vampire. One night he told me he was tired of existing, tired of . . . of everything. In the morning, he walked out into the sunlight. I couldn't stop him, couldn't do anything but watch. . . ."

I shuddered at the image that rose in my mind. "What a horrible way to die."

"It was quick, like flash paper. One minute he was there, the next he was gone."

I couldn't imagine such a thing. And even if it was quick, it must have hurt.

Rafe spoke to the car's computer, telling it where to go, and then he drew me into his arms. Utterly weary, I rested my head on his shoulder and slept.

The slowing of the car roused me. Feeling as though I had been asleep for hours, I lifted my head, looked out the window, and frowned. We were in the middle of nowhere. A tall mountain thick with trees and brush rose up on our left.

"Where are we?" I glanced at Rafe, and in spite of myself, felt a little frisson of fear slide down my spine. It was foolish to be afraid. I knew he would never hurt me and yet . . .

"You'll see." He grabbed a large canvas bag out of the backseat, then got out of the car.

I waited, my heart pounding, while he came around to open my door. Taking my hand, Rafe started walking toward the mountain.

"Where are we going?" I asked, unable to disguise the tremor of unease in my voice.

"It's a surprise."

I hoped it was going to be a pleasant one.

As we drew closer to the mountain, I saw the opening to a cave. When I tried to hang back, Rafe tugged on my hand. All I could do was follow as he moved unerringly into the darkness.

"There aren't any bats in here, are there?" I asked, and my voice echoed off the walls. "Or bears?"

"No."

Gradually, the cave grew brighter, though no light was visible, and then, as the cave grew taller and wider, I saw a large flat area covered in dun-colored sand. Several warm, furry blankets were spread on the ground. Dozen of candles in all shapes, sizes, and colors sat on a narrow earthen shelf cut into the cave wall. I guessed that Rafe had lit them with the power of his mind.

He dropped the bag he was carrying on a corner of one of the blankets.

"What have you got in there?" I asked, my imagination working overtime.

"Food," he said with a grin. "I can't have my bride going hungry."

Bride. Warmth spread through me. With all that had happened in the last few days, the fact that I had pledged my heart and soul to Rafe hadn't been uppermost in my mind.

I glanced at our surroundings. "I never thought I'd spend my honeymoon in a cave."

"It's not where you are," he murmured with a roguish grin, "it's who you're with."

"How did you ever find this place?"

"When I first moved to Oak Hollow, I did a lot of exploring to pass the time. One night I stayed out too long. I was about to bury myself in the earth when I saw the cave. I spent the day in here. I came back whenever I needed to be alone, away from the temptation of too many beating hearts. And no," he said, reading my thoughts, "I've never brought anyone else here. Only you."

And so saying, he took me by the hand again and led me deeper into the cavern. The walls grew closer together as we left the light behind. I thought I heard the sound of falling water, and then, abruptly, the cave grew wider again, and I saw a small waterfall that spilled into a placid blue pool. A profusion of night-blooming flowers and lacy ferns grew around the edge of the pool. Looking up, I saw that there was an opening overhead, revealing a patch of indigo sky dotted with stars.

"It's beautiful," I murmured, enchanted by the fairy-like wonder of the place.

"Feel like a swim?" Rafe asked.

I glanced dubiously at the pool. "Isn't it a little cold for that?" I asked, but Rafe was already undressing.

A familiar excitement unfurled deep within me as more and more of his body was revealed to my gaze. Had there ever been a man with shoulders that wide, a chest so irresistibly touchable, a belly so hard and flat and muscular? My cheeks warmed as he stepped out of a pair of black briefs and stood fully naked before me.

He flashed a knowing grin and then dove into the pool. He swam to the other side and back, then, treading water in the middle of the pool, he lifted a hand, beckoning me to join him.

At his look, heat flooded my body. A chilly dip to cool my heated flesh suddenly sounded very inviting. Besides, how could I resist a chance to be in his arms?

Acutely aware that Rafe was watching my every move, and feeling suddenly daring, I undressed as slowly and provocatively as I knew how. I had never done anything like it before, had never dreamed of such a thing, but now, with Rafe watching, it came as naturally as breathing. I only wished I was wearing something a little sexier than a pair of blue and white pajama bottoms, a T-shirt, plain white bikini panties, and fuzzy blue slippers. But if the look in Rafe's eyes was any indication, he didn't seem to mind.

Naked, I stood poised on the edge of the pool, took a deep breath, and dove in.

Expecting to plunge into cold water, I was pleased to find it was bathtub warm.

When I came up, Rafe's arms enfolded me. What a wondrous feeling, to feel his body next to mine, the sensuous slide of wet skin against wet skin.

With one arm wrapped around my waist, he kept me afloat easily. His free hand played over my body while he rained kisses on my cheeks, my brow, my chin, the tip of my nose. I tilted my head back, affording myself a view of the stars overhead while granting Rafe access to my throat. I shivered with anticipation at the feel of his tongue against my skin, tangled my fingers in his long hair at the touch of his fangs.

Pleasure shot through me from head to foot. Weightless, buoyant, I closed my eyes and gave myself over to the myriad sensations his kisses aroused.

"I want you." His voice rumbled in my ear, deep and husky with desire.

I looked at him through heavy-lidded eyes. "Do you?"

He growled low in his throat. "Don't tease me, woman."

"How much do you want me?"

He pressed his body against mine, letting me feel his erection.

"Ohhh," I purred. "That much?"

He growled again, lower, deeper. "Do you know what happens when you tease a Vampire?"

"No," I said, stifling a grin. "What happens?"

"This." He carried me out of the pool and into the cave, showering me with kisses every step of the way.

When we reached the blankets, he sat down, holding me so that my legs straddled his thighs and then, very slowly, he reclined, drawing me down with him so that my body covered his.

He stroked my cheek, ran his fingertips over my lips. "You're beautiful," he murmured.

"So are you." His body was firm, his skin was unlined, his hair was black and thick, and he would always look this way. When I was gray and wrinkled, he would still be beautiful. When I grew old and feeble, he would still be young and strong. I tried to shake the troublesome thoughts aside, told myself it didn't matter. I didn't want to think about such things now, when I was in his arms, but I couldn't stop. He would never change, never grow old or frail. Would I start to hate him when I began to age and he didn't?

"Ah, Kathy, it doesn't have to be that way."

"Yes, it does." I knew he was thinking about Susie. She liked being a Vampire, and that was fine for Susie, but she'd had no choice in the matter. I did, and I didn't want to be a Vampire.

"Do you want to live with one?" Rafe asked quietly.

"Is there any way for me to keep you out of my mind?" I asked, exasperated that he read my thoughts so easily.

"You can try."

"How do I do it?"

"Erect a wall around your thoughts."

"How do I do that?"

"Imagine it in your mind. Build it a brick at a time, as high and as thick as you like."

"And that will keep you out?"

"If it's strong enough." He stroked my cheek with his fingers. "You didn't answer my question."

"I don't know." Tears stung my eyes. Only moments ago, I had been sure Rafe was everything I had ever wanted, but now . . . Tears of doubt dripped down my cheeks and fell on Rafe's face. He didn't wipe them away, only looked up at me through fathomless black eyes, waiting for me to go on. "Make love to me, Rafe. Hold me tight and don't let me go."

Desperate and afraid to face the future, I needed to be held, needed to feel his arms around me, to hear his voice telling me that he loved me, that everything would be all right.

For a minute, I thought he would refuse, but then he cupped my face in his hands and kissed me, slowly, deeply, each kiss longer and more intense than the last. Closing my eyes, I surrendered to his kisses, to the sweet seduction of his hands moving over my damp skin, large hands that gently caressed me. His voice moved over me like rough velvet as he whispered love words in my ear, sometimes in English, sometimes in a language I didn't understand.

I clung to him, holding him tight, tighter, afraid that if I let go, I'd be lost. When I was ready for him, when I was sure I couldn't wait another minute, he wrapped one arm around me and rolled over, carrying me with him, so that he was on top. I cried out with pleasure as his body merged with mine.

And even then, I knew he was saying good-bye.

Chapter Twenty-Nine

When I woke in the morning, Rafe was gone. The words *gone for good* echoed in the back of my mind, and I knew I had lost him and it was nobody's fault but my own. Even though I loved him, I didn't have enough faith in myself, or in our love, to believe it would last. I wasn't brave enough to face the future at his side. I couldn't keep from thinking that the day would come when he would turn to someone younger and prettier, or worse, to a Vampire who could share his whole life, who would understand him in ways that I never could or would.

I sat up, noting that Rafe had covered me with a blanket and left the candles burning. His thoughtfulness brought quick tears to my eyes.

I spent the day in the cave. When I wasn't crying, I swam in the pool or napped in the shade. Late in the afternoon, I rummaged in the sack to see what Rafe had brought. I found apples and oranges, some string cheese, a box of crackers, a couple of bottles of water, and several of my favorite candy bars.

Toward evening, I got dressed, and after gathering up

the food sack and my handbag, I left the cave, wondering how I'd get back to town.

I should have known Rafe wouldn't leave me stranded out in the middle of nowhere. His car was still parked at the bottom of the hill.

Driving home, all I could think was, how had things gone so bad so fast? One minute everything had been wonderful, and the next, I was pushing Rafe away because I couldn't stand the thought that he would never change. People in love always talked about growing old together, and while I wasn't looking forward to growing old, I knew I didn't want to grow old by myself. But did I want to grow old without Rafe? It seemed a moot point now.

It was still early when I pulled up in front of my house. I sat there for a minute, staring blankly out the windshield. There was nothing here for me now, I thought. I would put the house up for sale and close up the store, maybe go home and spend some time with my folks.

With my mind made up, I got out of the car.

At the front door, I put my key in the lock, but there was no need. The door swung open on its own. A closer look showed the lock had been broken.

Turning on my heels, I ran down the stairs and climbed into Rafe's car. I didn't know who had broken into my house, but I had a pretty good idea. I doubted if they were still inside, waiting for me, but I wasn't about to find out.

Without a backward glance, I drove out of Oak Hollow just as fast as I could.

I drove until I reached River's Edge, and then I pulled into the parking lot of the first motel I saw.

Five minutes later, I locked myself in Room 9. I pulled the drapes over the windows before I turned on the lights. I stood there a minute, wondering if I had overreacted, but my mother had always said it was better to err on the side of caution than wake up dead in a ditch.

I smiled at the memory, then sat on the edge of the bed and switched on the TV. I was surfing through the channels when I heard a reporter say, "This just in from Oak Hollow."

As I listened to his report, I knew that leaving Oak Hollow had been the smart thing to do.

Two photographs were flashed on the screen. I recognized Jennifer and Gary immediately, listened with mounting horror as the reporter related how the two had been found dead in their homes, both dispatched by a single gunshot to the back of the head while they slept.

Pulling my cell phone from my bag, I quickly punched in Susie's number. She answered on the second ring. "Kathy?"

"Hi, are you all right?"

"We're fine. I just heard about Gary and Jennifer on the radio. Where are you?"

"I'm at a motel in River's Edge. Where are you?"

"With Joe. We're on our way to pick up my kids, and then we're getting out of town."

She was probably smart to take her kids. I doubted if either Edna or Pearl would have any scruples about using three innocent kids to get to Susie.

"What about your folks?" I asked. "They could be in danger, too."

"I convinced them to take a little vacation."

"Good. Listen, we need to warn those two men that

were with us that they're in danger," I said, "but how? I don't even know their names."

"I don't know. Joe thinks it's probably too late."

Just then, pictures of the two men appeared on the screen.

"Local police are calling the killings the work of a serial killer," the reporter said. "If you have any information . . ."

I turned the volume down. "Cagin was right," I said. "We're too late."

"Joe wants to know if you're with Rafe. He wants to ask him . . ."

"I don't know where he is."

There was a moment of silence, and then Susie said, "Keep in touch, all right?"

"I will. If you hear anything . . ."

"We'll let you know. Joe wants to know if you want to meet us somewhere tomorrow. He thinks we should stick together."

Safety in numbers. Ordinarily, it was a good idea, but I couldn't help wondering if that was true now. "I'll let you know tomorrow," I said. "How's your face?"

"It burns like the very devil, but at least it won't leave any scars. Be careful, Kathy."

"You, too."

I watched the rest of the news, relieved that there was no mention of Jimmy and Gina or Rafe, and then switched off the set.

Of the twelve people who had been subjected to Pearl's formula, two of the Werewolves had died from the injection. Four of the others had been executed. There was no doubt in my mind that Edna and Pearl were behind the killings. Clearly, the women intended to do away with those of us who had survived as quickly as possible so there would be no witnesses, no one left to go to the police.

Where was Rafe? Had he left town? Did he know what was happening? I wished he was with me. Closing my eyes, I tried to find the link that we shared, but either he was blocking me, or I was too far away to contact him. Or . . . I refused to consider the possibility that he was dead. I would know it if he was. I was sure of it. After all we had shared, I would know.

Sitting there, with the phone still in my hand, I wondered where it would all end.

Chapter Thirty

Rafe prowled the outskirts of the town. He had fed earlier, but it had done nothing to ease his inner torment. He should have known it wouldn't last, but he had let himself believe that Kathy was different, that she was strong enough and brave enough to share his life. How could he have been such a fool? No matter how hard he pretended otherwise, he was a Vampire, Nosferatu, Undead. He was a hunter, a killer by nature, a drinker of blood. He might play at being mortal, but that didn't make it so, would never make it so.

Giving free rein to his anger and his hurt, he stalked the shadows. The night closed around him, clouds gathered overhead, lightning scorched the skies, and a cold, bitter wind whipped the land.

And once again, he was alone, as he had been alone since Rane disappeared.

Ah, Rane, he thought, *where are you now?* His brother had long ago ceased pretending to be anything other than what he was. Rafe had followed him one night, stood in the dark, and watched his brother drain the blood and the life from some streetwalker. He had watched, and had been sorely tempted to push his brother aside and take the woman for himself, but he had not. He had known his mother would not approve, that his father would be disappointed. His grandfather had understood and sympathized with him.

He remembered sharing his thoughts while walking with his grandfather late one night.

"You can be man or monster," Roshan had said quietly. "It's up to you."

"You've killed," Rafe had said. "Many times."

His grandfather had nodded. "In the course of my existence, I have killed many men, sometimes in self-defense, sometimes because the temptation to drink my fill and ease the pain was more than I could bear. I have often wondered if I'll be called to account for all the lives I've taken."

"Judgment?" Rafe had asked. "Damnation?"

His grandfather had nodded again. "I've often wondered if I'll writhe in the flames of an unforgiving hell forever, or if there might be redemption for someone like me."

"Do you think that's possible?"

"I don't know." Roshan had laughed softly. "In all these centuries, I've not found an answer. I didn't ask for the Dark Gift. It seems unfair somehow that I should be punished for doing what I did to survive. And yet, the people I killed are just as dead. What right did I have to take their lives to prolong my own?"

"A Vampire with a conscience," Rafe had murmured. "A rare thing indeed."

And yet, in Rafe's family, not so rare, except for Rane. *Ah, Rane,* he thought again, *where are you now?*

But it was Kathy he yearned to see. His mind replayed every moment they had spent together, from the night he had first walked into her bookstore to that last night in the cave. He missed her smile, the sound of her voice, the love in her eyes, the touch of her body against his. His heart, his dead heart, twisted inside his chest. How long would it take to forget her? A century? An eternity? Where was she now? He knew she had left Oak Hollow, no doubt for good. For a moment, he was sorely tempted to open the link between them, but he shook it aside. She had left him, left town. He would not go after her, would not beg for her love and hope she would take pity on him.

He paused to stare into the darkness. The raging storm called to something primal within him, something dark and feral that yearned to be set free.

A jagged spear of lightning pierced the clouds, unleashing a torrent of rain. A rumble of thunder shook the earth beneath his feet.

He lifted his head to the rain, rain that soaked the ground around him even as the voice of thunder rolled across the heavens.

"Go," it seemed to say. "Go and be what you were born to be."

Muttering an oath, he pivoted on his heel and headed back toward the town. He couldn't get Kathy out of his heart, but maybe he could drown her memory in blood.

Chapter Thirty-One

I stood at the motel window, staring out at the rain. Too restless to stand still, I turned away from the window and paced the floor, my thoughts in turmoil, my heart aching. I was angry with myself for driving Rafe away, and angry with Rafe for walking away without an argument. Had he loved me so little?

I slammed my hand against the wall. That was unfair. It wasn't Rafe's fault that we were apart, it was mine. I had thrown our happiness away with both hands because I had let my doubts and fears get the best of me. There were no guarantees in life. Yes, the odds were good that Rafe would outlive me by hundreds of years, but what if he didn't? And what difference did it make? Life was uncertain, and more so every day. I could get run over by a car while crossing the street. Rafe could be destroyed by a Vampire hunter. Instead of accepting that and holding fast to whatever time we could have together, I had let my fears of an unknown future drive us apart.

Resting my forehead against the cold window pane, I closed my eyes.

Rafe, Rafe, where are you? Please don't shut me out. I was wrong. I'm sorry. Please forgive me.

Chapter Thirty-Two

The inside of the club was dark, quiet at this time of the night save for the clink of glassware and the murmur of voices.

Rafe stood to one side of the entrance, his gaze moving over the room, skipping over couples in his search for a female who was there alone.

After a time, he choose a woman sitting by herself at the end of the bar. She wore a white sweater and an ankle-length green skirt. He told himself the fact that her hair was golden blond and her eyes were green, like Kathy's, had nothing to do with his choice. Lots of women had blond hair and deep green eyes.

"Lying to yourself again," he muttered as he walked toward her.

She glanced up as he approached.

"Is this seat taken?" he asked.

"No."

He gestured at her glass, which was nearly empty. "Can I buy you another?"

"Sure."

"What are you drinking?"

"Scotch and water."

He ordered another drink for her and a glass of red wine for himself. Her name was Sonja and she had just turned thirty. She worked for a real estate company, had recently ended a two-year relationship, and lived alone.

She was ripe and ready for the taking, Rafe thought, but he wasn't interested in her body, only her blood.

It took little effort to convince her to leave with him. Once outside, he led her into the shadows and drew her into his arms. She was soft and pliable, her skin warm beneath his hands. The hunger rode him with whip and spurs, urging him to take her, to take it all, to give up the fight and surrender to the reality of what he was.

His power flowed through him, heightening his senses. The scent of her blood, warm and vital with life, filled his nostrils. The beat of her heart was echoed in the thunder that rolled across the skies.

He was a Vampire, and she was his for the taking.

He ran his tongue over his fangs, then bent the woman backward over his arm.

She was prey, and he was the hunter.

He was lowering his head when Kathy's voice, thick with tears, whispered through his mind. *Rafe, Rafe, where are you? Please don't shut me out. I was wrong. I'm sorry. Please forgive me.*

Lifting his head, he glanced over his shoulder, almost expecting to see her standing there.

Rafe, please come back to me. . . .

With a low growl, he released the woman from his thrall and then, thinking he was a damn fool, he followed the sound of his beloved's voice.

Chapter Thirty-Three

Fighting the urge to cry, I went into the bathroom and turned on the light. After undressing, I stepped into the shower. With hot water sluicing over my body, I could pretend the wetness on my cheeks was water and not tears.

Once started, the tears came harder, faster. How long could a person cry before they dehydrated?

So, I'd made a mistake, but it wasn't irreversible. It couldn't be. In spite of the danger, I would go back to Oak Hollow and find Rafe. I'd tell him I loved him, that I would always love him, and hope that he would believe me, and forgive me.

Unwrapping a bar of soap, I washed my face. When I rinsed away the soap and opened my eyes again, Rafe was standing outside the shower door.

I blinked at him, wondering if he was real or if I had been so desperate to see him again, I had conjured his image from my imagination.

I watched him undress, my gaze moving avidly over

every inch of exposed flesh, and then he opened the door.

"You want to get rid of that?" he asked, gesturing at the silver chain and cross that I now wore day and night.

Happiness bubbled up inside me like warm champagne. He was here, and by the look of him, he wasn't mad at me. I ran my fingertips over the chain. "I don't know if I should take it off," I said, as if I was giving it serious thought. "A girl can never be too careful."

"Take a chance," he said, flashing a wicked grin. "Walk on the wild side with me."

"You tempt me, sir." Batting my eyelashes at him, I lifted the chain over my head, leaned out the door, and placed the cross and chain on the sink top. I grinned inwardly when Rafe dropped a washcloth over them.

"That's the idea," Rafe said, and stepping into the shower, he closed the door. Taking the soap from my hand, he began to wash me, first my neck, then my shoulders and my arms.

I trembled at his touch, afraid to speak. If this was a dream, I didn't want it to end.

I had never felt anything as erotic as Rafe's strong, soapy hands sliding over my flesh. Once, I had imagined what it would be like for the two of us to shower together. The reality was better than my wildest fantasies. Desire stirred within me, hot and slick. A glance at Rafe showed that my nearness was having a similar effect on him.

When he had washed me from neck to heel, I took the soap from his hand. "My turn," I said, surprised at how breathy and sexy my voice sounded. It was an amazing feeling, running my lathered hands over his taut flesh, feeling his muscles quiver with longing at my touch, watching his eyes grow hot as my hands moved over his body, lower, lower . . .

With a growl, he turned off the water, swung me up into his arms, and carried me to bed.

He made love to me without a word, and I reveled in it.

He was here, and he was mine. There was no need for words. The look in his eyes, the sweet caress of his hands said it all eloquently.

Later, satisfied and sated, with my head pillowed on his chest, I whispered that I was sorry.

He covered my mouth with his fingertips. "Don't," he said quietly.

"But . . ."

"You don't need to apologize for being human, for being afraid of the unknown, for wanting a home and a family."

"Yes, I do."

Rafe turned on his side so that we were lying face-to-face, our legs intimately entwined. "I knew what you were thinking, feeling." He pressed his hand over my heart. "I knew how you felt, in here, but I let my pride get in the way of my good sense. I told myself I didn't need you, and I walked away." He lifted one hand, his fingertips sliding over my lower lip. "I'll never leave you again," he said, and I heard the promise in his voice, "unless you tell me to go."

"It'll never happen." The short time we had been apart had been enough to convince me that I never wanted to be parted from him again. "Will you promise me something else?"

"Anything."

"Please don't ever shut me out again. I tried to find you and I couldn't."

He stroked my cheek, brushed a lock of hair from my brow. "I'm sorry. It will never happen again." He blew out a sigh. "You saved me, you know."

"What do you mean?" My hand slid over his chest. I loved the feel of his bare skin beneath my palm, the fact that I could touch him and taste him to my heart's content.

"I was leaning toward the dark side," he said with a wry grin. "I had decided to stop fighting what I am and take what I wanted. I was about to feed when I heard your voice." He paused, his jaw tight. "Another minute, and I would have taken her. I would have taken it all."

"But you didn't. That's what's important. You didn't."

"You can't know how hard it is," he said, and there was no humor in his expression now, and none in his voice. "How hard it is to forever deny yourself that which you crave most, to smell it and taste it and not touch it."

I didn't know what to say. I couldn't begin to imagine what it was like for him.

"That woman owes her life to you."

I didn't know what to say to that, either.

He shook his head. "If I'd taken her, I would have regretted it the rest of my life."

"From now on, we'll be strong for each other. Just promise me one more thing."

"Whatever you want."

"Promise you'll never turn me against my will."

"I promise."

I snuggled against him. I hated to ruin the moment

between us, but it couldn't be helped. "On the news tonight . . ."

"I heard. You were smart to leave town."

"I didn't know about that until later. Someone broke into my house. They broke the lock on the front door. I didn't wait around to see who it was, or if they were still there."

He squeezed my shoulders. "Like I said, smart."

"What'll we do now?"

"You're going to stay here."

"What are you going to do?"

"I'm going back to Oak Hollow to put Edna and Pearl out of commission."

"Why can't Mara and Clive do it?"

"Clive took off for South America last night to take care of the last of the rebels. Mara's gone to Texas to put a certain school out of business."

"And she left you here to clean up the town?"

"More or less."

"I need to go home," I said, "and since you're going back to Oak Hollow, I think I'll just go with you."

"Dammit, Kathy, don't you listen? Didn't I just say you were staying here?"

"Yes, you did, and I said I was going with you."

"Stubborn woman."

"So you've said. Now, do you want to spend the rest of the night arguing with me?" I trailed my fingertips down over his chest, lower, lower. "Or making love?"

"Is that a trick question?"

"Speaking of tricks, don't even think of trying to leave without me. No turning into mist and sliding under the door."

Laughing softly, he rose over me, his dark eyes glowing

with desire. "I have a trick or two I think you'll like," he murmured, his voice husky.

I locked my hands behind his neck and drew his head down. "Show me," I whispered. "Kiss me and make the world go away."

"It would be my pleasure."

I thought it was just words, but the walls around us shimmered and disappeared, and in their place I saw rolling hills and fields of flowers and trees. Fluffy white clouds drifted lazily across a pale blue sky, and in the distance, I heard music that was both soft and sensual.

"More Vampire magic?" I asked.

"You like it?"

"It's perfect. Tell me you love me."

"I love you as I've loved no other." He rained kisses across my cheeks and my brow, the tip of my nose. "I love you as I will never love anyone else, in this life or the next."

"And I love you."

"I know. And I'll never let you forget it."

I ran my fingertips over his shoulders and down his arms, my hands measuring the width of his biceps. Sliding my hand between our bodies, I caressed the hard ridges in his belly, then slid my questing fingertips down to the juncture of his thighs.

"Careful," he said, his voice low and husky.

Lifting my head, I nipped at his chin. "I'm through being careful."

"That's my brave girl."

Turning my head a little to the side, I brushed the hair away from my neck. "Make love to me, Vampire."

A hint of red glowed in Rafe's eyes. He lowered his head until all I could see were his eyes. He uttered a low growl, and I felt the scrape of his fangs against my skin. When his mouth found mine, the real world melted away. Every touch was heightened, every sense intensified. The brush of his skin against my own was like nothing I had ever felt before, sensuous and erotic. I trembled at his touch, as he trembled at mine. His mouth was hot as he showered me with kisses. My hips arched to meet him, my body quivering with anticipation, and then we were no longer two, but one. One heart, one mind, one body.

I love you, I love you. The words whispered in my mind, over and over again.

I writhed beneath him, wanting more of him, wanting all of him. I sobbed his name, reaching, reaching for that which eluded me. I gasped as his body quivered, shuddered, exploded deep within me, filling me with warmth, carrying me over the edge of desire into ecstasy. Sated and utterly content, I clung to Rafe's shoulders while aftershocks of pleasure rippled through me.

Murmuring his name, I closed my eyes as sleep carried me away.

I woke to the sound of someone calling my name. I opened my eyes and closed them again, certain that I was dreaming.

"Wake up, dear."

Fear shivered through me. I took a deep breath, determined not to let it show, "Pearl, what are you doing here? How did you get in?"

Sitting up, with the sheet drawn up to cover my nakedness, I glanced around the room, looking for Rafe, but there was no sign of him. Instead, I saw Edna standing inside the doorway with five men; I recognized two of them from the lab. They had come loaded for bear this time. The men were armed with short-barreled rifles that I was pretty sure were loaded with silver bullets. Edna held a large vial I assumed was filled with holy water. My stomach clenched as I remembered the effect it had had on Susie and Rafe. Pearl held a snub-nosed pistol in one hand, and a sharp wooden stake in the other. Men and women alike wore heavy silver crosses on thick silver chains around their necks.

"Did you really think we'd let you get away?" Edna asked. "You've seen too much, know too much." She moved toward the bed, her eyes narrowed. "Where's Raphael?"

I shrugged. "How should I know?"

Pearl slapped me hard enough to make my ears ring. "We don't have time for games, dear."

"I don't know where he is." That much was the truth. I had awakened in his arms a few hours before sunup, and we had made love until dawn. I had no idea where he was now.

"Bring her," Edna said. "He won't get away from us this time."

One of the men used his rifle to gesture toward the door. "Let's go, sister."

I looked at Edna. "Do you mind if I get dressed first?"

She muttered something unladylike under her breath, then said, "Make it quick."

Holding the sheet around me, I went into the bathroom and shut the door. My clothes were folded on the sink top where I had left them the night before.

I dressed slowly, my thoughts racing. Where was Rafe? When had he left the motel, and why? I slipped the cross and chain over my head, then sat on the edge of the bathtub and put on my shoes.

Tapping my fingertips on the rim of the tub, I looked up at the window. It was small, but I thought I might be able to fit through it. My purse, my keys, and my phone were in the other room, but that couldn't be helped.

Taking a deep breath, I climbed on the edge of the tub and unlocked the window.

"Going somewhere?"

I scowled at the man standing in the alley. He made a shooing gesture with his gun. "Back inside with you now."

With a sigh of defeat, I closed the window just as someone knocked on the bathroom door. "Time's up, dear."

Muttering an oath, I opened the door, wondering if this nightmare would ever end. Once again, I found myself sitting in the back of a van, my heart in my throat as I wondered what Pearl and Edna had planned for me now. At least I hadn't been drugged this time.

I had expected our destination to be the lab in Oak Hollow; instead, I found myself back in the silver-lined room I had been in once before. Edna tossed me a pillow and a blanket and told me to make myself comfortable. Before she closed the door, I overheard Pearl say something about rounding up another group for more tests as soon as they dispatched the last of the previous subjects.

Dispatched. The word had a nasty ring of finality to it.

I didn't know where Rafe had gone, but I was glad he hadn't been there when Edna and Pearl and their henchmen arrived. Although he could be active during the day, I didn't know how strong his powers were when the sun was up, or if he could have taken on Edna and Pearl and five men at the same time.

I blew out a sigh and closed my eyes. I was getting awfully tired of being used as bait. I just hoped Rafe wasn't foolish enough to try to rescue me again, because if they got him in here with me, I didn't know how we would ever get out.

Chapter Thirty-Four

Rafe stood in the doorway of the motel room, his hands clenched at his sides. He had known before he opened the door that Kathy was gone, just as he had known that Edna and Pearl had been there. He caught the scents of five men, two that he recognized from the lab.

He swore softly, thinking he had been a fool not to end this sooner. He had intended to settle things with Edna and Pearl the night before, but then he had heard Kathy's voice in his mind. Her unhappiness had been more than he could bear. That, coupled with his own need to see her, to hold her, to make sure she was out of danger, had sent him to the motel in River's Edge. He should have gone back to Oak Hollow as soon as he knew Kathy was all right. Instead, he had spent the night making love to her, and now, because of him, her life was in danger again.

It took only minutes to follow her scent to the deserted meat-packing plant on Oak Tree Road. Muttering an oath, he paced the shadows, then dissolved into mist and slid under the door. He sensed Kathy's presence immediately.

Hovering near the ceiling, he saw Edna and Pearl sitting at one end of a long table, several notebooks and folders spread out in front of them. At the other end of the table, six men were playing poker. A number of rifles, handguns, and wooden stakes were piled on a smaller table, along with several glass bottles that Rafe assumed held holy water.

"I still don't know what they did to Travis," Pearl was saying. "But they're going to pay for it. He was the best hunter in the business!"

"Except for you and me," Edna remarked.

Pearl smiled fleetingly, then slammed her fist on the table. "I can't wait to get my hands on Cordova! I'm sure he's behind this. All our records in Texas have been destroyed, and all our files at the lab. Damned Vampire, sticking his nose in places where it doesn't belong! Well, he won't get away this time. As soon as we take care of him, we'll find Cagin and the McGee woman, and that'll be the end of it."

"Almost seems a shame to destroy Cordova," Edna said. "Such a good-looking man."

"Oh, for heaven's sake, Edna Mae Turner, you're just saying that because you think he has a cute butt!"

Had he been in corporeal form, Rafe would have laughed out loud. Cute butt, indeed!

"It's a good thing I had the formula in my head," Pearl muttered. "It made it a lot easier to concoct the new one. You know, instead of destroying Cordova, maybe we should just try the new formula on him and the girl."

"Whatever you want," Edna said agreeably, "but I still think you should write the new formula down."

"Maybe later."

"Do you think whatever Vampire whammy Cordova put on Travis is permanent?"

"I don't know. Did you see how he acted last night? One mention of the word Vampire and he practically went into hysterics."

Pleased with what he had heard, Rafe left the building and assumed his own form, then reached for his cell phone. All the rats were in one trap. All he needed now was a little backup.

Susie ran her hands over her face, then glanced at Cagin. "Does it look as bad as it feels?"

Joe shook his head. "No, it looks a lot better." He ran his finger down her cheek. "There's only a small red place here."

"What about the other side?"

"It's healing."

Susie sank back on the sofa. She had planned to get her children and leave town, but she couldn't let them see her like this. Instead, she had convinced her mother to take the boys on a little vacation for a few days. She hated for her sons to miss school, but it couldn't be helped. With a sigh, she rested her head on the back of the sofa. Sometimes she felt like she was living a nightmare from which there was no escape. She didn't know what she would have done without Joe. He was her only comfort these days.

When her cell phone rang, she picked it up, expecting it to be her mother or Kathy.

Instead, she heard Rafe's voice on the line.

"Susie, is Cagin there?"

Rafe stepped out of the shadows when Cagin and Susie arrived. "Thanks for coming."

"Wouldn't miss it," Cagin said with a grin.

"Is Kathy all right?" Susie asked.

"Other than being cold and scared, she's fine."

"So, how do you want to handle this?" Cagin asked.

"Like I told you, there are six men in there with Edna and Pearl. Lots of hardware." Rafe glanced at Susie. "And holy water. I figure the best way to play it is to go in hard and fast. We should be able to break down the door and take out the men before they know what's happening. Once the men are out of the way, we'll take the women. Cagin, you'll have to dump the holy water."

Cagin nodded. "No problem."

Rafe looked at Susie. "You up for this?"

She lifted a hand to her face. "Are you kidding? After what they did? Just try and keep me out. Besides, Kathy's in there, and good friends are hard to find."

Rafe winked at her. "Let's do it."

It went like clockwork. Cagin undressed and then shifted, Rafe kicked in the door, and the Were-tiger sprang inside, with Rafe and Susie right behind him.

The people inside the building looked up as the door flew open, the surprise on their faces quickly turning to fear. Edna and Pearl scrambled away from the table, apparently trusting that the men would protect them, but the men were too slow. By the time they reached for the guns on the table, it was too late, although one of them managed to fire a round that struck Cagin in the thigh.

With a growl, Cagin sprang across the table. Three of the men went down amid a flurry of growls, teeth, and claws; Rafe dispatched two of the men, leaving Susie to deal with the last one. It was swift and brutal and over in a matter of minutes.

Shifting back into his own form, Cagin grabbed the bottles and dumped the holy water outside while Susie and Rafe backed Edna and Pearl into a corner.

When Cagin returned, Rafe noted that he had taken the time to get dressed again.

"Now what?" Cagin asked, glancing from Rafe to the two women.

"Keep an eye on these two while I get Kathy," Rafe said, "and then we'll decide what to do next."

Chapter Thirty-Five

I was pacing the floor, my mind in turmoil, when the door swung open. At first, all I saw was a dark silhouette that looked familiar.

"Rafe? Rafe!" I flew into his arms, thinking I had never been so surprised or so happy to see anyone in my life.

"Rescue party's here," Rafe said, giving me a hug.

"How did you find me?"

His gaze moved over my face. "I'll always be able to find you. Are you all right?"

"I'm fine, now. Are you all right? How'd you get in here. Where are Edna and . . ."

He silenced my questions by kissing me. When I came up for air, I saw that we weren't alone.

Susie and Cagin had Edna and Pearl trapped in the far corner of the room. For the first time since I had met them, Edna and Pearl looked subdued, their faces pale. Moving deeper into the room, I stared at the six bodies sprawled on the floor at one end of a long table. The scent of blood and death made my stomach churn. The bitter taste of bile rose in the back of my throat.

I looked up at Rafe. There was no remorse in his eyes when he looked at me. I could only hope it had been self-defense.

"Let's get this over with," Cagin said.

I followed Rafe across the room, my stomach churning with apprehension. "What are you going to do with them?" I asked, though I was dreading the answer.

"What do you think?" Cagin asked, a growl in his voice.

"But . . ." I looked up at Rafe. "Are you just going to kill them in cold blood?"

His gaze met mine. "Don't you think they deserve it?"

I didn't know what to say. Edna and Pearl had killed innocent people. True, some of the ones they had killed hadn't been people in the true sense of the word, but they had taken innocent lives. I remembered the fear and humiliation I had felt while I waited in that awful cage, the horror that engulfed me when they injected me with their formula, the pain that had wracked my body. I could have been killed. We all could have been killed.

I looked at Edna and Pearl. You had to admire their courage. They were both glaring at Rafe, as though daring him to do his worst.

"Kathy?" I felt the weight of Rafe's gaze as he waited for my answer.

"I don't know." Maybe they deserved it, maybe not. Who was I to make such a decision?

"Well, I know!" Cagin said. "Look at Susie's face!" His power filled the room, and I knew he was eager to shift into the tiger and rip out their throats.

"Wait." Rafe's voice, soft as dandelion fluff, stopped Cagin in his tracks. "I have a better idea."

"Better than killing them?" Cagin asked. "I don't think so."

"Call it poetic justice," Rafe said.

Taking a step forward, he reached for Edna's hand. Lips compressed in a thin line, she recoiled from his touch.

In a blur of movement, Rafe grabbed her by the forearm. "Time to pay the piper," he said. She struggled in his grasp, but she was no match for Rafe's strength as he propelled her across the room. For the first time since I had met her, she looked old and scared.

I stared after him. I knew suddenly what he was going to do. It gave me a sick feeling in the pit of my stomach.

I didn't want to watch, but I couldn't look away. Preternatural power filled the room. It made it hard to breathe, lifted the hair along my nape.

Edna's eyes grew wide with revulsion when she realized what he intended to do. "No!" She tried to escape his grasp. "No, damn you!"

"Oh, yes," Rafe said.

His fangs extended, and his eyes went red as he pulled Edna into his embrace. She sobbed once, a sound that tore at my heart, and then she fell silent. Though it seemed he drank from her forever, in reality only a few minutes passed before he lowered her body to the floor. Kneeling beside her, he tore a gash in his wrist and then held the bleeding wound to her mouth. When she resisted, he forced her to drink. After the first swallow, she grabbed his wrist and held it to her mouth as though she were drinking from the fountain of youth. How quickly revulsion turned to need.

Sickened, I turned away to find Susie watching

avidly. Her eyes were bright, her body quivering, as she watched Edna drink from Rafe. Cagin's expression was impassive.

Realizing what her own fate was going to be, Pearl darted toward the door, only to be stopped by Cagin. She put up a good fight for a woman her age, but, like Edna, her strength was as nothing when pitted against a creature with Supernatural power.

She renewed her struggles when Rafe stood and walked toward her.

She stared at Rafe, her eyes narrowed with hatred. "Damn you," she said. "May you rot in hell for all eternity."

"Most likely," Rafe said.

When Cagin dropped her arm, Pearl backed away from Rafe, but there was no place for her to go. When her back hit the wall, she let out a high-pitched squeal, like a rabbit caught in the jaws of a lion. She glared at Rafe, her expression one of mingled fear and defiance when he pulled her into his arms. Knowing it was useless to fight, she squeezed her eyes shut as he bent his head to her neck. And then, like Edna, she went limp in his arms.

And, like Edna, she took one drink of his blood and wanted more.

When it was done, Rafe helped both women to their feet.

For a minute, they looked at each other as if they were strangers, and then they joined hands.

"I don't guess I need to tell you what happens next," Rafe said, glancing from one to the other. "If you don't want what I've given you, the sun will put an end to it. If you decide to accept it, I wish you well in your new life. Oh," he said, glancing at the bodies behind the table, "you might want to clean up the mess."

"Wait!"

Rafe looked at Pearl, one brow raised.

"Travis," she said.

"What about him?"

"If I bring him across, what will it do to him?"

"I imagine he'll be the same arrogant ass as a Vampire that he was as a hunter," Rafe said with a shrug. "Just keep him the hell away from me."

With their heads together and their arms around each other, Edna and Pearl staggered to the far side of the room. Clad in bulky sweaters, jeans, and comfortable shoes, they were the most unlikely-looking Vampires I had ever seen. I couldn't help wondering how they would fare in their new life, and if being Undead would have any effect on their wardrobe. I laughed when I heard Pearl say this would be the best Halloween ever.

Rafe looked at me, and then he held out his hand, a question in his dark eyes.

I looked at Edna and Pearl. I looked at the bodies on the floor. I thought about what it would mean if I went with him. I thought how dreary my life would be without him. And because I loved him, because I couldn't imagine a future without him in it, I put my hand in his and we left the building.

Susie and Cagin followed us outside.

"Well," Cagin said with a wicked grin, "that was worth the price of admission. Now what do we do?"

Rafe looked at me and smiled. "Now," he said, "I'm taking my bride home. How about you?"

Cagin looked at Susie. "What do you say, beautiful? Do you wanna get married?"

Susie smiled at him. "I think I'd like that."

"Thanks for your help," Rafe said, glancing at Susie and Cagin. "And keep in touch."

"Will do," Cagin replied.

Susie and I hugged, then Cagin took her arm and they disappeared into the darkness.

Rafe lifted me into his arms. "Told you they'd wind up together," he said, and the next thing I knew, we were at Rafe's house, in Rafe's bed.

It was where I wanted to be, where I wanted to spend the rest of my life.

"No regrets?" he asked. "You're sure this time?"

"I'm sure. I just wish . . ."

"What do you wish, love?"

"That we could get married, really married."

"Means that much to you, does it?"

"I know it's silly. It's just a piece of paper, but . . ."

He put his fingers to my lips. "If it's that important to you, then we'll do it."

"How? It's against the law. No minister is going to marry us."

Rafe grinned at me. "Hey, you're forgetting who you're talking to."

I batted my eyelashes at him. "Don't tell me. You're going to arrange a little Vampire hocus pocus."

"Something like that," he said. "But first . . ." He drew me into his arms and kissed me and, as always when Rafe touched me, I forgot everything else. The past few days, Edna and Pearl, my close call with death, none of it mattered now. Rafe's kisses were like liquid fire, heating my blood, melting my bones, leaving me breathless with wanting, trembling with desire.

Our clothing disappeared as if by magic, and then we

were lying side by side in a delicious tangle of arms and legs and deep, wet kisses. When he rose over me, I was more than ready. I felt the welcome prick of his fangs at my throat as his body melded with mine, and then there was only pleasure, endless sensual pleasure, and Rafe's voice whispering that he loved me.

I was getting married. I didn't know where, I didn't know who would perform the ceremony. Rafe said I shouldn't worry about anything but buying a wedding gown, and I took him at his word. I chose a floor-length dress with a square neck and long, tapered sleeves. My veil was also floor-length, as delicate and beautiful as butterfly wings.

Susie and Cagin had agreed to act as best man and maid of honor.

It was near midnight when Rafe and I arrived at the place where we would exchange our vows. I was surprised when he pulled up in front of a church. It was a lovely old place, surrounded by tall trees, shrubs, and flowering plants. The fragrant scent of evergreens and flowers filled the air.

A priest was waiting for us inside the doors. He was of medium height with warm hazel eyes. His hair was black and wavy, laced with silver at his temples. And he was a Vampire. A very old Vampire. Power radiated off him like heat from a fire.

Rafe introduced him as Father Giovani Lanzoni.

"This is indeed a happy occasion for me," the priest said with a smile. "Many years ago, I officiated at the marriage of Rafe's grandparents and, more recently, at the marriage of his mother and father. And now this." He beamed at us. "Truly, a happy day."

I smiled back at him, momentarily saddened to think that I would never have children, never see them marry or have children of their own. Just then, Rafe squeezed my hand, and I wondered if the same thoughts were running through his mind.

A few minutes later, Father Lanzoni directed me to a room where I could change into my wedding gown.

I grew increasingly nervous as the minutes passed. I wished my parents could be there, but it just seemed easier this way. Getting married at night, while uncommon, wasn't all that unusual. However, if my parents had been invited, they would have expected a reception with food and drink. And then there was my father, who photographed every occasion, large or small. Trying to explain why the groom and my maid of honor didn't eat or drink and why they didn't show up in the wedding photos was just more than I could handle.

My heart skipped a beat when I heard a knock at the door.

"Are you ready?" Susie called.

"Yes, come in."

"Oh," she murmured, "you look beautiful!"

"Thank you. So do you." She wore a long green dress that flattered every curve, and a pair of white gloves. I stared at the mirror as Susie came to stand beside me. I was there, as plain as day. There was no image of Susie. "Does it bother you?" I asked. "Having no reflection?"

"It was kind of freaky at first," she said with a shrug. "It made me feel like I didn't really exist, but I'm getting used to it, like everything else. Come on, your bridegroom is waiting."

I picked up the bouquet Rafe had given me, a single red rose surrounded by a froth of white roses and baby's breath, and followed Susie out of the room.

The chapel was filled with old-world charm. The altar and the pews were carved from oak. Shafts of silver moonlight shone through the stained glass window above the altar. The carpet was a deep blue. A sad-faced Madonna stood in one corner, her arm out-stretched.

Rafe was waiting for me at the altar. He had always been the most handsome of men, but now, clad in a black tux that complemented his dark good looks and emphasized his broad shoulders, he was devastating. My insides melted like hot wax when he smiled at me. Cagin stood beside him.

It wasn't until I was following Susie down the aisle that I realized there were other people in the chapel. Rafe's grandparents sat together, holding hands. Brenna wore a long-sleeved white blouse and a bright yellow skirt. Her only jewelry was the amber and jet necklace at her throat. Roshan wore a black suit that made him look dark and a trifle mysterious.

I didn't recognize the other three people in the room, although I knew the man had to be Rafe's father, Vince. There was no mistaking the resemblance between them. They both had the same thick black hair, the same straight brows, fine straight nose, and full, sensuous lips. The only apparent difference was the color of their eyes—Rafe's were black while his father's were dark brown. I assumed one of the women was his mother, Cara, but which one? The lovely blonde with the beautiful blue eyes and flawless skin who sat at his right, or the stunningly gorgeous creature on his left? I couldn't help staring at her. Her skin was like smooth porcelain, her hair was thick and black and fell over her shoulders in rippling waves. She wore an elegant emerald green dress that exactly matched the color of her extraordinary eyes. Her only adornment was a heart-shaped ruby pendant. She, too, was a Vampire.

It was amazing. All the Vampires looked to be in the prime of life. If I hadn't known that Roshan and Brenna were Rafe's grandparents, I would have thought that everyone in the room was the same age, for none of them looked older than thirty, and yet I knew Roshan had been a Vampire for hundreds of years.

My nervousness ratcheted up another notch. What if his parents didn't like me? What if they hated mortals? That seemed unlikely, since his grandfather and his father had married mortal women. Still, I couldn't help feeling out of place.

All my worrisome thoughts vanished when Rafe took my hand in his. His voice whispered through my mind. *I love you now, forever and for always.* For a single crystal moment in time, I saw only Rafe, his eyes dark with love and desire, his lips curved in a smile that was for me alone. His hand held mine, warm and firm and reassuring. He loved me and nothing else mattered.

"Shall we begin?" Father Lanzoni asked. His gaze moved over those sitting in the pews and then rested briefly on my face and then Rafe's. "My children," he said, his voice low and yet filled with authority. "You have come here this night seeking a blessing on your marriage, and I commend you for it. The secret of a long and happy marriage rests with the two of you. Always remember to put your loved one first and your own wants second. Treat your spouse as you would be treated. Remember how you feel this night, and I promise you that the love you have for one another will grow stronger with each passing day.

"I will pronounce the words that bind you together legally, but the true joining must take place in your own hearts, your own souls.

"Katherine McKenna, do you promise to love and cherish Raphael Cordova, here present, for as long as you shall live?"

For as long as you live. A few short years, I thought, when he might live for thousands. With a sigh, I murmured, "I do."

"Raphael Cordova, do you promise to love and cherish Kathcrinc McKenna, here present, for as long as you shall live?"

Rafe gazed deep into my eyes, and I saw forever waiting for me there. "I do."

"Then, by the power vested in me, I pronounce you husband and wife. You may kiss your bride."

Slowly, deliberately, Rafe drew me into his arms. My heart raced with anticipation as he lowered his head and claimed my lips with his. Sensual pleasure washed through me as he deepened the kiss, his tongue dueling with mine in a heady foretaste of what was to come when we were alone.

I was breathless when we parted, and a little embarrassed when we turned to face his parents and grandparents, all of whom were beaming at us. Susie was grinning. Cagin gave Rafe a thumbs-up.

Father Lanzoni cleared his throat. "May I present Mr. and Mrs. Raphael Cordova," he said, a smile in his voice. "I suggest congratulations be swift so that the newlyweds can find a room."

My cheeks grew hot as laughter erupted through the chapel, and then we were surrounded by Rafe's family.

The blond woman drew me into her arms and kissed me on both cheeks. "Welcome, daughter. I'm sorry we didn't get to meet earlier."

"Yes, me, too."

"My turn," said a deep male voice, and the next thing I knew, Rafe's father was giving me a bear hug that threatened to crack my ribs. "If he doesn't treat you right, darlin', you come and see me."

Roshan and Brenna hugged me in turn, and then Rafe's mother took me aside. "Don't be intimidated by us," she said with a kindly smile. "And don't let Rafe force you into anything you aren't ready for, if you know what I mean."

"He already knows I don't want to be a Vampire."

Cara nodded. "It should be your decision, of course."

"Are you ever sorry that you asked Mr. Cordova to bring you across?"

"No. Oh, there were times, in the beginning, when I missed being able to enjoy a summer day or a good meal, but they were small sacrifices to make when compared to what I gained." She took both of my hands in hers and gave them a squeeze. "I wish you every happiness. If you ever have any questions you don't want to ask Rafe, please call me. I hope we can be good friends."

"Thank you, Mrs. Cordova, I'd like that."

"Please, call me Cara."

"Thank you, Cara."

"Okay, that's enough," Rafe said, coming up behind us. Slipping his arm around my waist, he kissed me soundly. "From now on, she's all mine."

"Raphael, aren't you going to introduce me?"

The question came from the black-haired woman who had been sitting beside Rafe's father.

"Of course," Rafe said, smiling. "Mara, this is Kathy. Kathy, this is Mara. You've heard me speak of her."

I could only stare at the creature before me. This, then, was the queen of the Vampires, the woman who had bestowed the Dark Gift on Rafe's father.

"I'm pleased to meet you at last," Mara said.

I nodded, still too stunned to speak. She hardly looked a day over twenty-five, yet she had lived for thousands of years. It was mind-boggling to think of all she must have seen in her lifetime. What had it been like for her to watch the whole world change, to see everyone she had ever known pass away while she remained forever the same? I had a million questions I would have liked to ask her, but of course, this wasn't the time or the place.

A faint smile curved her lips, and then I heard her voice in my mind, soft and low, like a welcome breeze on a summer day. *When you tire of being a mortal, call me and I will bring you across. It will be quick and painless.*

Startled, I blurted, "Why would you want to do that?"

Rafe frowned at me. "Do what?"

Mara turned her gaze on Rafe. "I was merely telling her that if she decided to join us, I would bring her across." Looking at me again, she answered my question. "As for why I would do it, you might say I have a certain fondness for my godson and his father. As my fledgling, you will not be bound by the Dark Sleep." Her gaze burned into mine. "Think about it."

She bid Rafe's family good night, kissed Father Lanzoni on the cheek, squeezed my hand, and vanished from our sight. The priest wished us well, and then he, too, simply disappeared.

Cagin swore softly, then muttered, "I don't think I'll ever get used to that."

Susie laughed, and after giving me a hug and promising to call soon, she and Cagin left to pick up Susie's kids.

With their parting, I was the only human left in the group. Of course, technically, Cagin wasn't human, either. I wondered if Rafe's family looked at me and, subconsciously, thought of me as prey. Were they all as happy to be creatures of the night as they appeared to be? Except for the blood thing, their lives didn't seem much different than anyone else's.

"Are you ready to go?" Rafe asked.

I nodded, and after another round of hugs and kisses, we left the chapel. There were more good-byes as his family followed us outside, and then Rafe and I were alone in his car.

"You're very quiet," he said after a time.

"I'm sorry, I'm just a bit overwhelmed by it all, I guess."

"You were uncomfortable with my family."

"No," I said quickly, though in truth, I had felt like a newborn lamb among ravenous wolves.

"No?" He glanced at me, one brow lifted.

"Well, maybe a little," I conceded. "Can you blame me?"

"No, love."

"What will our life be like, Rafe? Will we celebrate Christmas and Easter and birthdays?"

"Of course."

"I'll have to call my parents and let them know about

the wedding," I said, thinking aloud. "Maybe we can go and visit them in a month or so."

"If you wish."

"Don't you want to?"

"Of course."

I wondered if he would feel as awkward with my parents as I had felt with his. My parents would expect us to stay with them, to have breakfast and lunch and dinner with them. How would I explain it when Rafe didn't eat? One wall in the family dining room was mirrored. What would they think when Rafe sat at the table and cast no reflection in the glass?

"I think the easiest thing to do would be to tell them the truth, don't you?" Rafe remarked.

I shook my head in exasperation. There was no point in telling him to stay out of my head. One day I was going to have to learn how to build that wall!

"I guess you're right," I said. "I can't imagine what they'll think, though." With a sigh, I rested my head on Rafe's shoulder. I'd worry about it later, I thought. Now, all I wanted was to be alone with my husband.

Rafe pulled into his driveway, then came around to open my door. Lifting me into his arms, he carried me into the house. When we crossed the threshold, dozens of candles sprang to life.

"Oh, Rafe," I murmured, "it's beautiful."

There were bouquets of roses and daisies everywhere. Dark red rose petals covered the floor of the entryway, releasing their fragrance as Rafe stepped on them.

He carried me into the bedroom. There were more flowers there. The covers on the bed were turned down, the sheets were covered with hundreds of white rose petals. Candles lit the room with a warm golden glow. Soft romantic music played in the background. A bottle of red wine and two crystal glasses waited in a white wicker basket on the nightstand.

Rafe put me down ever so slowly, so that my body glided intimately over his. "I think I've been waiting for you all my life," he said, his voice husky. "I can't believe you're really here, that you're mine." His knuckles stroked my cheek. "I think I loved you the minute I saw you in the bookstore. I know I couldn't think of anything else once I saw you."

"It was the same for me," I said. "I tried to fight it. I kept telling myself you were a Vampire, that we could never be together, but here we are."

"I will love you and cherish you for as long as you live." His hands slid up and down my arms, his touch sending ripples of anticipation racing through me. He kissed me gently, sweetly. "I will never love another."

"Rafe . . ." I couldn't bear the thought of his being alone after I was gone, couldn't bear the thought of leaving him. If I lived to be a hundred, it wouldn't be long enough.

"One love to last a lifetime," he murmured, and sweeping me into his arms, he carried me to bed.

We undressed each other slowly, savoring each shared moment, each tender touch, each gentle caress, our passion building, building, until the pleasure was almost more than I could bear, our bodies so hot, our need so intense, I was surprised the sheets didn't go up in flames. I ran my hands over his heated flesh, loving the way his muscles quivered at my touch, the harsh rasp of his voice when he cried my name, his body trembling convulsively as he buried himself deep inside me and carried me to paradise.

One love to last a lifetime, he had said, and as he kissed me, I knew the day would come when I would find the courage to cross the abyss that separated us. I would accept the Dark Gift and truly join my life with his.

Reading my thoughts as always, Rafe gazed at me, his dark eyes glowing with love and affection, and when he smiled, I saw forever waiting for me in his eyes.

Epilogue

And so Rafe and I were married. We decided to stay in Oak Hollow. With the war over between the Vampires and the Werewolves, and Edna and Pearl no longer a threat, Oak Hollow became the quiet haven I had come looking for. Pearl brought Travis across shortly after she had been made. As Rafe had predicted, Travis was as arrogant as a Vampire as he had been as a hunter. Strangely, he had no recollection of his former life. It was almost as if he had been born the night his grandmother gave him the Dark Gift.

Rafe and I often spent time with his parents and his grandparents, and I grew to love them all, especially his grandfather, Roshan, with his courtly manners and wry sense of humor. Rafe's mother and I became good friends.

As for my parents, I called to tell them of my marriage the day after the wedding. My mother was naturally disappointed that they hadn't been invited. I explained that Rafe had swept me off my feet and we had been married on the spur of the moment. Romantic that she was, my mother had assured me that she understood. For the next month, we received gifts from my mom and dad every other day. We had been married a little over six months when I finally told them that Rafe was a Vampire. I had expected the worst but, as they had so often in the past, my parents surprised me. My mother said it didn't matter. My father said he had known it all the time.

"Being able to identify the Undead is a family trait," he had remarked nonchalantly. "Your mother and I wondered if you had inherited it, since it usually passes from father to son."

Parents. Just when you thought you had them pegged, they threw you for a loop.

Susie and Cagin were married a year to the night after Rick's demise. Her children took to Joe immediately. The Cagins made an unusual family, with a Weretiger for a father, a Vampire mother, and three mortal children, but they all seemed extraordinarily happy together. Sometimes I envied Susie her children, but, for the most part, I was blissfully content with my life.

I continued to run the bookstore. I only worked four days a week, from ten in the morning until four in the afternoon, until I received an e-mail from Edna and Pearl complaining about my hours and asking me to stay open later since they couldn't shop until after dark. When Susie voiced the same request, I hired a young man to open the store from 7:00 P.M. to 10:00 P.M. one night a week.

Because my nights, all of them, belonged to Rafe.

If you liked this Amanda Ashley book,
check out her other titles
currently available from Zebra . . .

AFTER SUNDOWN

He Has Become What He Once Destroyed

Edward Ramsey has spent his life hunting vampires. Now he is one of them. Yet Edward's human conscience—and his heart—compel him to save beautiful Kelly Anderson, and soon their growing love is his reason for living. And as the ancient, stunning, and merciless vampire Khira seeks supremacy among Los Angeles's undead, Edward and his former nemesis Grigori Chiavari, once Khira's lover, must unite to stop her—before the city, and everything they cherish, is in her power . . . After Sundown.

A WHISPER OF ETERNITY

In Amanda Ashley's compelling, lushly sensual novels, vampires exist alongside humans—but their desires are not relegated to the shadows. Now, a timeless passion is shattered by dangerous immortal ambition—unless an eternal kiss can hold back the darkness of true death . . .

He Will Not Lose Her Again

When artist Tracy Warner purchases the rambling seaside house built above Dominic St. John's hidden lair, he recognizes in her spirit the woman he has loved countless times over the centuries. Drawing her into the fascinating, seductive world of the vampire, he aches to believe that this time she will not refuse his Dark Gift. But when Dominic's ancient rival appears in Sea Cliff, hungry for territory and power, Tracy becomes a pawn in a deadly game. To save her—and the passion that burns between them—Dominic must offer . . . A Whisper Of Eternity.

DESIRE AFTER DARK

Vicki Cavendish shows she should be careful. After all, there's a killer loose in town—one who drains women of blood, women with red hair and green eyes just like her. She knows she should tell police about the dark, gorgeous man who comes into the diner every night, the one who makes her feel a longing she's never felt before. The last thing she should do is invite the beautiful stranger into the house . . .

Cursed to an eternity of darkness, Antonio Battista has wandered the earth, satisfying his hunger with countless women, letting none find a place in his heart. But Victoria Cavendish is different. Finally, he has found a woman to love, a woman who accepts him for what he is— a woman who wants him as much as he wants her . . . which is why he should leave. But Antonio is a vampire, not a saint. What is his, he'll fight to keep and protect. And Victoria Cavendish needs protecting . . . from the remorseless enemy who would make her his prey . . . and from Antonio's own uncontrollable hunger . . .

NIGHT'S KISS

He Has Found His Soul's Desire . . .

The Dark Gift has brought Roshan DeLongpre a lifetime of bitter loneliness—until, by chance, he comes across a picture of Brenna Flanagan. There is something haunt-ingly familiar about her, something that compels him to travel into the past, save the beautiful witch from the stake, and bring her safely to his own time. Now, in the modern world, Brenna's seductive innocence and sense of wonder are utterly bewitching the once-weary vampire, blinding him to a growing danger. For there is one whose dark magic is strong . . . one who knows who they both are and won't stop till their powers are his . . . and they are noth-ing more than shadows through time . . .

NIGHT'S TOUCH

One Kiss Can Seal Your Fate . . .

Cara DeLongpre wandered into the mysterious Nocturne club looking for a fleeting diversion from her sheltered life. Instead she found a dark, seductive stranger whose touch entices her beyond the safety she's always known and into a heady carnal bliss . . .

A year ago, Vincent Cordova believed that vampires existed only in bad movies and bogeyman stories. That was before a chance encounter left him with unimaginable powers, a hellish thirst, and an aching loneliness he's sure will never end . . . until the night he meets Cara DeLongpre. Cara's beauty and bewitching innocence call to his mind, his heart . . . his blood. For Vincent senses the Dark Gift shared by Cara's parents, and the lurking threat from an ancient and powerful foe. And he knows that the only thing more dangerous than the enemy waiting to seek its vengeance is the secret carried by those Cara trusts the most . . .

DEAD SEXY

In The Still Of The Night

The city is in a panic. In the still of the night, a vicious killer is leaving a trail of mutilated bodies drained of blood. A chilling M.O. that puts ex-vampire hunter Regan Delaney on the case, her gun clip packed with silver bullets, her instincts edgy. But the victims are both human and Undead, and the clues are as confusing as the vampire who may be her best ally—she hopes . . .

Master of the city, Joaquin Santiago radiates supernatural power like heat from a blast furnace, but he's never met a creature like Regan Delaney. She intrigues him, fires his hunger, and unleashes his desire, but before he can enter her world, or she his, they must confront a vicious, elusive killer who is an enemy even to his own . . .

DEAD PERFECT

Be Careful What You Wish For . . .

Only a woman with nothing left to lose knocks on a vampire's door and asks for help. Shannah Davis is convinced that the mysterious dark-haired man she's followed for months can save her life—if he doesn't kill her first. But though Ronan insists he can't give her what she needs, his kiss unleashes a primal hunger that makes her feel truly alive for the first time.

After centuries of existence, Ronan has done the unthinkable. He has fallen in love with a mortal—and one with only weeks to live. Sensing the fear and reluctance beneath Shannah's request, he offers her a different bargain that will keep her near him during the time she has left. Every hour spent together leaves him craving her touch, her scent, her life's essence. Soon, only Shannah can satisfy his thirst. But if he saves her from death, will she love him for it—or spend eternity regretting what she has become?

And turn the page for a sneak peek at Rane's story,
NIGHT'S ILLUSIONS,
coming in February 2009 from Zebra . . .

"I still want to know about you."

"There's not much to tell. I'm a reporter for the Kellton Chronicle. I live at home with my father. And I'm not very good at getting interviews with magicians."

A slow smile spread over Rane's face. "If I was going to tell anyone my secrets, Savanah Gentry, it would be you."

"That's very flattering, but I still don't have a story."

"Maybe there isn't one."

"I don't believe that."

She ran the tip of one finger around the rim of her glass. "What do you do when you aren't mesmerizing audiences and ignoring reporters?"

He shrugged. "Nothing very exciting. Watch the sports channel. Go to the movies. Take long walks . . ."

"Walks? Really?"

"Why do you sound so surprised?"

"I don't know. I guess I pictured you more as the zero-to-sixty type."

"Can't I enjoy both?"

"I knew it! So, what do you drive? Something incredibly fast, I'll bet."

"Fast enough." He had tried his hand at racing for a while, until he got into a monumental wreck that no mere mortal would have survived. They had pronounced him dead at the scene. He hadn't raced under his real name, of course. There had been quite a stir the following day when his body turned up missing at the morgue. The newspapers had had a field day speculating on what had become of his corpse. "Would you like to go zero to sixty with me?"

He wasn't talking about cars and they both knew it. For one impulsive moment, Savanah was tempted to go with him, to indulge in one crazy, wild, once-in-a-lifetime night of passion, to bask in the sound of his voice, to do something totally outrageous and out of character. And then her good sense kicked in. "I don't think so."

"Afraid of me?" he asked, a challenge lurking in his dark eyes.

"Not exactly."

"Then what, exactly?"

"I don't make a habit of hot rodding with men I hardly know."

He learned forward. "Afraid I'll make you disappear?"

Savanah nodded. That was exactly what she was afraid of. She had covered too many stories where women got involved with seemingly nice, wholesome guys and were never heard from again. Sometimes their bodies turned up in a ditch, sometimes they were discovered by joggers in remote areas of the mountains, and sometimes their bodies were never found. When Savanah got her name in the paper, she wanted it to be in the byline of a great story or as the recipient of the Nobel Prize for literature, not as the victim of a violent crime.

He grunted softly. "Smart girl." He gestured at her glass. "Can I buy you another?"

"I don't think so. I'd really like to know how you transform into the wolf."

"You and a couple hundred other people."

"Would you tell me if I promise to keep it a secret?"

"I'll show you," he said, "but it will cost you."

"How much?"

"No money involved."

She canted her head to the side. "What do you want?" she asked suspiciously.

His gaze slid across her lips. "A kiss."

She blinked at him. "A kiss? That's all, just a kiss?"

"Along with your promise that this is completely off the record."

Her expression betrayed the battle between her hunger for a good story, her ethics, and her curiosity.

He leaned back in his chair, his elbows resting on the arms, his chin resting on his folded hands as he waited for her to make up her mind. Even if she wrote the story, most people wouldn't believe her. The wars between the Vampires and the Werewolves had ended more than eighteen years ago. Mortals being what they were, they had quickly brushed aside what they couldn't explain once the conflict was over. Since that time, the Supernatural creatures had been keeping a low profile. But it would only take one sensational story to bring the hunters out again.

"So," he said, "do we have a deal?"

"Yes."